Oh, God, it was *him*.

Flushing hot enough to ignite her own eyebrows, she slowly glanced up.

Towering over her stood six and a half feet of masculine perfection and irritation, a man so unspeakably virile he'd make Zena and her band of Amazons look like petite-size zeros.

Thunderstruck, Amara stared like an idiot, her mouth hanging open.

This was the closest she'd ever been to him and she almost needed a shield or lead blanket to deflect some of his unholy chemical effect on her. Things had been bad enough from a distance, but now she could smell him, too, and oh, what a thrill that was. Sandalwood, spices and the fresh, healthy musk of a man. Just his scent alone was enough to peak her nipples and get the honey flowing between her thighs, but she still had to assimilate the face and the body.

Like that was possible.

Looking at him gave Amara the kind of violent visceral response she'd never in her life had for anyone else. If he smiled or crooked his finger at her, she, Amara Clarke—defense attorney extraordinaire and fiercely independent woman who prided herself on never needing anyone, didn't believe in casual sex and hadn't had a date in three years or sex in four—would probably follow him into the back room, or the bathroom, or his car, or the nearest hotel, and let him do whatever he damn well wanted to do with her.

Yeah, she wanted him *that* much.

Also by Ann Christopher

Risk

Trouble

Published by Kensington Publishing Corp.

DEADLY PURSUIT

ANN CHRISTOPHER

DAFINA BOOKS
Kensington Publishing Corp.
http://www.kensingtonbooks.com

DAFINA BOOKS are published by

Kensington Publishing Corp.
119 West 40th Street
New York, NY 10018

All Kensington Titles, Imprints, and Distributed Lines are available at special quantity discounts for bulk purchases for sales promotions, premiums, fund-raising, and educational or institutional use. Special book excerpts or customized printings can also be created to fit specific needs. For details, write or phone the office of the Kensington special sales manager: Kensington Publishing Corp., 119 West 40th Street, New York, NY 10018, attn: Special Sales Department, Phone: 1-800-221-2647.

ISBN-13: 978-0-7582-3544-2
ISBN-10: 0-7582-3544-5

First Dafina mass market printing: November 2010

10 9 8 7 6 5 4 3 2 1

Printed in the United States of America

To Richard, always.
And to Kate Duffy, who told me
it was time to write a bigger book,
helped me through the murky process
of figuring out what that was,
and bought the results.

Acknowledgments

It takes a village to raise a child and to produce a book, and I owe a huge debt of gratitude on this one. To Deputy U.S. Marshal Brian Babtist, DEA Special Agents Richard Isaacson and Steven M. Robertson, Assistant U.S. Attorneys Kenneth L. Parker and Robyn Hahnert, my deepest thanks for answering all my questions with patience, good humor and enthusiasm. To Kevin Schad, criminal defense attorney extraordinaire and old friend (really old!), thanks a million for brainstorming with me.

Any mistakes are, of course, mine.

To Eve Silver, thanks for your hand-holding, beta-reading and extraordinary friendship.

And to all those on the front lines in the war against drugs—thank you.

Cincinnati

Kareem Gregory settled deeper into his leather chair and listened to his attorney do so much worthless yap-yap-yapping that he wanted to shove his fist down the man's throat. Every overpriced word that came out of the dumb-ass bitch's mouth only made Kareem hate the man more.

Fucking lawyers.

But for them and their incompetence, he'd be out of this mess by now.

Thanks to them, he was still hip-deep in shit.

What kind of shit? Entrapped by the feds, for one. Arrested on bogus money-laundering charges, for another. All his assets, from his million-dollar estate down to his last pair of diamond cuff links—pretty much everything he'd ever worked for—threatened with seizure and currently being eyeballed by the DEA *and* the IRS. Convicted and sent to a phone-booth-sized cell in federal prison when he had a business to run.

Well . . . two businesses.

His string of auto-customizing shops because, yeah, he liked to pimp rides.

And his real empire. The drug one.

Not that the feds had ever been able to nail him for it, because he was too slick and clever for them and he compartmentalized his organization so that the right hand never knew what the left hand was doing, and only he had both hands.

Only a few people knew he was the top dog, and he intended to keep it that way.

The feds' best efforts had only led to a money-laundering conviction. Even so, he'd gone to prison—and prison was prison.

He was lucky he'd survived one day on the inside, much less a year. Lucky for the fine wool of the suit he now wore and for the soft cotton of his undershirt instead of those coarse prison rags that scratched his skin.

The only good thing a lawyer had ever done for him, despite the tens of thousands he'd paid in legal fees, was winning his appeal. Now, after all the suffering he'd endured, God had finally smiled on Kareem again and sent him a few blessings, no doubt as a sign of greater things to come.

A retrial. Release on bail. The opportunity to crack a few heads and make sure everything ran smoothly within the organization. Renewed success in his hunt. The chance to expand his wine collection and screw every woman in sight.

Well . . . every woman but the one he really wanted.

Kareem shot a quick glance at Kira, his tight-lipped wife. She sat beside him in her designer dress, looking the way she always looked: icy and beautiful.

Funny, huh? The one woman he should be able

to have at will hadn't given him any since he was arrested nearly two years ago, and here he was, still sniffing after her. Back in the day, she'd loved him and given him that delicious body enthusiastically and often. She'd been his moon and stars. His freaking sun. Kira wouldn't let him touch her for now, but he'd get her back as soon as they worked out the whole trust issue.

In the meantime, there were plenty of other fish in the sea—damn sexy little minnows, too—and Kareem had several of them on retainer. Why not take full advantage? It made sense to store up a little in case his latest lawyer turned out to be as incompetent as all the rest, lost the retrial, and landed Kareem back in prison.

Not that Kareem had any intention of going back to prison.

Ever.

Which was one of the reasons he'd taken matters into his own hands.

That, and revenge, which was going to be oh so sweet.

"The U.S. Attorney's Office sent over their final witness list. A lot of familiar people on it." Jacob Radcliffe, who looked barely old enough to be out of diapers but was one of the best criminal defense lawyers in the city, flipped through his thick file, found some papers, and slid them across the enormous carved desk to Kareem. "No real surprises."

Ignoring the sudden, slight tremble in his hand, Kareem scanned the alphabetical list for the names he wanted, ignoring the others. He found them right away, and each one jacked his blood pressure up another thirty notches, sent his thundering pulse into overdrive.

Jackson Parker. Ray Wolfe.

Feds.

A searing rage rose up his neck and burned his cheeks before it prickled in his scalp. To think that *he,* Kareem Gregory, a world-class judge of character with enough savvy and street sense to sniff out every liar within a twenty-mile radius, had trusted them. Liked them. Let his guard down around them.

And what had his good faith gotten him? Betrayal by the kilo.

To add insult to injury, those men had eluded him and his inevitable retaliation for months. *Months.*

That, fortunately, was about to change.

"So that's the plan." Jacob showed signs of wrapping this shit up, thank God. "We're going to do our best to get an acquittal this time and make sure you never have to go back to prison."

How touching. As if Kareem would leave his future in this punk's pristine hands. Not in this lifetime. He thought of his plans, which were in motion even now. He thought of the bit of crucial information that had recently and unexpectedly fallen into his lap. He thought about how difficult it would be for his former business associates—Parker and Wolfe—to testify against him at the retrial if they were dead. He thought of their deaths, one of which was imminent.

Best of all, he thought about doling out the punishment these men had coming, and he smiled.

If you betray Kareem Gregory, even if you're a fed, you pay the ultimate price.

Simple as that.

"I'm going to do my best to stay out of prison, too," Kareem told his lawyer. "My very best."

Chapter 1

Lawrenceburg, Indiana

The irritating, nostril-burning smell of cigarette smoke woke Payton Jones from a sound sleep. Or maybe it was Mama's croaking bullfrog voice, or the violent thud as the old bat rolled into Payton's bedroom with enough force to bang the cheap door against the wall, no doubt leaving chip number three million in the puke yellow paint.

"Gitcher lazy ass outta bed. It's one-thirty in the afternoon."

Payton pushed the covers down and cracked a bleary eye open against the bright sunlight streaming in the window above the headboard. Unfortunately, Mama's wheelchair was parked directly ahead, and Mama, wearing her dirty red housecoat and as unavoidable as a sperm whale in a lounge chair, was in it.

Payton groaned. It was too early for this shit.

Muttering, head pounding due to the nine—or was it ten?—Jell-O shooters that went down the pipe last night, Payton dove under the blankets again.

This resulted in a smack on the leg sharp enough to clear the sinuses.

"Jesus." Good and awake now, Payton sat up and glared at Mama. "Who put a bee in your freaking bonnet?"

"I put me a list together, for the grocery." An inch-long strip of ash wavered and fell from the end of the cigarette onto Mama's lap, whereupon Mama brushed it onto the white sheet, one inch from Payton's hip. Payton yelped and swiped it to the floor. "Yer gonna need to stop at Walmart, too, and pick up my prescriptions."

"Why can't Al do it?"

"Because Al's working, like you should be."

"I can't find a job," Payton said.

"Helps when you look for one."

Of all the hypocritical bullshit Payton had ever heard, this running thread about looking for a job was the worst. How a woman could take one slight on-the-job hip injury, turn it into worker's comp benefits into perpetuity, and then have the nerve to complain about someone else not looking for a job was something Payton would never understand.

"I've *been* looking." This, as they both knew, was a lie, more or less, but what was left of Payton's pride required it.

Mama glared, her watery eyes squinched against the cigarette smoke that wafted up into them as she spoke. "You're nothin' but a big disappointment to me, Payton—"

"Shit." Payton got out of bed, stalked over to the closet, and rummaged through shirts and whatnot, scraping the hangers across the bar in the hopes of drowning out this latest recitation on the depths

of Mama's disappointment, but the noise didn't help. It never did.

"—a disappointment and a burden. Never gonna amount to anything, as far as I can tell. Dropped out of college. Dishonorable discharge from the army. No job. Out all night at the Argosy, drinking and gambling away the only two cents we got to rub together. What'm I supposed to do with you?"

"Beats the hell outta me," Payton said from the depths of the closet.

Payton had created this whole messed-up situation—no one else to blame there. Living at home in a trailer at twenty-four. Driving a piece of shit car that cost more than it was worth every fill-up. Saddled with the bitch here.

The army had provided two precious years of freedom, but that hadn't worked out in the end.

Blowing through the money from that last job wasn't the smartest thing Payton had ever done, but the blackjack table had been hot that night. For a little while, anyway. Still, betting ten large at once was a bad idea, so there were no real excuses.

Now Payton paid the price every time Mama played that same old broken record—*Payton Screws Up: Volume One*—and every time Mama swore that Payton would still be living at home decades from now.

Payton almost gagged at the thought.

Over near the bed, the bitch droned on, working up a head of steam, when a miracle occurred.

The phone rang, and it was the special ring tone—the Dixie Chicks' "Not Ready to Make Nice"—announcing that this was an important call, the kind that didn't happen often enough. Payton lunged for the leather jacket perched atop the teetering pile of clothes on the chair, fished the phone out of the pocket, and flipped it open.

"This is Payton."

There was a long pause, and then, "Someone's looking to hire."

The surge of gratitude and relief was almost blinding. "I'm available."

Mama watched with sharp eyes, mouth gaping open and cigarette stub dangling from the edge of her bottom lip by what could only be spit. Trying to look casual, Payton turned and stared out the window to that lousy battered blue car, which seemed to lose a foot or more of its body to rust every day.

"I recommended you."

"That so?" Payton now felt a little wary because Lady Luck generally wasn't this good or this timely. "Who needs me?"

"A friend of Travis."

Thank God. A referral from Travis was as good as gold, better than a personalized note from Oprah.

"So . . . you interested?"

Interested? Payton would gladly explore any escape option out of this pit, including an express train straight to the molten center of hell if one pulled up.

"Yeah. I'm interested."

Mount Adams, Washington

"You're wasting my time."

Amara Clarke gave the assistant prosecutor sitting across the table from her a pointed look, just for emphasis, and waited for the inevitable comeback, which didn't arrive immediately. Good. Maybe now she could eat her dinner in something resembling peace. Amara took a quick, desperate bite of the now lukewarm but still delicious chicken and noodles in her bowl, the only food she'd had since the brief recess at one this afternoon.

Katie O'Farrell watched her as she sipped her coffee, glowering and no doubt framing her rebuttal.

Amara didn't bother to hide her impatience; she had dinner to eat and work to do. Flapping a hand at her open laptop, she hoped Katie would take the hint and scram.

"Let's wrap this up. I need to write my closing, and so do you. And I'd like to get home before ice glues my car to the street."

A sheet of rain drove into the window at the end of the booth, chilling the air inside the diner and making the ominous *ping*s that could only mean sleet. Amara shivered, cold down to the marrow of her bones. If only she was home in a bubble-filled tub, breathing in the scent of lavender and letting Calgon take her away. She had better hopes of discovering a cure for cancer by tomorrow, but a girl could dream.

It was nearly ten and she was running on fumes. Her thirty-six-year-old body had started feeling the strain of the trial, which ended its second day today: tired, gritty eyes, empty stomach and a weird combination of sleep-deprived exhaustion and caffeine-driven agitation.

There was no explaining her case of nerves, even to herself. She ate prosecutors for breakfast, lunch and dinner. Thrived in the courtroom like an orchid in a greenhouse.

Why was she so antsy tonight?

The cook, whispered that insidious little voice in the back of her head.

No way, she thought, knowing she was a damn liar.

Taking another bite of noodles, she shot him a glance through her lashes. Being discreet was an unnecessary exercise, though, because he rarely looked at her. When he did look at her, it was with an unfathomable darkness in his eyes that made her feel like something he'd throw in the Dumpster out back.

Jerk.

Standing over at the grill on the other side of the long counter, flipping burgers or whatever it was he did, he had his white-T-shirt-clad, broad-shouldered back to her. This, fortunately, spared her from his cool-eyed disdain, but unfortunately treated her to an unimpeded view of the world's greatest ass, which was encased in faded, baggy jeans but still clearly tight and round.

Her face flamed. She looked away, irritated with her surging hormones.

That ass and that man, whoever the hell he was, had ruined the Twelfth Street Diner for her and, along with it, her trial rituals.

In the old days, she'd finish up after a long session at court and bring her laptop here to her favorite booth, where the hanging lamp over the table provided a soothing light, and the view of the arbor in the park across the street was more relaxing than watching the Travel Channel at home.

She'd order the pork chops and work late into the night, the comings and goings of the other regulars keeping her from the absolute loneliness she felt within the four walls of her house. She'd been well fed, content and as relaxed as a criminal defense attorney ever got.

All that had changed three months ago when *he* showed up.

Realizing she'd lapsed into staring again, Amara looked away, cleared her throat and tried to focus.

Katie O'Farrell, who was a friendly acquaintance even if she was Amara's current courtroom enemy, lowered her cup and clanked it on the table with unmistakable irritation. "You can't seriously believe I'm wasting your time. The jury's not with you. You should be glad to hear my offer."

"Oh, please."

"In case you didn't notice, you didn't make any dents in Detective Curtis today."

Amara *had* noticed, but she hid her scowl. Detective Curtis had emerged from her withering cross-examination smelling like a June rose, yeah, that was true.

It was also true that the *we hate you and the horse you rode in on* vibe from the jury didn't bode well for her client, Greg Kinney, accused low-level drug dealer and fumbling college student in his spare time. Poor dumb Greg stood better than a fair chance of spending some quality time in the pen, where he probably belonged.

Luckily for Greg, though, he had a U.S. senator for a father, and Daddy Dearest had enough money and sense to hire a good lawyer. Enter Amara.

She wasn't about to let Greg go down without a fight, no matter how stupid he was.

"Excuse me?" Amara slipped into full battle mode, her excess adrenaline fueling her outrage. "I'm supposed to have my client plead guilty and pack his bag for prison on the basis of your little hunch about which side the jury's on? Is this a joke?"

Katie shrugged. "Your client'll never get two years from the judge if he's convicted, and you know it. This is a decent deal."

Maybe. Probably. But Amara hadn't given up yet, nor would she. Tomorrow she'd deliver a closing argument to rival Clarence Darrow's in the Scopes Monkey Trial. Then she'd let the jury decide.

"We're not pleading out."

Katie, practically snarling now, put her elbows on the table and leaned in. "Are you holding out for one year? Is that what this is about? Because—"

"I'm not holding out for anything."

"—I'm not recommending one year. I know how you operate, Amara—"

"I'm not operating."

"—so don't even try it."

"I'm not trying *anything*."

Amara didn't bother trying to keep the annoyance out of her voice. What'd a person have to do to be left alone around here? Why couldn't she eat and work without harassment? "I don't want a deal of any kind, I'm not holding out for a year, and *I am not done with my noodles*."

A thick, muscular, brown arm had reached down to take her bowl, and Amara spoke without thinking. Her unnecessarily harsh tone registered with her brain a millisecond before the regret did, but by then it was too late.

Oh, God, it was *him*.

Flushing hot enough to ignite her own eyebrows, she slowly glanced up. Towering over her stood six and a half feet of masculine perfection and irritation, a man so unspeakably virile he'd make Zena and her band of Amazons look like petite-size zeros.

Thunderstruck, Amara stared like an idiot, her mouth hanging open.

This was the closest she'd ever been to him and she almost needed a shield or lead blanket to deflect some of his unholy chemical effect on her. Things had been bad enough from a distance, but now she could smell him, too, and oh, what a thrill that was. Sandalwood, spices and the fresh, healthy musk of a man who spent hours over steamy pots and pans. Just his scent alone was enough to peak her nipples and get the honey flowing between her thighs, but she still had to assimilate the face and the body.

Like that was possible.

The body was something she'd fantasize about for years to come. A pristine white T-shirt—how did he keep it so white, working in a kitchen?—stretched across broad, square shoulders and a rippling slab of chest and abdomen. One of those starchy chef's aprons, the kind Martha Stewart wore, had been folded down and tied around his narrow hips.

He had light brown skin and haywire curls the same sandy color. The brows, though, were dark and moody. So were the flashing eyes, which right now were expressing something fierce, like his fierce desire to dump the bowl of noodles on her head.

His five o'clock shadow had gone to seed a week or so ago, but that only added to his attractiveness, his air of surly attitude teetering on the edge of outright menace.

Looking at him gave Amara the kind of violent visceral response she'd never in her life had for anyone else. She wanted him. Had fantasized about his tongue in her mouth and her legs around his waist. Would love to have his scent and stubble marks all over her skin. Needed the slow, deep thrust of his body inside hers.

And then she needed it again. And again.

If he smiled or crooked his finger at her, she, Amara Clarke—defense attorney extraordinaire and fiercely independent woman who prided herself on never needing anyone, didn't believe in casual sex and hadn't had a date in three years or sex in four—would probably follow him into the back room, or the bathroom, or his car, or the nearest hotel, and let him do whatever he damn well wanted to do with her.

Yeah, she wanted him *that* much.

Their gazes locked and the cook looked her in the eye for only the second or third time ever. His dark brown gaze, so frigid it would no doubt cure the global warming problem if only someone would provide his transport to the Arctic, raked over her face and, in those fleeting milliseconds, one thing was perfectly, brutally clear:

He hated her.

He believed she was a snotty bitch who thought he was a peon well beneath her notice, and he despised her for it. There was no aspect of her that he liked; probably even the buttons down the front of her dress offended him. She had no hope of redemption against such absolute loathing, no possibility of him ever finding anything whatsoever worthwhile about her.

So it was no surprise when he slammed her precious bowl back on the table, turned his broad back on Amara and spoke to Katie.

"Who's the chocolate bunny?" He jerked his head in Amara's direction. "You should teach her some manners."

Oh, man. He was blessed with a naturally low, deep and sexy voice, the kind of voice that would keep a woman up all night with a vibrator in one hand and the receiver in the other if he worked for one of those phone sex hotlines.

Katie didn't miss a beat, smiling up at him with Nancy Reagan-esque adoration. "Amara can't be taught. But I'm happy to be your bunny if you, you know, need one in vanilla."

He grinned at Katie, and Amara seethed with something ugly, almost like jealousy, but then his words registered with her brain. That was a compliment, right? Chocolate bunny? It was also a condescending endearment offensive to anyone with a pair of ovaries, and of course she hated it on principle, but . . . did that mean she'd caught his eye?

"Where's Judy?" Katie wondered, referring to their waitress.

"Went home sick," Jack told her, still favoring her with the brilliance of his smile.

Amara tried to recapture his attention. "I—I'm sorry."

He glanced over at Amara, his jaw tightening.

"I just . . . I'm really hungry and the noodles are really good, so—"

The irritation vanished and he faced her, one corner of his incredible mouth creeping up into the wicked half smile of a man with one thing on his mind, and it wasn't food. To her utter astonishment, he gave her a pointed and assessing once-over, nearly searing the bodice of her dress off her body with the intensity of his gaze.

That look was about the rudest thing she'd ever experienced in her life.

It was also the sexiest.

"Why didn't you say so, Bunny?" he murmured. "I made the noodles. And I'm happy to let you taste anything of mine whenever you want."

If there was the teeniest doubt in her mind that he was trying to be as obnoxious and insulting as possible, the tiny wink he gave her cleared it up. Amara gaped at him, stammering. Her skin felt so hot it had to be purple by now.

Turning to Katie, who was also drop-jawed, the cook flashed a pleasant, dimple-revealing smile, the kind he sprinkled liberally on everyone else in the universe, but never Amara. "More coffee, Katie?"

Wait a minute.

Amara's belated outrage finally kicked in and, fuming, she eyed her own glass, which held only a couple of melted ice cubes and the sad dregs of a Diet Coke. How come his over-the-top nasty talk had her all hot and bothered? And how about a refill on *her* drink?

"Umm . . . yeah." Katie simpered under his attention until Amara wondered if she wouldn't slither onto the table and undress in an impromptu striptease for his special benefit. The killer prosecutor turned to vanilla pudding right before Amara's disbelieving eyes. "More coffee'd be great."

"How's the trial going?" The cook kept his back firmly turned on Amara and refilled Katie's cup from his steaming carafe. "Another conviction, you think?"

Katie seemed to recover some of her composure, which was more than Amara could do. "Absolutely. Unless I can get Amara to plead out."

Royally pissed off and telling herself it had nothing to do with being crudely propositioned by the world's haughtiest cook or jealousy over his attention to Katie, Amara let her quick temper get the better of her.

"I'm not pleading out," she told Katie, and then glared up at the cook. "I need another Diet Coke, if you can stop flirting with customers long enough to do your job. And my name's not *Bunny.*"

Oh, God. There was that look again, that flash of mischief that dried out her mouth and sent shivers chasing over her skin.

"No problem, Sugar. Just let me know what you want me to call you, and I'm there." With that, he strode back to the kitchen, leaving the women to admire his ass as he went.

"Oh, my God," Katie breathed. "He wants you."

Amara clenched her hands in her lap to stop the embarrassing tremble of her fingers. To think she'd been attracted to that jerk. Hah. He'd cured her of that, hadn't he?

And yet . . .

She felt hot-wired and unreasonably alive, as though someone had strung a power cord along her spine and it was shooting sparks through her body.

"He's only yanking my chain because he's a jackass." Working hard to sound normal, she waved at her laptop to remind Katie of the business at hand. "Can we wrap this up? I really have to get cracking here."

Katie frowned, looking resigned. "So no deal?"

"You know I've got reasonable doubt," Amara said with a conviction she didn't feel. "Otherwise you wouldn't be here doing your Monty Hall routine. Your office shouldn't have brought the charges in the first place, and it wouldn't have if this wasn't a senator's son and you weren't trying to show taxpayers how tough on crime you are. No deal."

Rolling her eyes, Katie slid out of the booth, flipped a couple of bills on the table, and grabbed her things. "See you in the morning, then. Tell Chef Hottie I'll dream of him tonight."

They both laughed, and Amara watched as Katie went through the glass door and disappeared into the night. The diner was empty now except for one of the other regulars, a senior citizen named Esther, who sat at the Formica counter flipping through the paper as she ate her pancakes. Amara was looking back at her screen when the cook reappeared with a new Diet Coke and handed it to her.

"What'd you do to Katie?"

Amara took a sip and tried not to bristle at the implication that she'd driven Katie away, which, she supposed, she had. "She left."

"Drove her away, eh? That probably happens to you a lot, Bunny. You should work on being less abrasive. You might make a friend or two."

Ouch. The mouthful of soda soured to vinegar on her tongue.

Though he couldn't know it and she'd die before admitting it, his barbed arrow hit its mark because people, generally speaking, didn't like her.

Her personality, it turned out, was a little caustic. Not that she was into self-analysis or anything, but it was probably because she'd grown up in foster care. Maybe she'd developed a defense mechanism to keep people away, not that crowds were knocking down her door trying to get close.

Anyway, that was how she was wired. If she wanted to get something, she got it, and if she wanted to say something, she said it. Sure, this turned some people off, but she didn't have time to smooth over people's hurt feelings. Plus, she couldn't easily turn off her defense attorney's fighting instinct outside the courtroom, which resulted in her plowing her way through life. Hazard of the job.

So, yeah, nobody liked her, but it was rude of him to say it.

Incensed, Amara recovered her speaking abilities and got over the whole intimidation thing. This guy may be a god sent down from Mount Olympus to torment womankind with lust, but he was still an arrogant SOB who needed a smackdown.

"I think you've got the market cornered on abrasive, *Honey,*" she said.

Uh-oh. Wrong tactic. Abort—*abort.*

That hint of wickedness came back into his expression, not so much a smile as the disquieting light of amusement in his eyes. Planting his palms on the table, he leaned down, right in her face. "I like the endearment, Bunny. Got anything else for me?"

"My name is Amara Clarke. Use it. *Honey.*" She extended her hand, wondering exactly how rude he was prepared to be.

The simple gesture took him by surprise.

For several long beats, he didn't seem to know what to do. For all his smirking bravado, she realized, he didn't want to touch her. His ambivalence was so strong she could almost stick her tongue out and taste it.

Dark eyes sparking, brows lowered, he glared, apparently cursing her to hell and back for all eternity. Then his gaze wavered and he looked down his straight nose to her hand. Finally, as though he'd never participated in a handshake before and wasn't quite sure how the procedure worked, he reached out and grasped her hand in his firm grip.

Holy God.

There was no preparing for the current of electricity that surged through her body when their palms connected. Nor could she explain the flow of blazing heat between them, which was disproportionate to anything a human being should be able to generate.

His expression was, for once, unreadable. "Jack. Patterson."

He pumped her hand twice, an unremarkable, socially acceptable handshake, and then let go. Without another word, he turned and walked back into the kitchen, leaving the door flapping after him.

Chapter 2

Sacramento

"Ooh, Baby, Baby" played over and over again in the car on the way home from dinner. The Smokey Robinson version first, of course, then Linda Ronstadt.

They sang together at the top of their lungs, being silly because this much joy refused to stay quietly bottled up inside. Only when they rolled down their quiet street and into the driveway of the duplex they rented did Ray Wolfe turn the music down a little; he didn't want the neighbors talking about them as they walked their dogs tonight. The car idled while they waited for the garage door to open.

"Why are we singing this song?" Joyce giggled. "It's about *breakups*."

"Yeah, well."

Shrugging, he lifted a hand off the steering wheel, reached under his wife's filmy flowered skirt, and slid his fingers up her smooth, bare thigh. Her low, throaty laugh and corresponding shiver tightened his groin.

"*Stop,* Ray." Squirming and darting a guilty glance

out the window and across the lawn to see if anyone was on the porch next door and within seeing distance, Joyce smacked his hand away. "Just focus on getting us inside the garage, okay?"

He laughed, navigated the Accord into the cluttered garage, and put it in park. She reached over and hit the remote clipped to his visor, and the garage door hummed again, lowering behind them.

"Let me see it."

Rolling her eyes, Joyce slapped the strip of shiny black and white photos into his waiting palm, and he frowned down at it. "I'm not sure this is a kid, Joy. Looks like a bean to me."

"Come on."

"I'm just saying." Leaning across the armrest, he kissed her smiling mouth. "Do we have any other proof you're pregnant?"

"Hmmm." She stroked her tongue across his bottom lip. "Well, the doctor said so."

"True." Opening as she demanded, he kissed her long and deep—until her eyes glazed and he felt his pulsing blood sizzle through his veins. "Anything else?"

"Well." She lifted his hand and pressed it to her newly enormous breasts, which, much to his fascination, now required a larger cup size. "Don't forget *these.*"

"How could I forget?" He smiled because his beautiful wife was pregnant, he was about to get some, and life was good. "Let's go, Joy."

He got out of the car.

And came face to face with a figure dressed head to toe in black.

A long beat passed. *There's someone in the garage,* he thought, bewildered.

Someone . . .

Then his sensual daze cleared.

Jerking to full attention, he dropped back into his seat and dove for the Sig Sauer he kept underneath it.

The assassin backed up a step and raised a steady gloved hand.

Joyce gasped with horrified comprehension.

Even as his fingers closed around his gun's butt, Ray knew it was too late.

He was a dead man, but then he'd been a dead man for months.

Staring down the length of a silenced pistol, his last thoughts raced through his head:

Why had he thought he could protect Joyce from Kareem Gregory?

Why didn't they ask the doctor whether the baby was a boy or a girl?

Was Jackson dead already?

"Run, Joyce!"

Ray raised his weapon and prayed he could buy her time to—

His world exploded with a muted *pop,* and there was nothing.

Payton Jones pumped a second shot into Ray's forehead, waited while he dropped and, being careful not to step in the blood and leave behind a footprint like the one in the Simpson/Goldman murders, edged around the man's crumpled body as it dangled half in and half out of the car.

There was more work to do.

The screeching wife had backed into a bike hanging on hooks against the far wall, her screams echoing off the concrete floor like cannon fire. She really needed to knock it off before a Dudley Do-Right neighbor stopped by to investigate, and time was a-wasting.

The first tap to her forehead shut her up and splattered the bike—damn, it'd looked like a nice one, too—with bits of brain and what looked like ten gallons of blood. The second tap wasn't really necessary, but was good procedure, just in case. Another quick squeeze of the trigger, and it was done.

Her face frozen in an eternal, wide-eyed grimace, she tumbled out of view behind the car. A long, crumpled strip of black and white paper—a picture, maybe?—fell out of her limp fingers and hit the ground with her.

Ahhh, *silence*.

Now it was time to clean up and get the hell out of Dodge.

All in all, this'd been a nice day's work. It felt pretty good, the satisfaction of an operation run by the book. The money would feel pretty good, too.

Payton smiled.

A nice rare steak would be great for dinner tonight, maybe with a baked potato. Oh, and chocolate cake of some kind, with ice cream. Yeah. That'd be nice.

But first things first: ditch the stolen car with its stolen plates and steal new ones for the long drive back home, all before the cops got wind of this nice handiwork.

Picking up the four shell casings and then the duffel bag from the corner where it'd been stashed, Payton walked to the side door leading to the backyard, which had a flimsy joke of a lock, and glanced around one last time, just to survey the scene and make sure there were no clues, no giveaways.

There weren't.

"Dumb fuck."

Who were these two? Payton didn't know and didn't need to know, just like there was no need to know who'd ordered this hit. You couldn't build too many layers of protection into these operations; keeping things on a need-to-know basis was better for all concerned. One fun fact had trickled down through the grapevine, though, and Payton squatted, considering it.

The man's vacant eyes stared off at the ceiling even as his blood formed a red halo around his head where it rested on the concrete. Payton leaned over the body and gave a bit of valuable, though posthumous, advice.

"Never go back for a funeral, dumb-ass. It'll trip you up every time."

He shouldn't have touched her, Jack thought, his arms immersed to the elbow in bubble-filled scorching water because the dishwasher, like the waitress, had gone home with a stomach thing. The diner's kitchen sink overflowed with a day's worth of cruddy, sticky stainless steel pots and pans, and he attacked each one as if it had done him a great personal harm.

This was where he belonged, hidden in the back. What'd he been thinking, going out there? Talking to her? Ruffling her feathers just to see the flash of passion in her eyes? What kind of plan was that?

He hadn't been thinking. That was the problem. He

hadn't had a clear thought since he first laid eyes on Amara months ago.

She was tall and curvy in all the right places, with legs, hips, and ass in abundance. Longish hair, wavy and black, piled on top of her head in a careless style that was sexy and easy. Smooth pretty skin about the color of his, but no doubt infinitely softer, not that he'd ever know.

Yeah, he'd noticed.

Even though he'd done a decent job of ignoring her up until now, he'd noticed.

He wanted that body curled around his with no daylight in between. He wanted the taste of her in his mouth and her sweat slicked all over him as he fucked her into next year. He wanted her cries in his ears and her scratches on his back.

But the bigger problem was that there was something else about her that called to him. That was why he'd gone out of his way to be obnoxious.

Was it the smile? It had to be. That smile transformed her face. She was beautiful without it, of course, but in the cold, flat, untouchable way a runway model was beautiful. The smile changed it all. Those sleek, high cheekbones became dimpled and cute, her cool dark doe eyes glowing and warm.

That smile. Yeah, it tied him in knots.

The pots finished at last, he crept back to the swinging kitchen door and peered through the round window. She was still there, typing furiously on her laptop, looking exhausted.

He checked the time: ten forty-eight. She was a hard worker. Tenacious, too. No matter how much he wished he didn't, he admired her. A lot.

On the other side of the door, Jonas Martin, aka

J-Mart, the retired army sergeant turned co-owner, along with his silent-partner brother, of the Twelfth Street Diner, looked up from the stack of bills he was counting from the register. He caught Jack in the midst of his pathetic Amara surveillance, gave him the *what the hell?* raised eyebrow, and jerked his buzz cut head toward the dining room.

Sighing and scowling, Jack pushed through the door and presented himself for the forthcoming interrogation.

"What the hell are you doing?" barked J-Mart.

"Minding my own business," Jack said. "You should try it."

Without missing a beat in his relentless counting of single bills, J-Mart snorted. "Why don't you grow a pair and go talk to her? What're you? Gay?"

"If gay means I want her thighs up on my shoulders, then yeah. I'm gay as the day is long."

J-Mart laughed while Jack, feeling like a shark on the other side of the glass from a juicy seal, stared hungrily at her. She was deep in her own world, muttering to herself as she typed, paying them no attention, and he couldn't absorb the details about her fast enough.

"She doesn't bite, Jack."

"She could bite me all she wanted. In another lifetime."

Jack couldn't keep the irritation out of his voice. Things were bad enough without J-Mart thinking he was a coward; he wasn't. In the old days, he would have pursued and caught Amara, enjoying both the pursuing and the having, but he couldn't do that now because he wasn't free and would never be free again.

And he wouldn't taint anyone else's life. That had

been his one promise, his vow to himself and to God: no collateral damage. Or, to be a hundred percent accurate: no *more* collateral damage.

"I'm not into relationships," he added.

"No shit." J-Mart, serious now, paused in his counting, with half of the bills in one hand, half in the other. "You've been here almost a year, and I don't know a damn thing about you other than you were a Marine. And I wouldn't know that but for the *Semper Fi* tat on your arm."

Jack lashed out, hating this shit. "Are you writing my biography, or what?"

"You let me know," J-Mart said solemnly.

"Know what?"

"If the trouble you're in gets too close, you let me know. I'll help."

He left, heading back into the kitchen. Jack gaped after him, floundering and speechless, his throat burning with suppressed emotion. Too late, he thought that he should've made another joke or issued another one of the easy denials he was so good at, but the moment had passed and he didn't have the heart for it anyway.

In the meantime, Amara was sitting over there, all by her lonesome.

Thinking fast, Jack poured another glass of Diet Coke and walked to Amara's booth. When he got there, she had her elbows planted on the table and her hands buried in her now-messy hair.

Startled, she looked away from the screen and up at him with bleary, bloodshot eyes. "Oh. Hi."

"Here."

Still feeling irritable and off balance from his interaction with J-Mart, knowing he was making a mistake and hating himself for becoming no better than a rutting stallion when she was in the room, he slammed the drink down and snarled.

"It's late. You should go home."

"Thanks." She took a grateful sip. "Can't, though. I've got to finish."

"Finish what?"

"My closing argument."

He couldn't help scowling, which seemed to amuse her.

"Let me guess. You don't like lawyers."

"No one likes lawyers."

She gave him a tired half grin. "You may be right."

Jack paused. Now was the time for him to go. He'd delivered her drink, told her to go home, and his mission was done. Too bad he was trapped in her gravitational pull.

"So you're representing some drug dealer?" he asked her.

"*Alleged* drug dealer."

Bullshit lawyer doublespeak. "Why're you wasting your time and talent on scum like that? I don't get it."

She blinked up at him. "Wow. You're right. When you put it that way, I should just skip the whole judicial process and try to get him scheduled for lethal injection right away. Is tomorrow soon enough for you?"

Damn. She was beautiful and funny. And people said miracles didn't happen.

The slope he was on got that much more slippery. First he talked to her and then he flirted with her. Crude flirting, but still flirting. Now they were laughing together, and who knew where that might lead?

Better to stop things right here, right now, and he knew just how to do it.

Dropping his voice, he gave her a smirking once-over and watched while her smile faded and disappeared. "Better go home, Bunny. It's late and some lucky man is probably waiting for you to give him his bedtime treat."

Chapter 3

Seething anew, Amara watched Jack head back to the kitchen. What was with that guy? One second he was a pleasant human being and the next he was leering and insulting her like it was an Olympic event.

Bastard.

He was right about one thing, though. It *was* time for her to go home, and the diner closed at eleven anyway. Her poor brain had done all the critical thinking it could handle for now, and she'd reached the point of diminishing returns. Might as well call it a night, go soak in that tub and have a glass of Zinfandel.

Standing, she twisted left and right to work some of the kinks out of her back, and then began the laborious process of cramming all the junk back into her overstuffed briefcase. Files, pens, the laptop . . . all of it went slowly inside while she tried to convince herself that she wasn't loitering.

Still, she couldn't help peering over her shoulder one last time, in the general direction of the grill, but the only sign of life came from Esther. The old woman pulled her woolly hat down over her ears, nodded a vague good-bye to Amara, and headed through the glass door and out into the night.

No Jack. Not that she ever wanted to see him again.

Now anxious to be gone, Amara jammed her fists into the sleeves of her black raincoat, belted the middle without bothering with the buttons, grabbed her briefcase, and stalked out.

Heavy night air, so cold it burned her sinuses on the inhale, cleared her head as she trotted down the salted steps to the deserted sidewalk. The sleet had stopped, thank goodness, but the street was shiny and dangerous, a sheet of black ice waiting to claim foolish victims who hurried across it. Mindful of her heels, she picked her careful way toward her car, which was to her right in front of the bank in the next block, directly under a street lamp.

It was darker than normal, though, and she glanced around an extra time or two, just in case. The familiar buildings—a brownstone, an office and a dry cleaner's—seemed gloomy and unnecessarily shadowy tonight, almost sinister. She wished she'd asked J-Mart to walk her to her car. Silly, yeah, but she wished it.

She kept moving, getting closer to—

Whoa. What was *that*?

With her face low against the roaring wind, it took her a moment to register the fleeting dark figure in her peripheral vision, but someone was out there where she couldn't quite see and—

A woman's shrill scream and a man's cry pierced the silence.

Oh, God. What was it?

Right there, two cars down from hers. Two people struggling.

A man—oh, God he was *huge* and he wore a knit cap pulled low over his eyes—had a woman trapped between her open car door and the driver's seat and was pummeling her with his fists, cursing her.

The poor woman shrieked and cowered, trying to shield her head with her hands.

"Fucking *bitch*."

Punch. Scream.

"Get out of my *fucking* way."

Kick, kick . . . punch.

"Please," the woman begged, sobbing, *"please, please,"* and Amara realized, with horror, three things:

The woman was Esther from the diner;

The man wanted her car; and

He was willing to beat Esther to death for it.

Desperate and petrified, Amara looked around for help, but there was no one to call and nowhere to go. The diner was too far away now, and nothing else was open. They were alone out here with a maniac. Panic kicked in, followed by the flight instinct.

Run, Amara, run.

She backed up several steps, ready to sprint to the diner for backup. Esther would have to fend for herself until Amara brought help back. But then Esther dropped to her knees, moaning, and Amara knew Esther would be dead long before help arrived.

Amara took a deep breath and screeched even as she dug in her briefcase for her cell phone, punched 9-1-1, and prayed the call had connected.

"Help! *Help!* There's a carjacking at Twelfth and Main!"

The man paused in his kicking of Esther and looked around at her with murder in his beady eyes. "What the *fuck*?"

Amara locked her knees and stood her ground. "L-leave her alone." She flashed the cell phone as if she meant business. "I called the police. They're coming! And if you don't leave me alone, I'll take your picture."

The man stared at her, clearly weighing his options, and then took a step in Amara's direction. *No, God. Please no.* Amara was taking a big breath, gearing up for another round of screaming, when, to her complete astonishment, a floodlight came on in the building nearest the man, shining on them like an angel's glow.

The man wavered, glancing between the buildings, where voices could now be heard, Esther, who was on her knees groaning, and Amara. In his wild, flashing eyes, she saw rising panic and indecision.

Clammy sweat dripped under her arms and down her sides as she considered two horrifying new possibilities. What if he was a crazed druggie? What if he had a gun?

More voices rose up, behind her this time. She didn't dare turn and look.

The man heard them, too. Galvanized, he hurried to Amara, hand outstretched. "Gimme that phone, bitch."

If she'd been thinking, she'd have just tossed the phone to him. But there wasn't time for thinking, only instinct. Raising her left arm, she swung it in a vicious backhand, slamming him across the face and shoulder with her thirty-pound briefcase.

Reeling, he roared with rage.

"Oh, God." Amara braced for the attack and raised her arm again.

He leapt at her.

She glimpsed the glazed, feral eyes of a habitual drug user and smelled his fetid breath in the quick seconds before his rough, cold, brutal hands closed around her throat and squeezed until agony sliced through her body.

Jerking her knee up as hard as she could, she connected with his groin and he let go, howling with pain. Free now, she staggered back, coughing and wheezing, and thought she heard someone call her name. The voice sounded remote through her fear, as though someone in China was yelling at her, but this was no time for listening.

The man rounded on her again.

Amara prepared to swing the briefcase again because she wasn't going to die. Not like this.

From behind her came an animalistic sound that was somewhere between a yell and a roar. Afraid to glance away from the druggie to identify this new monster, Amara froze and waited, her view of her attacker occluded by the steaming puffs of her panting breath.

The druggie looked around, flinched, pivoted, and finally ran off. At the corner he turned left and disappeared just past the bank.

With a weak cry of relief, Amara's boneless legs gave way and she collapsed to the pavement. "Thank you, God. *Thank you.*"

Running feet in jeans and hiking boots came into her field of vision, and then she saw the same muscular brown forearm that had tried to take her chicken and noodles earlier. Never in her life had she been so happy to see a limb.

"Jack."

Raising her head, she saw a twisted face full of

worry layered over a killing rage. No wonder the attacker had run off. Jack looked capable of ripping the man apart with his bare hands and eating his flesh while it was still warm.

Mustering every ounce of strength, she flashed him a weak *I'm okay* smile.

"Amara." All the anger leached away from his expression, leaving naked fear. "We heard you screaming."

"Esther," she began. "Is she—"

"J-Mart's with her. She's sitting up. Don't worry."

Amara sagged with relief as Jack came closer, and she finally let go of her briefcase. With awesome strength and a surprising tenderness, he reached down and pulled her to her feet. His hands ran across her arms and back and then up the sides of her neck to her face and hair, checking for an injury.

"I'm fine." She planted her hands on his forearms, steadying herself. "Really."

This was a lie. She felt like either vomiting or collapsing, she wasn't sure which. But she'd be damned if she'd do either and embarrass herself in front of Jack.

Finding no lumps or breaks elsewhere on her body, Jack stroked her cheeks and studied her with a penetrating, unfathomable gaze. When he spoke, his voice sounded scratchy and weak.

"He choked you."

Adrenaline still pumped fast and furious through her veins, numbing her a little, but Jack didn't look so good. That, to her surprise, worried her. Shrugging, she tried again for a smile.

"I'm fine. *Really.* I think I got him pretty good. I hit him with the MacBook."

Jack let out a startled bark of laughter and then quickly choked it back. His face darkened again, and this time there was something new in his expression, something powerful and irresistible but well beyond her skills at identification.

It happened quickly.

One second she was standing there, looking up at him, and the next she was in his arms with no idea how she'd gotten there, clinging to a thrilling wall of warm muscle unlike anything she'd ever touched before.

They swayed together, grappled to get closer. Beneath the soft cotton of his T-shirt, his skin felt hot and hard. *Right.* Murmuring something comforting that she couldn't quite hear, he pressed her closer to his thundering heartbeat. His fingers slid into her hair again, caressing her scalp, and she felt *alive* and, better than that, *saved.*

Which was a great consolation for being attacked.

"How is she?" asked a strange female voice out of her line of sight.

Jack's arms tightened around her. "She says she's okay. I think she should still be checked, though."

Amara groaned a protest that Jack and the woman both ignored.

"The police are coming," the woman said.

In confirmation, Amara heard the distant but growing wail of sirens and knew it was time to return to the real world. Slowly, with reluctance, she stepped out of Jack's hold, but he kept her at arm's length and that was fine with her.

She looked around and registered the non-Jack parts of the scene. Ten or fifteen people had gathered nearby, most hovering around Esther. A couple of cars had pulled up, headlights blazing. There was no sign of the attacker.

"I've got to go." His voice sounded harsh now, tense. "Will you be okay?"

"Yeah. Sure." Nodding, she tried to hide her disappointment. "But the police will want to talk to you since you're a witness."

An odd, twisted expression crossed over his features. "I'm not sticking around. I'm not wild about the police."

"Oh." What the hell was that supposed to mean? Nothing good, for sure. Jack's issues with the police probably went well beyond them giving him a ticket or two for Driving While Black. She ought to know, having represented more than a couple of cop-o-phobic people in her day. "Right."

"And there are enough other witnesses," he continued.

"Right."

The sirens got louder, and now she saw flashing lights out of the corner of her eye. Several vehicles, including a satellite truck from the local news, raced into view. She stifled a groan. By the time she finished talking to the police and reporters, it'd be three A.M. Wonderful. It wasn't like she needed any sleep before closing arguments began at nine.

Jack's tight face told her he wasn't any happier with the new arrivals than she was. That was some consolation. He didn't seem to want to let her go. That was another. His glittering gaze held hers for so long she was sure her features had begun to melt and blur.

"Take care of yourself, okay?" he asked, low. "No need to be so brave."

This unearned praise startled her. "Oh, no." Better set the record straight lest he think she was something she wasn't. "I'm not brave at all. It's just that Esther needed help and I was the only one around."

He stared, at an obvious loss for words, and this time she recognized the look on his face without any problem at all. It was something she'd never seen from him before: the brief but thrilling gleam of admiration.

As the first ambulance screeched to a halt at the curb, he backed up a step or two, his hands slowly slipping down her arms and away. When at last the contact between them was broken, she felt hollow and alone, which was ridiculous because she was always alone anyway and probably always would be. Even so, she shivered and wished she had his touch back, his warmth.

"Good night." Just like that he melted into the darkness and was gone, leaving her to face the swarming crowd by herself.

Chapter 4

"Ahhh . . . *shit.*"

Kareem Gregory tightened his grip on Marcella's silky black hair as her head bobbed over his lap. Her laughing dark eyes smiled up at him, as if she knew exactly how skilled she was, how freaking *unbelievable* those full lips felt around his dick, and he decided he'd pick her up a little something extra at Tiffany this week.

After a minute, he reached toward the end table, found his glass of Le Gay Pomerol 2006 (he'd always been partial to Bordeaux) and silently toasted himself before he took a sip.

A little celebration was definitely in order because he was a genius.

His plan was ticking along better than he could ever have expected. The feds had had a few questions for him—they always had a few questions for him—but his alibi had left them nothing to go on. They'd never again have anything to go on, assuming he didn't trust the wrong people again. He was too smooth for that.

Marcella, taking a little initiative, climbed up and straddled him.

He flipped her a condom from the end table. Enthusiastic as always, she went to work while he adjusted his boxers for her, and that was when his cell phone, which was sitting on the coffee table next to the mirror with the lines on it, rang.

Undeterred, Marcella tossed him the phone and, impaling herself, began to ride hard and fast. The world swam out of focus and opening the phone and pressing buttons suddenly got a whole lot trickier. He managed by the fifth ring.

"Yeah." He balanced the phone between his shoulder and cheek, freeing up his hands so he could hold on to Marcella's big ass as it flexed.

"Turn to CNN," said one of his three lieutenants, Roger "Yogi" Watkins, whom Kareem liked to refer to as his VP of operations.

"I'm *busy*." Groaning, and trying not to lose focus at this crucial moment, Kareem licked a nipple as it bounced past his mouth.

"You'll want to see this."

His vision growing dim with pleasure, his eyes half closed, Kareem couldn't see much of anything at the moment. "This better be good."

Grabbing the remote, he punched a couple of buttons and waited while the wall-mounted TV switched over from *Scarface*—Al Pacino was a genius—and then . . .

The anchors yakking while in the window they showed one of those grainy security tapes, which was an overhead shot of a woman clocking a man with a briefcase and being attacked and choked.

The crawl said BRIEFCASE BRAWL: PROMINENT

WASHINGTON DEFENSE ATTORNEY GETS SENATOR KINNEY'S SON OFF ON DRUG CHARGES, FIGHTS CRIME IN SPARE TIME.

Big deal.

"Why am I watching this?" he said into the phone.

"See anyone you know?"

Kareem kept watching, and that was when God smiled on him again. Because there, with long, curly hair and the beginnings of a beard that, all in all, made a lame-ass disguise, was none other than Special Agent Jackson Parker.

No. No fucking way. He couldn't get this lucky.

But it was and he could. Same build. Same eyes. There he was, talking to the briefcase woman, copping a feel, his face as familiar as Marcella's tits.

All business now, Kareem pushed her off him. "Where is this? *Where?*"

"Washington State," said Yogi.

Kareem did a few quick mental calculations, afraid to get too worked up. "Our friend is still on the coast, right?"

"Yeah."

"Good. I want this taken care of. Tonight."

"Tonight? But—"

"Tonight," Kareem said. "Get it done. You got me? Offer a bonus or some shit."

"Yeah, but I don't know exactly where—"

"Isn't that an apron dude's wearing? Motherfucker's working as a busboy or something. Find the restaurant. And if that doesn't work, find the woman. Follow the tail trail and he'll be sniffing on down it. You feel me?"

"Yeah."

Clicking the phone off, Kareem stared up at the TV and watched as they showed the security video two more times, and then finished the segment and went to commercial. When Jackson Parker's face disappeared for the last time, he stood there for a moment, stunned, and then laughed and sank back onto the sofa.

Marcella climbed back onto him, picking up where they'd left off.

Frenzied with triumph now, not bothering to be gentle, he flipped her onto her back so he could fuck her good. She got louder and louder as she moved against him, and he couldn't tell whether she was crying with pain or pleasure, not that it mattered to him either way. All that mattered was that he was the man and each sharp thrust of his hips felt like another nail in Jackson Parker's coffin.

J-Mart wiped down the last strip of counter and watched the stragglers file out the door and disappear into the darkness. There'd been several new customers here tonight, mostly young, female and hot—not counting a couple of obvious fruity-toots.

He'd seen two redheads, a blonde, a pretty young thing with the brightest baby blues he'd ever seen and an ugly gray GIVE PEACE A CHANCE sweatshirt that couldn't hide a pair of world-class tits, and two fine black women he wouldn't have minded being sandwiched between.

None of the beauties—male or female—had come for the food.

They'd all come to see Jack, the local hero who'd been plastered all over the news today, and pretty face after pretty face fell with disappointment when he told them Jack was off tonight.

The press had been here earlier, too, but, knowing

how Jack liked his privacy, J-Mart had shooed them out and refused to give either Jack's last name or his address, both of which were none of their business.

They'd be back tomorrow, though, and so would Jack. Maybe he should call the kid tonight and warn him about his new fans. Give him a heads-up so he'd know what was waiting for him.

It was a good thing Jack'd been scheduled off tonight; something told J-Mart he wouldn't have appreciated the groupies.

J-Mart, on the other hand, loved groupies.

Baby Blue came up to the counter and handed him a ten. "Great pie."

J-Mart rang her up and got the change out of the register. "You'll have to come back and see us again."

"I might just do that."

Flashing a smile that had parts of his body sparking with the kind of interest he hadn't felt in years, she turned and went to the coat rack for her jacket.

If only he were thirty—no, forty—years younger.

Sighing, he watched her leave and turned to the only remaining customer.

Amara.

That one had balls of steel. He'd commanded a soldier or two who hadn't shown one-eighth of the courage she'd shown last night. She also had a wounded streak a mile wide, and it had gotten wider when she realized Jack wasn't coming in tonight.

Edging around the counter, he stood at the end of her booth and gave her a kindly smile as he watched her pack up her briefcase. Truth was: he felt sorry for her. If there was anything going on in her life other than work, he'd never seen any sign of it.

Something was brewing between her and Jack

though, and J-Mart intended to fan that flame as much as possible. Lord knew Jack needed somebody in his life. In all his seventy-four years, J-Mart had never met a lonelier soul than Jack Patterson.

"You get a new laptop already?"

Amara grinned and reached for her scarf. "This one is fine, believe it or not. My files are so thick, I think they made a nice cushion for the computer."

"Heard you got that snot-nosed senator's kid off scot-free."

Her grin widened. "*Allegedly* snot-nosed."

J-Mart laughed. Yeah. This one was perfect for Jack. She'd keep him laughing and Jack needed to laugh. "He'll be back tomorrow."

Amara ducked her head, flushed until her ears glowed and made a production out of tying her scarf. When she looked up again, the grin was gone. "Who?"

"Don't kid a kidder, girl. You know damn good and well who I'm talking about."

"J-Mart," she said sourly, "I know you're older than dirt and you make the best pie in the city, but if you call me *girl* again, I'm going to have to take you off at the knees." She hefted the briefcase for him to see. "Don't make me use my computer on you."

This time he roared, his heart lighter than it had been in what felt like years.

"He likes you, girl. Don't let him fool you."

An unmistakable flare of interest lit her eyes but she tried to hide it behind a scowl.

"If anything, Jack wants to screw me. There's a difference."

"I thought you didn't know who I was talking about."

"Funny." Her lips thinned with enough irritation

that he knew he'd hit a sore point. So she wasn't immune to Jack Patterson. Good. "You're a regular Richard Pryor, aren't you?"

Chuckling, he took her elbow and steered her to the front door, where he paused to flick out the lights, flip the black and white sign to the CLOSED side and snatch her jacket off the coat rack and his from behind the counter before he locked up.

As always, he felt a surge of affection for the Twelfth Street Diner, his tiny kingdom. No one would ever mistake it for a five-star restaurant, but the food was good and the Formica and linoleum were his and his brother's, bought and paid for. The work was hard and the pay pitiful, but it sure beat the hell out of getting shot at in the jungles of Vietnam.

"I'll walk you out."

"I don't need a babysitter, J-Mart."

"Great. Think of me as your bodyguard then."

For a second he thought he was going to feel the business side of her briefcase for sure, but after huffing and glowering she gave up the fight and let him lead her down the steps to the sidewalk. Maybe last night's experience made her thankful to have an escort to her car even if she was too proud to admit it.

The night was crisp and fresh after yesterday's sleet, the air still with waiting for tomorrow's rain. After five or six steps the relentless cold penetrated his bones and he felt the familiar dull ache of his arthritis. If he'd been smart, he'd've worn a heavier jacket today, but of course if he'd been smart, he'd've moved to Orlando twenty years ago.

The prospect of another winter here in the great Northwest was every bit as appealing as his next prostate exam. He stepped up the pace to Amara's black Saab SUV and walked her around to the driver's side.

"I'll see you in the morning, girl."

The wry twist of her lips told him that this additional *girl* was duly noted, but she didn't call him on it. "Actually, you won't see me in the morning. I just finished up some paperwork and now I'm taking some time off."

"Time off? Don't tell me you've got a life . . . ?"

She opened the door and tossed her briefcase inside. "No life. What I've got is fifteen vacation days that I'll lose if I don't use before the end of the year."

"Why don't you use that time over the holidays and go visit family?"

But he knew she didn't have any family and the telltale flicker of sadness behind her eyes confirmed this before she hid it behind a careless shrug. "I'm not big on holidays."

"Me neither, girl." He thought of his daughter Jenny back in Boston, with her buttoned-down corporate husband and big house that had six bedrooms, none of which ever seemed to be available for a broken down army sergeant at Christmas.

Loneliness echoed through him. "Me neither."

Settling into her seat behind the wheel, Amara shut the door, started the engine and rolled down the window. "Where'd you park? Need a ride?"

"Oh, I'm not leaving. I've got another hour of prep work for the morning and then payroll after that."

"Looks like I'm not the only one with no life, eh?"

"I'm too old for a life." Grinning, he smacked his palm on her hood, shooing her on her way so he could get back inside where it was warm. "Get outta here."

With a beep and a wave she rolled off. Taking a

moment to appreciate the purr of a powerful engine, he watched her go until her taillights disappeared around the corner at the light.

Once she was safely gone, he zipped his jacket up to the neck and scurried back down the sidewalk at a pace that had his knees protesting. He fumbled with his keys and got them into the lock by the third try. A rush of blessed warmth hit him in the face as he went back into his haven, but he kept the jacket on for now. With his luck, it'd be noon tomorrow before he got his creaky bones heated up again.

He headed through the swinging door, past the kitchen and down the narrow hallway to his office. Paperwork first, while his mind was still fresh, and then he'd start in on the—

Clink.

J-Mart froze, listening, halfway between the kitchen and the broom closet.

The diner was full of late-night sounds and he knew them all. The hum of the refrigerator, the rumbling grind of the ice machine, the nonstop trickle of the world's most stubborn toilet, which resided in his men's room and wasted enough water to fill a small pond. There was no *clink.*

Clink.

Shit.

Nerve endings crawled to life up and down the back of his neck and he felt the sudden and still-familiar clammy wetness in his armpits even though he hadn't experienced it—not while awake, anyway—since he left the mosquito-infested humid heart of hell that was Vietnam.

It was coming from his office. Where a lamp that he'd left off was now on. He could see the narrow line of yellow light seeping under the door, which was ajar. He'd left it shut and locked because the cash box was in there.

Double shit.

Kids. Why didn't they learn? Sort of a thug's rite of passage, was robbing the Twelfth Street Diner.

J-Mart had caught the last two hoods six months ago, and he'd catch this one.

Adrenaline pumping, he hugged the wall and edged toward the office door. At the broom closet he paused to reach inside for his Louisville Slugger, which he kept propped in the corner for just such an occasion.

Holding it cocked and ready over his shoulder—he didn't want to hurt the kids, just surprise them enough to wet their pants and scare them straight—he poked his head inside the office door and assessed the scene.

The corner lamp was on.

The cash box was sitting, untouched, atop the pile of crap on his desk.

A slight figure stood in front of the tall file cabinet at the far end of the room, the one where J-Mart kept his employee records, trying to jimmy the lock with controlled, efficient movements.

Sweatshirt. Jeans. Knit cap pulled low so no hair was visible.

Purple rubber gloves—the kind the technician wore whenever he had blood drawn—covering small but steady hands.

Those gloves puzzled him. Worried him.

That wasn't a neighborhood kid.

The burglar made an indistinct noise of unmistakable triumph, slid the top drawer open and, after pocketing the metal tool, began to rifle through J-Mart's files.

In his surprise—*what kind of dumb fuck of a burglar ignored the cash box so he could rummage through employment and insurance records?*—J-Mart forgot himself and spoke.

"What the hell are you doing?"

The burglar wheeled around.

J-Mart tightened his grip on the comforting weight of his Slugger, but then their gazes connected and his jaw dropped.

It was Baby Blue, the cute little cherry pie eater with the GIVE PEACE A CHANCE sweatshirt and world-class tits. Only her cuteness had been swallowed up by a cold intensity that had him wondering, with increasing dread, if maybe he should've called the police.

"You shouldn't have come back, old man," she said, and there was something in her icy eyes that made his bowels loosen.

"What do you want?" If he'd been in his right mind, he'd've been embarrassed by his croaky voice, but he had more important things to worry about because he had the strong feeling he was about to die.

"Where's Jackson Parker?" asked Baby Blue.

Who the hell was Jackson Parker?

For one uncomprehending moment J-Mart stared at her, but then he understood with a sudden violent clarity. There was no Jackson Patterson. It was *Parker*. And here was Jack's past, caught up with him at last.

She'd broken into the file cabinet to find Jack's address.

Only—funny thing. Jack's real address wasn't in there; the one he'd listed on his employment application belonged to a pizzeria two blocks from here. Jack had told him he'd had some problems in his past and J-Mart didn't give a damn about his fake address because he was a fine cook who showed up for work when scheduled.

Maybe he should have asked another question or two about Jack's troubles, but it was way past too late now, wasn't it? Now the only thing that mattered was protecting Jack. As long as he didn't crack, Jack would remain safe from this little demon. And J-Mart had promised he'd help.

The prayer came back to him though he hadn't stepped foot in church in a thousand years. Whaddaya know. The nuns had drilled a little religion into him after all.

Hail Mary, full of grace . . .

"I've never heard of Jackson Parker."

This was technically true, not that he expected it—or anything he said or did—to save his life now that he'd seen this woman's face.

That expression didn't change. Those wide blue eyes didn't blink. That small body didn't have one ounce of mercy in it, but then assassins weren't known for their tender hearts.

J-Mart thought of Jenny. He thought of children she might one day have that he would never see. He hoped his son-in-law would take care of them.

And he prayed.

The Lord is with thee, blessed art thou amongst women . . .

Reaching behind her back, Baby Blue produced a weapon and, without hesitation, aimed it at his leg and fired.

Pain exploded through his knee, shooting out the top of his head and through the soles of his feet to the floor. He dropped like a concrete slab, yelling with agony and pissing himself, curling into the fetal position before he'd even finished falling.

His vision dimmed, went dark, and came back again. Now she was standing over him, looking down with what might have been regret, but you had to have a soul to feel sorry about anything.

Anger slowly penetrated his consciousness. Through the groaning and the slobbering and the agony, one persistent thought gave him strength: he would not go out like this. He was a retired sergeant with the United States Army who'd served two tours of duty in Vietnam and he would not fucking go out like this.

So he unclenched his hands from the bloody and ruined remnants of his knee, uncurled his body, and glared up at his killer. Shaking convulsively, he unclenched his jaw and willed his voice to be clear and strong.

Hail Mary . . . Hail Mary . . . Pray for us sinners now and at the hour of our death . . . Hail Mary . . . Mary . . .

"Fuck. You."

Annoyed, Payton Jones stared down at the old man. Not because she cared if the crazy fuck bit it on the office floor now rather than in a hospital with prostate cancer or some such shit a few years from now, when his time came naturally. She didn't.

The problem was: this job was beginning to require a lot of legwork and a fair amount of collateral damage. Collateral damage meant more risk to her. Under normal circumstances she'd lie in wait until she had a clear shot at the target and would never show her face to anyone. This whole *break-into-the-file-cabinet-to-find-Parker's-address-so-she-could-kill-him-tonight* operation was riskier than she'd been told.

More risk meant she was entitled to more money.

More than the bonus she'd been promised a little while ago if she took care of this Jackson Parker character ASAP.

She'd find Parker. If the old man didn't tell her before she clipped him—and it was beginning to look like he wouldn't—then she would surely find him in the file cabinet over there as she'd originally planned, or maybe in the old man's phone and cell phone records of recent calls.

If *those* turned up nothing, then she had Plan C, pretty little Amara Clarke, to follow up with, and she knew how to find Amara Clarke. But no matter how things unfolded, this job was a lot more work than she'd expected, and the pay needed to reflect it.

Impatient now, she raised her weapon and stared down the length of her arm to the old man, who was now babbling and crying, his face a disgusting mess of snot and tears.

"Hail Mary, Hail Mary, *please*—"

"Let's talk about Jackson Parker," she told him.

Chapter 5

Luck was with Jack. There was an empty parking space on the street in front of his five-story brick apartment building, and he slipped his battered red Jeep into it. The usual suspects were loitering on the sidewalk despite the late hour: prostitutes who knew better than to approach him over there, drug dealers and their apprentices over there.

They all watched with interest as he unloaded his mountain bike, the only quality thing he owned, from the rack, hefted it over his shoulder and climbed the steps. He could almost see the *cha-ching* of easy money in their greedy eyes as they stared at the bike, which was exactly why he kept it safely inside his apartment.

He'd stayed out longer than he'd planned, but the weather was good and the trails were clear if a little muddy after yesterday's sleet, and he hadn't had a day off in three weeks. So, after a sleepless night filled with images of Amara, the images all the more graphic because now he knew the silky-smooth texture of her fragrant hair and the scent of berries and flowers on her skin, he'd gotten up at the crack o' dawn, thrown some protein bars, trail mix and water bottles into his backpack and driven for hours up into the mountains.

Now it was after eleven and he was back, bright-eyed, bushy-tailed, and ready for a second restless night with a hard-on the size of Plymouth Rock in his pants.

Flipping on the cheap overhead fixture to illuminate the four-walled shit box that was home sweet home, he leaned his bike against the table and tried to be grateful he had a spot to lay his head.

The place had all the comforts: Formica kitchen with harvest gold icebox circa 1962; folding card table with matching chair; one knife, one fork, one spoon and a big stack of white paper plates; a king-sized bed on the other side of the room, close enough that he never had to worry about tiring himself out during any middle-of-the-night hunts for a snack, but also close enough that he could never cook bacon unless he wanted his sheets to smell like pork for the rest of the week.

In pride of place on the wall opposite his one window: a forty-two-inch LCD HDTV with a picture sharp enough to cut diamonds.

He clicked it on to the local news, crossed to the bathroom to start the water running in the shower in the hopes that it would be hot by this time tomorrow, and backtracked to the fridge for a Gatorade.

He'd just bent to reach for the Styrofoam clamshell filled with out-of-date lasagna from the diner—he'd brought it home last week, but it probably had another forty-eight hours or so before the bacteria really took hold—when he thought he heard something that made his heart stop and his blood run icy.

Had someone said Amara's name?

Straightening, he let the refrigerator door slam shut and turned to watch the big-haired and shellacked anchor continue with her story. "Prominent local defense attorney Amara Clarke had a busy day yesterday," she began, but that was all Jack heard because his carefully constructed world was dropping out from under his feet.

There, in the window over the anchor's shoulder, was a grainy-ass black-and-white surveillance video that showed, among other things, the kind of close-up of Jack's face that Kareem Gregory could have only dreamed of.

Stupefied, Jack watched until it went to commercial.

Then he picked up the remote, punched Rewind and watched it again.

Then he blinked, shook his head and tried to think.

Fuck.

He stood there for one more bewildered second before his training kicked in, and then he sprang to life because he knew this drill. He'd done it once before, in New Orleans, and he could do it again.

Ten minutes. He had ten minutes.

Dropping to his knees, he belly-crawled halfway under the bed and emerged with his huge black duffel, which was already filled with most of the things he would need: a prepaid cell phone, his backup weapon, the keys to his storage unit and extra car, which was housed in said storage unit, clothes, shoes, books.

Yeah, his life was a train wreck, but it'd have to get a damn sight worse before he'd leave *The Autobiography of Malcolm X* and *To Kill a Mockingbird* behind.

His hunting knife and sheath, which he'd strap to

his ankle. A wallet filled with cash and a selection of fake but convincing driver's licenses in a variety of identities. Maps.

Straightening, he looked around at the rest of his pitiful belongings.

The bike was toast. Nothing he could do about that. Same with the TV.

Okay. What else?

The picture of Mama over on the nightstand. Snatching it up, he wrapped it in his underwear and found a secure place for it inside the duffel.

That was it.

Sad commentary on his life that it only took him thirty seconds to pack it all in a bag.

Of course this meant he'd never see Amara again.

Better for her, woe-is-me for him.

And J-Mart. He'd never see him again either. But he owed the old man a good-bye. It was the least he could do after all J-Mart had done for him: giving him a job, not asking any questions, offering a shoulder to lean on.

So he'd sneak into the diner—J-Mart was there right now, he knew, chopping romaine for salads and baking muffins for breakfast—and then he'd take off for parts unknown.

Again.

Once he got where he was going, he'd call the people he needed to call.

As he headed into the bathroom, he ignored the sickening ache of loss in the darkest pit of his belly. Loss? Get real. Amara had never been his, never would be his, and his disappearance from her life was the best thing that could ever happen to her—even though it felt like a crushing blow to him.

* * *

Jack's simmering dread intensified as he crept through the alley to the diner's back door and discovered it unlocked and ajar. J-Mart never kept the heavy metal fire door unlocked. And he was here somewhere because his gleaming black pickup was still parked by the Dumpster, the Ronald Reagan bobble head doll looking oddly forlorn in the rear window.

Something told Jack not to go inside. Pocketing the extra set of keys J-Mart had given him when he began working at the diner, Jack eyed the ancient Honda Accord that he'd retrieved from his storage locker and parked behind J-Mart's truck. He should leave and call J-Mart from a phone booth in a day or two. That made the most sense and was the safest option.

Except that he couldn't do it.

Pausing only to pull the forty-caliber Glock semi out of the waistband behind his back, Jack eased the door open a crack, slid inside and made it two steps before the smells slapped him in the face, nearly knocking him on his butt. Not the familiar savory scent of beef stew, the cinnamon-y fragrance of hot apple pie, or even the scorch of the microwave popcorn that J-Mart liked so well and occasionally burned.

No.

The coppery tang of blood leached into his nostrils and settled, heavy and unwelcome, on the back of his tongue. Above that was the unmistakable stench of shit. Above that was a sinus-clearing layer of ammonia. No, not ammonia. Piss.

Jack gagged, knowing what he was about to find.

He crept down the hallway on silent feet even though he didn't need to bother because the place was empty. His senses would have been screaming at him if anyone was around, but the hair on his arms lay flat, telling him there were no intruders.

Not now, anyway.

The light was on in J-Mart's office but Jack's feet refused to go in there. Swiping at his eyes—*shit, God, SHIT*—he took a deep breath, flipped off the pistol's safety, kicked the door all the way open, and scanned the room from the threshold.

J-Mart was lying face-up on the floor. What was left of him.

It wasn't pretty. His glazed eyes were open with a tiny bloody hole between. His legs—both of them—were a mangled mess of tissue, cartilage and jagged bone below the knee. His mouth gaped and his tongue lolled.

Dead. No. Not just dead. Dead could mean died peacefully of heart failure in bed.

J-Mart had been tortured and slaughtered because of Jack.

With a wounded-animal roar, Jack let the pain come and helped it along by pounding his forehead against the wall hard enough to split the skin.

Jesus. Hadn't he sworn there'd be no more collateral damage on account of him?

Another head pound. And another. Only when he felt the warm trickle of his own blood and the corresponding relief did he pull himself together and stop the pity party by sheer force of will.

Swiping his eyes again, he took a quick look around to see what else this scene could tell him. There was nothing other than what he already knew—this wasn't a robbery gone bad. J-Mart's watch was still on his arm, the cash box still on his desk. Nothing whatsoever was out of place.

No—wait.

The file cabinet was open. J-Mart kept it locked. Jack's employment records were in there, but big freaking deal. Jack had never put his real address on the paperwork and, even if he had, he'd just left his apartment, never to return.

Once he got back in that Accord, drove off and disappeared into the night, there was no way he could be traced, nothing to tie him to Mount Adams or anywhere. J-Mart was dead, but Jack was safe—for now, at least—and there was nothing and no one anyone could use to get to him.

Relieved and ashamed of himself for it, he turned to go.

Then he thought of Amara and the way he'd held her on camera, as though they were lovers and she meant the world to him, and the breath choked off in his lungs.

People did this for fun? And relaxation?

That was getting harder to believe by the second.

Amara eyed her stupid little knitting project with increasing irritation. On one end was an enormous ball of fuzzy-soft purple yarn, every inch of which she had personally and painstakingly unraveled from the skein. Why this was necessary, she had no idea. But the instructions said do it, so she'd done it. Then she'd "cast" one end of the yarn onto one of a pair of enormous wooden knitting needles that looked more like drumsticks than craft implements.

Now she was supposed to begin knitting the actual

scarf, which the lying bastards at the yarn manufacturer had claimed, on the back of the yarn wrapper, was a basic project. *Basic.* Yeah, sure. Basic for anyone with thirty years' previous knitting experience.

Lowering the needles, she looked around her house and wondered how she'd survive for the full three weeks of her mandatory and unwelcome time off.

The blue and yellow pillows on the off-white Pottery Barn sofas and miscellaneous rattan chairs were fluffed and arranged because she was compulsively neat and used a cleaning service on a regular basis. The hardwood floors and rugs were immaculate, and so were the kitchen and the closets.

Putting the knitting aside, she clicked off the lamp on the side table nearest her and un-muted the TV so she could watch the Travel Channel, where they were doing a special on—she squinted at the screen so she could read the blurb at the bottom—Costa Rica. Perfect. She'd never been to Costa Rica or, frankly, anywhere, and, with any luck, the image of the lazy sway of palm trees would lull her to sleep sometime before dawn. She settled her head on the pillow at one end of the sofa, snuggled under her favorite angora throw, and tried to veg.

She hated vegging.

Still, she tried for ten seconds, until she heard . . . a sound.

Mute and indistinct, it was nothing describable, just . . . a sound.

Cocking her head, she listened and heard only the hiss of the ancient but exceedingly efficient radiator in her bedroom and . . . yeah, the gentle *ding-ding-DING, ding-ding-DING* of the brass bell wind chimes outside her bedroom window, which sounded a little louder than they needed to.

Hold up. Had she left the window open? Yeah. There was the cascading clatter of her wood blinds against the window. Now she'd have to get off her butt and close it.

Great.

Halfway down the hall, a prickle of . . . something . . . skittered up her spine.

She hesitated. She listened. And then she told herself she was being stupid.

Shaking off the silliness, she stepped into the carpeted blackness of her bedroom and identified the shadowy shapes looming on all sides: entertainment armoire, comfy chairs, desk and bed.

No boogeyman. Dummy.

The blinds clattered again, and she slid the sash closed, locked it, and peered through the slats at eye level to see if there were any other poor souls awake at this ungodly hour. There weren't. Only the ghostly shapes of several enormous oaks lining the street, all of which seemed sinister tonight, close cousins of the evil tree from which the Headless Horseman had sprung in the Johnny Depp version of *Sleepy Hollow.*

Too much coffee was the problem. That and no sleep for the last oh, say, four years. No more caffeine for her, starting tomorrow. And she needed to work harder on the whole sleep-relaxation thing. For now, she'd get some warm milk in a mug, top it off with two or three inches of Kahlúa, just to make it drinkable, and she'd be good to go.

Guided by the blue digital clock displays on the range and microwave, she walked back down to the kitchen and—

A slight movement registered with her peripheral vision, the fragmentation of a silent mass that was bigger and blacker than the darkness surrounding it.

The signal was still en route to her brain—*run!*—when a pair of arms circled her from behind, capturing her, and she screamed, struggling for her life.

Chapter 6

The more Amara fought, the more trapped she became, as though the person holding her was the solid and vertical equivalent of quicksand, sticking to her and dragging her under to certain death.

She screamed. A hard hand clamped over her mouth.

She bit. Those digging fingers tightened, hurting.

She tried to free her useless arms from her sides. The living manacles embracing her in an immovable grip clenched, compressing her ribs.

She kicked out and was swung off her flailing feet.

Roaring with suppressed fear, growing desperation and a white-hot rage at being a crime victim in her own damn kitchen, she resorted to her only remaining weapon and jerked her head back—determined to knock out as many teeth as possible—and connected with someone's nose with an audible and, she hoped, painful crunch.

"Christ."

Ignoring the pinpoints of light blinking before her eyes and the ache that would soon be a goose egg on her scalp, she hung her head again and prepared for another assault, but the intruder was ready for her this time and jerked away.

This led to overcompensation and a wild moment during which they staggered together, teetering between remaining upright and becoming victims of gravity.

Gravity won.

They hit the cold slate floor with a skull-jarring crash that was made worse because Amara had no hands free to catch herself and the man weighed a ton. His unforgiving body was every bit as hard as the tile beneath her belly and she gasped for breath even as she waited for her ribs to splinter.

And there was a new threat.

The unmistakable bulge of a fearsome package—flaccid now, yeah, but still fearsome—wedged against her butt, which was covered only by the insubstantial floss of a pair of thong panties and the negligible film of a cotton nightgown.

Oh, God.

Their minds seemed to be following the same path because Amara renewed her struggle, writhing and twisting, at the same time that the intruder tensed his muscles, tightening them to stone against which she had no prayer.

She screamed with frustration against his palm, the sound muffled and impotent, and then something extraordinary happened.

"Amara." The crushing weight against her lessened and he shifted enough for her to suck in a strangled breath. "I'm not going to hurt you."

The hoarse voice penetrated her panic and she froze with astonishment.

Wait a minute. She knew that voice.

"It's Jack from the diner."

"Juuck?" she asked into his hand.

"Yes." She heard the relief in his voice. "I'm letting you go. Don't hurt me, okay?"

She nodded.

His hand let go of her face and he braced atop her body in push-up position as though testing her new-found compliance. From there it took him an unaccountably long time to climb the rest of the way off her and she became aware, with excruciating sensitivity, of the cool air against her bare hips and butt, her spread thighs and single bent knee as she tried to get a toe-hold against the floor, the rasp of his pants against her legs, the flat hard lines of his belt buckle, his strength, his scent, the overpowering heat he generated.

With slow and deliberate movement, he eased down the length of her body.

And was gone.

Amara waited, trembling, not daring to breathe, this sudden respite from death too good to be true, but then her near-nudity below the waist spurred her to action. Scrambling into a squat, she skittered backward, away from him, until her back thumped the dishwasher.

Standing now, he stared down at her. She stared up at him. Then he reached out a hand for her to grab. When she hesitated, he bent at the waist, caught her under the arms, and hauled her up. The soft slide of her nightgown back into place covered her up, but she tugged at the ruffled bottom around her knees, just in case, and then squared her shoulders, gripped the counter for support and tried to look like she was a woman to be reckoned with even though she was scared out of her freaking mind.

They eyed each other warily, both panting. Something obscured her vision and she belatedly realized it was her wild hair, which was in her face and down around her shoulders. She shoved it back, aware of him watching her, marking her every movement.

Tired of the darkness, she reached behind, not daring to break eye contact, even for a second, fumbled for the over-the-sink switch, and flipped it.

This was a mistake.

He'd looked scary enough in the dark, when she'd seen only flashes of the wild light in his eyes, but now he was downright terrifying for a variety of reasons. First was the gash on his forehead that would eventually turn into a Harry Potter scar. Second was the bloody nose, for which she claimed full responsibility. Third was the full-body makeover he seemed to have undergone since she last saw him.

The overgrown face scruff was gone and so were the sandy curls she'd imagined fisted in her hands. No sign of the white apron. What was left? A clean-shaven man with hard-edged granite cheekbones, a skull trim and a *don't fuck with me or you might not live to tell the story* bad-ass expression she didn't want to test unless she had to.

This was not the laid-back fry cook whose biggest issue was whether the day's order of eggs had arrived safely from the dairy. This was a focused and fearsome warrior. She'd caught a flicker of him last night when he rescued her from her attacker; now she was staring at a raging inferno.

Though he wore the usual baggy jeans, a sweater and a puffy jacket, nothing special or remarkable, her instincts screamed that this man was a soldier or mercenary. If someone needed rescuing from a South American jungle, this was the guy you'd send for. It was all in his eyes and the way he carried himself, the absolute stillness and relentless focus with which he watched her, analyzing and strategizing.

And then he blinked once, twice—she had the feeling he was struggling with himself, trying not to do something he desperately wanted to do—and his unreadable gaze traveled lower.

To her body in its filmy cotton nightgown, backlit now by the light she'd flipped on in her foolish haste. One sweeping glance left her feeling naked and vulnerable, as though he'd arranged her on satin sheets for his slow inspection and ultimate enjoyment.

It was all over in less than a second, but her flesh responded on a primal level she was helpless to control. Her breasts grew heavy and ached and her dark nipples peaked until the harsh rise and fall of her chest against the cotton tormented her. The curve of her hips, her thighs and the deep cleft between them all felt a touch of that intense gaze and responded.

Sheer defiance kept her from crossing her arms and covering herself.

Or maybe it was idiocy.

After three or four of the longest beats of her life, he caught his breath and became aware of the blood trickling from his nostrils. "Jesus." Looking her up and down once more, this time with clear irritation, he swiped the back of his hand under his nose. "I knew you were nothing but trouble."

Incensed, she sprang into motion before she knew what she was doing. This SOB broke into *her* house, tackled her in her own kitchen, scared her half to death when she was minding her own business, not bothering anybody, and now he had the unmitigated gall to call *her* trouble?

Oh, *hell* no.

Her hand had just closed around the well-balanced and satisfying hilt of her favorite piece of cutlery, a two-hundred-dollar chef's knife from Williams-Sonoma, yanked it down from the magnetized strip on the wall, and raised it toward his face—if he thought he was going to have a scar on his forehead now, just wait till she got done with him—when he vaulted across the room to stop her. One second he was safely over there and the next he was in her face, snarling.

His huge hand clamped down around her wrist and squeezed. "Drop it."

"Screw you."

She knew she'd regret those two words and she did. Immediately. That hand tightened until streaks of pain shot up her arm and cleared her head. Yelping, she let go and the knife clattered to the floor. He kicked it away with one booted foot.

Fine. There was a complete set up there on the wall, starting with a lovely meat cleaver. Glaring at him, she calculated the best way to twist her body and reach the cleaver with her free hand. But before she could execute what she thought was shaping up to be a brilliant plan, he read her mind.

"Don't even think about it," he warned, pulling her by the arm until she was in the center of the kitchen, well away from any weapons.

Furious, she jerked free and they faced off. Coming to the slow realization that he could have killed and/or raped her three or four times by now if that was what he'd had in mind, she focused on her anger rather than her fear.

"What the hell do you want?" she snapped.

"I need to talk to you."

"Talk? Really? You ever hear of a telephone, Jack? Or what about this: doorbell. Say it with me: *door-bell*. How did you get in here anyway? How did you even know where I live?"

"It was real tricky. I looked you up in the phone book. And I came in through the kitchen door."

This was outrageous. That door had a damn fine dead bolt lock that she'd installed with her own two hands and trusty cordless drill. "You picked my lock?"

He didn't answer.

"Why not try knocking on the front door? At a decent hour?"

"This is an emergency." He hesitated. "And I didn't want to be seen."

"By who? The boogeyman?"

The sarcasm bounced right off his flat demeanor. "The people who are after me."

"Okay, I'll bite. Who's after you, Jack?"

"I can't get into that. But they're going to come after you, too, and I need to get you out of here. Now."

Well, she'd known there had to be something seriously wrong with a person who looked like Jack and could cook, but she'd chosen to nurse the ridiculous girlish hope that she'd actually met an interesting man. A jerk, clearly, but still interesting. Not that she wanted to marry him or anything, but it was nice to know that such a man existed.

Now she had to face the ugly reality that he was bat-shit crazy and probably off his meds. Hell, it was worse than that. No doubt there was a padded wagon roaming up and down the streets of Mount Adams right now, driven by uniformed men with giant nets, looking for him.

It figured.

Tragic, but he was in her house and she needed to get him out without him killing her, which he could still decide to do.

"Jack," she said, trying to keep the condescension out of her voice, "if someone's after you, you need to call the police."

"The police can't help me. And they can't protect you."

There was no reasoning with the unreasonable, but she tried anyway. "Okay, Jack. I'm going to take it on faith that someone's after you. What does that have to do with *me*?"

"If they can't find me, they're going to use you to get to me." He paused long enough to analyze her uncomprehending look and answer her unspoken questions with rising impatience. "Because of the video, which makes it look like we're lovers. Look—we don't have time for this. I want you to get dressed, throw a few things in an overnight bag and—"

"I'm not going anywhere with you."

"—let me take you to a hotel or someplace safe—"

"You're insane." Damn. She hadn't meant to say that. There went her whole *don't piss him off* plan. "I'm not going anywhere with you."

"—and then I can touch base with my contacts and we can figure out how to keep you safe." Crossing to the sink, he turned on the water and splashed his face, getting rid of most of the blood.

"Hey—"

Ignoring her protest, he grabbed the bar towel from the ring, dried off and tossed it onto the dish rack.

"Don't just stand there. Get going."

"No."

He treated her to a string of curses on a growl of

increasing frustration and Amara decided she'd had enough. If he'd wanted to kill her, he'd have done it by now. The fact that he hadn't gave her the courage she needed to march to the kitchen door, which was, sure enough, now unlocked—*thanks for breaking into my house, jerk*—and hold it open in the hopes of facilitating his speedy departure.

"Thanks so much for the warning about the . . . you know . . . bad guys." God. How stupid did she sound? Bad guys. Right. "I'm going to lock the door again after you leave, keep my eyes open, and if any of them show up—"

"Don't patronize me." He did another one of those vaulting across the room maneuvers—how did such a big man move so quickly and silently?—snatched her away from the door and closed it. "I'm not talking about people who will key your car if they get mad at you. These people will torture you to find out what you know about me and then they will kill you. You feel me? Kill. You."

Amara jerked her arm free and opened her mouth to argue.

And the lights went out.

Not just the lights. The hum from the refrigerator stopped. The low murmur of voices from the Travel Channel in the living room fell silent. For no reason at all, the world went dark, quiet and scary.

An angry accusation formed on her lips and she looked to Jack, ready to demand an explanation.

But then she caught a shadowy glimpse of his wide-eyed expression and read it with no need for interpretation. *Oh, shit,* said that grim face, and Amara's fear hiked several notches higher.

They stared at each other, frozen and waiting, and

heard it at the same time: the soft but unmistakable sound of a footstep.

On the hardwood floors in her hallway.

In her house.

Then came the pinpoint flash of a light on her wall, and Amara knew.

This was no random power outage, and if she glanced out her window she would not discover that her neighbors' houses were also dark. This was the very same bad guy Jack had just warned her about, and he'd cut her power for the express purpose of coming in here to kill them both. He had a flashlight and probably a gun and she and Jack would be dead within minutes.

Panic propelled her to take a step toward the door, but Jack touched her arm and then raised a finger to his lips.

Shhh.

The *oh, shit* was gone from his face and he didn't look scared or even worried. He looked calm and cool, as though he'd been through this drill a million times before and was counting the seconds until his next coffee break. That obvious and unshakable confidence gave her strength enough for a deep breath.

She nodded.

Using hand signals she'd seen in some military TV show or other, he motioned for her to get down and crawl under the kitchen table. She obeyed without hesitation, hanging on to one sturdy oak leg and angling her body so she could keep him in sight.

A half smile of approval flickered across Jack's face as he reached behind his back and produced . . .

Oh, my God.

Was that a *gun*?

The floor creaked. Right outside the kitchen. That pinpoint of light danced across the kitchen door . . . the range . . . the baker's rack.

Oh, God. Fear clamped down on her, prickling her scalp, burning her throat and constricting her lungs. *Please, God. Please, God, pleasegod, ohgod, ohgod, please—*

Praying for survival, she watched Jack blend into the wall to the right of the archway from the hall, and then the floor creaked again, too small a sound to warn of this new evil in her peaceful sanctuary, and a figure came into view, a phantom, an intruder.

Shaking, Amara clamped her free hand to her mouth and tried to control her raspy breathing.

Stealthy and deadly, lit only by the moonlight filtering in from the shades, nothing but black upon black upon black, with no discernible eyes or even face, the intruder crept forward with the flashlight in one hand and a gun in the other.

It was a big gun—longer than Jack's.

No, wait.

That gun had a silencer on it. That was an assassin's gun.

Which meant that . . . that was an assassin.

Not a garden-variety robber or would-be rapist, the kind of criminal who could possibly be talked out of committing a violent act.

An assassin.

Please, God, don't let us die.

The assassin lingered in the doorway and looked back and forth, surveying the room, and that light circled the walls, ceiling and floor in a relentless sweep.

And then Amara saw it inches from her crouched knee: the hard stainless steel glint of the chef's knife she'd tried to use on Jack. Oh, thank God. Not that a knife would be much good against a silenced gun, but it was sure better than nothing.

Reaching out, she clutched the knife's hilt and picked it up.

The blade's ring, like a tiny sword being drawn, echoed in the kitchen's utter silence.

Amara cringed; the assassin cocked his head; Jack struck.

With moves Amara had only ever seen in a James Bond movie, Jack sprung forward and elbowed the assassin in the face. Crying out, the assassin dropped to the floor and his gun clattered away.

Amara scrambled for it.

The assassin drew his knees into his belly and kicked out, catching Jack squarely in the thighs. Jack yelped with pain, hit the floor on his butt and kept rolling until he got back to his feet as though the whole move had been choreographed by a stuntman.

The assassin, meanwhile, was up and running and had apparently decided that, given the loss of his gun, it was time to call it a night. Darting down the hallway in a full retreat, he ripped open the front door—Amara heard the telltale squeak of the hinges she never remembered to oil—and ran off.

Cursing, Jack took a few steps after him and paused long enough to aim his gun in a two-handed hold and fire. The sound exploded through the kitchen and ricocheted off the walls until it felt as though Amara's ears were bleeding.

Apparently it was a miss because Jack cursed again and yelled at Amara over his shoulder, a wild light in his eyes. "Stay here. I'll be right back."

Amara nodded and watched him go. The second he

was out of sight, she crept out from under the table, reached for her cordless phone on the counter and punched three buttons that she really hoped were 9-1-1. Nothing happened. Bewildered, she tried again, but then it hit her: no power meant no cordless phone.

Shit.

Glancing wildly around for her cell phone, she remembered she'd left it in her briefcase and hurried into the living room to find it. The second she fished it out, running footsteps approached outside her front door and she froze, debating whether to run back to the kitchen for the gun and wondering why she'd been stupid enough to leave it there in the first place.

Jack reappeared, shutting the door behind him, and glared at her. Even though he was panting—they both were—he managed enough breath to chastise her.

"Believe me now?"

"Absolutely."

His sharp gaze latched onto the phone in her hand. "What the hell are you doing? I told you we're not calling the police."

Something inside Amara snapped. She hadn't slept in days, she was running on fumes, she'd endured two break-ins tonight and feared for her life three times in the last eighteen hours.

You didn't mess with a woman on the edge.

"Listen, jackass." She used the phone to gesture in his face, beyond caring that she was yelling like a banshee. "I don't know what planet you're from, but here in the United States, when someone breaks into your house in the middle of the night and tries to kill you, you call the police."

Jack reached out and neatly snatched the phone from her.

After one disbelieving second, Amara growled with outrage.

Jack cut her off by planting his hand over her mouth, jerking her to him and speaking quietly in her ear.

"As I have been trying to tell you since I got here," he said, "some bad people are after me and I'm afraid they're coming back right this second, as soon as they get another weapon."

Amara whimpered at the thought.

"If you'll be so kind as to throw on some clothes, pack a couple of things in a bag and come with me," Jack continued, "I'll be happy to take you somewhere safer until we can contact the authorities and figure out what to do with you. Does that work for you, or should I leave you here to deal with the killer yourself the next time he comes back?"

Shoving her away, he turned her loose and she rounded on him, opening her mouth, itching to finish the verbal castration she'd started and make sure he didn't manhandle her again in this lifetime.

But then she tamped down her hot temper and realized that while he may be a jackass, he'd saved her life once tonight and she sure hoped he'd do it again if the time came.

"Let's go." She hurried down the hall toward her bedroom and clothes. "What're you waiting for?"

"You've got two minutes," Jack told her grimly.

Chapter 7

"I need to make a phone call," Jack said.

Amara, who was sitting in the motel room's single chair, looked up from the spot she'd been staring at on the floor and blinked. Her face was so expressionless that he doubted she'd heard him and wondered if she was in shock.

They'd driven twenty miles down the interstate and found a no-tell motel with a vacancy. No one had followed them; Jack made sure of that, and it was easy to track the people behind you on a deserted highway in the middle of the night.

The motel, one of those sprawling ranch types with an actual neon sign, didn't look promising. A bored clerk who could barely be bothered to look around from the online poker he was playing checked them in. Cash didn't seem to be a problem, though, and the room smelled clean, so Jack was grateful for those small blessings.

Amara, on the other hand, was a first-class, grade-A problem of the highest magnitude, one he needed to wash his hands of as soon as possible. Her silent routine in the car didn't fool him for a minute, nor did those big, unfocused eyes and the bewildered way she'd noted the ugly blue and green flowered bedspread, matching drapes, black-velvet wall art and threadbare carpet, as though she didn't know where she was and couldn't understand how she'd gotten there.

Any moment now, she'd get a second wind and come out swinging, as much of an unmitigated pain in the ass as she'd ever been.

"How come you get to make calls and I don't?" she demanded.

Sure enough.

Jack stared at the intransigent line of her mouth—nothing bewildered or unfocused there, not now—and wondered why God had sent this woman to torment him. Was it because his life wasn't screwed up enough already? He needed a few more trials and tribulations to test his mettle as a man—was that it? Or was it a slow day out there in the universe and God just needed a good laugh?

"Well, Amara." He took care to strike the exact sarcastic tone he needed to make her stubborn chin jut at him—there it was. Funny how he took time out from a life-threatening situation to press her buttons and let her press his. "If you have a prepaid cell phone that's registered in a false name like this one"—he found the phone in his jacket pocket and flashed it at her—"that won't lead any killers to our door, feel free to use it."

The words struck a chord with her and her eyes widened with unmistakable fear. "That was a killer, wasn't it?"

"That was a killer."

"How did he find me? Did he follow you?"

"I know how to blend in. No one followed me."

"Then how did he find me?"

Jack shrugged. "Probably the same way I did. You're in the phone book."

She managed an ironic smile. "I wanted potential clients to be able to find me. I guess that worked a little too well, huh?"

"Looks like."

"I think he got in through the garage. The circuit box's in the garage."

Jack wanted to tell her not to dissect the intricacies of a contract killer's standard operating procedure—if a professional had been hired to find and kill you, he'd find and kill you because it wasn't that hard—but he let it go for now. She'd get the picture soon enough.

"Yeah. The garage. Makes sense."

Nodding with grim satisfaction, she stared down at the floor again, but something was still nagging at her. He could see it.

"I personally installed locks on all my doors when I moved in. Good dead bolts. I'm not one of those people who leave their doors unlocked for the kids when they get home after school—"

"Some people can't be kept out with locks, Amara," he said simply.

This seemed to make sense to her, which was strange because all these months later it still didn't make sense to him.

She stared off across the room, lost in her troubled thoughts.

And then, without warning, she jerked her head around and nailed him with a narrowed gaze that was as clever as it was unrelenting. Uh-oh. He tried to hide his growing unease by taking off his jacket and tossing it on top of their bags, which he'd placed next to the wall, but it was hard because any minute he'd break into an outright nervous sweat.

Damn woman.

Of all the people in the world to be saddled with, he had to choose a brilliant criminal defense attorney who was probably known nationwide for her blistering cross-examinations.

"Who are you?"

He arranged his features, aiming for an expression of uncomprehending innocence. "I told you. Jack Patterson."

"Jack Patterson. Fry cook." The icy derision in her voice was enough to cover everything in the room with a layer of frost. "Who just happened to—*what?* Piss off a neighbor in a fence-line dispute and make him angry enough to hire a killer to get you? Is that what you're telling me?"

"You don't need all the details."

"What about some of the details?"

"You don't need those, either."

"My life is on the line here, too, and I'm entitled to—"

"You're not entitled to jack shit," he told her.

He didn't expect any of his evasions to fly, and they didn't. Spitting mad now, she surged to her feet and got in his face, her eyes bright and wild and her wavy black hair skimming her cheeks.

"I'm asking the wrong question, aren't I? Instead of wondering *who* you are, I should be wondering *what* you are."

Shit. Was it getting hot in here? Jack scrolled through a series of lies and excuses in his mind, hoping he'd come up with one that would satisfy her without putting her in any more danger.

"You're in organized crime, aren't you?"

Irritated and agitated, Jack stripped off his sweater and tossed it on the bed. "Yeah." He tugged at the bottom of his white T-shirt and wondered why he didn't feel any cooler. "Me and the Gottis and the Gambinos and the Genoveses. We're like this." He held up a hand with his first two fingers crossed. "I'm godfather to all their kids."

She snorted with a repressed laugh. "Yeah, you're right. That's stupid. The way you moved tonight, the way you carry yourself—"

"Drop it, Amara."

"—the way you handle your weapon—"

Jesus. Staring into her eyes, he'd swear he could see the neurons firing in her clever brain, feel the connections being made. Why didn't someone put her in charge of the world hunger problem? With a mind like this, she'd have it solved by the end of the week.

"—you're a cop, aren't you? No—wait. You're a fed."

He turned away, his careful explanations scattering like grains of sand in a hurricane. For the life of him, he couldn't think straight when this woman was in the room. Hell, he could barely breathe half the time and he wasn't doing so great managing the in-out lung thing right now.

"You ever try novel writing with that imagination?" he wondered.

Edging around until she was in his face again, she gave him a sharp jab in the chest with her index finger. "That's it, isn't it? You're FBI, aren't you?"

"I'm not FBI and you need to back off. I'm trying to protect you."

The sudden sharpness in his voice didn't make a damn bit of difference because she'd scented blood and zeroed in for the kill. He'd've had better luck extracting his thigh from the jaws of a rabid pit bull.

"Homeland Security? Immigration? ATF?"

"I said, *back off,*" he roared.

Amara didn't back off in the face of his fury, didn't flinch, didn't so much as blink one long eyelash. Instead she stared at him with her unwavering vision and the kind of courage that even a couple of his toughest colleagues had lacked. Despite his frustration, he felt a grudging respect for her, an admiration he'd sooner die than admit.

"No, wait," she whispered, the light of comprehension illuminating her face. "I remember what you said. You wondered why I was wasting my time defending an accused drug dealer, didn't you?"

Jack looked to the ceiling and let the defeat wash over him.

It was almost a relief.

To be who he was, just this once. To tell the truth, just this once.

Nodding and triumphant, Amara connected the last dot. "You're DEA, aren't you?"

Exhausted now, Jack looked her in the face, held her gaze, and said nothing.

That was all the answer she needed. The thrill of her momentary victory leached away as the enormity of his situation sank in. Her expression sobered by slow degrees until finally she was looking at him the way he imagined she'd look at a man with inoperable lung cancer.

Empathy was there in her warm brown eyes. Much as anyone else's empathy would have set him off with proud indignation, there was something about *her* empathy that felt like absolution.

With this one woman, he didn't have to explain. She understood the path he'd chosen and that he'd been doing his job. She knew that tracking down drug dealers wasn't the thrilling escapade they showed on TV, where the daring agent nailed the bad guys in an hour and headed home for a shower and a nice dinner. She knew, without his explanation, that the work he'd done was hard, that he'd made enormous personal sacrifices, that he'd had to get his hands dirty and, worst of all, that he'd had to make tough moral choices that he questioned to this day.

She got it.

The weight of his unexpected gratitude threatened to knock him flat on his butt.

Tears shimmered in her eyes and they were so beautiful and so terrible that he felt them in the pulse thundering in his ears and the blood beating in his heart—she affected him that much.

"Oh, Jack," she said, and then a crease furrowed her smooth brow. "That is your name, isn't it? Jack?"

This one didn't miss a beat, did she? He almost had to smile. "Jackson is my first name."

"But Patterson?"

He said nothing. He supposed this was the new code between them: when she stumbled onto something that was a little too dangerous and a little too close to home, he kept quiet rather than lie to her.

Funny thing about this irritating woman. He had a real hard time lying to her.

"How long have you been in hiding, Special Agent?" she asked.

None of your business. That was the correct answer, the one he should hurl at her with enough force that she finally backed off and let the whole dangerous topic of his unfortunate career choices drop. *None of your damn business,* he should say. *Now sit down and shut up while I make that phone call I've been trying to make for the last ten minutes while you've been interrogating me.*

Instead, he opened his mouth and said, "Several months. I'm on a leave of absence."

"Sooo . . . you're in WITSEC?"

"Huh-uh. I'm a big boy. Special agents like me with weapons training and a gun are supposed to be able to take care of ourselves. We don't get put in the Program. We get transferred to another office."

"Oh."

She reached out to touch his arm and suddenly all that touching empathy was more than he could stomach without lapsing into dry heaves. Wheeling away, he snapped at her over his shoulder.

"Now if you're done with the third degree, I need to make that phone call so I can get you out of my hair as soon as possible. You're a royal pain in the ass."

Some devil made him glance back in time to see the hurt streak across her face and it stabbed him with the kind of pain he deserved for being such a bastard after she'd shown him such kindness.

But Amara Clarke was only a temporary visitor to his fucked-up world, and it was best that they both remembered that and kept a nice distance from each other. Best for her and definitely best for him. Emotional attachments weren't his thing and never would be as long as Kareem Gregory was alive and had the money to put out a contract on him.

Aware of Amara hanging her head and collapsing back into her chair, Jack pulled his cell phone out again and punched the numbers he had memorized and only used in case of emergency. He figured his current boiling cauldron of trouble qualified.

"I'm calling Dexter," he said.

"Who's Dexter?"

Cincinnati

"Dexter. Oh, God, *Dexter.*"

Belinda, thought Dexter Brady, really overdid it when she came, especially when they did it doggy style, like now. The whimpers, the operatic screams, the endless loud calling of his name, so bad that he'd had complaints from his irritated upstairs neighbors on more than one memorable occasion. He appreciated enthusiasm as much as the next guy and, let's face it, he could fuck a woman like nobody's business, but Belinda really needed to tone it down.

As soon as he came another three or four times, he intended to tell her so.

She went limp at last and it was his turn.

Both hands on her hips, he used one knee to nudge her thighs wider, until she collapsed on her belly and he could thrust as deep as he needed to. He came in a surge of weak relief that in no way corresponded to the frenzied workout he'd just put himself through. Letting his head fall back, he reached for the pleasure and tried to prolong it, tried to embrace the relief and let it be enough, but it wasn't. It never was.

Sated and disappointed—Jesus, why did he think every time would be different and why was he always so disillusioned when it never was?—he pulled out and collapsed onto the pillows next to her. He'd just reeled her in and covered her mouth with his, licking deep, when his cell phone chirped on the nightstand.

"Ignore it, baby." She nipped his bottom lip, sucking it, and he would have ignored it because not much in life was worth interrupting for a phone call and sex definitely wasn't one of them, but then he decided he should do his job.

"Sorry." Giving Belinda one last kiss, he kept one hand on her tits and reached for the phone with the other. "Brady."

"It's Jack. I've got a situation."

Climbing out of bed, he turned his back on Belinda's wide eyes and paced over to his dresser in the corner. "Parker, you stupid fuck. What happened to you?"

Chapter 8

Jack tried to stay calm, which was a major project at the moment with his frayed nerves and the squared lines of Amara's jaw as she stared across the room and refused to look at him even though he knew darn well she was listening to every word.

"I've got a situation and I've got a new phone," he told Dexter.

"Yeah, well, I've got a situation, too." Dexter's voice softened a little and this terrified Jack because he was pretty sure Dexter hadn't shown any softness since the first Bush administration. "It's bad news. Wolfe's dead. His wife too."

The words hovered in the air, heard but unregistered.

Jack waited for them to sink in, but they didn't. Amara, apparently sensing a change in him, looked around with concern in her eyes. Jack turned his back to her, swallowed hard and struggled with words. None came, but the knowledge settled in his gut with the weight of a thousand boulders.

"Parker?" Dexter said in his ear. "You there?"

"What—" Realizing he was croaking in a pretty good imitation of a bullfrog, he tightened his grip on the phone and cleared his throat. "What happened?"

"They were hit execution style in their garage."

Standing up suddenly became way too much effort. So did sitting down. In a pathetic compromise, Jack rested his forehead against the wall and sucked in a breath that did nothing for him except give him enough clarity to imagine Ray and his innocent wife—hell, they were all innocent, but she'd *really* been innocent—sprawled and bleeding on the concrete floor of their own damn garage.

Emotion erupted from him in an unstoppable blast and, with a roar of agonized anger and frustration—*why Ray, God, WHY?*—he banged his head on the wall.

Behind him, Amara cried out and hurried to his side but he shook her off and focused on the warmth of his blood as it flowed anew from the split in his forehead, and embraced the beautiful release that physical pain gave him from emotional pain, which was always so much worse.

"Stop it, Jack. What are you trying to do to yourself?"

Amara wheeled around for a washcloth from the stack on the counter a few feet away. Next thing he knew she was back, pressing the scratchy cotton to his head and caring for him in a way no one else had for longer than he could remember. He submitted, wanting to shake her off and, more than that, wanting to pull her closer.

Meanwhile, Dexter was talking in his ear. "What's going on, Parker? Who's that? Where are you?"

"I've got it," Jack told her, taking the cloth and keeping it in place with a firmer pressure than she'd been using, not to stop the blood but because when he held it this way the pain continued in a steady throbbing ache that gave him the focus he needed.

Hovering within touching distance, she watched him with worried eyes.

"It's Amara Clarke," Jack said into the phone. "She's a local defense attorney and she's caught up in my mess. We were caught on surveillance video together and it wound up on the local news—"

"What?" Dexter said.

"National too," Amara murmured. "CNN called, MSNBC, the networks. Didn't you see it? Where have you been?"

Jack closed his eyes with sudden nausea. Well, that sure explained a couple things. How ironic was that? After all the skulking in shadows he'd done trying to keep himself alive, his face wound up plastered all over the country anyway. Yeah. Real funny.

"Do you want to tell me how this happened?" Dexter demanded.

"It's a long story." Jack's sudden weariness was so overwhelming it was an effort not to slur his words. "But he knows where I am." Aware of Amara's intense interest and her absolute focus on everything he said, his every breath and blink, he took care to keep things general, to not name names. "He sent someone to the diner tonight, looking for me."

Here Jack had to pause because the memory of J-Mart's body, ruined and dead on the floor of the diner that had been his great love, tormented him. He thought of those vacant eyes, that gruff voice, silenced forever, and the kind soul who'd never done anything wrong except befriend Jack without asking questions.

Amara, whose unerring instincts were beginning

to unnerve him, big time, shifted closer and put a steadying hand on his arm.

Jack looked at her as he spoke into the phone, trying to be gentle as he told them both because he knew Amara had liked J-Mart. "They shot the diner owner earlier."

Amara emitted a choked wail that hurt him—actually felt as though it reached down his throat and ripped off a piece of his heart—but Jack continued, needing to say it and get it over with. "He's dead."

"No." Amara clenched her fists and jerked them up and down in angry slashing gestures that punctuated her grief. *"No, no, no!"*

Jack watched as her bright eyes filled and overflowed with sparkling diamond tears that trailed down her cheeks. The right thing to do would be to hold her, comfort her, but there was no comfort in him, not for himself and certainly not for anyone else.

So he focused on the pain in his head, the negligible weight of the phone in his hand, a place near the light switch where a corner of the faded wallpaper had peeled. Anything but her.

"They went to Amara's house tonight looking for me," Jack told Dexter. "We barely made it out of there alive."

"Parker," Dexter muttered. "Could anyone but you scare up this kind of trouble?"

Jackson snorted, keeping one eye on Amara, who snatched a tissue from the box on the counter, dabbed at her eyes and, after a deep breath or two, seemed to pull herself together. "Sorry to wake you up, Dex. I know how you value your beauty sleep."

"I'll call Seattle. Get them to put together a couple of guys. Where are you?"

"Yeah. About that." Jack toyed with what he needed to say, trying to figure out the best way to broach the topic, and then decided, screw it. "I'm a big boy. I can take care of myself—"

"I know you're a big boy," Dexter said. "Get to the point."

"I'll be fine until I head back to Cincinnati. I want to know what you're going to do to keep Amara safe."

Dexter's sigh was so harsh Jack had to pull the phone away from his ear. "Look, Parker. It's not that I'm not sympathetic. I am. But that woman is not our responsibility."

Jack, who'd expected exactly this kind of response, still couldn't suppress the low growl of angry frustration rumbling in his throat.

Amara watched him, unblinking and emotionless.

"If you want," Dexter continued, "I can make a call to the local police and see what kind of temporary protection—"

"Local police?" Jack snarled. "I'm not sure you understand what's going on here, Dex. This woman was minding her own business and she stumbled across a robbery. She risked her life to save the victim. Because of her bravery and through no fault of her own, she was caught on security camera *with me.* Tonight she was nearly killed in her own fucking house by a contract killer who's looking *for me.* My boss was killed execution style—did I mention that his knees were shot out before he died?—by probably the same contract killer who's looking *for me.* Do you get that?"

"Parker—"

All but breathing fire now, infuriated by the injustice to Amara and the hornet's nest he'd introduced into her life despite all his efforts not to, Jack raised his voice several notches.

"So you'll have to forgive me if I think this problem is a little too serious to just hand her over to the local Keystone cops and hope for the best. You feel me?"

A pause, then, "Is her shit that good, Parker?"

"Fuck you." Cheeks burning because Dexter was right—he wasn't thinking with his big brain, not entirely—he turned to Amara.

God knew he wanted her.

She stood there, shoulders squared, eyes dry and resolute, looking like she was braced for anything and ready to be brave. Hell, she *was* brave; that'd already been demonstrated twice over as far as Jack was concerned.

But being brave, as he knew firsthand, didn't amount to a fly's piss when you were facing down a professional killer who was backed by a drug kingpin with deep pockets and a thirst for vengeance as nasty as he could make it.

And Jack didn't want Amara to have to be brave. He wanted her to be back safe in her own house, where she could work on her cases, install fresh dead bolts, and live a peaceful and violence-free life before dying in her bed at the age of a hundred and six.

She held his gaze, knowing her future was in his hands. And she didn't look worried, foolish woman.

"Who is she to you, Parker?"

"Someone I want to keep safe." There was a hall-of-fame-worthy understatement. "And since you're the only person I can trust, I'm counting on you to help me out."

Dexter kept quiet for a minute and Jack could feel

his wheels spinning, plans formulating. When he spoke again, it was with the decisive tone and determination Jack had long respected over the years.

"Give me your location. I'll call Seattle and have them put a team together to come get you. We'll get the woman sorted out later. I'm thinking it'll take a couple hours. I assume you can stay out of trouble for that long . . . ?"

The basic plan sounded good, but there were always weak spots, always human error to be dealt with. "Who're you sending? We don't need a whole parade—"

This sensible question earned him the predictable response from Dexter. "Don't tell me how to do my job. You just sit tight until they come knocking on your door."

They ironed out a few more details and then Jack hung up, weary to the depths of his soul and wishing he could postpone the inevitable next confrontation with Amara, who was surely gearing up for another grueling cross-examination of him. But when he tossed the phone on the nightstand, she surprised him.

"Is Dexter your boss?"

"Yeah."

"Someone's coming for us?"

"Yeah."

"He's not happy about me, huh?"

This almost made him grin. "No one's happy about you, Bunny."

In what he supposed was a one-time only thing, she let both the sarcasm and the nickname pass. "How's your forehead?" she asked quietly.

"What? Oh." Peeling the washcloth away, he poked at it with his fingers, trying to assess the damage.

Amara jerked his hand away and scowled. "Brilliant. Be sure to infect it with as many germs as possible, genius."

He laughed, which was proof positive that this whole adventure had rendered him insane. Actually cracked his lips open in a smile and let it play out to its natural conclusion, which was laughter. It almost felt good. Almost eased some of the pain.

"Amara," he said. "We're running for our lives. We'll be lucky to see the sun come up in a few hours. Do you think we might have a few more important things to worry about than a little cut on my forehead?"

Snatching the washcloth away, she went to the sink, ran some water on it, wrung it out, and came back to gently wipe his skin with it. "With brains like that, I'm surprised you've managed to keep yourself alive for this long. This guy who's after you must be a real idiot, huh?"

He laughed again and the sound was strange to his own ears. His laughter didn't get much of a workout these days and hadn't for years. There'd been more than one or two dark moments when he'd thought he'd never laugh again.

Forgetting himself—he always forgot himself when she was around—he stared down at her wry smile and felt connected to another human being in a way he wasn't sure he'd ever been. But then he remembered and the moment became too intimate and delicious.

Don't get too close, man.

He turned away on the pretext of grabbing his bag from the floor, slinging it onto the dresser near the TV and rummaging around for some fresh clothes. With tremendous effort, he focused on the hot shower he was about to take and tried not to feel her silent presence behind him.

She'd be gone soon, so it was best to concentrate on that.

The problem was, she was here now.

Don't look at her, he told himself. *Don't look . . . don't look . . . don't—*

Angling his body just slightly and cursing himself for a fool, he kept her in his line of vision because you could lead a horse to water, but you couldn't make the dumb bastard drink.

Having peeled back one corner of the spread to reveal a bright white sheet—the Princess wouldn't want to put her precious ass on any soiled linens, now, would she?—she sat with one leg tucked under her and did that vacant-stare thing again.

There was something forlorn and exhausted about her, poor thing. He was used to this lifestyle, but she wasn't and never would be. Compassion reared its ugly head and he wanted to tell her that she should take a nap, that it would be a couple of hours before the cavalry rode in, but he wasn't sure what the sight of Amara lying in a bed within touching distance would do to his limited reserves of self-control.

Besides.

He sort of liked her company. Sort of liked not being alone for once.

He'd be alone again soon enough, so there was plenty of time later for that.

Digging through the bag, he tried to remember what he'd been doing. What was he looking for? What was he about to do? Oh yeah—shower. That was it.

With his hands wrist-deep in his clothes, he couldn't

think of the first damn thing he needed. How could he think when it was so much easier to stare at Amara?

Yeah, he hadn't been so busy fighting professional killers that he'd failed to notice the fine details of Amara's *Penthouse*-worthy body. And she'd flipped the light on and backlit every inch of herself. It wasn't that he'd been trying to see everything, but Jesus—what was he supposed to do? Ignore those dark-tipped tits and shapely legs? Pretend he didn't see the soft curve of her belly and enticing triangle between her thighs?

What was the point of that ridiculous sheer nightgown she'd been wearing? He'd seen Band-Aids that provided more coverage than that. Why not just go to bed nude?

Amara. In bed. Nude.

Now there was an image he wanted to back away from before he got hurt.

But . . . her face. He could watch it for days and never get bored, maybe weeks. It was all big eyes, cute nose and fantasy-come-to-life lush mouth. That mouth could do a guy some serious damage—if he was lucky.

And where'd all that hair come from? All that long, wavy, silky-sexy black hair. What was she thinking, hiding hair like that by piling it on top of her head? Although . . . on second thought, maybe it wasn't such a bad idea. It didn't stretch his imagination too much to imagine her sparking car accidents and/or riots by walking down the street in all her glory.

Her drop-dead looks. Yeah. That was the problem.

And yet . . . her beauty wasn't the problem at all—wasn't even a fraction of the problem. The problem was way more than he wanted to admit, ever.

As though she finally felt the hunger of his gaze on the top of her head, Amara looked up at him and he saw, to his pained surprise, that a new sheen of tears sparkled in her eyes and her bottom lip trembled.

Aw, fuck.

There was childlike hope in her expression.

"Is J-Mart really dead?"

He hesitated. "Yes."

"Are you sure?"

He swallowed. Wet his dry lips. Wished he could die on the spot rather than cause that light in her eyes to go out. "Yes."

She nodded, accepting the worst.

In the echoing silence, he ignored the crushing pain in his chest and turned back to his bag. Underwear. He needed underwear, deodorant and—

"What's going to happen now, Jack?"

"Well . . ."

Extracting the kit with his toiletries, he tried to think. "For now, they're sending someone—a team—to pick us up. They'll figure out how to protect you—"

"They didn't seem too enthusiastic about that, did they?"

"I plan to help them along with their enthusiasm level," he said flatly.

"And you're going to Cincinnati? To testify?"

Oh, shit. Had he said that? Out loud? Why couldn't he remember that this woman was a sponge with a clever brain worthy of a CIA operative?

He said nothing, and she knew. She always knew.

"When can I go home?" she asked.

"Soon. I think."

"When can you go home?"

He opened his mouth to say it, but it wasn't so easy

getting the words out. They clogged his chest, swelled in his throat and tasted bitter against the back of his tongue. "I don't have a home."

That lip of hers trembled again and she twisted her mouth in her effort to control it. When she spoke again, her voice was hoarse. "When can you stop hiding?"

"When he's dead," Jack told her.

"What about if he's convicted?" she persisted.

Was she joking? Could anyone really be that naive? Was her middle name Pollyanna or something? "When he's *dead*."

The information finally seemed to penetrate her stubborn brain, thank God. Nodding, she wiped her eyes. He, meanwhile, tried to pretend he didn't see her crying, tried not to know that those precious tears were for him.

"I'm scared," she whispered.

"I know."

"You're not?"

He shrugged. "I'm used to it."

"Can you ever get used to this?"

Opening his mouth, he tried to activate his voice. It took a long time. "No."

Another nod. They stared at each other for a couple beats, neither speaking, and then she did a snort-laugh thing that had no humor in it.

"Want to hear something sad, Jack?"

"Sure. Because I haven't had enough sadness in my day yet."

This time her laughter was the genuine article. Quick but genuine, then gone like a streaking comet. "When I was throwing my stuff in the bag, I kept thinking I should call to let them know I'm okay—"

"Who?"

"That's the sad part." She looked exhausted and empty suddenly, as tragic as the sole survivor of a nuclear holocaust. "There's no one to call other than the office, and I'm on vacation anyway. If I'm gone, they'll replace me by the end of the week. They won't find a better lawyer than me, but I'm thinking they'll round up someone who doesn't piss everyone off like I do."

"You're irreplaceable."

She stared at him and he gave himself a swift mental kick in the ass.

Because he hadn't meant to say it and definitely hadn't meant to say it like *that,* with all the enthusiasm and fervor of the president-elect taking the oath of office.

Stammering, he changed the subject. "W-what happened to your parents?"

"I don't have parents."

"Everyone has parents."

"Forgive me." Her lip curled in an ugly smile, an abomination. "I never knew the man who donated the sperm on my behalf, but he was one of my mother's"—she swallowed hard—"clients."

No. Oh, no.

"She was a prostitute. Before she died of AIDS."

She hitched her chin up, waiting for his reaction, daring him to feel sorry for her, and he suppressed that urge only with great difficulty. Instead, because he knew she needed it, he shrugged and finally fished a pair of boxers out of his bag.

"Forgive me if I don't pull out my violin. We've all got our hard-luck tales, don't we? Maybe we should run a contest, see who wins."

She glared, looking as though she could happily smash his face with the butt-ugly lamp on the nightstand. After a minute, she continued.

"While my mother was, uh, *busy,* her younger sister watched me. But then she got into drugs and I got into trouble at school. One of my teachers called protective services. They put me in the system—"

"The system?"

"Foster care."

"Oh."

"I was ten."

"Oh," he said again because there was nothing else to say.

"I went to Washington State on an academic scholarship. And then to the University of Washington for law school."

What else? He'd expected nothing less. This was not a woman who could be held back and he was damn proud of her for it. "Good for you."

"Do you have family, Jack?"

Family. Looking to the plaster-chipped ceiling for some kind of divine intervention, he wondered if this night could possibly get any worse and if he could have just a few more reminders of the things he'd lost and the things he'd never have.

But God was, per his usual practice where Jack was concerned, silent.

Fine, God. Fine.

Angry again, Jack yanked the bag's zipper closed, threw the whole thing to the floor and kicked it into the corner as he stalked to the bathroom.

"I'm taking a shower," he called before he slammed the door.

Chapter 9

Kareem Gregory got home just as the first yellow rays of sun were cracking through the trees. Man, it was late. He checked his watch again, wondering why he hadn't gotten a call yet from Yogi, telling him they'd dealt with Parker. He'd better hear soon.

Meanwhile, it was good to be home. It was a great crib—a Tuscan-style villa, 10,000 square feet and $1 million of it—in one of Cincinnati's best neighborhoods, surrounded by a solid brick wall and security cameras.

All in Mama's name, of course, because that was the way these things were done when you ran a string of customized auto shops, the customers often paid in cash, and the feds were therefore constantly breathing down your neck, wondering where all the money came from.

The DEA would love to seize this house. They still might. God knew they were working on it. Too bad he was always one step ahead of them.

He tried not to make too much noise and wake

anyone up, not that he was creeping in. He didn't *creep,* not in his own damn house.

Although . . . if Kira'd give him what he wanted, he wouldn't have to step out, but Kira wouldn't let him touch her. Why? He hadn't been exactly honest about some of his business dealings before they got married. Hadn't really mentioned that his auto shops didn't account for the bulk of his income. Why should he? Did a man have to fill out a disclosure form before he got married? Hell, no. He was an entrepreneur; he owned some businesses; he had some money. That was what he'd told Kira, and that was all she needed to know.

He was a businessman. Maybe he didn't have a college degree with his name on it, but he was a visionary, the same as Bill Gates or Warren Buffett, who had an organization with rules and layers, profits and projections and losses.

But he'd lied.

Partially because Kira had been trying so hard to escape the ugliness from her childhood that she'd never marry into a situation that might send her back down the same road. Mostly because he needed to see that innocence in her eyes, to know that she looked to him as some kind of knight with the shining armor and black stallion and shit, an honest man who would rescue and protect her.

An honorable man. That's what she'd wanted and that's what she'd gotten. He had ethics and principles that he lived by and that he required of those who worked for him. They just weren't the ethics and principles that she thought.

So they'd gotten married and they'd been happy.

Two years after that, it all went to hell. Thanks to the DEA and their undercover agents, assorted snitches and entrapment, his beautiful life had gone south on an express bullet train riding greased rails, and she'd turned away.

He hated her for that.

What had happened to the *for better or for worse* part? Huh? Her pretty little manicured hands weren't clean in this mess. Oh, no. She'd played her role. She'd been—what was the word?—complicit. Yeah, that was it. She'd pretended she didn't know that drugs were paying for her house and her clothes and her college education, but she *knew*. She saw guns and the bodyguards, the feds and their warrants and their searches and their Big Brother routine.

Kira was complicit, the same as Carmela Soprano was complicit in Tony's business activities, the same as Kay Corleone was complicit in Michael's. Wives *knew*. They always knew. And they accepted.

So why wouldn't Kira act like his wife?

Halfway down the hall, he heard the light jangling of tags and the click of nails on the polished floor, and met up with the stupid little dog she'd gotten while he was in the pen. Fucking beagle. She'd named the little yapper Max, which was idiotic.

But Kira liked Max, and Kareem wanted the privilege of screwing his wife again, so he pretended he liked Max, too. "Hey, doggy."

Inside the kitchen, the smell of coffee had already alerted him that someone was awake. It was Kira, sitting at the built-in desk, dressed already with her curly black head bent over her homework.

Nursing.

While he'd been rotting away in federal prison, she'd been working on her degree, and getting damn good grades, too. She'd graduate soon, with high honors. He didn't know whether to be annoyed or proud.

She ignored him for as long as possible, then troubled herself enough to look up from her notes and give him a vacant Stepford wife smile.

The blank expression irritated him like sand in the crotch of his trunks when he went to the beach, because she never looked at him the way she used to.

"Good morning," she said, like she was glad to see him.

It was all part of the game, so he'd play. "How's my baby girl?"

Part of the game was that she pretended that whatever he did didn't bother her, and this worked to his advantage a lot of the time. Like now. He ran his hand over the soft fluff of her short and natural hair, soaking in the apple-fresh scent of her skin. And then, because that wasn't enough, he leaned down and kissed the mocha satin of her cheek and pretended he didn't feel her stiffen.

She wanted to pull away, but rejecting him outright wasn't part of the game, so she didn't do it.

One day, he knew, she would do it. When she'd finished her degree and could make her own financial way in the world, she'd ask for a divorce and try to break free. Even though there was no breaking free of Kareem Gregory for anyone who touched his life, no liberation for anyone, friend or enemy, until he said so (and he never said so; like Cosa Nostra, this was a lifetime thing with him and you didn't just say *See ya, Kareem* and hand in your resignation letter), she would ask him for a divorce and hope he agreed.

She knew better, but she'd ask anyway.

Either way, that day was coming and the confrontation

between them was as inevitable as the Mexicans trying to short him on the latest shipment of his shit.

But today wasn't the day.

"Coffee?" She was already up and on her feet, heading to the coffeepot.

"No, thanks. What'd you do last night?"

"Studied. I thought I'd make some pancakes, if you're hungry—"

"Maybe later. You ready for your test?"

"Yep."

That was the game. He asked her about school; she offered to cook him something; sometimes they mentioned the weather. That was it. Whoever dropped the illusion of them being a happily married couple first, lost. Right now, they were stalemated and had been for a while.

"Later, Baby Girl."

He left. He was almost out of the kitchen and about to head up the back steps to the bedroom, when something happened.

"Hey, cutie." Kira was using the voice she used to save for Kareem on the dog. Fucking *Max*. "Hey, cutie. You want some kibble?"

Kareem paused in the doorway, hot anger seething to life in his chest, and watched her bend down, scoop up the dog, and kiss his furry forehead with the same lips she wouldn't let anywhere near Kareem.

Kissed. The. Fucking. Dog.

Time to up the stakes.

Determined to provoke a genuine reaction out of her, he wheeled around, walked back, and did something he hadn't done in forever: gave her the once-over that let her know what he wanted.

He let his gaze heat up several notches and ran it

over her face . . . her titties . . . her hips, her crotch. Hopefully this reminded her of a couple things. That he still wanted her, for one. That she still belonged to him, for another. That he could do any damn thing he wanted to do to her and there was nothing she could do to stop him.

Nothing.

He flicked his gaze back up to her face and saw the flare of panic in her eyes before she blinked and hid it. He leaned past the dog and kissed his wife on the mouth.

If she could kiss the dog, she could damn well kiss him.

Kareem brushed his lips back and forth over hers and then slid his tongue inside the hot silk of her mouth, tasting her revulsion, her hatred, and he reveled in it. If hatred was the only true reaction he could get from her, he'd take it.

When he was good and ready, he ended the kiss, breathless now.

She was breathless, too, with a spark of heat and remembrance in her eyes.

That spark gave him hope. "How about dinner tonight?"

"I've got more studying—" she began, but the automatic refusal trailed off when she saw what he was doing.

"Hello, Max." Using that same singsong, Kareem scratched the dog's head and then under his chin. "You want to go for a walk?"

Max, the dumb canine, licked Kareem's hand.

Kira held the dog a little closer, as though she wanted to protect him.

Unsmiling, Kareem held her gaze. "I like this little guy. You don't mind if I take him for a walk, do you?"

Kira stared at him, comprehension making her pale. "No."

Kareem held her gaze for an extra beat or two, just to make sure she understood. Deep down, where it counted, she needed to know who was in charge and who would always be in charge. "What were you saying about dinner?"

"Dinner sounds great."

Bingo. The game was back on, with Kareem five points ahead.

Cincinnati

Empty.

Marian Barber shook the bottle again, just to make sure, because it was early and she hadn't slept well and, let's face it, she didn't think well until she'd had her first morning dose of her pills, but the bottle remained stubbornly empty.

Oh, God. No pink tablets. No OxyContin. None. *Oh God Oh God Oh God.*

Panic made her lash out. She hurled the bottle across the room, where it hit the slate shower tile and ricocheted to the floor with a clatter loud enough to wake the dead.

Frozen and panting, Marian waited and hoped Dwayne hadn't heard.

Just wait. Just wait. Just—

"Marian?" called Dwayne's sleepy-hoarse voice from the bedroom. "You okay?"

Shit.

Hurrying to the bathroom door, she peeked out and saw her husband levered up on his elbows in the middle of the rumpled bed, with slashes of weak sunlight across his bare chest from the drawn blinds.

"I just dropped a bottle," she told him. "Go back to sleep."

"Come back to bed." He reached out a hand to beckon her.

Jesus Christ. Marian tried to tamp down her sudden rage, but it was hard because her skin was crawling and she could barely stand still. Under her armpits she could feel the steady trickle of clammy sweat, and cramps were starting low in her belly; in another minute or two she'd have diarrhea foul enough to melt the toilet. Drop dead, she wanted to say, but she kept her voice sweet and tried to sound like his offer was remotely tempting.

"Can't." Something invisible with icy fingers skittled up her spine and she shivered, crossing her arms over her chest and trying to conserve body heat so the shivers wouldn't turn into shakes. "I've got to take my car in for an oil change this morning, remember?"

"Take it to the dealership. That quicky lube place can't handle a Land Rover."

"I will," she said.

Brilliant, asshole.

Here she was, about to crawl out of her skin and quite possibly tear the house apart in her desperation for some relief, and the clueless idiot she'd married, Sherlock Fucking Holmes, wanted to get serviced, and then he wanted the car serviced, too.

If she tried, she couldn't hate him more. For sleeping like a baby when she couldn't keep her mind from churning about how she'd divert more money from their accounts, how she'd cover up another diversion and then, assuming she got that far without discovery, where she'd get more Oxy.

Back in the bathroom, she clicked on the light so she could see better and caught sight of a haggard figure in the mirror. She paused, gripping the sink for support.

Was that her?

Death warmed over didn't really cover it. She'd have to get a little color in her face to look that good. She looked sweaty and gray—yes, gray—with ringed and sunken eyes that looked like they belonged to a cadaver. Her silky brown hair was wild around her face, brittle, and she had the haunted, feral appearance of an escaped convict with bloodhounds baying at her ankles.

God, she needed the Oxy. Her hair could be fixed once she had the Oxy. Everything would be fine once she had the Oxy.

Dropping to her knees on the cold tile, she scuttled for the bottle, ignoring the protest in her aching back, the painful slipped disk that had started her down this road in the first place. She took the bottle and shook it. Held it up to the light just to be sure.

Empty. Still empty.

Crouching back on her heels, she tried to think. Dwayne. That bastard had taken her shit. That was it, wasn't it? He knew how good it made her feel, how it boosted her through her endless days listening to Mommy-this and Mommy-that and trying to be everything to every fucking body, and he wanted some for himself.

That was it. That was what was going on here. She'd kill him for this.

She surged to her feet and lunged for the door, and then a memory hit her.

She'd come in to use the bathroom last night. She hadn't felt so hot. She'd chewed those last two Oxys and washed them down with tap water. This was her fault.

She braced her hands on the sink again and, lowering her head, sobbed silently until long strands of spit ran from her mouth to the bowl. Maybe the pharmacy would—

No. The pharmacy wouldn't. She knew that. The doctor had prescribed a thirty-day supply of the shit and she'd chewed and swallowed her way through the tablets in—she ran through it in her mind, trying to count—six days. Only six days? Yeah. It'd been the day she took the girls for their checkup, and that was six days ago.

If she went to the pharmacy, they'd call the doctor.

If they called the doctor, he'd know.

Help. She needed help.

This was the time to tell Dwayne that she might have a problem. That she'd been taking several tablets a day even though she hadn't had any serious pain in months. That she might be a little out of control.

But then she thought of the look on his face when he realized that she was a druggie. He'd want to send her to rehab. And then everyone would know.

And the girls. What would she tell the girls?

This last thought galvanized her and she dropped to her knees and scurried around the floor, looking in the far corners and ignoring stray hairs and dust bunnies.

She didn't have a problem and she didn't—

There. Under the far corner of the embroidered rug. Was that—was that pink?

A quick flip of the edge of the rug and there it was, the most beautiful thing she'd ever seen in her life: a little pink tablet, dropped and forgotten, just waiting for her to discover it.

Laughing, she ignored the layer of lint on it and chewed it happily.

Thank God.

No, she thought, staggering to her feet and wiping the lint off her tongue, she didn't have a problem at all. She just needed her medication. She was like a diabetic, not a drug addict.

But . . . she would need to do something she'd been avoiding.

She'd have to call Jerome on his cell phone and pray he'd sell her some shit.

Again.

Chapter 10

Jack came out of the bathroom with a towel around his waist and *don't mess with me* etched deep in his face. If Amara had any doubts about his mood, it was cleared up by the tight-lipped glower he shot her as he strode past on his way to his bag in the corner, pausing only to toss his black toiletries case on the nightstand.

She'd been lounging against the pillows, wondering if she should try to get a little sleep, but now she sat up straight and watched him, reading his body language, which was like an open book with large print, pictures and helpful commentary in the margins.

So he didn't want to talk to her and was trying to block her out. That was just too freaking bad. She had a couple of things on her mind, and staring death in the face had a real good way of putting things in perspective. If she was going to die soon, the least he could do was answer a couple of questions and tell her the truth.

Somehow the world had shrunk down to her and Jack, the walls of this room and the experiences they'd shared together. Sharing a hotel room and seeing his toiletries, not to mention facing down an assassin together, forced the kind of intimacies on them that would have been unimaginable a couple of days ago, back when she wasn't certain he'd ever voluntarily looked at her and was positive that he hated her.

Her jaw opened up the way it was supposed to, but her mouth was dry suddenly, her voice tight, and it had nothing to do with any danger, which seemed momentarily far away from this cozy hotel room.

It had everything to do with Jack and his soapy-fresh scent layered over the sporty smell of deodorant. The muscular lines of his back and shoulders didn't help. Neither did the flex of his hard butt as he stooped over the bag or the gleam of his caramel skin stretched taut over a powerful thigh where the white towel fell away.

He had the shapely calves of someone who'd played soccer at some point in the not-too-distant past, and even his feet, as well-kept as his strong hands, were nice in their flip-flops, with high arches and strong toes.

He rose and faced her, yanking another white T-shirt—he seemed to have an endless supply—down over the heavy slabs of a chest that had flat nipples and a narrow streak of hair disappearing to southern parts whose bulkiness couldn't entirely be explained away by the knot in the towel.

He was perfection. Six-plus feet of everything a woman could ask for and more than she could dream of. The kind of man whose mere presence made other men superfluous if not outright invisible.

Jack pulled on a new pair of jeans and tossed the

towel aside without ever giving her a glimpse of what was beneath the towel, damn him. "You're staring."

Yeah, she was, but she couldn't seem to stop.

If the killer knocked on the door right now, poked his head in, and announced that they had better say their prayers, Amara wasn't certain she could stop.

Maybe it had to do with the heightened adrenaline. Maybe it was because she hadn't had sex during the current president's administration and the sex she'd had before that had been forgettable in the extreme. Maybe it was because Jack's skin looked so warm and inviting and the thought of never touching it before she died suddenly seemed more tragic than never going on safari or seeing the whales off Nova Scotia.

Mostly it was because there was always something in Jack's eyes when he did look at her, something unidentifiable but disturbing, hot and cold, untouchable and irresistible, all at the same time.

Like right now.

"What's on your mind, Amara?"

"Can I ask you a question?"

"Could I stop you?"

No, he couldn't stop her, but now that her chance had come she couldn't quite get the words out. It seemed so melodramatic, like she'd been caught in a Bette Davis movie and had three months to live or something, and she'd never been an emotional person. Not really. But there was a growing weight in her heart—it felt like a boulder now and would soon be a solid wall of insurmountable rock, like Gibraltar—and she needed to know.

"Will we ever see each other again after tonight?"

"No."

The way he refused to look at her hurt almost as

much as the answer. *No.* Just like that. With no signs of regret or even recognition, as though he was thinking right now, for the very first time ever, *hmm, yeah, I guess I won't ever lay eyes on Amara again—I wonder what's on ESPN?*

And here she was, sick.

As always, when she got upset, she got mad. The focal point of her anger at the moment was his stupid black duffel, which he'd placed on the bed and was now rummaging in. Again. What the hell was so important in that duffel bag that he couldn't be bothered with looking up at her and acting, even if he had to pretend about it, like she was a worthwhile human being to whom attention should be paid?

Feeling huffy and itching for a fight, she jumped to her feet, marched around to stand in his face and shoved the bag across the bed—man, it was heavy—and out of his reach. She was taking her life in her hands, she knew. The warning rumble in his chest confirmed it, and so did the sudden lowering of those heavy dark brows. Even the vivid red gash of his cut forehead, which had thankfully stopped bleeding, seemed pissed at her.

"I'm talking to you," she snapped.

"I answered your question," he told some vague point off to the left of her face, his voice roughening with each choppy syllable.

"Maybe you could look at me."

Ah, but he didn't want to. He hardly ever wanted to. Jaw tightening, he looked heavenward, no doubt cursing God for saddling him with Amara. Looked to the floor. Looked to the wall behind her. Then, finally, met her gaze with slow murder flashing in his eyes.

"We'll never lay eyes on each other again after tonight?" she asked again.

"No."

"That makes me sad. Even though you're a jerk, it makes me sad."

His lips twisted with such derision that she flinched. "It should be the best news you've ever heard. Since I'm such a jerk."

"It's not."

He stared at her for several beats and then, oh, God, and then something shifted in his expression, and that *thing,* whatever it was, streaked across his face and was gone, but not before she felt it in her breasts and her suddenly aching sex, low in her belly and in her soul.

"What do you want, Amara?"

This wasn't a growl. Oh, no. It was a purring murmur; it was the husky voice of a man who wanted to give her what she wanted, whatever it was.

"I want you to tell me why you hate me so much and why you've gone out of your way to be as offensive as possible to me."

There it was. Her hidden vulnerability and the thing that had kept her awake more nights than she'd ever admit. No one else much liked her. Fine. Jack didn't like her and it was a devastating injury, the kind that might make her bleed out before help could arrive to save her.

She'd expected her question to surprise him, to make him uncomfortable, and it did. Color rose up over his cheeks and he naturally tried to hide his discomfort by distracting her. "What do you care? I'm just the cook."

Amara shifted closer, until the zone of heat surrounding his body engulfed her from head to toe and just another inch or two would brush her up against the heavy slabs of his chest.

They were close to something here, a breakthrough or a breakdown, she wasn't sure which, and all she knew was that she needed to keep pushing his buttons, no matter how much it scared her to do so.

"You're not just the cook. And I want you to be a man and tell me why I bother you so much."

Unblinking, he stretched his lips in a crooked approximation of a smile that struck terror in her heart and hitched up her breathing with something that wasn't terror at all.

"You don't want to question my manhood, Angel Eyes. It puts me in a bad mood."

Angel Eyes.

Amara's heart, which had been stuttering along, skipping some beats and doubling up on others, stopped altogether. They stared at each other, the tension between them notching slowly higher, a roller coaster with a peak way up in the clouds somewhere, still well out of sight.

She became aware of the rasp of his breath, the tiny cleft in his chin, the faint scent of minty toothpaste that lingered around his mouth, which wasn't so tight anymore, but full. Lush. Infinitely inviting.

"Angel Eyes." Her whispery voice was giving her trouble, so she paused to clear her throat. And when she licked her lips, his hot gaze tracked the movement the way a starving cat would track a mouse he wanted to swallow whole. "That sounds a little better than *Bunny.* Your hatred is slipping, Jack."

An invisible force was operating on them, some pull like gravity that had them drifting closer together without conscious movement. All Amara knew was that now his brown eyes took up the whole field of her vision, and they were dark and turbulent, splintered with black and gold and filled with the kind of desire that, if unleashed, would flatten her to paper-thinness.

She wanted it unleashed and wanted, just as much, to unleash her own passion.

"Amara." The huskiness in his tone screamed at her but the note of warning barely registered. "I'm trying to do the right thing by you, but I'm no saint. Not even close. So if you're offering me something, I'm going to take it."

His words of caution didn't interest her. She was a big girl.

"I'm offering." God, it felt good to say it and stop pretending she didn't feel the effect he had on her. "If the worst-case scenario is that we're both going to die soon, and the best case scenario is that you'll go your way and I'll go back home and never see you again, then . . . yeah. I'm offering."

That was as clear as she could make it.

A blank check. The keys to the kingdom. The whole enchilada.

He could have her now, however he liked, and she was sure her enthusiastic sincerity was shining on her face like an airport beacon.

Still, he hesitated.

Some internal struggle was going on inside his sharp brain, some epic battle that looked as though it might tear him in half. Because his breathing was harsh now, his face strained. And his body all but vibrated with the force of his simultaneous restraint and need to reach for her. Her peripheral vision caught the pulsing action of his fists clenching and unclenching at his sides, opening and closing, again and again.

"You don't know what you're doing. You're going to regret this."

"Yeah," she agreed. "I probably will."

His face fell but he nodded, as though this was exactly what he'd expected her to say and he didn't blame her for choosing the smart option.

"But I'll regret not doing it more."

Jack gaped at her for one frozen moment, and the tension between them peaked. Amara felt the precise moment that roller coaster summited and knew the ride had begun in earnest.

With a hoarse cry, Jack reached for her and yanked her against his body.

Chapter 11

There he was.

Twenty minutes late for work now and on her fourth circuit around the block in one of the worst sections of downtown Cincinnati's Over-the-Rhine, where every moment without being eyeballed, leered at or questioned by the police was cause for celebration, Marian Barber finally saw Jerome.

Cursing everything about him, from his collection of thuggish friends, all of whom probably had an early violent death and/or prison time in their immediate future, to his insolent black stare to his baggy jeans, black skull cap and pristine athletic shoes—green today; they'd been orange last time—she pulled the Land Rover up to the curb in front of a shabby brownstone and rolled the passenger side window down to talk to him.

The SOB took his own sweet time about sauntering over to her. She checked her watch, impatient to get to work and, more than that, to take her meds so she could face work.

The more time she spent in this shithole, the more

chance there was of getting caught, but she couldn't worry about that. If the cops ran her plates, they ran her plates. She could say she was lost and asking for directions. She had bigger problems to deal with today, namely, what kind of payment Jerome was going to demand for the Oxy. She had the strong and terrible feeling that the bills she'd grabbed from the ATM—there went this month's Visa payment—weren't going to be enough this time.

Jerome finally made his way over and leaned one hand on the roof. "Hey, Jerome."

" 'S'up?"

Bastard. Like he didn't know what was up. Like there was some chance she'd driven down here and risked getting caught just for the pleasure of asking him how his day was going so far.

"Like I told you on the phone, I need some Oxy."

He shrugged. "I'm not sure I have any today."

Marian waited. Her skin stretched so tight she felt certain that her flesh would explode out of it any second and ooze, glistening, like a slug. "Well, could you check?"

He yawned with a flash of gold and a loud cracking of his jaw. "How're you planning to pay me?"

"Cash."

Dread wrapped its fingers around her throat and squeezed, especially when his lazy gaze drifted lower, to her breasts. "Maybe I want to lay a little pipe." He smiled, revealing a hint of dimples. "Or maybe I want to have a seat in your ride so you can suck me off. You up for that?"

"No."

He laughed.

She tried not to vomit.

Because she was lying. To get her shit right now? Yeah, she'd suck him off. Probably let him fuck her, too, as long as he let her take her meds first and used a condom.

"Well, Marian," said Jerome, "this is your lucky day today because all I want is that information we talked about. And the cash."

"I don't have it." Her gut cramped again, hard, and even though she'd thought her earlier episode of diarrhea had cleaned her out nice and good, she apparently had enough left inside her to make an embarrassing mess any second. She shifted, trying to hold it in. "I can't get it."

"Okay." Jerome wheeled around toward his sniggering friends. "Buh-bye."

Marian lost it. "Fuck. Fuck, fuck, *fuck*." Punctuating each curse by smacking her hands against the wheel, she gave herself over to one moment of despair, one moment where she considered how far she'd sunk, how much she still had to lose, especially if she did what he asked, and how much she needed her shit.

The shit won.

"Okay," she called after Jerome. "I'll get it for you."

Jack didn't mean to do any of it. Not respond to the naked heat in Amara's eyes, take her up on her self-destructive offer or even touch her. He especially didn't mean to lose control to the point that Kareem Gregory and his contract killers and vendettas seemed like a minor irritation that he should think about some day when he had the time.

But all of it happened anyway.

There was one moment when it wasn't too late and he could have turned back. A single second where they stood there, frozen with the sudden shock of being in each other's arms, twined together like wisteria around a trellis, hip-to-hip, thigh-to-thigh, with one of his hands squeezing her butt and pressing her closer to his rigid erection and the other in her hair, feeling that wavy silk—ah, God, it was so soft, so thick, and her scalp was warm beneath—and she had her arms around his neck and one hand on the top of his head as though she refused to take even the slightest risk that he might pull away, and he wasn't too far gone yet.

His presence of mind was slipping away but enough remained for him to notice the fan of her sweet breath against his lips, the tiny curve of her mouth in a smile, the glow of joy, no matter how temporary, in her face, and he thought, *no, this is wrong, I can't have her one time and then never see her again; one time is never going to be enough.*

Some of his turbulence must have broken through because her expression darkened as though she knew she was losing him. And Amara, street-fighting defense lawyer that she was, played dirty by murmuring, "Don't think, Jack," and then licking her way into his mouth.

In that one heartbeat, it was too late.

But of course it had been too late for him the second he laid eyes on her.

All kinds of crazy sounds erupted from some hidden place inside him—broken sounds, euphoric sounds—and he gathered her closer, kissed her deeper, because if he had to die he damn sure wasn't going to do it without tasting the hottest depths of Amara Clarke's mouth.

There was no guarantee that there was a heaven waiting for him on the other side or that God wouldn't laugh and throw him out on his butt when he showed up at the pearly gates, but that didn't matter because heaven was right here, in his arms.

But . . . he needed to take this slow and not miss anything, to mark this moment for the rest of what was sure to be a cursed and lonely life.

So he peeled back enough to look down into her flushed face and glittering, heavy-lidded eyes. Catalogued her trembling breathlessness. Absorbed the thrilling heat of her passion for him as it hit him in wave after wave. Best of all, he didn't pretend not to see her. This one time he could stare at her to his starving heart's content, drown himself in her eyes and then, when he'd recovered, drown himself again.

Aware of her writhing against him with growing impatience, the thrust of her hips and the need in her breathy little cries, he slowed down and touched her. Ran his fingers over her smooth forehead and traced the fine arch of her brows. She watched him with wide eyes as he studied her face and stroked her cheeks with his thumbs.

So soft she was. So incredibly, unbelievably soft.

Too awed to speak, Jack stared, helpless.

And, still struggling for breath, she smiled at him. Despite all the danger he'd brought into her life, there was a glow in her face that she didn't try to hide, a light in her eyes when she looked at him.

"You're beautiful," he told her.

"So are you."

No, he wasn't, but he wasn't about to enlighten her.

Magnetized by the pull of each other's skin, they couldn't stay apart. Couldn't get close enough. Kissing her and backing her toward the bed, he paused only long enough to rip his T-shirt off over his head, a task she didn't make easy with her clutching fingers and sharp little nails that scratched at him in her desperate efforts to keep him close.

No problem. Let her scratch him. Let her rip him to shreds. This woman could chew him up and spit out his splintered bones if she wanted to. He was that far gone.

They hit the bed and tumbled down with him on top, but she didn't seem to mind his weight. Gripping his ass, she shifted until he was between her legs and his brain melted down even as his swollen dick threatened to shoot off like a rocket with no further stimulation.

Again he peeled himself away and it was harder this time. Infinitely harder. Standing, he kicked off his jeans and underwear and lunged for his toiletries kit on the nightstand and a condom.

She, meanwhile, sat up to see what he was doing, caught sight of his erection, and stared with open appreciation. "Oh, God."

Her movements frantic now, she jerked her sweater over her head, kicked off her shoes and socks and went to work on the button on her jeans.

He took over because she was moving too damn slow. Grabbing her waistband and nudging her fumbling hands out of the way, he ripped the jeans down her long legs while she stretched out on her back and helpfully lifted her hips for him.

The sight nearly knocked him on his ass: Amara, naked but for a virginal white satin bra and skimpy white lace bikinis contrasting with that gleaming brown skin, her hair wild and free, her hands reaching for him, his name on her swollen lips.

"Jack. *Hurry.*"

Hurry. Yeah. Great idea.

Crawling over her, he flicked the front clasp of the bra and her breasts spilled free, heavy and round, with jutting dark nipples so large he nearly came at the sight of them.

Rubbing his hands all over her breasts, squeezing and plucking, he thought vaguely that he needed to taste them but he had more important things to taste now.

Scooting lower, he dragged his tongue over her taut abdomen, dipped it into her belly button, and enjoyed her squirming as he pulled the lacy panties down and off.

He looked up then, and there she was. Waxed and bare as the day she was born, with the ruddy cleft that was the new focal point of his life engorged and glistening, wet and fragrant with a delicious earthy musk and all for him.

She spread her thighs, arched her hips and invited him.

Pausing only to lick that hard nub, to taste her this one time, while he could—she cried out in response, her body jackknifing—he rose up over her and settled in that cradle that he'd been waiting for. Dying for.

Their gazes locked and she stared at him with such want in her eyes, such need and, most terrible of all, such joy. As though he was the best thing that had ever happened to her rather than the worst.

And he knew he shouldn't do it. That this moment was as dangerous and irrevocable as a first hit of heroin. But, Jesus, right now he needed this woman more than he needed to live another day.

And he was a dead man anyway.

Taking the head of his penis, he stroked it in that slick river, back and forth, lubricating both of them, and then, with a single hard thrust, buried himself as deep as he could humanly get.

Ah, shit. Shit, God, *shit.*

The pleasure stole his breath and streaked straight to his brain.

The unbearable friction scared him for a second. He froze, paralyzed by the blinding ecstasy and the fear that if he so much as flexed his hips he would hurt her. She was stretched so tight there was no way he could avoid ripping her to shreds, but it would kill him to stop now when he had so little control left.

Bracing on his forearms, he trembled, waiting for a sign from her.

To his astonished relief, her features twisted into a breathtaking look of such euphoria that he didn't need to ask if she was okay. Hell, if she felt a millionth of what he was feeling, then she was the luckiest woman on earth.

Experimenting, with her and himself, he rotated his hips in a tiny circle and they both unraveled. Amara arched backward, incoherent and uncontrollable cries pouring from her mouth in an endless stream . . . or was that him?

She wasn't done with him yet.

Smiling and whispering, panting and meeting him thrust for thrust, she locked those plump thighs around his waist and palmed his cheeks to bring him in for an openmouthed kiss.

As her body's sweet suction milked him, he cried

out, over and over again until—Jesus, was that him? Shouting her name like that?

He couldn't help it. In this woman's arms he just couldn't help himself.

Payton Jones pulled the car into the parking lot and turned off the headlights. She circled around back, past the chain-link fence and black pit that was no doubt a swimming pool covered with a tarp for the winter, and parked outside room 112. Thanks to the GPS device she'd slipped into Amara Clarke's coat pocket back at the diner, Payton could put her finger on them anytime she wanted to.

Selecting a space both for its view of the long row of room doors—the lovely Highway 8 Motel was only one level, nothing but first class all the way, so that made things easy—and for its easy access to the highway on-ramp, which was a quarter mile down the road on the left, Payton parked, cut the engine and waited.

And seethed.

By now she should be on her way to the Argosy, where her luck was about to change. Instead, she was still here. And Jackson Parker was still alive.

Keeping one eye on the row of doors, Payton reached for her case and pulled out the rifle's butt with hands that were, she realized with annoyance and dawning humiliation, unsteady.

Never once in her life had she lost control of a job like this or been taken by surprise. Never once in her life had she lost her weapon. Never once in her life had she been so royally *fucked*.

But it was all good because her little mistake could be rectified soon. And the tables at the Argosy would still be hot and still be waiting for her when she returned to Lawrenceburg.

Caressing the rifle's shaft, she attached it to the butt, the weight comforting in her hands, the wood smooth and solid. Reliable. And then she reached for her scope.

Chapter 12

Jack was ignoring her again.

After ruthlessly possessing her with the kind of skill and passion that had damn near disintegrated her body, he'd all but jumped out of the bed. While she was still reeling with reverberations that probably registered on Richter scales in both Beijing and San Francisco, wondering if her legs would ever solidify enough for her to walk upright and unaided again, he'd shoved away from her and begun to dress.

This was no surprise, so she tried not to take it personally. They were still being stalked by a killer, after all, and still in grave danger.

Her semihysterical brain dredged up that courtroom scene from *A Few Good Men* where Tom Cruise grills Jack Nicholson on the witness stand. "Grave danger?" Cruise asks. "Is there any other kind?" wonders Nicholson, the asshole.

So, yeah, she and Jack were still in grave danger and having the sex of a lifetime didn't change that. Knowing that she'd never see Jack again after tonight, never know whether he was alive and well and cooking at, say, a Galveston diner or dead, shot execution style two days from now, didn't change that. The fact that Jack meant something to her and she meant nothing to him didn't change that.

It probably made sense for her to get dressed, too. The cavalry would be here any minute, after all, but in her current dazed state she wasn't sure she'd be able to correctly identify the body parts that needed socks, for example, so she decided to stay put for another minute or so.

And watch Jack.

He didn't shower again. It wasn't that she was trying to attach undue importance to this little detail or anything, but they were sharing a hotel room and it was hard not to notice: he didn't. Her scent was, therefore, all over his body and would be there until he showered. Did he know that? Did that register with him? Probably not.

She, on the other hand, wasn't going to shower either, and it wasn't because of time constraints or panic or anything else like that. It was because she wanted to carry any little part of Jack—as much of Jack—as she could with her for as long as possible.

His musky-fresh scent, the accidental marks from his nails or teeth, the delicious ache he'd left between her thighs. She only wished his hands had tattooed their prints all over every inch of her body because she didn't want to forget anything.

"Jack?" she began.

"Get dressed."

It was an order barked over his shoulder as he bent to pull his gray boxer briefs up over the flexing globes of his incredible ass. In front—and, again, it wasn't that she was being nosy or anything, but it was hard not to notice with the way his body was angled—his thick length was still ruddy and engorged and took a little adjusting after he slid into his underwear and jeans and tried to pull up the zipper. Finally, with a muttered curse, he gave up on the bottom half of his body and reached for his T-shirt and sweater, yanking them over his head in choppy movements.

"What are you doing?" Startled, Amara glanced up to see him—hey, what do you know?—glaring into her face. Well, no. Apparently he could only look at her as long as she wasn't looking at him. That was how it worked. The second their gazes connected, his skittered away and he began the all-important search for his shoes and socks. "I told you to get dressed."

"So sorry, Special Agent."

That got him, just like she'd hoped it would. Waiting until his head whipped around in her direction again and she saw the glinting anger in his eyes, she threw the sheet back and got up, giving him a full and unobstructed view of her naked body.

The effect on him was immediate and satisfying: his mouth opened and closed, all but choking on whatever sarcastic retort he'd meant to fling her way. To his credit, he tried not to look and then, when that failed, tried not to gape. But a naked woman was too much for most men and Jack turned out to be mortal after all. Who knew?

His expression black and thunderous, he looked his fill, lingering on her still-swollen parts, namely her jutting nipples and slick sex. Unfortunately, winning this one small point with him was torture for her, and it was all she could do not to writhe and beg—she wanted him that much.

Even so, her momentary discomfort was well worth

the look on his face. The starving, needy, half-crazed look that told her he wasn't immune after all. She may be unlikeable but she was amazing in bed and therefore unforgettable.

Hah. Take that, jackass. Good luck with that zipper now.

Feeling triumphant though still lost and empty, she turned her back on him, found her panties, and bent to pick them up.

Behind her, Jack made a strangled noise.

"What now?" she asked.

Jack didn't answer.

"Jack?"

Glancing over her shoulder, she had the pleasure of seeing him try, with what looked like a lot of difficulty, to peel his gaze away from her ass. Then he cleared his throat and reverted to Jack the Untouchable and Unreachable, all business and as approachable as an armed nuclear warhead.

Finished with his clothes and jacket, he shoved his weapon into the waistband behind his back and threw his few remaining belongings in his duffel.

"The team'll come. We'll run out, get into their vehicle and be on our merry way. You'll be questioned, I'll be questioned, they'll figure out how to protect you for a little while, and we'll go our separate ways. The end."

He was leaving; why did that hurt so much? Of course he was leaving. Her mother had left, and so had her aunt. People always left. It was the name of the game and there was nothing she'd ever been able to do about it.

And yet she still had to ask. "You'll go back to Cincinnati for the trial?"

He checked his phone and didn't answer.

God, she hated him sometimes.

"You do understand," she said through the uncontrollable flexing of her tight jaw, "that I am a lawyer, right? I know how to get information about dockets and trials and stuff. I can make one phone call to a contact in the U.S. Attorney's Office in Cincinnati and find out all I need to know—"

"You don't need to know."

"Don't tell me what I need."

Jack the Cool and Unruffled now looked furious. "What you need is to forget that you and I ever crossed paths and go back to your life."

Yeah, sure. Like she could do that.

Fully dressed, she jammed her hands on her hips and faced him, itching for a fight. "No problem. Consider yourself forgotten."

A muscle ticked in his jaw as he focused the full might of what looked like a killing fury on her. "Great."

"But it would be *nice,*" she continued, "if you sent me a message to let me know that you're okay—"

"No."

"You can send a message. That's not a huge deal. Send it through the U.S. Attorney's Office or—"

"No messages."

"—use a code or something so I'll know you're still alive, *you bastard.*"

Well, so much for her brilliant and simple plan to not let him know how she felt. The ringing hysteria in her last two words was pretty much a dead giveaway.

She squared off with him, which was like having a staring contest with Lincoln's image on Mount Rushmore, all granite and no emotion, no flicker of humanity. She was ready to say, *screw it, Jack, I'm begging you,* when his phone vibrated and, with obvious relief at the distraction, he pressed a button and listened.

"Got it," he said.

Lowering the phone, he stared at her and she knew this was it—the have-a-nice-life part of the proceedings—and her stomach plummeted with a lurch so sickening that she wondered if she'd vomit.

"They're here."

"Oh," she said. "Okay."

To her surprise, he didn't seem so steely all of a sudden. She'd expected him to fling open the door, plant a foot on her butt and kick her outside, thrilled for her to be someone else's responsibility now, but he didn't.

Hesitating, he stared down at her and she edged closer and stared up at him, miserably aware that she'd never have another stolen moment with him and would probably never be alone with him again.

This was it and anything she didn't say now would never get said.

You've infected me and I don't know what to do about it.

Could you please reverse the spell you've put on me so I can live a normal life?

I could never forget you, even if I wanted to.

"Stay safe, okay?" she whispered.

His lips curled into a crooked line so heavy with irony that it could never be called a smile. "I always do."

Neither of them moved.

Amara was dying to touch him again, would have sacrificed a limb just for the pleasure of cupping her hands on his hard cheeks the way she'd done when he'd been buried deep inside her and they'd watched each other come, but she knew that he wouldn't tolerate her touch now.

"I lied," she told him. "I'll never forget you."

"You should. It's for the best."

Turning, he slung their bags over his shoulder and reached to unlock the bolt on the door, and it was this loss of his attention that spurred her into action. Screw it. She needed to know and in another thirty seconds the chance would be gone forever. They couldn't leave it like this.

"Jack."

Taking a huge emotional risk, she put a hand on his arm and squeezed.

He froze, his head bent low, and didn't look at her. Beneath her fingers she felt the iron flex of his muscles as they stretched tighter and tighter.

"This thing with us. It was . . . it was something, wasn't it? It could have been something . . . couldn't it?"

There it was. She, Amara Clarke, queen of emotional distance, put her heart on the line and he, bastard that he was, didn't answer. Didn't even *look* at her.

"Please," she said, because, hey, if you were going for complete humiliation, why not go big? "Please, Jack."

He stared at the floor and shook his head.

Rage flooded her. Rage and sudden embarrassing tears that she would not—would never—let him see. Why was she even bothering to be upset? Wasn't this the one unchangeable constant she'd experienced since birth?

It was the story of her sorry existence: people left her the first chance they got.

Sorry, Amara, buh-bye. Try to have a nice life now, you hear?

Snarling, she tightened her grip on his forearm, hoping to make him bleed, to mark his skin and leave a permanent reminder that Amara Clarke had once been in his life.

"You son of a bitch, you can leave me with that much."

He looked at her then and, oh, God, she had to let go of his arm and cover her heart because she wasn't ready for the glittering agony and quiet desperation in his brown eyes. It was an abyss, a bottomless hole of black emptiness that made her pain look like a walk down the beach on the brightest, clearest day of summer.

"I can't leave you with anything," he said.

Amara was still reeling with shock and disbelief when he drew his weapon and peered through the ugly curtains. And then, when he decided it was safe, he opened the door, letting in a blast of icy-wet air and a figure so dark and silent he might have been a phantom.

"Parker, you punk, dragging me out here in the middle of the night," said the man by way of greeting.

Parker, Amara thought. Jack's last name was *Parker*.

"Good to see you, too, Mateo," Jack replied. "Did that rash ever clear up?"

"I didn't say it was good to see you. And your sister gave me another rash, but I had fun getting it."

They glared at each other.

And then, by some silent and invisible signal, they reached out and pulled each other into one of those back-slapping male hugs that looked more like a punishment than a sign of affection.

Mateo was fully suited up for a raid, Amara saw,

which meant that he wore the full DEA fearsome warrior ensemble: dark knit cap, dark DEA jacket, bulletproof vest, gloves, boots and gun. It was like the room had been invaded by an occupying army of one. Lucky thing this was a good guy. Amara sure wouldn't want to be on his bad side.

"Who's this?" Mateo asked.

"This is Amara Clarke," Jack said. "She's with me. Amara, this is Mateo Garciaparra, a sorry specimen from the Seattle office. We trained together back in the day."

Mateo shot Jack an indecipherable look and then focused all his energy on Amara, who locked her knees lest they start shaking. Mateo was, in his own way, almost as tall, dark and handsome as Jack. He had sleek raven's-wing-black curls that were long and unruly beneath his cap and skimmed the back of his turtleneck sweater, olive skin and cheekbones carved to such masculine perfection as to leave no doubt about the existence of God. His slashing brows and flashing eyes, sharp with intelligence, were black as midnight in hell, and his lush red lips were straight-line pissed.

"Oh. She's with you. Has she got a note from the pope vouching for her?"

"She's got *me* vouching for her," Jack told him with a darkening-cloud face that warned of Armageddon unleashed if Mateo didn't shut the hell up ASAP.

"How do you know she's not the cause of all your problems?" Mateo wondered, checking his weapon. "I'm thinking this one's got you doing most of your ruminating below the waistband."

Amara opened her mouth to blast him but, at a

narrow-eyed warning look from Jack, snapped it shut again.

"If Amara wanted me dead," Jack said, "she could have managed it by now."

"Maybe she's not that bright."

Yeah. Okay. Calling her a Mata Hari was one thing; calling her dumb was unforgivable. "Listen, jackass—" she began.

Mateo inflated with irritation until he looked even more fearsome than before, but if he was going to dismember her he was damn well going to get a piece of her mind first.

"I'm plenty bright enough to take down your friend *Jackson Parker from Cincinnati* here—"

Mateo shot Jack a *you dumb fuck* look; Jack grimaced.

"—if I wanted to. And if you keep talking about me like I'm invisible, I'm going to reach down your throat and pull your tongue out by the roots."

The men gaped at her and their mutual silence went a long way toward soothing her bruised feelings.

Mateo recovered first. "I think I'm in love," he told Jack. "I'm going to fight you for her when we get out of here."

Jack snatched her to his side and flipped out the overhead light. "Just get us out of here. That's all you need to worry about."

Checking their weapons again, the men opened the door and headed out, sandwiching her in between.

The street beyond the motel's grounds was damp and deserted, a ghost town of hulking businesses and a gas station or two shut down for the night. The only sign of life was the quiet purr of an SUV engine as it idled several feet away, perpendicular to the row of parked cars outside their room, and the quiet swoosh of another dark figure, a smaller one this time, as it approached.

Oh, God.

The danger was real, and it was back in all its nightmarish glory. Being curled around Jack with him deep inside her—that was the moment out of time. This was the reality.

Her adrenaline spiked, heightening her awareness of the cold . . . the silence . . . that faint prickling feeling of being watched by unseen eyes. She clutched her purse, prepared to duck, run or hide, whatever they told her to do.

They hustled her to the SUV and met the new figure at the trunk.

Oh, wow. It was a woman.

Blond underneath the baseball cap, with a wry smile and a gun as big as the men's. "Nice," she told Jack. "I can see why you want to keep her safe."

Jack snorted. "Amara, this is Daisy Reed, one of the DEA's finest, believe it or not. She's here to save our asses."

"Thanks for, ah, saving my ass," Amara told her.

"Don't mention it." Daisy, all business now, hurried around to the trunk and swung it open. "Let's get these bags—"

But Amara wasn't paying attention because something funny was going on with Jack's forehead as he stooped to help Daisy.

He had a bright red dot right between his eyes.

At first Amara thought some weird trick of the neon motel sign was reflecting off the dried blood on his cut, creating a strange effect, but then her brain, already bewildered and overwrought from the night's events, came up to speed with a burst of horrified clarity:

There was a bead on Jack's forehead.

Bead. Rifle. Sniper.

"Jack," she screamed.

Jack's head whipped around and his wide eyes reflected his alarm, but that bead was still there. Daisy had seen it, too, and was already in motion, moving with an Olympic sprinter's reflexes and taking a running step and then a flying lunge for Jack.

"Parker! *Get down*."

Amara got there first, shoving Jack out of the way with an almighty burst of strength.

"Amara," roared Jack, and then there was the unmistakable crack of gunfire.

Crack. Crack-crack.

Jack dropped and rolled, then came up again with his weapon ready and his mind focused on one crucial thing: *Protect Amara no matter what.*

Mateo shouted.

More armed agents jumped out of the SUV, fanning out across the parking lot.

Then came another *crack,* a sickening fleshy *pop,* and a shower of warm rain that Jack knew wasn't rain at all.

Sudden, screaming terror stopped his heart. No. Jesus, no. Not Amara.

Afraid to look, to know, he prayed to a God he'd stopped believing in years ago and fell back on his training to assess the situation.

There was her shoe, stretched out in front of her, with the toe pointing to the sky.

Horror expanded in his throat, locking down the yell that wanted to rise up out of his mouth and continue for the rest of his life.

No, no, no.

Moving forward with only his fear to propel him, he saw her sprawled legs, one bent, and realized that she was moving. Moaning. He looked up the length of her body and saw her chest heave, her head move.

"Jack," she said weakly.

Thank you, God.

Galvanized and acutely aware of more shouts and *cracks,* he kept one eye on his surroundings as he squatted beside her on the concrete, grateful for the negligible but better-than-nothing cover of the SUV.

Was . . . was the side of her sweater wet? It looked wet, but it couldn't—

He checked again, holding his breath. Yeah. Blood.

"Fuck," he said.

Fuck, FUCK—oh, shit. She was looking at him, focusing on his face and trying to blink away her stunned confusion. *Don't scare her, Parker. Don't make this worse for her.*

"Hey." He tried to smile.

She spoke in a voice so faint it scared him all over again. "I think I'm shot."

"I think you're right. Let's see."

Being as gentle as he possibly could, he rolled her to one side just enough to inch up her sweater and discover a clean exit hole through her back, down near her waistband. It didn't look like the bullet had gone through a kidney or anything, but who the hell knew? Everything he knew about gunshot wounds came from watching *ER.*

Keep it calm, man. Low key. "It's not that bad, Bunny. We'll get you patched up."

She didn't look reassured. She looked fretful and sweaty. "Where's Daisy?"

Yeah. Daisy. About that.

This whole time he'd been aware of another set of legs stretched out on the concrete nearby. He'd seen the creeping black stain in the periphery but he'd blocked it because his fried brain could only take one heart-stopping crisis at a time.

But the time for procrastinating was over.

Amara levered herself up on her elbows, and they saw Daisy at the same time:

She'd been reduced to a body, spread-eagled and obscene, with bloody pulp for a head.

Chapter 13

There he was.

Kira Gregory saw Supervisor Dexter Brady of the DEA the minute she came through the vestibule and into the red and white over-the-top cheerfulness of the T.G.I. Friday's restaurant nearest campus.

It was late morning, and the not-quite-lunchtime crowd provided enough chatter to cover up the forthcoming conversation. The chirpy hostess walked her up the steps past the bar, giving Kira a quick glance of Brady, who was sitting alone in a booth and had his skull-trimmed head bent low over the thick menu. Though she'd been prepared not to make eye contact with him, it didn't matter because he idly flipped a page as she passed, yawning as though he hoped to crack his jaw clear through to the base of his neck. On the table in front of him was a half-full glass of something that looked suspiciously like pink lemonade.

The hostess kept going and headed straight for one of the freestanding tables at the far side of the bar, but Kira stopped her.

"Excuse me." She pointed over her shoulder to a booth. "Can I sit here?"

"Sure."

Kira slid into the seat nearest Brady and sat so they were back to back.

"Your server will be right over to get your drink order," the hostess said.

"Thanks." Kira smiled and flipped her menu open as the hostess left.

"You're late, Mrs. Gregory," murmured Brady.

Irritation combined with the excessive tension she was already feeling and made a disquieting cocktail. Big deal, right? Everyone called her Mrs. Gregory. It was a sign of respect for the drug lord's wife, the same way people called Diana Ross *Miss Ross*.

Except that she hated her married name, her marriage and, most of all, her husband. So she could do without the constant reminder of her status, especially when it came from that low voice that infused each syllable with a Richard Pryor concert's worth of sarcasm.

"Sorry." Kira unwrapped her silverware and opened the napkin onto her lap. "I had to double back a couple of times to make sure I wasn't—Sprite, please."

"Great." The server who'd materialized at the edge of Kira's table detoured back to the bar, barely breaking stride.

"Fascinating." There was a flapping sound and Kira pictured Brady turning the page of his menu, trying to decide between the steak and baked potato or burger and fries while checking his watch to see how soon he could be done with her. "I would have thought a wealthy trophy wife such as yourself would have her own driver and bodyguard."

Kira fumed in silence until her temples began to throb. It was a crime to kill a federal agent, sure, but what about jabbing him in the back of his head with a fork while in a public place? How much time would she get for that?

But . . . no. She needed him. No matter how big a jerk he was. Taking a deep breath, she opened her menu and refused to rise to his bait. "Kareem wants me to use a driver, but so far I've held him off."

"You do realize that there's probably a GPS device hidden under the buttery leather seats of your luxury car . . . ?"

Was that a minute amount of concern she heard, layered in with the sarcasm? "That's why I wanted to meet you here rather than downtown at your office."

"And your dear husband won't be suspicious when he studies your credit card bill and discovers you've been slumming at a Friday's?"

Kira shrugged even though she knew he couldn't see it. "They've got a great turkey burger. And apparently I can't quite rise above my humble beginnings."

"Are you ready to order, sir?" The server was somewhere out of her line of sight, apparently talking to Brady now.

"How's your turkey burger?" he wondered. "I hear it's good."

Kira bent over her menu and tried to smother her unexpected smile.

"It's great," the server told Brady. "Especially with cheddar and barbeque sauce."

"Let's do it. With fries."

"Will do." The server walked the two steps to Kira's

table and handed her the Sprite, which Kira sipped. "What would you like?"

"I'll have the bacon cheeseburger with extra bacon, fries and a Brownie Obsession for dessert," Kira said. "Just keep the food coming."

"On the healthy heart plan, are you?" asked Brady as the server headed back toward the kitchen, and this time Kira could almost swear she heard genuine amusement in his voice. It was hard not to twist at the waist and try to catch a glimpse of this rare event. Had she ever seen him smile? More importantly, could he smile without imploding his face?

"What can I say?" Kira replied. "Sometimes carnivores need meat."

"Much as I love a great turkey burger, I'm not sure why I'm here, Mrs. Gregory. So why don't you enlighten me?"

Oh, God. The moment of truth at last. "I need your help. And I can help you."

There was a long and painful pause. If he wanted to make her squirm by not answering, it was a brilliant plan. Fidgety and nervous, she eased her head into a slow glance over her shoulder, making sure he was still there.

He was. Sipping his pink lemonade, the SOB.

"So sorry, Mrs. Gregory," he finally said. "As I told you the last time you contacted me, and the time before that, if you need help, you need to go to the Red Cross because I'm not interested."

Okay. So she'd expected this. He didn't trust her and he was determined to make her walk over a few more hot coals before he committed to anything. She understood. And still the hysteria hovered in her throat, suffocating her by degrees.

"I need *protection*."

She could almost feel the bastard shrug behind her. "They've got battered women's shelters for that. If you're trying to disappear, you need to talk to the U.S. attorney about qualifying for WITSEC. So there you go. You've got lots of options available. Good luck."

There was such boredom in his voice, such absolute lack of empathy for her situation and what it cost her to sneak out and meet him here and the risks she was taking that she forgot herself in her desperation.

Turning at the waist, gaping at the back of his head and ready to climb over the booth until she landed in his lap and forced him to look at her, she pulled up short only when she saw that the server had reappeared with both of their plates.

Kira whipped back around and, no longer able to get enough air through her nose, floundered, her mouth opening and closing like a caught trout's. *Breathe, Kira. Breathe.*

"Turkey burger." The server clunked the first plate on Brady's table.

"Looks good," he said. "Can I get some ketchup?"

Ketchup. Kira nearly burst into maniacal laughter and wet her pants with the panic. She was caught up in an endless black vortex of drugs, lies and violence, living with her convicted felon of a husband, a man who probably killed a person a day on a good day, two on a bad one, and every second she survived was a small miracle and an enormous personal triumph—and this man wanted *ketchup*?

"Ketchup. I'll be right back with that." The server stepped closer and presented Kira with her plate. "Bacon cheeseburger for you."

"Thanks." Kira stared at the food, trying not to gag.

The server started to move off, but then double-taked when she caught a closer look at Kira's face. Shit. Kira swiped at her nose and tried to perk up, but too late.

"You okay, honey?"

How funny. The Friday's server was willing to help her if necessary, but Brady, whose help Kira really needed, wasn't.

"I'm fine. Thanks."

The server moved to the next table, leaving Kira free to notice the loud and appreciative smacking going on behind her.

"What's wrong, Mrs. Gregory?" Brady asked around what sounded like half his sandwich. "A fly in your food? The turkey burger's great, by the way. Thanks for the recommendation."

God help her. "He's going to kill me. When I try to leave him, he's going to kill me."

This ugly truth, at least, stopped the chewing. There was another pause.

"Probably."

Brady's honesty, for some reason, calmed her. Finally, at long last, she could acknowledge the situation. Stare it down and formulate a survival plan beyond trying to keep her husband out of her bed every night.

She wasn't stupid. She wasn't paranoid. She wasn't delusional. She was right.

"So that's it, then? I'm on my own? You're going to stand by and let him kill me?"

Brady didn't speak . . . didn't speak . . . didn't speak for so long that she began to let herself hope that maybe her life or death mattered to him because, hey, if he hit a dog in the street with his car he'd probably stop to see if he could help the dog, right? But then his voice, lower now but no less resolute, shot her hope all to hell.

"You're not my responsibility. Mrs. Gregory."

Stunned, she sat there with paralyzed limbs and listened to him slide out of his booth. Then she heard the flick and flutter of what was probably a bill as he left it on the table. Finally, heavy footsteps trailed off toward the front of the restaurant and he was gone.

And she was alone. Again. Still. Always.

Seconds passed. She stared at her gooey hamburger. She thought about the efforts she'd made to become a worthwhile person even if she was a drug kingpin's wife, the studying she'd done and the nursing degree that was almost hers. She thought about the secret bank account that was in her name alone and the pitiful remnants of her spending money that she'd managed to save in it because Kareem gave her only a little cash and encouraged her to shop with his platinum card so he could track her spending and keep her short leash in his firm grip.

She thought about how she'd landed herself in this situation in the first place by being the dumbest and most desperate nineteen-year-old who'd ever walked the face of the earth, and how she had no intention of spending the rest of her no-doubt short life paying for that mistake.

Most of all, she thought about how far she'd come and how much farther she had to go, and how she could get there—she knew it—if only someone would help her, just a little.

And then she got mad.

Snatching up her purse and jacket, she tossed her

own bill on the table and raced out into the parking lot. It took point-two seconds to spot Brady, who was sitting three spaces down in an idling and unmarked black sedan that screamed federal agent to anyone who cared to notice.

He didn't see her because he had his head bent low over his phone, checking e-mail or some such.

Kira threw caution to the wind. If Kareem had someone following her today, she was pretty much screwed, but at the moment she was screwed no matter how she looked at it. So she marched up to his car, jerked the passenger side door open—what kind of self-respecting law enforcement official left his door unlocked?—and climbed inside.

Brady gaped while she dropped her stuff on the floor and pulled on her seat belt.

"Drive," she barked.

"Fuck," he said, and drove.

Funny thing about hospitals: they were all the same. Every last one of them smelled of alcohol and fear, industrial strength bleachy cleaners and death. The personnel all wore Crocs in every twisted color under the neon rainbow and smiled those quiet smiles of concerned comfort when they knew damn well that they were going off to break in a few minutes and you'd still be stuck in the plastic chair in the waiting area, hanging on until you got word that your loved one was going to live or die. The fluorescent overhead lights, colored tape on the pristine linoleum floors and buzzing activity at nurses' stations universally scared him to death.

Oh, yeah. Jack and hospitals went way back.

Resting his elbows on his knees and his head in his hands, Jack tried not to think, which was hard since he had a whole brain full of fucked-up shit to consider.

Like how his whole No More Collateral Damage rule had been shot to hell.

Like how Amara had been shot saving his life and he, true to form, hadn't protected her worth a damn.

Like how he was pretty sure he'd have to take the elevator up a couple flights to the psych floor and check himself in for a permanent stay if she . . .

He'd vomited, which was pretty funny.

Not right away. He'd held off during the race to the hospital in the back of the ambulance, when he held Amara's hand and told her she'd be okay. He'd been through that drill before, so he did a real good job of sounding convincing. Then he held off until they wheeled Amara down the hall and into the exam room. He even managed to wait until the doctor came back out and told them she'd need surgery to patch the hole.

And then he calmly went to the nurses' station and asked where the nearest bathroom was. Following the red tape on the fucking floor, he located the men's room and an empty stall.

Whereupon he puked his guts out for, oh, about ten minutes or so.

Then he pounded his forehead against the plastic door six or eight times—yeah, that'd hurt—and sobbed quietly until he puked again.

Now here he was, waiting, her smell still on his skin, and he didn't know if he could struggle through one more second of life and then face another second after that.

He heard footsteps and then someone appeared in his peripheral vision and sat in the chair next to him. It wasn't the doctor, so he didn't give a shit who it was and didn't bother looking.

"How're you doing?"

Mateo. Jack didn't answer.

Silence for a few minutes.

"We got the shooter through the belly. Turns out she was a cute little thing with a GIVE PEACE A CHANCE sweatshirt on. Funny, huh? She had a stolen car with enough firepower in it to kill two or three hundred people and a GPS setup that looked like it came straight from the CIA. Anyway, Kareem'll have to find someone else to do the shooting from now on. She's dead."

Fascinating.

"We searched Amara's stuff. She had a little pen-sized GPS tracker in her coat pocket. We figure that's how the shooter found you at the motel."

Again—fascinating.

Who cared about the whys and wherefores at a moment like this? Amara was shot. Debriefing the circumstances wasn't going to make her any less shot.

Then he thought about the moving force behind all this violence and jerked his head up with a bitter fury strong enough to tear this whole hospital apart.

"And how's our friend Kareem?" Jack asked. "Safe at home in his million-dollar mansion with his beautiful wife getting ready for his retrial with another top-notch lawyer?"

"Last I heard, yeah."

If he'd had any contents left in his stomach, Jack would've vomited again.

Kareem was still free and sitting in the lap of

luxury because his fast-talking lawyer, who was nothing more than a prostitute in disguise, selling his wares to anyone able to pay without regard to the moral implications of what he did, had won him a new trial on procedural grounds.

Despite all his team's hard work and sacrifices—and there'd been plenty, both personal and professional—the most dangerous drug kingpin Jack had ever encountered in his career was roaming the streets again, free to continue selling drugs, expand his evil empire, murder people and generally contaminate everything that came within the gravitational pull of his malevolent life—and all because of *procedural grounds.*

Renewed agitation had Jack jumping to his feet to pacing, which was difficult in the tight row between chairs. Luckily the waiting area was deserted and there was no one nearby to complain about Jack's relentless cursing. After a minute he wore himself out and collapsed back in that torture rack of a chair.

Mateo took another stab at conversation. "Sooo . . . Amara. She seems like the compliant type."

An unexpected snort of laughter contracted Jack's ribs, but this was no time for jokes, not when Amara's safety was still at issue. "She needs to be protected when she gets out of here." Jack hoped none of his feelings for Amara showed on his face because he *really* wasn't up for an interrogation right now. "I don't want Kareem going after her again, trying to get to me. Once the retrial begins and he can get a clear shot at me, I figure she'll be safe to go back home and resume her life. Until then, I'll need to look out for her because she doesn't have a family."

"Huh," Mateo said. "You gonna let her go?"

Trying to look bewildered and pissed off by such a random question, Jack glared. No way was he in the mood for twenty questions. "What the hell are you talking about?"

The good thing about Mateo was that even if he didn't always keep his big mouth shut, he generally knew when to back off, like now. "Huh," he said again.

Jack shot him a final glare, just to put a lid on the subject—forever—when a woman in blue scrubs walked up. Jack teetered on the edge of cardiac arrest, but then she smiled and he nearly passed out with relief.

"Which one of you is Jack? She's asking for *Jack*."

Chapter 14

Down the street and around the corner they went, a muscle in Dexter's tight jaw ticking down the time remaining before he unleashed the full might of his undoubtedly explosive temper on her. After about two minutes, he pulled into an alley between two brick apartment buildings, parked behind a Dumpster and cut the engine.

His eyes were hot and cold at the same time, full of a flashing fury. His nostrils flared and his lips sneered. And despite all her internal pep talks about being brave, she cowered in her seat, afraid of this man in an unidentifiable way that was entirely different from the way she was afraid of her husband.

In all her desperation to recruit someone to her side, to balance the scales a little because Kareem had all the money, the personnel and the weapons and she had nothing, she'd forgotten that Dexter Brady was a man. At least fifteen years older than her, he was big and strong but not infallible or impenetrable, as she'd thought, with flesh and blood feelings that she'd never in a million years thought she could tap into.

"What the hell do you want, Mrs. Gregory?" he roared.

"*Please*. Help me."

"Why should I trouble myself to save your pretty hide? When did you ever try to save anyone but yourself?"

Now wasn't the time to lie, much as she wanted to. "Never."

This truth, perversely, made him angrier, until his walnut skin glowed red and he ejected the words from his mouth as though from one of Kareem's semiautomatic weapons. "Never. You never did, did you?"

Without waiting for her answer, he snatched up her left hand and waved it in her face, reminding her of the unforgettable. A diamond eternity band, ten carats total weight. Snuggled next to that, a flawless five-carat Asscher-cut diamond engagement ring worth a quarter of a million if it was worth a dime. She intended to take it to a discreet jeweler as soon as she left here and find out exactly because this ring was her only nest egg for when she finally left Kareem. Once, when she'd been too young and stupid to know better, this ring had been her most prized possession. Now she saw it for what it was: a beautiful symbol of Kareem's ownership and her status as a mercenary who'd done anything for money and what she'd thought was security.

Or was she a plain vanilla prostitute?

Most days it all blurred together.

"Did you ever think where the money for your bling came from, Mrs. Gregory? Did you ever think about all the kids who were using and dying because of your husband's illegal activities? Did you ever think of any of that while you were living in your million-dollar house and driving your Benz to church every Sunday?"

"Do you think you can accuse me worse than I can accuse myself?"

The righteous Dexter Brady didn't like that. His eyes widened with unmistakable surprise and he flung her arm away, turning to his window, propping his elbow against it and staring out at the Dumpster. "Why should I help you?"

That deep voice was calm now, barely audible and back to its bored cadence, but Kira wasn't fooled. She'd won. She knew it even if he didn't. "We can help each other."

"I don't need your help," he said to the window. "My boys ran a clean investigation. We got an indictment and a conviction. I'll bring Jack back in, he'll testify again, and we'll get another conviction. Easy as pie. What are you going to do? Bake cookies for us to eat on the way home from the courthouse?"

"Kareem is still dealing, same as ever. I don't think he's even broken stride."

"And you know this—how? Because he discussed his distribution network the other night in bed after he'd finished fucking you?"

She deserved that, yeah. But she didn't like it.

"You don't know what it's *like,*" she cried. "I'm doing the best I can and I am trying to become a better person. I know the great and perfect Dexter Brady has never come down off his mountaintop long enough to mingle with us mortals and make a mistake, but try to understand what I'm going through."

He stared at her. "You're wrong about that. Being in this car with you is the biggest mistake I've ever made. Mrs. Gregory."

There was something new and disquieting in his eyes now, something that wasn't hostility or disgust and that gave her the courage to push him a little further.

"Kira," she told him.

Mistake. She knew it even before he blinked and looked to the Dumpster . . . the dashboard clock . . . anything that wasn't her.

"What proof do you have that he's up to his old tricks?"

"None," she admitted. "Not yet."

"Brilliant."

"Look. Kareem's hired a whole new legal team and they might get him off this time. Don't you want to have as much spaghetti to throw at the wall as possible to make sure some of it sticks? Or do you want to risk Kareem staying out on the streets forever?"

"What about you testifying against him in open court? You ready for that? And that's assuming you can testify and Kareem's lawyer doesn't block you on account of the husband-wife privilege."

"I'm ready to do anything that'll get Kareem out of my life for once and for all."

His jaw dropped in a gape and he whipped his head back around to face her. "You don't get it, Mrs. Gregory. He'll never be out of your life until one of you dies."

Oh, she got it. "I'm not asking that much."

He snorted. "And all you want in return—?"

"Is protection when it's all over. A chance. Which is more than I've got now. Do we have a deal?"

"How are you planning to get said proof without getting killed in the process?"

"How the hell should I know? I'm making this up as I go. Do we have a deal?"

"Depends." He was all business now. "You bring me something to get excited about, and we'll talk. I'm not going to bat for you on the basis of all the great information you might bring me one day if your schedule permits. You want to be an informant, you need to inform me of something I don't already know."

"I'm on it," she told him.

"Jack," Amara said groggily.

She was in the curtained-off recovery area with all the tubes, IVs and monitors that went along with it. One of those ugly-ass speckled blue hospital gowns was visible above the white sheet, and she struggled with the oxygen thing in her nose while he crept closer.

He was forcibly reminded of another hospital, another patient, another outcome.

And yet this moment was almost more unbearable because her eyes were still clever and bright and her will strong—he could see it—and she was still Amara.

There was a real danger that he'd embarrass himself. Just drop to his knees and sob with relieved joy until there was no water left in his body. Swallowing hard, he worked on not doing that. "Hey, Bunny."

Just as she pulled the cannula out of her nose, a nurse swooped in and replaced it.

Amara scowled. "Tell her I'm a lawyer, Jack. I can sue her for this."

Jack snorted with something that was more laugh than sob but definitely a little of both. "You have no idea what you're up against," he told the nurse. "You should make it easy on yourself and let her take it out."

The nurse didn't look worried. "You need to tell *Bunny* here that I'll cut her pain meds if she keeps it up."

"There's no need to get nasty," Amara said.

Laughing, the nurse winked and bustled off.

And Amara held out her hand, the one with the IV line in it. "Come here."

Jack hesitated. If she had any sense, she'd eject him immediately, and he almost felt it was his moral duty to tell her so. On the other hand, he would die if he didn't touch her. Hurrying up, he took her hand and it was so soft, warm and *alive* that he lost it. Pressing his lips to the back, tubes and all, he cried, with shaking shoulders and the whole humiliating deal.

"I'm sorry about Daisy," she said.

"I'm sorry about you."

"Hmmm." Her lids drooped and he could tell he was losing her to the drugs. "Don't worry. Next time I'm going to duck behind you. I've already decided."

He laughed again and there was less cry in it this time.

"What time is it?"

"I have no idea," he told her.

"Did you take a nap? You look tired."

Was this a joke? *He* wasn't the one with extra ventilation in his side. "I don't sleep."

She cracked her bleary eyes back open. "What does that mean, you don't sleep?"

"I snooze. I catnap. I don't sleep."

"Why not?"

"Would you sleep if someone wanted you dead?"

"Good point. They're letting me go in the morning," Amara murmured, her eyes closing again.

"I know," Jack said. "You're coming with me."

Nightmarish as dinner with Kareem was, with Kareem's hand skimming her bare thighs under the table, making her hot and wet no matter how much she hated herself for it, Kira wished she could extend it. What would he do when they got home? What would she do? Open her arms and legs to welcome him back?

At this rate? Yeah, she probably would.

Because she was a slut.

On the ride home, her jumbled thoughts nearly overwhelmed her. Dexter Brady's image flashed through her mind, a bolt out of nowhere that lingered when she wanted him gone. His features were harsh, unforgiving and utterly fascinating, and his fingers, unlike Kareem's, were the plain, unbuffed but neatly trimmed and strong fingers of a man who worked rather than a man who lied, cheated, killed and primped.

Don't think about him, Kira.

Until she found some evidence to use against Kareem, she had to focus on hanging on. Had to be as cunning and cold-blooded as her husband. Had to somehow keep him out of her bed, which was damn near impossible when her weak body wanted him there.

Something intangible had changed between them today and suddenly the rules were different and the stakes were higher. Her whole *I need more time to rebuild the broken trust between us* gambit was no longer working. He wanted her back, *now,* and she was so scared she could barely breathe. Every hour, minute, second and nanosecond of every single day of her miserable life, she was scared out of her freaking wits because an impatient Kareem Gregory was a dangerous man.

She had to play her cards exactly right. There was no room for error.

So when they got home and Kareem suggested a drink, she plastered that damn good-wife smile on her face and said, "Great," like she meant it.

And, wouldn't you know, just when she thought the night had gotten as bad as it was going to get short of Kareem barging into her bedroom in the middle of the night, it got worse. Wanda, Kareem's mother and Satan's Gucci-clad surrogate here on earth, waited for them on her perch in the leather armchair in the corner.

Kira pretended she was Halle Berry and really started to act. "How was your evening, Wanda? I thought you were playing cards tonight."

Wanda sipped her scotch before she answered. "Betty canceled on us, so we didn't have a foursome."

"That's too bad."

Wanda turned to Kareem, stood, and received his kiss on the cheek. Kira tried not to snort because they did the whole kissy routine every time they saw each other, which was several times a day.

"How was your steak, Baby Boy?" Wanda asked him. "Was it cooked right?"

Kareem grinned. "Wasn't bad. Wasn't yours, though."

Kira worked on not rolling her eyes. Neither Kareem nor Wanda had ever seen the need to cut the apron strings, so Wanda's living here with them was the perfect arrangement. That way, Wanda could fawn over Kareem's every burp, fart, and sigh, and receive, in return for her never-ending devotion even in the face of the mounting evidence of Kareem's evil, unlimited access to Kareem's platinum cards, luxury cars, furs, and enough diamond jewelry to have a collection to rival the queen's.

Kira was the only outsider here, but she was used to the feeling.

Kareem sat next to Kira, bringing the sporty scent of his cologne with him and frowning at the dog, who'd trotted in and climbed on her lap. "You're getting hair on your dress, baby."

"Leave the girl alone, Kareem," Wanda said. "You know she doesn't worry herself about clothes."

Translation: your ungrateful wife doesn't appreciate the expensive things you buy for her, son, but I appreciate you enough for both of us.

Kareem put Max on the floor and ignored his mother. "It's time for bed." He stroked Kira's nape and, God, it felt good. All he had to do was touch her there, and she unraveled. She was sick, obviously. Her ongoing lust for this man was a sickness that could kill her, the same as AIDS or malaria.

With rising desperation, she scooted to the edge of the sofa and stood while Kareem tracked her every movement. His white-hot gaze scraped over every inch of her body, stripping away the dress, the bra and the panties until only his remembered intimate knowledge of her body remained, offering no protection whatsoever.

Kareem stood and extended his hand; she took it. What else could she do?

"Good night," they both told Wanda, who craned her neck to watch them with sour interest as they headed down the hall to the enormous curved staircase, and then they were climbing toward God knew what with Kira leading the way.

On the fourth step, he skimmed her bare thighs.

Eleven more steps to the top . . . ten . . . And then there was the cool rush of air below her waist as he raised her skirt high, baring her to the waist.

"Have mercy, Kira," he muttered.

The black lace of her expensive panties drove him wild. That was why he'd bought them for her. It didn't explain why she still wore them, though. Maybe she needed the physical reminder of her moral decay. If she had any integrity at all she'd burn everything he'd given her with his drug money and replace every last stitch with Walmart selections, but her integrity had evaporated years ago.

Besides. What other kind of underwear should a slut wear?

They walked in silence to the closed door to her bedroom, which was part of the master suite. "Kareem," she began.

He was too busy turning her in his arms to listen. With utter focus, he kneaded her ass with one hand, bringing her up against the unforgiving length of his heavy erection, and stroked her face with the other.

Kareem had always known what buttons to push. He'd always aroused her in a way no other man ever had. Add her forced abstinence to that mix and she was a powder keg looking for a lit match.

She hadn't had sex in almost two years, ever since his arrest. Her young body was alive and awake, and her breasts needed a man's hands and lips. The throbbing core between her thighs wept for a man's possession and she wanted it to be hard and fast, rough and unforgettable.

Kareem knew all about her wants and needs because he'd introduced them to her.

Looking into his brown eyes now was a mistake, but she did it anyway.

The connection was still there.

He was as beautiful as he'd ever been, no question. If anything, the years had only sharpened his features. He had smooth walnut skin warm over slashing cheekbones, sleek black hair and brows and lush lips framed by a neat mustache and goatee.

Kareem had the face of an angel. A fallen angel, yes, but still an angel.

"I miss you, baby."

In that weak moment, she missed him, too. So when he lowered his perfect, perfect lips to her mouth, she raised her chin to meet him.

Chapter 15

Like the worst kind of street hooker, spreading her thighs for whoever had twenty bucks to spend, Kira moaned for him, opened her mouth wide and took him deeper. She couldn't help it. Only when his entire body tightened reflexively around her and she felt his control slipping and hers along with it, did she remember.

The memories slammed through her with the force of a forked lightning strike. This man was a murderer—if not with his own hands, then with his deeds, his very existence. This man distributed drugs to children and he'd never lost a single night's sleep over it. This man was a parasite who belonged behind bars if not six feet under.

Didn't she have a little control here? Couldn't she exert it? Just because she'd prostituted herself during their entire marriage didn't mean she had to prostitute herself *tonight*. Right?

Stiffening, she pulled back and lied because she was a good liar.

"I can't." God, was that her voice husky with all that lust? "I'm on my period."

This may not work, of course. There were many ways she could satisfy him short of intercourse, and he might demand one because his erection was full and insistent.

Had he even heard her? Probably not, judging from the way he kept kissing her.

Or was she kissing him?

Stop, Kira. You've got to stop.

"Kareem."

This time he heard her. Letting her go, he took one step back and clamped his skull between his own hands, frustration radiating off him in waves. But he wasn't angry. His joyous smile was blinding and beautiful and she, against all reason, felt guilty for doing this to him and for what she was about to do.

It hurt to see him like this, to feel the responsive pang in her heart. Why couldn't she stamp out all feelings for this man? Hadn't she learned enough about his true nature by now? What else would it take?

Destroyed, she couldn't even look him in the eye. How crazy was that?

"I love you, baby," he told her.

"I know."

She did know. He loved her as much as a sociopath was capable of loving, which was probably right around zero percent.

"Does this mean we can try again?"

No. Not in this lifetime. Never. "Yes," she said.

That beautiful smile widened, killing her, and then it seemed to dawn on him that an apology might be appropriate, given that he'd lied about pretty much everything he'd ever told her.

"I'm sorry. About . . . everything—"

"I know," she said again.

"—and when the trial is over and I'm acquitted, we're going to start all over. Maybe a second honeymoon—"

Oh, no. She couldn't let him get too far down that road because it would only make things worse in the end. It was better to divert him.

"Are you so sure you'll be acquitted?"

Whoa. There it was. A hint of the darkness in his soul, so subtle and fleeting she would have missed the ugly flash in his eyes if she hadn't known what to look for.

"I'm sure."

"How do you know?"

His smile shifted and changed into that secretive and malicious abomination that was the reminder she needed. She was dealing with evil here. She wouldn't forget that again, not even for one weak second.

"You know I don't leave things to chance, Baby Girl."

"No."

He took her back into his arms and nuzzled her temples. "How was your test? I forgot to ask."

Test? What test? Oh—the test she'd lied about to get out of the house this morning. Yeah, she remembered. She also remembered the thing she'd discovered when she went to the jewelers, another gambit in the cat-and-mouse game between them.

"Great. I think I got an A."

"Good girl."

"Kareem." She kept her voice sweet even as she rested her arms on his and locked them so that he couldn't pull her any closer. "I took my ring to the jeweler's today."

Suddenly he was all business and the languid passion disappeared even though his hands continued their slow circuit of her body as though he couldn't help himself.

Sharp with focus, he narrowed his eyes. "Why?"

"A prong was loose."

"And what happened?"

"They told me this ring is a fake."

They stared at each other, each playing their part.

He kept his expression benign, as though he hadn't switched her ring with a fake because he knew she'd try to sell it to get the money to leave him, and she kept hers wide-eyed and honestly bewildered, as though she hadn't taken it to the jeweler for that very purpose. As though she was a dutiful wife who wanted to take good care of the jewelry he'd bestowed upon her in all his benevolence.

Her performance was better.

He backed down, the hint of belligerence slipping away and leaving what seemed to be guilt. "I should have told you. I didn't want to take the chance on someone trying to, ah, steal the ring—"

Right. Like there was anyone stupid and suicidal enough to try to steal the engagement ring off a drug kingpin's wife's finger.

"—so I, uh, had another one made. With CZs."

"Oh." Nodding as though this made perfect sense, she pressed her luck a little bit more. "Where's the real one?"

"In a safe place."

Kira knew a brick wall when she saw one and she also knew that she could kiss the real ring good-bye.

She'd never see it again. She should have sold it when Kareem was in prison, but she'd thought she had more time. That was the story of her life, apparently. She always thought she had more time.

But she didn't.

One day soon her cat and mouse game would be over and Kareem would know exactly what she was doing. Which was why she was trying to form this alliance with Dexter Brady, the only man in the world who could possibly help her.

If she could hold on long enough.

"Well. Good night."

She started to open her door and escape into the room. Not that it was safe in there or anywhere in this house, but it was safer than being in the hall with Kareem's hands all over her body. Before she could get two steps away, though, he grabbed her back for another kiss.

And she wondered, with Kareem's tongue deep inside her mouth and her body boiling hot, how soon she could find evidence that would send him back to prison, where he belonged.

Amara woke and stared into the darkness, knowing he was there even if she couldn't see him. They were in a hotel suite with a guard posted outside the door. Mateo and Jack were in one bedroom, Amara in the other.

They'd let her go this morning and they'd leave for Cincinnati tomorrow, where she could stay in the safe house while she recovered. Jack insisted on it because he felt sorry for her pitiful lack of anyone in her life to give a damn that she'd been shot.

If she hadn't been so anxious to spend more time with him any way she could, her pride would've demanded she read him the riot act for his charity. Who the hell did he think she was? Did he think she couldn't stay in bed to rest and feed herself a bowl of chicken soup every now and then? Did she look like an invalid?

Not for the first time, though, her pride shut right up where Jack was involved.

Where was he? She knew she wasn't imagining things. "Jack."

Nothing for a few seconds, and then a shadow detached from one side of the drapes and came to stand at the foot of the king-sized bed.

She levered up on her elbows but couldn't see his face. "What are you doing?"

"Nothing."

There was a trace of defensiveness in his voice and she realized he'd been watching her—watching over her—probably for a while. "You should get some sleep."

"I told you," he said. "I don't sleep."

"Oh."

O-kay. Now what?

She stared at his dark figure. She checked the blue lights of the digital clock: one forty-three. She thought about how tired she was and how she needed her rest. She felt sad for him that he didn't sleep well. She looked at the vast expanse of bed to her right, all fluffy pillows and down comfort.

And she wanted.

If she had a single ounce of common sense, she'd ask him to leave. It wasn't her rule that there should be a thousand brick walls between them, but the rational part of her could see that it was a good rule and should be observed.

They weren't going to build a relationship. They should, therefore, put the kibosh on any further touching, snuggling or encounters in a horizontal position, gunshot injuries or no. Jack's sex appeal was so overwhelming and her attraction to him so strong he could probably make her come while she was in a coma.

He should leave. Tell him to leave.

She opened her mouth. "Come here."

At first, she thought he'd refuse, but then he sprang into action and got in the bed, bringing all his wonderful warmth with him, stretching out alongside her, being careful to spoon her gently so there was no risk of touching or injuring her side.

Those arms came around her, strong and secure, and pulled her closer, until they were molded together like two pieces of a giant jigsaw that had been cut from a single piece of wood and reunited.

And even though she'd nearly been killed a couple times since she met Jack and, for all she knew, a killer was walking down the hall to their suite right now, gun in hand, Amara felt safe.

"Thank you for saving my life," he whispered.

She smiled. "You're welcome."

"Sleep, Bunny." He pressed a kiss to her temple.

And she slept.

DEA Supervisor Dexter Brady braced his hands on his desk, tried to ignore the blinding headache skewering him between the eyes, and concentrated on not shitting a brick.

Leadership came with responsibilities, one of

which involved not killing the people who worked for you even when they needed killing on account of gross stupidity. Being a leader also meant keeping cool and making levelheaded decisions in the face of adversity, when what you really wanted to do was hop the next plane to Cancún and hope things turned out okay in your absence. Most of all, being a leader meant dealing with rogue special agents who were at turns brilliant saviors and, just as often, royal pains in the ass.

One of the biggest pains in the ass he'd ever had the misfortune to manage had just arrived in his office, looking surly enough that he wanted to vault over his desk and backhand his scowling face into next week: Jackson Parker, accompanied by a new transfer to the Cincinnati office, Mateo Garciaparra.

If only he'd listened to his mother and gone to business school.

Jackson Parker, who had extensive weapons training and the guns to go along with it, needed to be installed in a safe house and babysat. Normally the DEA didn't do safe houses. Normally they only babysat snitches, not their own agents who, theoretically, were able to defend themselves. Never under any circumstances did they babysit agents' girlfriends. Despite all this, they'd set up a safe house, sent over a small task force of babysitters, and let Parker's girlfriend move in and unpack.

Yeah, the world had turned upside-down and dogs and cats were living together in harmony here in the Cincinnati office. Soon it would probably be raining gum balls.

Dexter watched and waited as the special agents who'd been assigned to the task force guarding Parker escorted him into his office and lingered, looking to Dexter for instructions.

"Wait outside," he told them.

They filed out, leaving Dexter alone with Parker and Garciaparra and still too angry to deal with Parker.

He stuck out a hand to Garciaparra. "Welcome to Cincy. I'm Brady."

The new guy pumped Dexter's hand. "Garciaparra. Thanks."

Dexter waved a hand at the chairs in front of his desk. They sat. He sat. He stared at them. They stared back. None of them spoke.

He hadn't laid eyes on Parker in a long time, not since Gregory was convicted and Parker went into hiding. In theory he should be happy to see him again, still alive and healthy. In reality he was thinking this'd been one of the quickest periods of his life.

He studied Parker and decided the ass chewing could wait a minute or two. The brother looked the worse for wear, as though he'd been burning the candle with blowtorches at both ends. A little haggard, a little gaunt, he had heavy bags under his eyes and appeared to need a sixteen-year nap.

"Is there a reason you gave your escort such a hard time when they picked you up at the airport, Parker?"

"I didn't trust them."

Dexter snorted. "Didn't trust them? There's a shocker, Garciaparra. Did you hear that? Parker doesn't trust people."

Both men kept quiet, which only pissed Dexter off more.

"I assume you trust me, Parker." Dexter worked hard to make his voice as sarcastic as possible. "Or did you want to give me a once-over and make sure I'm not really Kareem Gregory with a mask and a voice-alteration device like they use in all the *Mission: Impossible* movies?"

Parker flattened his lips and said nothing.

This continued silence when a fight would be so much more satisfying infuriated Dexter. "It'd be nice if you were smart enough to know who to trust and who not to trust, Parker."

Parker shrugged and stretched his lips into half of the most insolent smile Dexter had ever seen. "I make it easy on myself and don't trust anyone."

"Interesting. So how come you're glued at the hip now to this Amara Clarke woman? You trust her? Or is she your new adoptive daughter?"

Aha. Pay dirt. Parker flushed an angry red and glared at Dexter with slow murder in his eyes. "I have no reason not to trust her."

"Wow. Even though you've had—what?—two attempts on your life since you laid eyes on this paragon of trustworthiness. You don't see any possible connections there? Or is it all a giant coinky-dink?"

Parker seemed frozen with rage, but that was just too bad. He could go fuck himself in the corner for all Dexter cared at this moment.

Finally Parker spoke, heaping dry kindling on the smoldering flames of Dexter's temper. "I know you're busy, what with pushing papers from one side of your desk to the other all day—"

"Jesus," Garciaparra muttered to the ceiling.

Parker was a dead man. Dexter was going to call Kareem Gregory and tell him to come get Parker now. Hell. At this point he'd even pay for Gregory's gas to get over here.

"—and you probably haven't had time to read one more report and keep yourself up on current events and all," Parker continued, "but Amara Clarke has been caught in the crossfire of this fuck fest. The contract killer that our good friend Kareem Gregory sent to kill me went to her house looking for me and would have killed her if I hadn't gotten there in time."

"That's really tragic." Leaning his head back against his tall chair, Dexter yawned, patting his mouth. When he was done with that, he made a show of checking his watch. "Tragic. Really, but—"

Parker went purple.

"—what's it got to do with the DEA and her staying in the safe house we set up to keep your precious hide safe while you're in town?"

"Not a goddamn thing," Parker snarled. "I paid for her flight here and I'll pay for her groceries. Just think of her as my private bodyguard or spiritual counselor for the duration. Satisfied?"

"Well, I'm sure you see God every time you fuck her, so that makes sense," Dexter said.

"Dios," Garciaparra breathed.

Parker was on his feet bracing his hands on the desk to lean down and stare Dexter in the eye with a rabid-dog primitive wildness. "Here's what Amara Clarke's got to do with you: the government needs my testimony. I need Amara Clarke to be kept safe. If you can't let her sit in the safe house, recovering from her gunshot wound and not bothering anybody during the trial, you're going to find that my memory is going to suffer—"

"What?"

"—and I'm not going to be the most convincing witness in the world. You feel me?"

So much for being a calm, effective leader. Fuck it. He was going to reach down Parker's throat and rip his lungs out through his mouth.

Jumping up and only vaguely aware of his chair toppling and crashing to the floor behind him, Dexter reached out and grabbed the collar of Parker's sweater. Parker erupted, trying to break away in a flurry of swinging arms and bared teeth, and it looked like there was going to be a fun time up in the office tonight.

But before things could really get going, Garciaparra dove between them and pulled Parker back, pinning him against the far wall and holding him there with one elbow in a choke hold across the man's throat. Parker snarled and spluttered but couldn't break free to kill Dexter as he clearly wanted to do.

Taking advantage of his captive audience, Dexter came around his desk and got right up in Parker's face. "If you threaten me again, Parker, I'm going to call in my friends from the marshal's office and have them put you in full lockdown until the trial. Okay? That's number one."

"Fuck you," Parker spat.

Dexter decided to ignore this ongoing rudeness. "Number two: if your testimony is anything other than stellar and convincing, I'm going to call in the U.S. attorney and see if we can't charge you with perjury and/or obstruction—"

Parker gave a mighty heave and nearly came loose, but Garciaparra shifted his hold and squeezed Parker in the hollow between his neck and shoulder and Parker yelped and settled down a little but still strained to get free.

"—but I know it won't come to that because no one

wants Gregory back in prison more than you do. You built the case against this parasite and you're too much of a professional to blow it now even if you are apparently thinking with your dick."

"Low blow, man," Garciaparra muttered as Parker's renewed outrage gave him a fresh surge of adrenaline and he struggled harder.

Dexter ignored them both. Enough. This was stupid. They were all on the same side and it was time they remembered it. He went back to his desk and sat.

"Here's what we're going to do: the woman can stay in the safe house with you for now, and I don't want to hear a peep out of you or her. The only thing I want to hear about your continued existence is a series of daily reports from the U.S. attorney telling me what a good boy you're being and how hard you're working on preparing for your testimony.

"And then, Parker, I want you to get the hell out of Cincinnati and go somewhere where I, hopefully, will never have to lay eyes on you again. We're working on getting you out of here and finding a new home for you, far, far away. Okay? So keep your bags packed. In the meantime, I don't have time for this bullshit because we've got a dead agent in Sacramento, a shooting in Seattle, nothing that could tie the dead shooter to Gregory, and—"

"I can help you with that," Parker said.

What the fuck? "Did you need an engraved invitation from the director to tell your story, or were you planning to share this information with me any time this morning?"

"The shooter dropped her weapon at Amara's house. We can't tie it to Amara's shooting, but maybe ballistics can show that the same weapon was used on my boss at the diner and Ray Wolfe and his wife."

"Where's this weapon?"

Parker, stubborn and paranoid to the end, squared his jaw. "Do I have your word on Amara Clarke?"

Dexter rolled his eyes. This woman's shit must be pure magic. Truly. "Yeah, Parker, you've got my word."

"I'll get it to you," Parker said.

"Do that. Immediately."

Dexter set his chair upright, sat, leafed through his paperwork and wondered if taking another Extra Strength Tylenol on top of the four he'd downed in the last hour would be too much. His head was killing him and Kira Gregory's beautiful image was hovering at the corner of his mind, demanding attention.

"Now get out of my office," he barked.

Kareem Gregory left his lawyer's office and met up with his bodyguards, who'd been waiting for him by the SUV in the parking garage. Keeping their eyes open to make sure they weren't being followed, they drove to meet two of his lieutenants, Yogi Watkins and Kerry Randolph, in the deserted, weed-overgrown parking lot behind some bankrupt piano manufacturer's deserted warehouse.

Not exactly a well-appointed conference room with hot coffee and pastries, but it was the only place where he was reasonably certain he couldn't be caught on tape, assuming the feds were watching him, which was always a safe bet.

"Stay here," he told his lazy-ass boys.

They grunted, only too happy to sit inside where it was warm.

Dumb fucks. What was he keeping them around for? Seething, Kareem jumped out of the Land Cruiser, slammed the door and strode past Kerry Randolph, who stood at attention beside his BMW.

"What's up, man?" Kerry asked.

What? *What?* Did that bitch just speak to him? Stopping dead—he didn't have any problems with Kerry at the moment, but it was early yet and that could change—Kareem wheeled around and gave him a look that had the brother turning white with fear.

"Don't speak unless spoken to," Kareem told him.

Kerry snapped his jaws shut.

That's right. Keep quiet. Now to deal with Yogi.

Kareem stalked over to where Yogi stood waiting by his Lexus sedan, looking worried with his brow crinkled and shit. The brother needed to be worried because Kareem was *pissed.* He was cold, tired and fed up with the incompetence that surrounded him on every side. His freedom hung on the line, he had a business to run and, most of all, he had a wife that he wanted to hook up with again, as soon as this trial was behind them and their future was free and clear.

He didn't have time for this ongoing *shit* and he didn't have time for traipsing around the city for secret meetings to crack heads.

"Kareem," Yogi began, all cautious, like he was tiptoeing through a minefield.

Kareem stared at him, saying nothing.

A semiautomatic handgun was a nice weapon to have in his arsenal, but so was silence. It made the strongest people, like Yogi, shrink and wither like an eighty-year-old's dick. Made them wonder when Kareem was going to go ape-shit and dole out a severe punishment for a job poorly done. Half the time

Kareem never had to do any follow-up because the stare was enough.

Follow-up was definitely in order today, though.

Yogi seemed to know it, too. Tall and doughy, nicknamed Yogi because of his unfortunate resemblance to the bear, he was looking nervous and sweaty even though it was gray and icy today and their breath made clouds of white steam.

Yogi's face screamed bad news. Kareem didn't want any more bad news.

Ever.

"Don't *Kareem* me." Keeping his voice low and rough, Kareem watched his best man swallow hard and wanted to take him off at the knees for showing fear. "Maybe you can explain why I haven't heard any news about that project not being completed the other night like I asked."

As always, Kareem spoke in code.

"Maybe you can explain to me," he continued, "why I just got finished being questioned about some shooting in Seattle where some special agent was killed, and I didn't know anything about it. Maybe you can tell me why the feds are now talking about bringing the wrath of God down on me for something I didn't authorize and had nothing to do with. Maybe you can tell me *what the fuck is going on*?"

Yogi looked pale but stood his ground. "Our friend out West hasn't checked in."

"Hasn't checked in," Kareem echoed.

The incompetence was mind-boggling. This punk was too stupid to live and every breath the man took was a waste of the free air. Kareem turned, paced away a few steps and then came back. The wind was on his face, blowing heavy and wet and promising snow, but all he could feel was heat and rage and the desire to damage something, to kill.

"Hasn't. Checked. In."

"I've been calling—"

"Shut the fuck up," Kareem roared.

Yogi shut up, damn near shaking like a leaf.

Good. He had plenty of reason to be scared.

Kareem pulled his hands out of the pockets of his wool overcoat and ticked his points off on his black leather-gloved fingers. "So we've got an unfinished project. We've got a shitload of money paid out with nothing to show for it. We've got a missing friend on the West Coast who's probably hopped a plane to Bali with my funds. And we've got my retrial starting in *a couple fucking days.*"

Yogi kept his yap shut.

"What about that project here at home, since we're going to need a Plan B? We get that information from Jerome yet? How's he doing on getting his little suburban druggie to talk?"

Yogi, who had his head hung low like a dog waiting to be kicked, shook his head and confirmed what Kareem already knew. It was no surprise, right? Why should this one thing be going well when everything else was a big pile of steaming elephant shit?

Goddamn it.

All conscious thought left Kareem's brain until only two things remained: Yogi's throat and his driving need to wrap his fingers around it.

He lunged. Snarled. Grabbed.

Chapter 16

The next thing Kareem knew, he had Yogi up against the Lexus and the brother was flailing with the effort to escape the beating, his eyes bulging. He didn't fight back. He knew better than that. All the men knew that raising a hand or a weapon against Kareem was an automatic death sentence.

But car doors were slamming all around them and Yogi's men were climbing out the other side of the Lexus, and running feet finally penetrated Kareem's screaming rage as he pummeled his right-hand man.

No one dared touch him, but someone had the balls to speak his name.

"Kareem. You don't want to do this, man."

Wrong choice of words. He *did* want to do this.

Kareem punched Yogi one last time across the nose and then, because that punch hurt his knuckles and, worse, spurted blood into Kareem's face and probably got some on his coat and scarf, punched him again. Yogi spluttered, swallowing a cry.

With disgust, Kareem turned him loose.

Coughing and gripping the car for support, Yogi doubled up and gasped for breath.

The men said nothing and concentrated on looking at their shoes in between nervous glances at Kareem and Yogi.

Kareem paced away, flexing his sore fingers and trying to calm down.

Shit. He hated losing control. Hated being reduced to this. Why couldn't people be professional? Why couldn't they do their jobs? It wasn't that hard. Why did they force him to get ugly? Did they think he enjoyed having to enforce discipline?

Several gulps of the frigid air cooled him off and he turned back to the group. Everyone shifted and hung their heads. That made him feel better because they looked sorry and he knew they'd work harder next time.

Running a business was really like being a father. These men were like his children. They just needed occasional guidance and instruction, and, as the saying went, it hurt him worse than it hurt them. But rules were rules and business was business.

Kareem shook his head because the whole scene made him sad.

And he used the silence again to make sure he had everyone's attention.

He did, but he glanced around the loose circle anyway, taking a long beat to look everyone in the eye and make sure they were all on the same page and all knew what he expected of Yogi and of them.

Then he turned to Yogi, cupped his face in his hands and kissed his cheek because he loved him like a brother and when you doled out the discipline you needed to make sure you did it with kindness and love.

"Why do you have to make me do this, man?" Kareem wondered. "Huh?"

Yogi didn't answer.

Kareem fished a linen handkerchief out of his breast pocket and passed it to Yogi. "Clean yourself up. And do your job. You feel me?"

"I feel you."

Yogi's voice sounded hoarse, but it was loud and clear and Kareem knew the man wouldn't fail him again, not if he wanted to live.

Good. So they understood each other.

Kareem felt much better. Light and hopeful, with a big weight taken off his shoulders. Yogi was back on the job and would make sure Parker didn't live to testify against Kareem again. It would all come together. If Parker didn't testify, Kareem would be acquitted. And once Kareem was acquitted, he and Kira could start their marriage over.

It was all connected. Circle of life and all that shit.

The sooner he was found not guilty, the sooner he could get back where he belonged: in bed with a wife who believed in him and looked at him with love and trust shining bright in her eyes.

Jesus. The image damn near made him cry.

Smiling at the men, he jerked his head toward the Land Cruiser and started walking.

"Let's go. I've got a business to run."

So this was a safe house.

Safe was, Amara supposed, a relative term.

Her house back in Mount Adams was beautiful, with flower boxes in the spring, matching colors and textures, and accent pieces with the furniture, but it was right on the corner of a tiny intersection and had flimsy locks and was not, therefore, safe.

The safe house of her imagination was an impenetrable fortress carved into the side of a mountain that was accessible only by a three-day journey by four-wheel drive SUV and then by helicopter. It had bulletproof windows, security cameras that covered every inch of the house, retinal scans for entrance from one room to the next, massive guards who had all been Navy SEALs in a former life, and roving packs of Dobermans—no, pit bulls—that were trained to kill intruders on sight. That was the ultimate in safety.

This house was . . . somewhere in between.

No cameras, no dogs, no bulletproof windows. They didn't *look* bulletproof, anyway, but what did she know? It was just a plain old house, two-story brick traditional with three bedrooms and two baths, about thirty years old, on about an acre of land at the end of a lane.

That was it.

Well, and the guards. Two inside and two outside. There'd apparently been some discussion of putting two more in a surveillance van down the street, just in case, but they didn't have the money or manpower to spare for that.

The four guards were DEA agents who'd either drawn the short straw to get put on the safe house protection task force or were on some sort of grievous punishment for past misdeeds. This gig couldn't be on the list of most coveted assignments for anyone, even the local traffic cop.

Jack was out and about in the world doing God-knew-what sort of DEA secret agent business. He'd left earlier and she'd watched him go, feeling forlorn and all but pressing her hands and nose to the nonbulletproof windows and wishing she could go with him.

Because Jack was her only link to anything approaching normalcy. With him, it was easier to convince herself that everything was under control. Without him, she was scared to death.

The irony of the situation didn't escape her. You'd think she'd have a little more backbone by now, but no. Despite all the alleged criminals she'd represented over the years (and who was she kidding with the *alleged* part? Most of her clients had been guilty of the crimes they'd been arrested for and at least a dozen others for which they'd managed to fly under the radar), she was a coward at heart.

She'd never been in the military. Never handled a gun. Never feared for her physical safety, unless she counted the five or six times growing up when she'd had to defend herself against her mother's johns when they'd looked at her with a little too much interest and she'd locked herself in the second bedroom of their tiny apartment.

They were dealing with a hired killer financed by a vengeful drug kingpin. You didn't reason with these people. There was no begging and no mercy, no negotiation tactic that could possibly work. It was only a tiny comfort that Jack was the real target and she was only temporarily caught in the middle. There was a light at the end of her tunnel, yeah. One day soon, hopefully, she could go home and resume her real life.

Jack never could.

This last thought started the walls closing in on her. That, and the lack of fresh air combined with her increased restlessness now that she was feeling better.

"I'm going for a walk," she announced.

There was a little more sharpness in her voice than she'd intended, and Special Agent Samantha Martinez heard it. She'd been sitting at the dining room table working on some report or other, but now she glanced up.

Though she seemed young, no more than thirty-ish, with a pretty face and wavy black hair scooped back in a loose bun at the nape of her neck, Sammy looked like she'd seen and heard a lifetime's worth of bullshit and didn't plan to put up with any more from Amara. Word was she'd been with DEA for eight years and was a cop before that, so she'd earned a healthy dose of respect from Amara.

At the other end of the table, Special Agent Anthony Kelleher finished up his call and put down his cell phone. As though he sensed trouble in the making, he shot Sammy a warning look.

"No walks, Amara," said Sammy in a falsely pleasant voice that plainly said Amara was a pain in the ass she wished she didn't have to babysit. "Why don't you watch cable?"

"I'm not a TV watcher." This was a lie. Amara had already missed several episodes of her favorite Travel Channel shows, but she resented Sammy's trying to shuffle her off into the other room like a kid who could be tempted by an episode of *SpongeBob SquarePants.*

Sammy shrugged and resumed scribbling on her stupid little report. "How's your scarf coming?"

"I'm tired of knitting."

"Then it looks like this isn't your lucky day."

Amara was getting ready to jump down the woman's throat with both feet when Anthony cleared his throat and smiled.

"Ah, Amara," he said, all boyish charm and dimples with a hint of the South in the low drawl of his voice, "when you get a minute, why don't you go on ahead and put that grocery list together for us? And then we can send someone on over to the—"

"Tell you what, Billy Bob." She didn't mean to be rude, but, come on, was this guy for real? "You ease up on the southern hospitality a little, because I'm immune anyway, and I'm gonna take me a little ole walk. You hear?"

Anthony laughed, which was the scrape of fingers over the blackboard of Amara's raw nerves. "We're all in this together, Amara. We're going to have a lot of long, tense days here together if we can't work on getting along."

"I'll be in a better mood after my walk."

"That's a negative, ma'am." Sammy now reached for her cell phone and punched in a number. "We can't keep you safe for Jack if you're traipsing—"

"I'm not planning to traipse. *Ma'am.*" Amara looked around for her jacket. "I'm going to walk to the corner and back. There's no one around for miles—"

"That we know of." Sammy put the phone to her ear, dismissing Amara.

This was outrageous.

The security issue was one thing—Amara got that and she wasn't a complete idiot, after all—but the disrespectful treatment was something else and needed to be addressed. For all she knew, she'd be holed up here with Crabby Patty for another week or ten days, and Amara certainly didn't intend to put up with this rudeness.

Without any real thought, she reached out, snatched the phone and clicked End.

A startled moment passed during which even Amara thought, *wow, maybe I went too far that time,* and then Sammy jumped to her feet and got in Amara's face, looking surprisingly fierce, or maybe it was just the weapon strapped to the holster at her side.

"Excuse me," Sammy began.

"No, excuse *me,*" Amara said.

Anthony materialized between them, which didn't stop them from yelling at each other, but then a new voice joined the fray and Amara shut up the second she heard it.

"What's the problem?"

Oh, God, it was Jack.

After being gone for hours and hours, long enough for her to begin wondering if he'd been shot or had simply decided to take off on his own and never look back, he'd chosen now, while she was behaving like a bigger shrew than usual, to reappear.

Amara snapped her jaws shut and felt the flames of embarrassment burn her face.

Sammy, meanwhile, wheeled around, resumed her seat and looked dignified.

Jack's gaze locked with Amara's. Although he didn't smile, he didn't look especially angry, and she'd had enough experience with his dark moods to know. There was a fresh bandage on his poor abused forehead, so she took that to mean he'd had it checked out.

"Alienated everyone already, Bunny?" he asked. "That didn't take long."

Oh, sure. Blame the prisoner. Like it was her fault. Furious, she pointed to the offenders. "These two clowns," she said, "Billy Bob and Crabby Patty, are refusing to let me get any fresh air."

"Oh." Jack said it with zero inflection, and yet

everything about him screamed reproach, as though he was apologizing for her childish behavior and wished she had the grace to do the same.

Effectively shamed, Amara sucked in a harsh breath and apologized. "I'm sorry."

Satisfied, Jack held out a hand to her and she took this lifeline, grateful for it. He reeled her in and held her against his side, his endorsement and support speaking volumes. These people respected Jack and would therefore give her the benefit of the doubt, even if she was behaving like a raving bitch.

"Amara takes some getting used to," Jack said.

Now wait a minute. She didn't need a spokesperson to explain her behavior to the world. Hadn't she just been woman enough to apologize? Frowning up at Jack, she snatched her hand free.

"Kindly do not talk about me like I'm not here, Special Agent."

Still seething, she stormed up to her bedroom to find her coat, slamming the door behind her. These people could not keep her locked up indefinitely with no fresh air and no fresh food and nothing—

The door opened and Jack came in.

"I need a minute, okay? And please knock before you come into my bedroom."

"It's our bedroom."

Abandoning the walk idea, she went to the window and concentrated on pushing the awful flowered drapes back so she could get as much sunshine as possible. It'd been sleeting for days in Cincinnati and now it was cold but sunny and she couldn't even see the light with these nightmare drapes.

"There are two other bedrooms here," she told Jack. "Pick one."

"I've already picked whichever one you're in." Unperturbed, he leaned against the cheap plywood dresser and crossed his ankles and arms. "What's this about?"

That impenetrable calm of his just drove her through the roof. So did his stupid questions, as though he'd thought and thought about it and just couldn't fathom why she'd be upset about anything.

"*What's this about?* This is about my house being broken into and me being shot. This is about flying all the way across the country to hide in a tiny little safe house for God knows how long—"

Jack did his best statue routine, absorbing her histrionics with nary a flicker of his eyelids or a ghost of an expression on his face.

"—and all you stupid DEA agents with your rules and your secret handshakes and your little nonverbal signals that make me feel like more of an outsider than I already am, and you marching in here and telling me that I can't even choose a bedroom without you controlling my selection. That's what this is about."

Spent and breathless, she brushed her flyaway hair out of her face and waited for him to level her with his temper and call her ungrateful for their protection. Maybe he'd go so far as to say that if she didn't like the minor inconveniences of temporary living in a safe house, she should go back to Washington by herself and good luck with that.

She was prepared for that reaction.

She wasn't prepared for him to reach out and grab her, but that's what he did.

The shock took a long time to register—how could he go from standing there, looking bored, to quick handwork that would make Muhammad Ali proud? By the time she thought to flail and struggle, it was too late and he was all over her. She overcompensated and they toppled to the bed, or maybe that was what he'd had in mind all along.

He favored her wounded side, but still managed to damage her equilibrium. Every part of him was so strong and hard and healthy, and she was infuriated, flat on her back and helpless. Not helpless to get away, but helpless to resist her body's insane reaction to him.

She tried anyway.

Arching back, she worked to get her arms between them, to plant her hands on the marble-hard slabs of his chest and push. No dice. His gentle hands—God Almighty, how was it possible that such a big man had such an unspeakably tender touch?—cupped her face, stroked it, and she was lost in the sensation and, worse, the emotion.

"I'm sorry," he said.

That rumbling croon set off wave after wave of shivers down her spine and pooled in her belly and lower, until her thighs were parting because they needed to and there wasn't a damn thing she could do about it.

"This is exactly what I never wanted to happen. I didn't want your life to be turned upside down because of me."

In no mood to be gracious, she tried to pull free and said, "Well, it is."

"I'm trying to make it right," he told her. "I'm trying to protect you."

"Protect me?" A laugh came out of nowhere and it was bitter, borderline hysterical. "I'm sure I'm safe from all the killers and drug dealers in the neighborhood. But who's protecting me from you?"

No one liked to be confronted with his own hypocrisy, Jack least of all. Those heavy brows came together over eyes glittering with splinters of brown and gold, desire and anger.

"We're helping each other through. That's all. We can't make it more than it is."

"More than what?" She raised her brows, wanting to hurt him, to smash his face in the mess he'd made of her so he'd have to deal with it. She shouldn't have agreed to come. She should have stayed in Washington. She should have stayed as far away from this man as possible because the more time she spent with him, the more time she wanted. "More than me screwing you on demand and then you walking away when you decide the time is right without looking back or giving me a second thought? I think I'm clear on that, thanks. Now get out."

Chapter 17

She'd pushed him too far, and his retaliation was swift and merciless. Without warning, Jack jerked her sweater up to her chin and ripped her bra down. Her breasts, bared to the cool air, bounced free and her nipples tightened down to hard little buttons of throbbing sensation.

She cried out with some combination of affront and need, and he answered by lowering his head. Taking her in his hands, he rubbed and squeezed, licked and nipped.

He couldn't have been more insulting.

She couldn't have loved it more.

Arching for him, she widened her legs further and he was right there, slipping a hand beneath the low waistband of her jeans and stroking her until she went up and up and her panties were soaking wet. As if he hadn't proved his point to his complete satisfaction, he withdrew his fingers from her greedy body, wiped her juices around first one nipple, then the other, and suckled.

Amara bowed over backwards, desperate to get away but more desperate to come.

And then, when she was teetering on the brink of an explosion that would shatter her and then blow the roof off this safe house, he stopped. Let her go, pulled back and stood up, staring at her with the grim satisfaction of a man who had a woman right where he wanted her and planned to keep her there for a while.

Exposed, both physically and emotionally, Amara knew she'd never been more vulnerable in her life. Only the heavy bulge in the front of his jeans and the sheen of sweat on his forehead saved her from complete devastation.

He wasn't immune to this thing between them, thank God.

"You need to get this straight, Bunny. I'll be in this bed with you tonight and every other night until the trial is over and we go our separate ways." His voice was low and untroubled, his tone absolute. "If that's not what you want, all you have to do is tell me no the next time I reach for you. But I don't think that word has ever come out of your mouth when I'm touching you."

Pausing, he looked her up and down, smiled a crooked smile, and stroked himself with a rough grip that had her hips writhing and her mouth watering. "And I don't think it ever will."

Infuriated with him but more with herself, she yanked off her shoe and aimed it right at the bandage in the middle of his forehead.

Without any appearance of hurrying, he ducked in time for the shoe to hit the door as it closed.

* * *

Where?

The word raced through Kira Gregory's mind, faster and faster as the hours crept past, fueled by her paranoia and agitation and the knowledge that Kareem's retrial started in a couple days and she'd found no evidence of Kareem's illegal activities to give Dexter Brady.

Which meant that, despite her desperate plea for help, Dexter Brady, her Plan B, hadn't worked, and she was on her own. Again. Still. Always.

Well, she had Max, didn't she? He was over in the corner under the table, gnawing on a bone. Too bad the little devil couldn't take his ass out in the world and get a job to support the two of them.

No. It was up to her. Which was why she was here, in Kareem's darkened study in the dead of night.

Where did Kareem keep the combination to the safe, the information about the offshore bank accounts she knew he had, and the unregistered weapons he collected the way boys collected manga?

Where?

It was all here in this house somewhere, probably in this room. She could smell it.

Where, where, WHERE?

A scream of frustration rose up in her throat, but losing her cool wouldn't get her anywhere. She had to be as cunning as Kareem if she wanted to make it out of here alive.

Think, Kira.

She glanced around the big room, which was illuminated only by a small lamp on the console in the corner, and tried to put herself in the shoes and mind frame of a drug dealer.

Yeah. Good luck with that.

The thing was: Kareem had two conflicting considerations. On the one hand, he knew the feds were after him, knew his property was subject to warrants and searches and seizure at any time, knew that there could be wiretaps and hidden cameras all over his precious house, recording his choice in food, underwear and toilet paper.

He wasn't stupid. He had all the trappings of respectability, and he tried, whenever possible, to keep his hands clean and present that face to the world. On the other hand, wasn't it basic human nature to keep treasures close? To bury your money in the backyard where you could get it quickly if you needed to skip out of town unexpectedly? To sleep with your favorite gun under your pillow just in case one of your bodyguards fell asleep on the job and a bad guy—like, say, a competing drug lord who'd like nothing more than to slit your throat and take over your territory—broke into your house and tried to kill you?

So—yeah. It had to be here. Somewhere.

The computer screen glowed blue and the mocking little window asked for a password. Kira wanted to smash her foot through it. Password. Yeah. Like she knew it. Fuck you.

It wasn't that she thought she'd turn up anything more than the DEA's best had back when they'd executed their search warrant when Kareem was arrested. They'd found some money in the safe, a registered nine-millimeter that was pristine as the first winter snow atop Mount Everest, and nothing else.

But that had been a long time ago and they hadn't been back since. She'd hoped—prayed—that Kareem had become complacent since then, or maybe outright sloppy or lazy. Maybe he'd temporarily stashed something in the room with the hopes of removing it to a safer place quickly, when he had the chance. Maybe, she'd thought, she'd be lucky enough to stumble onto something during that narrow window of opportunity.

She should have known better.

Just then, the clock on the mantel chimed to life and began the belabored process of dinging the hour. Eleven o'clock.

Oh, shit. Kareem would be back from the meeting with his lawyers soon, if he wasn't already on his way.

If he caught her in here, she was dead.

He had a study, she had a study, and both areas were clearly delineated and off-limits to the other. What would she say? That she had a sudden and urgent need to borrow paper clips at eleven o'clock at night?

And Wanda—what time had Wanda said she'd be home from playing cards tonight? Midnight? Or had she said eleven?

Okay. Check the room, girl. Make sure everything's in its place.

The rug was laid flat, with the fringe pointing in the right direction, nice and straight. None of the artwork was crooked. One of the earthenware pots was about half an inch off center, so she corrected it. There. Perfect. The computer screen still glowed blue, but it would hibernate in a minute and Kareem would never know she'd been here.

She snatched Max up, along with his bone. Thirty-ish silent steps down the crypt-dark and deserted hallway, past the kitchen and up the stairs, and she'd be home free.

Swinging the well-oiled door on its hinge, she

peeked over her shoulder toward the mud room—no sounds of a car in the garage, thank goodness—left the office and took care to tiptoe around a couple of creaky spots on the floor. Picking up speed, she glanced into the kitchen as she passed.

And came face to face with her mother-in-law.

Jack rested his palms on either side of the white sink, leaned in and studied his reflection in the mirror. He didn't like what he saw. He never did.

The fluorescent light fixture threw shadows over his face and emphasized the dark patches under his eyes. That jagged-ass cut on his forehead was now scabbed and crusty. Ten o'clock shadow and a desperate glint in his expression rounded out his look, which was a twisted hybrid of *The Fugitive* and *Dead Man Walking* in a pair of blue plaid flannel pajama bottoms and nothing else.

He reached out and flicked the switch anyway.

The darkness comforted him a little, but it was the difference between hanging by your thumbs for twenty-four hours straight or hanging by your thumbs for twenty-four hours with periodic five-minute breaks. Didn't matter much. In the light or in the dark, he was still the man who used to see the world in black and white and now saw only gray in every direction. He was still the man who knew what the right thing to do was, but couldn't make himself do it. He was still a weak man grasping for whatever brief shining moments of beauty, peace and normalcy he could get.

Did that make him a selfish bastard? Then he was a selfish bastard.

But he was ashamed of his selfishness. It ate him from the inside out, a piranha with razors for teeth and intractable jaws that held on for dear life and sliced at him until he was wounded, bleeding, and too cowardly to look in the mirror and face his demons for what they were.

He couldn't make sense of anything.

Not the continued bitterness he felt about giving up the life he'd known and the life he'd wanted for a mission he wasn't certain, even now, had been worth it. Kareem Gregory wanted to kill him. Quite possibly would kill him. Pursuing the man had cost Jack his life as he'd known it, and for what? A lame-ass money-laundering conviction that got overturned on appeal?

Yeah. Fair trade.

Most of all, he couldn't get to the bottom of his driving passion and need for Amara Clarke, however he could get her, for as long as he could have her.

This last part was the most unforgivable.

She wanted him to let her go; he should let her go. No mystery there. All he had to do was request that she be moved to another safe house. Easy, right? Just make that call to Dexter Brady, listen to his bitching and moaning about the cost, and it was done.

Amara would be safe somewhere else and untangled from the snake's nest of Jack's life. They'd never see each other again, which was best for Amara's physical and emotional health and, as for what was best for Jack, well . . . too bad, so sad. This wasn't about Jack.

He didn't get a vote. Shouldn't get a vote.

Only he was voting right here, right now, wasn't he?

Amara was staying here, he'd decided. With him. Period.

The time would come for them to say good-bye to each other soon enough. They didn't have to do it now. Two adults could maintain a consensual relationship for as long as they wanted, couldn't they?

As long as they knew what they were getting—and not getting.

Amara would be insane to get emotionally attached to him when he had an anticipated life span shorter than the shelf life of a carton of eggs. Amara was the smartest woman he knew. Ergo, she knew better.

Apparently he didn't, though. He longed for more time with her strength and laughter, wanted more slicing and dicing by her caustic tongue, wished he could die in her arms and buried deep inside her body rather than at the hands of one of Kareem Gregory's hired guns.

Jack gripped the hard porcelain and squeezed. He leaned his forehead against the cool mirror, closed his eyes, scrunched his face and reached for a little clarity. But clarity danced around the edges of his consciousness, just out of reach, and Jack was alone, like always. In a sign of how desperate he was, he even thought about praying, but why give God one more thing to laugh at him about?

And then it occurred to him. He'd happily hate and punish himself forever if he could spend a few more days and nights with Amara. It was a price he was willing to pay. They'd only made love once. *Once.* How could anyone—even the indifferent God who'd ignored pretty much every request he'd ever made in his entire life—think that once was enough?

Why worry about what God thought? He and God

had parted ways years ago. And Jack always hated himself anyway; if he sent Amara away he'd hate himself for not keeping her here.

So why not go down in flames?

As long as he kept up the emotional brick walls between them and kept warning her about the inevitable outcome—where was the harm? She was a big girl. She could make her own choices. If she didn't want him, she could say so.

Sudden euphoria made his head feel weightless and his breath fast and easy. Swinging open the bathroom door, he stepped over the threshold into the bedroom, and she was right there, standing less than ten feet away, waiting for him.

Jack's skittering heart gave up the fight and stopped altogether.

Her face was lit with a glow he didn't think could be explained by the ambient light from the nightstand lamp, at least not altogether. Her clothes were gone, all but a black satin bra and teeny-tiny panties skimming her hips and ramping up his imagination. Her gleaming skin, marred only by the bandage on her side, was smooth and warmly brown, a chocolate fantasy come to life right here within touching distance.

She was breathtaking.

Long legs with plump, biteable thighs, big breasts, wide hips and soft curves in every direction he looked. That wavy black hair that had always been up in those messy ponytails—how many times had he stared at her from the grill at the Twelfth Street Diner, dying to get his hands in that heavy silk?—was down around her shoulders, skimming them. Behind her, the door was shut and the bed turned down.

She waited, saying nothing.

There was so much he wanted to say. So much he could never say.

His thick tongue and dry mouth didn't work until he'd cleared his throat a couple of times. "Are you kicking me out?"

"No."

"Good."

As he reached for her and felt that first contact between them, the first slide of skin to skin, the first sigh, the first brush of lips, he acknowledged what he'd always known:

It was all a lie.

All the justifications and excuses he'd just given himself, that whole pep talk, were a shimmering mirage with no substance whatsoever.

There would be no emotional distance between them, at least not on his part. She wasn't the one who needed protection from this thing they did to each other; he was.

He was in love with Amara Clarke.

Maybe he could never tell her. But he could damn sure show her.

"I don't want to hurt you," he murmured.

"You won't."

Her lips skated across his chest as she said it and her hands slipped beneath the elastic waistband of his pajamas to grip his ass and bring him tight up against that soft, sweet spot between her legs.

Didn't want to hurt her. Huh. Wasn't he considerate? And who was on the lookout to make sure *he* didn't get hurt? Did she have any idea that his heart sang every time he looked at her and broke whenever he thought about leaving her?

He nuzzled her forehead and sank his fingers deep

into that fragrant hair, tipping her head back so he could see her face.

"Jack," she began.

"You talk too much," he said, and silenced her with a kiss.

Chapter 18

Wanda was waiting for Kareem when he arrived home, sitting in her leather chair in front of the fire with her feet on the ottoman, a blanket in her lap, and a snifter of brandy on the side table.

Time to set the ball in motion and see if she couldn't get rid of Kira, once and for all.

You couldn't get too eager with Kareem, though. He always knew. And if you ever acted like you really cared about something, he'd see it as a sign of weakness, so she didn't want to do that.

Best to be casual.

"Is that you, Baby Boy?" She looked around just as Kareem came in. "How you doing?"

"I'm all right."

He kissed her cheek on his way to the drink cart, looking tired. Dark circles ringed his pretty brown eyes, and if she didn't know better she'd think the spaces beneath his cheekbones were beginning to hollow out.

He opened a bottle of his expensive red and poured while she watched.

He sure did look like his daddy. It squeezed her heart to think how much. Of course, Kareem Sr. hadn't stuck around past the fifth month of her pregnancy. That partially accounted for the boy's relentless ambition and the occasional bursts of anger that flashed, white-hot, across his face. Kareem Sr. hadn't had that darkness. But she'd loved him and she damn sure loved his son. She'd do anything for their son.

Kareem was already sipping his wine, loosening his tie and looking around for his sorry excuse for a wife. Wanda could read the disappointment in his eyes like a large-print book. He didn't want to ask where Kira was and admit either that he couldn't keep tabs on her or that she didn't bother to stay up late and find out how his trial preparation had gone. He seemed to think that the separate bedrooms were a temporary setback and everything would switch right back to sunny days in paradise the minute the trial was over.

Poor boy. He was the only one in the house who didn't know that Kira didn't love him and never had.

It wasn't his fault for being blind. Kira was beautiful and she seemed sweet. What red-blooded male could resist that combination? Kareem was hardly the first man in the world to be manipulated with his dick. Just look at his daddy and the way he'd taken off after that skanky waitress when she crooked her little finger at him.

"How'd things go tonight?" Wanda asked.

"Pretty good." Kareem was now over at the desk, flipping through the day's stack of mail. "We met with the jury consultant."

"Does he know what he's doing?"

Kareem looked up from the envelopes long enough

to shrug and shoot her a worn-out smile. "That's the million-dollar question. And I do mean *million dollar.* Ask me again when the jury brings back the verdict."

He glanced toward the foyer, as though he could make Kira appear if he only wished it hard enough. The poor boy needed his eyes opened for him. That was why Wanda considered it her duty, as his loving mother, to help him out.

Kira was a bitch. She was selfish and arrogant. She thought that because she'd been raised in a big house in the suburbs, with a mama who was a doctor and a daddy who was an engineer, she was better than Wanda and Kareem, who'd grown up in the projects, where the fences were chain-link, not picket.

Her lack of gratitude for everything Kareem did for them was unforgivable. Even Kira's upcoming nursing degree (and getting a college degree was another reason Kira thought she was better than everyone else) was something that Kareem had paid for off the sweat of his back.

Was Kira grateful? Did she support Kareem and cook his favorite meals for him, the way Wanda did? Did she lay on her back and fulfill her most basic duty as a wife?

Hell no.

And this, among so many other reasons, was why Kira had to go.

Yawning, Wanda got up and stretched. "It's past my bedtime. I am *beat.*" She took her drink and headed toward the hall, blowing a kiss to Kareem as she passed.

Ask me, boy. Ask me.

"What time did Kira go to bed?" Kareem asked.

With her back to her son, Wanda gave herself a

quick second to smile. And then she locked that smile safely away and did a slow about-face as she tried to look thoughtful.

"Hmm," she said. "Last time I saw her was around eleven, I guess. She was coming out of your office with Max."

Kareem stilled, the wine halfway to his parted lips.

"Good-night, Baby Boy."

Wanda continued on her way. Easy as pie.

Jack gathered Amara in his arms and touched her. Face, neck, shoulders . . . back, breasts, hips . . . butt, thighs, face again, then hair, and the endless caressing circles started over again, each more devastating than the last.

It was all over for her and they both knew it. He'd won and she'd lost. She couldn't tell him no and therefore he could screw her at will and leave her when he was ready with no emotional attachments. Whatever worked, right? Unfortunately, this little arrangement was proof positive that she was her mama's daughter. The only thing left was for him to flick a couple bills on the nightstand on his way out the door.

The worst part was, when she was in his arms she didn't give even the tiniest damn.

Not when the skin across his shoulders was so sleek and hot and the surging muscles beneath so hard and immovable.

And his sounds. God, his sounds.

She drank up his incoherent murmurs and rumbling purrs and soaked in his harsh, panting breath because it meant she was driving him as wild as he was driving her.

He kept the pace slow and easy and ignored her surging hips and implicit invitation, but his control was slipping away and she was happy to help it along and get him thrusting into her needy-slick body at the earliest possible opportunity.

So she flicked her bra clasp free, released her aching breasts and waited to see how he liked them apples, Mr. Controlled and Slow.

"Jesus," he said.

Hah.

They'd been kissing this whole time, but now he pulled back and stared, too far gone to hide behind his mask of indifference for once. Boy would he be pissed if he could see himself in the mirror right now. His face glowed with a rapt expression that she'd never thought to see on a man's face, not in this lifetime, and she knew—she *knew,* down to the marrow of her bones and up to the limits of the universe and beyond—that she wasn't her mama's daughter after all and she meant something to him even though he wished she didn't.

"Amara."

Her name was never as beautiful as when he said it, especially when his voice was choked and his tone reverent, as though he'd latched onto heaven and didn't plan to ever let it go.

She smiled a lazy smile because her body was so loose and easy, and his heavy-lidded gaze tracked her every sighing response as he filled his hands with her breasts and circled her nipples with his rough thumbs until her pleasure made the room swim.

"I knew I should have stayed away from you."

Something came over her, some inner courage she'd never had until now because God knew she'd never been a resounding success with men. Whatever it was, it wiped the smile from her face and made her speak to him with the utmost pity because, really, there *was* something between them and she was determined to keep him from walking out on her without a look back.

"Poor Jack," she whispered. "You don't really think you can stay away from me, do you?"

He froze, helpless to deny it or even to work up an evasion of some sort. "I've never been able to stay away from you—"

—and I never will be.

The words were there and she heard them even if he caught himself at the last second and snapped his jaws shut.

The meaningful silence was enough, for now. Touching him was enough—for now.

Straining on her toes, she wrapped every part of herself around as much of him as she could reach, anchoring them together with her arms around his neck and one leg hooked around his hip.

Ahhh, God. Crying out, she almost had to push him away so she could breathe.

Mostly she needed him closer and was ready to fight if he pulled back by so much as one-half millimeter. He didn't. She felt his driving need for her in the waves of heat off his body and in the trembling of his arms. Tasted it in his kiss as their mouths and tongues found their way back together, nipping and licking and then, finally, thrusting deep in time with the surging rhythm of their hips.

Deeper. Harder. Hot tears of pleasure and frustration collected at the corners of her eyes and she couldn't stop them from leaking out because it was so good with Jack, so damn good, and yet it was never quite enough and he would be gone soon and she'd be destroyed.

"Don't cry," he whispered against her lips, still watching her.

"I can't—"

"What, baby?"

She didn't want to confess anything damaging or waste time talking, not when her tormented body needed him now. Her aching inner muscles were rippling with faint contractions and the cream was thick between her thighs, but this was one of the many things he did to her: push her past caring, past pride, past dignity.

"I can't get enough of you."

His jaw tightened with grim and unmistakable satisfaction. "I know the feeling."

Planting his hands on her butt, he lifted her and she clung, and the next sensation she felt was the cool of the sheets sliding against her back as he lowered her to the bed and bent to take off his pajama bottoms.

He hadn't bothered with underwear, glory hallelujah, and she squirmed out of hers, getting ready, needing to hurry, *hurry,* even as she struggled against her heavy lids to keep an eye on him.

He was unspeakably beautiful, amazingly perfect. The mere sight of him threatened her with cardiac arrest, he was that thrilling. He had those wide linebacker's shoulders and arms rippling with the kind of definition that the flabby of the world spent millions on personal trainers trying to get. His taut torso narrowed down to square, notched hips, and his strong thighs and long legs looked as sturdy and powerful as the mightiest oak.

And in between that torso and those legs?

Amara levered herself up on her elbows, hardly knowing where to look. His ass was round and tight, and the thought of it flexing and releasing as he moved inside her was enough to dry out her mouth.

In front was a jutting erection. Ruddy and heavy, it strained for her and was big enough to give her more than a moment's pause if she hadn't already experienced the unspeakable pleasure it could bestow.

She parted her thighs, angling her hips this time just in case he was a little slow reading body language. His glittering gaze tracked the movement and a wicked half smile flickered across his lips and then disappeared. He reached out for one of the foil packets on the nightstand but took too long about ripping it open with his teeth and getting himself covered.

Waiting one more second was impossible, even as he crawled over her and settled his weight, so she reached down to stroke herself and moaned with the relief, letting her head fall back and her eyes roll closed.

"Are you ready?" Shoving her hand away, he replaced her fingers with his own.

"Oh, yeah."

Chapter 19

Everything about him was an invasion, like the way he took the plump head of his penis and stroked her with it, lubricating them both until there was nothing but a hot, slick readiness as he inched his way inside, stretching her and then waiting for her body to ease a little more to accommodate him, stretching and then waiting again, longer.

And the way he stared her in the eyes was an invasion because he saw too far inside the hidden parts of her soul and didn't turn away from the ugliness. The scared, pouty Amara was right there for him to see, and so was the Amara who cared way too much about him if she was at all interested in maintaining sound mental health.

And the way he'd crept under her skin and into the region surrounding her heart—that was the worst invasion of all.

The worry built, but so did the pleasure. The pleasure won. When he'd gone as far inside her body as he could go, which was both unbearably far and a hundred miles from far enough, and she was stretched and tight, gasping and trying to keep one little part of herself protected from this man, the ripples started.

As he greedily absorbed her every expression and every tiny whimpering cry, he circled those strong hips, driving her farther than she thought she could go.

Trying to get as much of him as she could, she wrapped her legs around his waist and then . . . oh, God, and then all that slow, easy friction zeroed in on the sweetest spot in her body. All that delicious rubbing condensed and coalesced into contracting waves of pleasure so powerful she wanted to run from it and drown in it, all at the same time.

He knew it, too.

"Now," he murmured against her lips and then nuzzled and licked his way as deep into her mouth as he was in her body.

Now.

There was one second of frozen waiting, and then Amara's body jackknifed and only Jack's protective arms holding her tight kept her in one piece. Piercing ecstasy ricocheted through her and her inner muscles gripped him with a pulsing wet suction that was rhythmic and endless.

And then Jack came, too. She thought her cries had been loud, but his were louder. His sounded choked and shocked, almost joyous. He gathered her closer as she scratched his back, clamped his hands on her flexing butt and thrusting hips and drove himself right into an orgasm that turned all his muscles to stone.

They lay there after, their limbs entwined in the kind of sweat-slicked and messy tangle that was the earthiest, most sensual thing in the world. His scent was all over her, musky but still fresh, intoxicating, and she thought that anyone coming within ten feet of the door to the room must smell it.

Jack raised his head and focused eyes on her that were half closed and drowsy with satisfaction, but there was a silent question in their dark depths: *Are you okay?*

Amara smiled with her swollen lips, pushed the tangle of hair back from her face, and gripped the tight round globes of his butt, bringing him closer.

"Again," she said.

"What would you be doing," she asked after a while, "if you weren't here?"

"Wishing I was here."

She laughed. Feeling his grin against the back of her neck, she wished she could see it. Jack never grinned enough.

They were spooned together in the bed, with Jack's groin—relaxed now, but she'd change that in a minute—molded to her butt and his arms and legs surrounding her with warmth.

It was somehow easier to talk in the dark. Maybe wheedle a secret or two out of the Sphinx here. While she had the chance.

"Let me clarify: what would you be doing if you didn't have to hide? Special agenting again?"

His muscles tightened, but he didn't head for the shower or demand that she shut the hell up, so she considered that progress.

"No."

"Then what? Open your own restaurant? Chez Jack?"

Another grin, this one accompanied with the unmistakable contraction of his belly against her back. Wow. A laugh. She was getting good at this.

"I, ah, had actually thought I'd go to law school."

What? This tidbit had her twisting around to see him, maybe turn the light on and get a good look, but he merely locked his arms and kept her in place.

"Law school?" she said. "Are you kidding?"

"Shhh."

He nipped the back of her neck, nuzzled it, and her foolish body shivered. She knew what he was doing, and it was a diabolically effective ploy, she'd give him that, but she wouldn't be diverted this time. "Don't try this distracting routine on me. It won't work."

He sighed. "It never does."

"Are you telling me you want to be a lawyer—like me?"

"No, not like you. I'd be a prosecutor, possibly look for something in the U.S. Attorney's Office. I'd leave the criminals to you and your ilk."

"*Alleged* criminals."

"Whatever you have to tell yourself to sleep at night."

This conversation was too important and interesting to have while she couldn't see his face. Ignoring his groaned, "Why can't you lie still for thirty seconds?" She turned to face him.

He sighed with obvious resignation but didn't seem too upset. *"What?"*

"Do you have family?"

To her astonishment, there was no stony silence. Just a very sad answer. "No."

"Have you given up on the idea of having your own family?" she continued.

Of course she was assuming facts not in evidence:

some people weren't cut out to be parents, didn't want a family and didn't need the excuse of being marked for extinction as a reason not to procreate. Maybe Jack was one of those, although she doubted it.

There was a long silence, and then, "Yes."

That single word held enough regret to fill an Olympic-sized swimming pool, but no particular self-pity, which surprised her. "Aren't you bitter about that? You didn't sign up for a life sentence of looking over your shoulder—"

"I knew there were risks with the DEA. If I wanted safe, I'd've been a dietician."

That was funny. She couldn't think of anyone she'd ever met who was less the white-coat type. Smiling because she was happy for this one second in time, she tipped her head back and let the laughter come.

Jack's breath hitched. "I can't stop staring at you. It's bad."

Obviously he wasn't the kind of man to fall into bed with a woman he thought looked like a rottweiler, and he'd told her she was pretty. No news flash there. But, *man,* the way he said it, with all that awed reverence shining in his eyes, as though he was witnessing a sunset wrapped in a rainbow from atop a spectacular seaside cliff, sent her imagination into overdrive. The words seemed pregnant with more meaning than she could comprehend.

Boy was she in bad shape. Her gut told her to believe while her practical lawyer's mind told her not to be such a flaming romantic idiot. "Thank you."

She kissed him, soaking up his expression and storing it away for later. In the meantime, though, she had more questions.

"Did you go to college? The DEA doesn't take dummies."

That got her the belly laugh she'd been looking for and it was stunning. All flashing white teeth, dimples, and that deep rumble of unrestrained amusement that was like a Frank Sinatra–Ella Fitzgerald duet, it was so wonderful to her ears.

"I have my degree, yes. Math," he added when she opened her mouth again to ask.

Math. Wow. "And you went to . . . ?"

"None-of-your-business university."

"You do realize that the second I can, I'm going to Google you."

"Good luck with that."

From the amused gleam in his eye she figured his past had been thoroughly erased before he went under cover and such a search would turn up only a look-alike farmer in Topeka named Jackson Parker, but she intended to try anyway.

"And you were in the Marines before that?"

"Uh-huh."

Now he was the distracted one. His rapt attention seemed to have snagged on the heavy swell of her breasts as they disappeared under the gaping sheet, and he stroked the curves, slowly . . . slowly . . . tracing across her skin until she felt the goose bumps rise.

Against her thigh she felt the hard ridge of something else rising too.

"Why did you go into the Marines?"

He flashed her a look of purest annoyance, at least a hundred-proof, before his attention reverted to the sheet and the process of pulling it away from her. "Because it was the best way to say *fuck you* to my father."

"Ah," she said, and then a soft, sighed *ahhh* as his

hand covered her breast and kneaded in the gentlest of circles until her swelling nipple sent streaks of pleasure to her wet sex.

Burying his lips in the hollow between her shoulder and neck, he kissed and inhaled his way up to her lips, where he hovered, levered over her with his chin on one hand.

"Any other questions?"

There was no time for an answer because he took her mouth in one of those deep but languid kisses that was more of a flowing of bodies together, a joining of something more important than tongues.

Pulling back just enough to speak, she looked up at him and hoped he'd keep answering. "Do you ever regret your choices?"

This seemed to be the one question too many. With a sudden intake of breath, he glanced off across the room, gathering his thoughts, and when he turned back and spoke again she could almost see the scalpel he used to slice away the words and feelings he didn't want to reveal, not ever.

"When I think about . . . this guy," he told her, "and I think about the damage he's done and the lives he's ended and ruined and the drugs he's put on the streets—heroin, crack, Oxy, you name it, he's distributed it, he's like the Walmart of drug dealers—no. I have no regrets. I'd do it all over again a hundred times. Someone had to do it. Why not me?"

The other half of this carefully worded sentence hung in the air, tantalizing her, and she prodded a little to help it along. "But . . . ?"

"Lately," he said, and the hand on her breast resumed its tender stroking, circling but never touching her nipple until the need nearly blinded her, "I've been spending a lot of time wishing I'd been a ditch digger instead of a DEA agent because at least then my life would have been my own."

When he raised his head and stared her straight in the eyes, the strength of his glittering bitterness and despair, the sheer volume of it, made her gasp, and everything she'd wanted to know was right there.

Even if his strict code of honor or protective streak or whatever it was demanded his eternal silence on the subject, he wished he could be with her for longer than these few stolen nights. She meant more to him than that.

Clinging to this quiet knowledge, she opened her arms and legs to him as he settled between her thighs.

Marian Barber didn't want to take the kids with her, but what could she do?

That shit Jerome sold her last time was good. Really good. So good it shot right through her with an extra head-lightening jolt of *don't worry about a thing* relaxation, as though Bobby McFerrin and Bob Marley had exploded inside her and spread peaceful calm in every direction.

It wasn't the same dosage she'd been taking. There were a couple extra grams of Oxy in there—thirty milligrams in the brown tablets instead of twenty in the pink. The old stuff hadn't done this for her.

The problem was: he'd only given her a few pills—the fucker. Now they were almost gone again and she needed more.

What were her options? She'd narrowed them down to shitty, shittier and shittiest.

Shittiest was telling her husband she might have an

issue. But why would she do that? So he could worry and lecture her, fret about the possible damage to his precious career and then send her to rehab?

Yeah, right.

And anyway—she didn't have a problem, so why make a whole big production out of it? A slight issue, yeah, sure. A challenge area for growth potential? Absolutely. A problem? No way.

So shittiest wasn't an option.

Neither was shittier, which was going back to her doctor or pharmacist or a new doctor and trying to get the Oxy the hard way. The legal way. But she'd seen the narrowed light of suspicion in the doctor's eyes the last couple times she was in the office, and now he was talking about more tests and/or additional rehab, both of which would reveal what she already knew: that her original injury had healed just fine, thanks, and there was no reason on God's green earth for her to take the Oxy anymore except that the shit made her high as the orbiting space shuttle and she needed it to get through every hour of her duty-filled mommy-mommy-mommy life.

Oh, and for a few extra laughs, the old stuff wouldn't do it for her anymore, even if she could get it legally. She could just see it now. After finagling an appointment with a doctor, suffering through the tests and the questions and the who-knew-what, the doctor finally whips out his prescription pad. And what would she do? Tell him not to waste her time with anything less than a thirty-milligram dose?

Yeah. That wouldn't raise suspicion or anything.

That just left the shitty option: taking the kids along for a quick little prework run to meet Jerome and get a few more pills to help her along.

It wasn't an ideal situation. She knew that. You didn't take your kids into a bar and you didn't take them to meet your street pharmaceutical supplier. Mothering 101. But they were two and clueless. They'd stay in the SUV munching Cheerios from their cups, as oblivious to this little errand as they were when she stopped by the dry cleaners.

Easy as pie.

But . . . she hadn't gotten the information he'd asked for.

That part might be a little trickier, but Jerome had been very pleasant when she called his cell and hadn't mentioned the information at all. So maybe he'd forgotten all about it. He wasn't exactly a Rhodes scholar, was he? You didn't become a dealer if you were that bright. So hopefully he'd forgotten about the request or decided to get the information some other way.

If not, her plan was to simply explain that she couldn't do what he'd asked because the risks if she got caught were too great. If she got caught and landed in trouble, he'd lose a paying customer, wouldn't he? Where was the win-win in that?

Nowhere. Surely he'd agree.

Still, when she pulled the Land Rover into the alley and cut the engine, her nerves skittered on her. The alley was still sort of darkish at this hour of the morning, and Jerome was already there, leaning against some unmarked doorway with his hands in the pockets of his puffy jacket and his ankles crossed.

Something about him was menacing.

Well, she knew what it was, even if the PC police would arrest her for thinking it. He was a young black man on the street. Period. That was enough reason to be scared shitless, but today there was something about the absolute stillness as he watched her that raised the scary factor just enough to make her sweat.

"I'll be right back, you two," she told the girls as she got out.

"Okay." Bethany flashed a quick smile filled with white baby teeth.

Veronica, who had her tiny fingers stuck in her plastic cup, just smiled.

Marian felt a sudden swell of unexpected emotion. They were so cute with their curly hair and chipmunk-on-steroids cheeks. At times like this it was hard to remember why it felt like these two sucked another gallon of her blood every day of her life.

The cold air hit with a blast as she slammed the door shut and headed toward Jerome. Though the doorway's overhang threw his face into shadow so that his eyes and the whole top half of his face were all but invisible, she could tell one thing:

He wasn't smiling.

"Good morning." Keeping her chin up, she hoped that the flat, disaffected look in his eyes—somewhere between Hannibal Lecter and *Night of the Living Dead*—was a figment of her overwrought imagination.

Then he smiled and she knew her nerves had been playing tricks on her. "'S'up?"

Her mouth was watering and she felt the familiar hum in her hungry veins but she tried not to sound too anxious or desperate. "Do you have some Oxy for me?"

"Depends." He shrugged. "You got my money?"

She patted her skirt pocket—she'd dressed for work, of course. "Got it."

That smile widened and so did her feeling of disquiet, but then, without another word, he turned and walked to his car, gesturing for her to follow. She did.

Was . . . was that it, then? Was he just going to sell her the shit? A wave of relief hit, bubbling up in an inappropriate giggle, and she choked it off because this wasn't a done deal yet.

But her mouth was all but dripping now, her heart racing with excitement, and she could almost feel the familiar crunch between her teeth, almost feel the rush of—

"Oh," he said.

Oh? What *oh*?

At the driver's side of his car now, a disappointing ten-year-old-ish Toyota Tercel with fancy hubcaps and not at all the drug-dealer-mobile black SUV with tinted windows that she'd imagined, he snapped his fingers as though he'd just remembered something and looked over his shoulder at her.

"I almost forgot. Did you get that information we talked about?"

Marian's heart stopped.

Okay. Okay, so this was a slight setback, true, but she'd expected something like this and had her explanation ready. "Umm . . . No." *Stop wringing your hands, fool. It's a dead giveaway.* "It's not that I don't want to do it or anything, but if I get caught—"

He backhanded her.

One minute she was talking and he was nodding and being a good listener, and the next her head was whipping around, her ears were ringing with a throbbing pain that shot out the top of her head, and her mouth was filling with the coppery taste of blood.

Had he . . . had he just hit her?

The panic was just knotting in her belly, just starting

to coalesce and grow, and the dots were connecting that, one: here was a violent black man twice her size slapping the shit out of her; and two: they were in a deserted alley where he could do anything imaginable to her and get away with it; and three: her children were here and she'd been the idiot who'd brought them; and four: how would she hide the mark that was probably blooming on her face right this second, assuming she lived to tell the story; and five:

Did this mean he wasn't going to sell her the shit?

All this ran through her mind and was adding up to a whole boatload of *Titanic*-sized trouble steaming her way when he backhanded her again, confirming that he really had done it the first time.

Screaming now, she tried to break and run but he was too quick and grabbed a hunk of her hair near the crown and swung her around by it until the Tercel's trunk cut into her belly and doubled her over.

Oh, shit. Oh, shit, shit, SHIT.

She struggled, but trying to break free was useless and she felt those huge fingers tightening, ready to rip her scalp off at any second. Terrified sobs rose up from her tight throat.

Jerking her head again, he spoke in her ear. "You want your kids to hear this?"

"Please don't hurt me," she cried. "I have money and I—"

Another jerk, this one accompanied by a "Shut the fuck up," and a thrusting thigh between hers, widening her stance.

She shut the fuck up, midsob.

And then she started sobbing again, harder now. Not that. Please, God, not that.

"Please." Tamping down her hiccuping wails, she

tried to talk, but the hand that wasn't holding her hair was sliding under the front of her skirt now, exposing inch after inch of her legs to the icy air. "Please don't do this. Please, please, please—"

"Shut. The fuck. Up."

She stopped talking but kept sobbing, making a pathetic and choked mmm-mmm-mmm sound, because that one hand, the one that was the real problem, was now sliding between her and the trunk, groping between her legs with searching fingers as though there was gold to be mined. Only the thin layer of her panties protected her from his invasion and that was no protection at all.

"Please." Opening her mouth was a mistake because it let loose a whole big strand of spit that embarrassed the one tiny part of her that wasn't scared.

"Relax," he said, still stroking. "I don't fuck crack hos and I don't fuck hopped-up soccer moms either. I want you to go to work today. Nod if you understand me."

She nodded, ignoring the resulting pain in her scalp.

"I want you to get that information without getting caught. Feel me?"

She nodded again.

"And I want you to bring it to me today. Got it?"

She nodded.

"Don't fuck with me," he warned.

Those hard fingers clamped down now, squeezing and mashing the most sensitive part of her body, hurting with a pain worse than childbirth. Her sobbing took on a higher-pitched quality but she couldn't move at all because moving only worsened the agony.

"Are you planning to fuck with me?"

She frantically shook her head.

"Because if you fuck with me, I'm going to show up at your house on Grand Vista Avenue—"

Oh, Jesus. Oh, Lord Jesus, he knew where she lived?

"—and I'm going to break down the door and I'm going to fuck you. And then I'm going to blow your brains out against your nice walls—"

The images were all right there, flashing before her eyes. She saw this monster on her quiet street, contaminating it. She saw him storming into her house with the gun he surely had. She felt, pressing against her ass, the unforgiving weapon he'd use against her before he killed her—

"—and I'm going to look around for a few more brains to blow out. Are we on the same page here, bitch?"

She nodded.

Done with her at last, he let her go with a final thrust that had her forehead banging against the trunk with a loud and cold *thunk* that unleashed stars before her eyes.

Bewildered by this sudden freedom, she edged away from his car and turned to see him sauntering to the driver's side with a smirking face and tented jeans.

"You better get going." Holding his left arm up, he tapped his watch. "Tick-tock. You don't want to be late for work, do you?"

Desperation fueling her fear, she pivoted, ran to her SUV and hurled herself into the driver's side. Slamming and locking the door—locking, heh, right, like that would keep the monster out if he wanted to come in—she twisted at the waist to look at the kids, who were both okay but kicking their feet, growing restless.

Bethany took one look at her face and started crying.

Veronica looked at Bethany, grabbed Bethany's pacifier and stuck it in Bethany's mouth.

Bethany stopped crying and Veronica returned to her Cheerios.

Marian continued to sob.

She was pulling out of the alley when a terrible thought hit her, one more to add to her growing list of terrible thoughts.

Jesus, God, how was she going to get through this nightmare?

Jerome hadn't sold her the shit.

Chapter 20

"Coffee?"

Dexter Brady watched Kareem go to the coffeepot over on the wet bar and fill several mugs. They were in the corner of Kareem's spectacular vaulted living room, which was in Kareem's spectacular house, which sat on a couple of well-manicured and spectacular acres. It really was amazing what the owner of a few auto-customizing shops could do with a few extra bucks. To hear Kareem tell it, all this was the legitimate result of his legal endeavors.

Sure. And Dexter had three twelve-inch dicks.

"This isn't a social call," Dexter told him.

A hint of amusement flickered across Kareem's face. "Just being polite."

A polite sociopath. Wasn't that nice?

Dexter eyeballed Kareem's attorney, Jacob Radcliffe, who sat on the buttery brown leather sofa. Mercenary bastard. Beside Dexter sat Assistant U.S. Attorney Jayne Morrison, because there were procedures to follow and she had to be involved in this little stop-by-and-say-hello questioning. Having it here at

Kareem's house was just for fun because, hey, the coffee downtown was nowhere near as delicious as the shit Kareem served.

They all waited, tense and silent.

Finally, after much stirring and adding of sugar and cream, Kareem sauntered back to the sofa and sat. Checked the fall of the razor-sharp crease in his slacks, crossed his legs, sipped, and waited with that poorly hidden glimmer of excitement in his eyes.

Kareem liked the hunt. Oh, yes. He preferred to be the hunter, true, but he didn't mind being the hunted every now and then, just for kicks. Distributing drugs and playing cat and mouse games were mother's milk to Kareem here. They got his juices flowing and made him tick. They completed Kareem.

And Dexter was going to take him down if it was the last thing he ever did.

"What do you want, Brady?" Radcliffe clutched his own mug and had the nerve to look annoyed. "My client doesn't have much time and you already questioned him."

"He came to see how many kilos he could spot lying around in plain sight," Kareem interjected before Dexter could answer. "Isn't that right, Dex?"

The roar of his rising blood pressure flooded Dexter's ears and he felt the heat under his skin, the fury. "Good guess, but no. I'm actually here to tell you the good news."

Kareem opened his mouth wide in an exaggerated yawn and added a stretch. "Don't keep us in suspense. Did your agents raid a crack house this morning? Get a gram or two off the streets and make the world a safer place?"

Dexter forced a smile but his face was burning

now, so hot with anger he was surprised his flesh didn't peel off in curled strips. "You remember that shooting in Seattle we talked about? One of our special agents was killed?"

"You consider that good news?" Kareem asked.

Dexter ignored that. "Couple things I forgot to mention before in all the excitement." He paused so Kareem could sweat it out a little. "Jackson Parker was involved in that shooting. You remember your old friend Jack, don't you? He ran the undercover op on you that led to the whole"—Dexter waved a hand—"money-laundering thing. This ringing a bell?"

There was no amusement in Kareem's face now, and the boredom also seemed to have evaporated. Was this a crack in Kareem Gregory's legendary control?

"Get to the point," Kareem said.

"Oh, don't worry about your boy Jack. Another agent was killed but Jack is fine." Dexter let just a hint of smugness creep into his voice now and, for good measure and knowing it would kill Kareem, allowed himself a tiny satisfied smile. "He's alive and well and well-protected. Anxious to testify and put you back behind bars where you belong."

Kareem blinked.

"Jayne." Jacob Radcliffe interjected, no doubt trying to prove his worth. "Is there some reason my client needs to be subjected to this silly cat and mouse game in his own house on the day before—"

Jayne showed complete disinterest at this whining. "Special Agent Brady has some questions. As a courtesy to your client, we're asking them here rather than dragging him down to the office. If you don't like it, we're happy to drag . . ."

Radcliffe lapsed into an impotent silence.

"Well." Kareem stood like he wanted to wrap things up and move on to the important part of his day. "Thanks for the news flash. If that's all—"

"That's not all," Dexter told him.

He thought of the dead agents, the waste and the wide path of destruction this one man had carved throughout his sorry, too-long life. Then he thought of what a pleasure—what an orgasmic, ball-busting, out-of-body experience pleasure—it would be to put this man behind bars or, better yet, in his grave, where he belonged.

Dexter leaned in so he could see every flash of emotion on this bitch's face, every pore and every bead of salty sweat. Kareem stilled as though he knew something terrible was coming and wanted to brace for it.

"Here's the good news, which we kept out of the press. The shooter was killed."

Kareem's eyes widened a fraction. Just a hair, but it was enough.

This was why they'd withheld the information this long. Dexter wanted another bite at the apple. He wanted to see Kareem's eyes dilate with fear and he wanted to see it in the house Kareem could lose if he wasn't careful. He wanted to get this slippery motherfucker and he planned to keep nipping at his heels until he did.

"And guess what she—yeah, it was a she; what a surprise, huh?—left in her car?"

Kareem didn't bite.

"Her *weapons*. Isn't that great? A whole bunch of them, too." Dexter counted off on his fingers. "A rifle with a scope, a silencer. Oh, and we recovered a nine-millimeter. And guess what kind of pistol Ray Wolfe and his wife were killed with? What—no guess? I'll tell you anyway: it was a nine-millimeter. Small world, huh?"

Kareem stilled, his face frozen into stone.

"Your time here is up, Brady."

Radcliffe stood like he was the bouncer or some shit, but Dexter didn't budge. He was here to see Kareem's reaction to this news and by God he was going to see it.

"Don't worry, Jakie, I'm almost done." Dexter waved a hand and kept his gaze on Kareem, whose skin was slowly turning ashen. "So we thought we'd run a ballistics test or two on the gun and see if it's the same one. And if it is—and I *think* it is—we'll have a connection between the contract killing of one federal agent and the accidental killing of a second agent. And then—and here's the really good news I want you to know, Kareem—all we'll need is one tiny connection to whoever hired the killer and we'll have the basis for all kinds of new charges. Meaty stuff, too. Murder, conspiracy . . . much more exciting stuff than money laundering. Carries longer prison sentences. I thought you'd want to be the first to know."

How do you like that, Kareem?

The brother didn't like it at all. For one brief second it was all naked on his face:

Shock, rage and, yes, fear.

The unmistakable light of truth: Kareem had, in fact, hired the killer.

The hard edge of Kareem's determination to do whatever he had to do to stay free.

And then Kareem blinked, and all that raw emotion disappeared, leaving only a beleaguered businessman being harassed by an overzealous fed.

Kareem shrugged, looking politely puzzled. "I'm not sure why you're telling me all this, but I do appreciate the personal attention. If you're finished—?"

"Actually, I think I *will* have that coffee now. Thanks."

Ignoring Kareem's hand, which was outstretched toward the foyer, Dexter strode to the wet bar, poured some coffee and sipped appreciatively. That drug money sure could buy the best. He put the cup down with regret and headed for the door with Jayne on his heels. He'd just passed Kareem and Radcliffe, noting their stupefied expressions with satisfaction, when the one thing that could ruin his triumphant moment happened:

Kira Gregory appeared.

There was no *click-click* warning of approaching high heels, no door slam or "Honey, I'm home," to tell him to play it cool. All he knew was that one second she wasn't there and the next she was, hurrying around one of the billion corners in this McMansion.

Shit.

Hadn't he scheduled this meeting at a time when she was supposed to be at class? Hadn't he and Jayne waited outside in his parked car until Kira drove off before they approached the house?

What the fuck was she doing here?

After nearly plowing each other down, they both pulled up short. Since Dexter was the one with his back to Kareem, he gave her a sharp warning look and saw in her bright clever eyes that she was already right there with him, pulling her story together.

"Special Agent Brady." Cool as a frozen cucumber, she gave him a look he imagined she'd use on a puddle of vomit on her floor. "What are you doing in my house?"

They'd officially met before, of course. On that unforgettable night nearly two years ago when they arrested Kareem.

"He was just leaving, baby." Kareem sauntered across the room, his speculative gaze evenly divided between Dexter and Kira. "What're you doing back here?"

"Forgot my book." She pointed to a ten-pound textbook on the kitchen table.

When he got to his wife's side, Kareem wrapped his hand around her back, settled it on the curve of her ass and reeled her in for a kiss. On the lips. As though he hadn't seen her in five years.

Dexter watched because he'd been forced into the designated audience role whether he wanted to be there or not, and tried to pretend he didn't hear the sudden angry rush of blood in his ears or feel every nerve in his body stretch to near invisibility.

Then they pulled apart and Kira smiled up in her husband's face, visibly melting the man on the spot. And Dexter kept his features neutral and wondered how the face of an angel could hide a soul that treacherous.

"You haven't seen Brady since the last time he was here, have you, baby?" Kareem asked, paranoid down to the last electron in the last atom in his body.

And Kira, without blinking, looked bewildered and said, "No."

Dexter suddenly felt a million years old, as though he was just a day or two away from disintegrating into a pile of dust and then blowing away with the breeze. For the first time in his life, he thought that maybe he wasn't cut out for this work. For the first time in his life, he didn't want to do this work.

"I've taken enough of your time," he said.

He thought he was talking to Kareem, but his gaze was drawn to Kira. To her defiance, her flushed skin, and those unfathomable eyes that hid more secrets than a password-protected computer at the CIA.

"A pleasure seeing you," he told her, adding, because he seemed to need the reminder, "Mrs. Gregory."

She didn't meet his gaze.

Chapter 21

Kerry Randolph got there first, a little early.

He had a bad feeling about this meeting with the boss, but bad feelings and Kareem Gregory went together, like peanut butter and jelly or guns and drugs. If you saw one, you expected the other. Kareem had summoned Kerry here, to "the place," an isolated field at the end of an isolated dirt road that branched off a two-lane highway thirty miles north of Cincinnati and, like clockwork, Kerry's gut started churning with a whole bellyful of bad feelings.

What did Kareem want now?

Another loyalty pledge? The simple pleasure of terrifying his men for no good reason? Someone to hold his dick while he peed and his tissue while he blew his nose?

You never knew with Kareem.

Cursing, Kerry cut the engine and climbed out of his BMW to wait for Kareem's arrival, which could be three minutes or four hours from now.

The weather wasn't helping his feeling of approaching doom. The sky was the kind of heavy slate gray that was perfect for funerals and ten inches or more of wet snow. The temperature was somewhere down in freeze-your-balls-off range, and his breath hung in the air, almost turning to ice before his eyes.

Nothing good ever happened on a day like this.

The location wasn't exactly good for morale either. If Kerry had to pick a place for, say, shooting someone in the back of the head and getting away with it, this shitty little hidden spot would be high on the list.

Overgrown with weeds, surrounded by trees, accessible only by that little groove of muddy tire tracks that would need at least a million-dollar upgrade before it could be called anything as grand as a road, this spot would never be a contender for scenic getaways.

Which was why Kareem had chosen it for meetings. The DEA couldn't creep up on you out here, and Kerry was positive that if he pulled out his phone right now and tried to get a signal, the phone would laugh at him.

The low purr of an expensive car's engine cut across his thoughts. With the reassuring weight of his Beretta strapped to his leg, he turned, expecting Kareem's Land Cruiser, but it was a Lexus.

Yogi, then. One of the other lieutenants.

Good. Misery loved company and it was always good to have another body or two around to absorb Kareem's malice once it started flowing.

Yogi parked next to the BMW and grunted a greeting as he climbed out. He looked as pissed off and vaguely anxious as Kerry felt. "The fuck is going on?"

Kerry shrugged. "No idea."

They both leaned against the BMW and Yogi crossed his tree-trunk legs at the ankles. The would-be casual gesture didn't fool Kerry; the man was like his brother and Kerry could tell: he was rattled.

The sound of a new car crunching on the gravel made them jump.

They both looked around and saw Kareem. In the Land Cruiser. Alone.

Usually he rolled with a couple of his boys with him, just in case. He didn't like being alone and vulnerable and hated driving himself somewhere when one of his boys could chauffeur him around like Tony fucking Soprano.

But he was alone now.

They straightened and stood at attention, watching while he parked and climbed out with that grim, *don't mess with me* face, partially hidden with his favorite black-ass wraparound sunglasses. His black topcoat flowed around him as he walked, like Darth Vader's cape.

There was no greeting for either of them. Through his growing unease Kerry wondered where Hector, the third and final lieutenant, was. Why wasn't he here for this little summit meeting?

"How're you coming," Kareem asked Yogi in a flat, other-side-of-the-grave voice, "with that little roach-killing project I gave you?"

Yogi winced and his brown skin went pasty. To his credit, though, Yogi kept his chin up and his voice steady. "It's coming," he said.

Right. If things were coming along as swimmingly as Yogi wanted Kareem to believe, they wouldn't be standing out here in the muddy middle of no-fucking-where, freezing their dicks off.

"Coming?" Kareem asked. "Really?"

Yogi fidgeted.

Bad move. Kareem had shark's blood running through his veins, and he could smell a drop of sweat from a mile out and a drop of blood from ten miles. And a man had a better chance talking a great white into showing some mercy than he did with Kareem.

"It'll take a little more time." There was a faint wheedle in Yogi's voice now. "But it's all under control."

"Under control?" Kareem walked a couple steps away and then came back, his thoughtful face turned up to the gray sky. This was what Kareem did. He played with his victims. Terrorized them. "I'm wondering how things can be under control when the exterminator is dead."

"What the fuck—?" Yogi's jaw dropped, nearly hitting the ground with his shock.

"I'm wondering how things can be under control," Kareem continued, "when I've had to answer questions about a dead roach exterminator I didn't know a damn thing about."

Yogi, whose wide eyes now showed white all around the pupils, had the good sense to keep his mouth shut. Or maybe he was too scared to speak.

An obscene smile lifted one corner of Kareem's mouth. An open grave was warmer than that smile; a grizzly on a killing rampage was more merciful.

When he spoke again, his voice was even quieter. "And I'm wondering why your roach exterminator, the one you hired—God rest her *stupid*, *incompetent* soul—took care of the wrong damn roach before she died. You got any explanation for that, Yogi, my brother? You got any explanation for why you couldn't handle a basic assignment? Anything to say on your own behalf?"

Yogi defended himself, but it was a pitiful sight that

made Kerry want to turn away. The dignity was gone. The bravado was gone. Yogi looked sweaty, sickly and scared enough to fall over backward in a dead faint.

He looked like a terrified and terrorized brother begging not to be punished.

And make no mistake, there would be punishment. There was always punishment, and with Kareem, anything was possible.

"I've got other people, man." Yogi held his hands out, palms up, but he may as well have dropped to his knees. "I can work this shit out."

Behind those black wraparounds, Kareem's face was expressionless. "How're you going to do that, Yogi? When we don't even know where the roaches have gotten off to? You got a magic wand I don't know about?"

"I'll get it figured out, man," said Yogi.

"So you think I should give you another chance?"

The light of hope flipped on in Yogi's face, a layer of brightness over the ugliness of desperation. "Hell, yeah, man."

Kareem stared at him, trying to look puzzled when what he really looked like was a cobra poised to strike and strike hard. "But you let me down when I trusted you with something important. Don't you need to be punished?"

Yogi took so long to answer that Kerry began to wonder if he was saying his prayers. "Naw, man," he finally said. "Let me make this shit right."

Kareem stared; Yogi sweated it out; Kerry tried to become invisible and backed up a step or two to facilitate the process.

And then, suddenly, Kareem smiled and shrugged in a *what's all the fuss about?* gesture. There was an arrested moment during which Yogi seemed unable to believe his luck, and then he grinned.

The sudden turnaround seemed too good to be true, but then Kareem was like the weather in Cincinnati and underwent a complete reversal every fifteen minutes or so.

"We—we cool then?" Yogi asked.

Kareem held his arms open. "My man."

Yogi walked forward and the two gripped each other, slapping backs and laughing. This went on until Kareem pulled back, patted the fleshy side of Yogi's face, and kissed him.

"What did you think I was going to do?" Kareem put his arm around Yogi's shoulder and steered him toward Yogi's car. Kerry, who wasn't sure what his role was in this love fest, stayed where he was. "I know you'll never let me down again."

"You had me going there for a minute." Yogi shook that big head and laughed again. "I was a little—"

Kareem dropped his hand while Yogi kept on walking and talking. Kerry sighed, looked up at that gray sky and worked his shoulders up and down, trying to get rid of some of the kinks. He wondered why Kareem had dragged him along for this odd little crime and punishment scene. Then he wondered when they could wrap this up and head back for some lunch.

And then, out of the corner of his disbelieving eye, he saw Kareem reach into the left breast pocket of his overcoat, pull out his forty-five, and shoot Yogi in the back of the head with it.

Kerry saw Kareem's arm rise and saw the gun in his hand. Heard the lightning-bolt crack of the weapon's fire. Witnessed the cloud of blood and gore and the sudden disappearance of Yogi's head. Saw the hesitation of Yogi's body, the slight pause while it decided whether to keep walking or collapse to the ground. Saw it crumple into a sickening heap.

He saw it all and he still didn't believe it.

And then he did.

"Jesus," Kerry whispered. "Oh, sweet Jesus, please, God, Kareem, no—"

Kareem stood over Yogi's body, the picture of regret and sorrow for this unnecessary loss. He even hung his head the way Kerry had seen him do at funerals.

Kerry liked to think that he was calm in a crisis, that he knew how to handle himself and could get out of any sticky situation, but he'd never seen one of his closest buddies get his brain blown out before, and the words poured out of his mouth in an unstoppable stream.

"Jesus, God, Kareem, why did you do that to Yogi—?"

Kareem looked up at last, and damn if there wasn't sadness in his strained face. "Do you think it's easy being a leader, Kerry? Making the tough decisions?"

"Jesus, man—"

"Do you think I wanted to do that to Yogi?"

"Why did you do that, Kareem, why did—"

"What should I do when one of my men—one of my closest advisors, one of my *lieutenants*—doesn't do his job and snitches on me? Turns me in to the *feds,* Kerry. Should I let that go?"

What? *What?* Oh, Jesus, was *that* what this was about? Kareem's paranoia had focused on *Yogi*?

"He didn't do it," Kerry cried, and he *was* crying now because he wasn't going to come out of this alive; no one could have the slightest dealing with Kareem Gregory and come out of it alive. "Man, you *know* that. Yogi didn't roll like that. He wasn't smart enough to—"

Standing over Yogi's dead body, Kareem pushed those sunglasses to the crown of his head so Kerry could see the stark loss in his face. "Everyone's smart enough to look out for number one when the feds come knocking."

"Kareem, man, no, Yogi didn't—"

But Kareem wasn't looking and it was too late for Yogi anyway. Hell, Kerry was beginning to think that Yogi was the lucky one because at least he didn't have to deal with Kareem's reign of terror anymore.

"Good-bye, my brother," Kareem told the mess of pulp that had been a man, their friend.

Turning, he strode off toward his car, unhurried as he put the piece back in his pocket and spoke to Kerry over his shoulder. "Check his pockets and his car. Make sure he hasn't got anything. And then we're going to talk about you taking over distribution for him."

Kareem got into his car, still upset. He drove back into town to his lawyer's office for the trial preparation meeting as planned. He accepted a cup of black coffee from the firm's receptionist, and asked to go into the conference room ahead of Jacob Radcliffe to use the phone. His cell's battery was low, he claimed.

The receptionist pointed him to the phone and told him to dial nine.

So he dialed nine and then dialed the other number and waited, still seething.

What was the world coming to? Why couldn't people be trusted? No—forget trust because he knew the only thing he could trust was that people always looked out for number one. Trust wasn't the issue. Professionalism was the issue.

Why couldn't people do their damn jobs?

Yogi, the man he'd trained and loved and brought up through the ranks with him—for *years* he'd groomed that man—couldn't handle the simple assignment of hiring someone to take care of Jackson Parker.

How hard was it? They'd found out where Parker was due to Parker's own stupidity. They'd done everything but drawn a map to Parker. Everything but leave a trail of bread crumbs directly to Parker's door.

And had the hit woman hit Parker? Hell no. The stupid fucking bitch had not only not hit Parker, she'd hit another federal agent and created one more goddamn thing for the authorities to come after Kareem for.

Hell, he didn't mind being in the hot seat every now and then as long as it served some greater purpose. But what was the purpose here? Huh? He was all for as many dead DEA agents as possible, but what the hell good did some nameless Seattle fed's death do for him or his organization? None. N-O-N-E.

And then the shooter had been shot. Not that he cared one way or the other because there was always another shooter out there, most of whom could be counted on to shoot the person they'd been hired to shoot. But this shooter, Yogi's shooter, had to go and get shot and leave her motherfucking weapons behind. Just leave them there.

So now it was a matter of time before the feds linked Ray Wolfe's death with the Seattle DEA agent's death. The feds needed a map and a flashlight to find their dicks half the time, true, but they could usually be counted on to run a few simple ballistics tests. So there'd be a link between the deaths of two federal agents and from there . . . from there all they needed was one small link to Kareem and he'd be facing capital murder charges rather than simple money laundering.

Had Yogi seriously thought he'd forgive that mistake?

And of course, Kareem had never been able to shake the feeling that Yogi had been the snitch who'd dropped that first dime on him to the feds. The one that first pointed him out and said you might want to look at this guy. Was there any solid evidence? No. Could Kareem prove it? No. But his gut told him that there'd been a snitch within his own organization and the snitch was Yogi.

So Yogi had to go.

But still. The waste just killed him. How was Kareem supposed to run an organization that required three lieutenants when he was down to only two? How could this fly? How could Hector and Kerry handle everything for him?

Well . . . they'd just have to step up to the plate, wouldn't they?

They were the best of the best, and the most trustworthy, not that anyone was trustworthy. So now Kerry could take care of distribution and Hector could get the information they needed to take care of the Jackson Parker problem for once and for all.

ASAP.

Parker wasn't the only problem on his plate. He also needed to figure out what, if anything, Kira was up to. But first things first.

Kareem held the receiver to his ear and listened to it ring.

"Yeah," Hector answered.

"It's me," Kareem told him. "I've got a project for you and I need it done yesterday. I need a roach killed. You know any good exterminators?"

"I'm on it."

"And I need you to follow up on some information one of Yogi's men was supposed to get. Check with Jerome on it, okay?"

"Whatever you say, man."

Chapter 22

She was really going to do this.

God help her.

Marian Barber's plan was to wait until lunchtime to sneak into her boss's office and get the information Jerome wanted from her. The problem was, "lunchtime" was a flexible concept around here, depending on the crisis of the moment, everyone's mood and, probably, the phases of the moon.

She only had a couple of pills left. Normally she'd've taken them an hour ago, but she didn't want to take them until she knew there'd be more. And there wouldn't be more unless she got it from Jerome because she was out of other options. Not to mention the fact that she didn't want to test out Jerome's threats.

Maybe he didn't mean them, but then again—maybe he did.

No matter how she looked at it, she was screwed ten ways from Sunday. The only way things could be worse was if the powers that be chose today for a random blood test, which was one of the downsides of working for a federal law enforcement agency. Her number hadn't come up for a while and goodness knew her luck wasn't holding. If she was tested, what would the results say? Did they test for prescription meds? And if so, did they test the level? Would they know she had enough shit in her bloodstream to tranquilize an elephant?

The despair in Marian's throat crept a little higher and burned a little hotter.

The one thing she tried not to think about was what Jerome planned to do with the information once she gave it to him. It was probably safe to assume it was nothing good, but that didn't have to mean it was anything *terrible,* did it? By acquiring this information for Jerome—she almost thought *stealing* but it wasn't *stealing* because she wasn't a thief—she wasn't taking part in anything dangerous or illegal.

Was she?

The possibility of getting caught in the act, of getting fired for what she was about to do, was too horrible for words, so she didn't think about that, either.

"You look terrible."

"Huh?"

Rhonda was standing there. "Your tooth must really be bothering you."

Marian belatedly remembered she'd told everyone she had a sore tooth to explain the single chipmunk cheek she'd acquired courtesy of Jerome and his lead-plate hands.

"It's nothing." Marian gave Rhonda's purse, which was slung over the woman's shoulder, a pointed look and tried to move the proceedings along. "You going to lunch?"

"Yeah. I'll be back in forty-five."

"Great."

The second Rhonda disappeared into the elevator,

Marian vaulted to her feet and ran into her boss's office. Having practiced the drill a thousand times in her mind, it ran like clockwork now.

Key: get it out of the pocket of the suit jacket, which was hanging on the hook on the back of the door and thank her lucky stars her boss had mentioned that was where he kept it and left his jacket while he went to grab a sandwich.

File cabinet drawer: unlock it.

Unmarked file shoved in the back: get it.

Address printed on the paper: memorize it.

2250 Stockbridge Lane.

That was it.

Oh, God. That was it.

She raced out of the office, home free.

Until she ran smack into the broad chest of her boss and almost landed on her butt.

No. Christ, God, no—

Dexter Brady reached out a hand to steady her. "Are we under attack?"

She opened her mouth and prayed she could produce a laughing sentence rather than nervous vomit. "I need to get out of here or I'll be late for . . . the dentist."

Somehow she grabbed her purse and managed a sedate walk out to the lobby area, but waiting for the elevator was out of the question. Hurtling through the fire door, she raced down the two flights, slowed up again through the atrium, and went through the glass doors to the parking lot, where she found her car, got in and called Jerome on her cell phone.

"Yeah," she said when he answered. "I got the address to the safe house like you wanted. And I need my shit."

"Good girl. I've got something extra special for you." The smile in his voice came across the line, loud and clear. "Call it a little thank-you for everything you've done."

Kerry drove up I-71 at eighty-five miles per hour, fifty miles north of Cincinnati. He was almost at the late afternoon meeting spot, but part of him hoped he'd lose control and wrap his car around a tree so he wouldn't have to be Kerry Randolph for another cursed minute.

This idea was gaining strength when his phone buzzed. He grabbed it from the cup holder, and one quick glance told him more than he wanted to know.

Caller unknown said the lighted display. If only that were true.

Could he not go two freaking hours without being tracked like a FedEx package?

Up ahead, another overpass zoomed into view, closer . . . closer . . . and he ignored the phone's second buzz and eyed the massive pillars. A car racing at this speed didn't have a chance against unforgivable concrete like that. All he needed to do was stomp the accelerator and loosen his fingers, just a little, and it would all be over. The constant fear, the minefields in every direction he tiptoed, the unwavering certainty that a violent death was sneaking up on him, waiting around every corner.

Except that then he was level with the overpass and too soon it was disappearing in his rearview mirror, and he was still alive and still the spineless punk that had stood there and watched his oldest friend get shot in the back of the head for an imagined crime that he hadn't committed.

And Kerry had nothing left except the flat green fields streaking by his windows, the sickening knot of cowardice and fear growing in his gut, and the buzzing phone.

Snatching it up, he answered on the fifth vibration. "Yeah."

"Where you at?" demanded Kareem. "I've got some shit for you to do."

The weight of Kerry's exhaustion pressed down on him, so heavy he was surprised it didn't push him through the bottom of the car. He was tired of the endless waiting for the shoe to drop. He was tired of the constant fear. Most of all, he was tired of himself.

"I'll be there in a minute."

"All right then," Kareem said. "Don't keep me waiting."

Disgusted, Kerry tossed the phone down and tried to focus on the highway. His exit came into view and he rolled off the ramp and turned right into a BP gas station that was deserted except for the silvery bright gleam of a fuel tanker.

Kerry drove around back, to the meeting place behind the freestanding men's restroom, and parked his car. He got out and stood where he was, taking a minute to enjoy the sunshine on his face and the cold air in his nostrils, clearing out the woe-is-me from his brain and letting him think clearly enough to remember one fact: he was doing the right thing for probably the first and last time in his life.

After three deep breaths, he turned to Dexter Brady's parked car, which was idling next to his, went around to the passenger side, and got in.

Chapter 23

"What've you got?" Dexter Brady asked without preamble.

Nothing, even if it was a lie, was the best answer because it was the one least likely to get Kerry killed, but his conscience wouldn't let him leave Yogi's headless body lying in that field for buzzards to eat. Funny, wasn't it? At the ripe old age of thirty, which was ancient by street standards, he'd chosen this moment to sprout a conscience and start feeling guilty about all the shit he'd done over the years.

Yeah, funny. Either that or criminally stupid.

He hesitated. Even now he wasn't sure he could trust Brady, and he was sure the brother would just as soon arrest him on some trumped-up charge as look him in the eye.

Still, Kerry had started down this road and might as well keep walking. He was now a confidential informant. A confidential informant was a snitch, the lowest form of human life—just beneath pedophiles and men who had sex with dead bodies—dressed up in an Armani tuxedo.

People who snitched on Kareem Gregory had the expected life span of amoebas, but those were the breaks. Snitching, like popping a cherry, was easier after you'd done it once. Having facilitated the money-laundering setup, it was easier to snitch on Kareem now. Easier, but not easy.

Brady glared. "Sometime before my pension kicks in would be nice."

"He clipped Yogi. Shot him to the back of the head this morning."

Brady's eyes widened with horror. "Christ."

There was no need to define *he,* nor did there seem to be any question about Brady believing him, which was a small consolation.

"What happened?"

Kerry shrugged. "He blames Yogi for screwing up on some roach-killing project. Killing the wrong roaches. That mean anything to you?"

Brady had his emotions back under control now, but he couldn't prevent a flicker of understanding from crossing his face. "Yeah. What else?"

"I was the only one who saw. Kareem shot him in the back of the head after acting like he'd give him a second chance." Kerry broke off because he couldn't speak. Brady looked away, out the driver's side window, giving him a minute to pull himself together.

"You can't leave him out there like that, man."

"Where is he?" Brady asked.

Kerry told him and Brady made a quick decision. "I'll arrange for an agent to find him. He'll make like a hunter with a dog or some such."

"Appreciate it," Kerry said.

"You know what he did with the weapon?"

"Yeah. He gave it to me for safekeeping. Why the fuck you ask me a question like that?"

In a trick that reminded Kerry uncomfortably of Kareem's ability to do nothing but look at you and somehow make you feel smaller than half a grain of sand and stupider than an ice cube salesman at the North Pole, Brady stared at him, eyes narrowed and jaw tight.

"I don't think you understand," Brady said, and his voice was low and rough, just like Kareem's, and his aura of power and invincibility expanded to fill the car, just like Kareem's, "that I'm the only one going to bat for you. I'm the only one willing to put in a word for you with the U.S. attorney, and I'm the only one willing to stick his neck out to try to keep you safe."

Yeah, Kerry got all that.

On the other hand, scarier men than Dexter Brady had threatened Kerry lately, and Kerry was tired of running scared. Plus, he was pretty sure that no matter how angry Brady ever got at him, Brady would never shoot him in the back of the head.

"And here's what you need to understand," Kerry said. "I'm the brother that can help you put Kareem away for the rest of his life. I know you've got a hard-on for the money-laundering charges, but that's nothing compared to the kind of shit he's gotten away with. If you don't want my help, good luck trying to get something on him. Maybe you can put together another task force and see if you can charge him with a parking violation or something."

Brady's cool finally seemed to be slipping because he all but growled at the sarcasm. "Have you got anything to place him in that field other than your version of events, which he's going to deny? Hell, for all we know he's planting the gun in *your* house right now and about to drop the dime on *you*. We need to give a jury something to work with."

"I don't have shit."

"Yeah, you don't have shit." Brady snorted. "You don't have shit and I don't have anything except a wasted afternoon spent driving up here and a murdered drug dealer in a field that I can't pin on Kareem. I told you we needed to get you wired up."

"I'm not wearing a wire. If Kareem catches me with a wire, I'm dead on the spot."

"Then what's the point? Why are we having these little meetings? So we can catch up on all the latest Kareem Gregory gossip and talk about his winter fashion selections? You haven't produced a single thing—"

Oh, hell no. Kerry wasn't going to sit quietly by while Brady rewrote history and erased all the parts where Kerry had stuck his neck on the line.

"I fingered him in the first place."

"Yeah, and like you said, that led to money laundering. I put a team in there, ran an operation and all we got was our dicks in our hands and money laundering. Now my men are either dead or in hiding and that motherfucker's still walking the streets. When are you going to give me something I can use? Where is his distribution center? Where does he store his shit?"

For the first time all afternoon—hell, it felt like the first time in his life—Kerry smiled. Because there was a tiny sign of hope that they might all be out from under Kareem Gregory's thumb sometime this millennium.

"Now you're asking the right questions," he told

Brady. "Guess who's been put in charge of distribution now that Yogi's gone?"

The words hung out there for several long beats and Brady tilted his head and his eyes slid out of focus, as though he'd heard the words but couldn't process their implications. But then, quite suddenly, Brady's gaze swung back to Kerry, and it was shrewd, narrowed and excited.

And he smiled back.

The loss of Jack's heat woke Amara up the next morning.

Groggy, her side sore but not terrible, she tried out a ginger movement or two and twisted beneath the tangled linens in time to see him get to his feet and stare down at her in the predawn light breaking at the curtain's edge.

Reaching out, she caught his forearm and they held on, and for that one second they were just a pair of lovers, the same as any other, trying to let each other go long enough to begin their day. But then he slid his hand down her arm and away and the connection was broken.

They'd only been using borrowed time anyway, but letting him go hurt every time. One of these times he'd leave and never come back. That was what people did, especially people who were marked for death.

They left.

She propped her head on her hand and watched him search the floor for his underwear. Looking at him aroused her, even now when her body felt sore but still delicious and satisfied. The gleam of his skin, the hard muscled curves of his long limbs, the thick nest of dark hair between his legs and the length of his penis, semiengorged and ruddy with a morning erection—the sight of all that resonated in her body.

"Go back to sleep, Bunny," he told her. "You need your rest."

"You didn't think I needed rest last night."

This lame attempt at humor fell flat because his lips thinned and he looked away, unable to hold her gaze. "Last night I was selfish. *Again.* I seem to have a problem with that where you're concerned."

"Don't." Ripping the sheet free from the bed, she stood and wrapped it around herself. Only she moved too fast—man, she really needed to take her pain meds, and soon—and couldn't hide her slight wince from Jack's eagle eyes. "I feel fine—"

"I should keep my hands to myself."

She could hear the recriminations building in his hoarse voice and feel the hot shame radiating off his skin. If this kept going, he'd be banging his forehead against the wall again, and she couldn't have that.

"Don't say that. I need you to touch me. *Need it.*"

Evidently there were no words that wouldn't pour out of her mouth when she was under this man's influence, nothing she wouldn't say or risk.

"Touch me." Rubbing against him, she grabbed his hand and clamped it to her breasts, urging him to caress, to squeeze. He did, hardly needing the encouragement. Despite the sudden rigidity in his body, she knew he wasn't in control. Neither of them was when it came to this thing they did to each other.

Groaning, he caught her mouth beneath his and kissed her deep. The desperation in his frantic movements—he ran his hands over her head, cheeks, shoulders, hips and butt—rocked her to the depths of her belly.

Or maybe it was only her own rising fear that she felt.

Just when she thought they were about to tumble to the bed and lose themselves in the oblivion of each other, he pushed her away, hard, and there was nothing frantic about him now, nothing undecided.

They stared at each other, their panting breath harsh in the morning's stillness.

There was regret in his glittering eyes, which was some small consolation. "I have to go, Amara."

"I know."

But he stood there watching her, the muscled slabs of his chest pumping like bellows, and he didn't go.

A dumb question popped into her head but she asked it anyway. How much longer would she have the chance to ask him questions, dumb or otherwise? "Did you sleep?"

An almost-smile touched his lips. "I don't sleep."

"You should."

"I have better things to do in that bed with you than sleep."

She'd noticed. "Today's the day, huh?" she asked, another dumb question.

That hint of a smile disappeared. He swallowed with a hard bob of his Adam's apple. "Today's the day."

The drill wasn't entirely new to her, having represented a protected witness or two in her practice. Jack would have an armed and uniformed escort of several officers that would get him safely to the federal courthouse's underground parking garage in an unmarked SUV. They would smuggle him to a secure holding area via some back elevator or other, and would get him to the courtroom through hidden hallways and staircases that the general public never saw.

He would testify under the watchful and protective eyes of his bodyguards but would also have to meet the eyes of the man who wanted him dead. The two men would be separated and have no opportunity to confront each other, except for when Jack testified, but Jack would be subjected to the man's malevolent presence and know that he was actively trying to kill him even if Jack couldn't prove it.

"Are you ready for this?" she asked.

"Past ready."

Yeah. It was there in his face, the hard glint of determination and maybe a little relief. That made sense to her. After hiding in the shadows trying to stay alive, he could finally do something active and was happy about it. A man like Jack could never be happy doing nothing other than cooking in a diner and pretending he was invisible.

"Are you scared?"

He shrugged, looking wry. "Scared and I are old friends."

That wasn't news, but she still hated to hear it. And the closer he got to leaving the safe house to testify, the more the fear clamped down around her throat. Her imagination kicked into turbo-overdrive and she had the sudden image, bright and clear as a full harvest moon on a crisp fall night, of him lying in the alley outside the courthouse.

Shot. Bleeding. Dead.

"You'll wear a bulletproof vest, won't you?" There was a definite note of panic in her voice now. She touched his arm, pressed it. "If they tell you to wear a vest—"

"Yeah, I'll do what they tell me to."

For some reason she didn't entirely believe him, but his unwavering gaze held hers for a minute and that was some reassurance. "How long will your testimony take?"

They were circling closer to something here and the tension level in the room reflected it, hiking up into the orange zone and bordering on red. His gaze skittered away and settled on some distant object over her shoulder. His light tone didn't fool her for one second.

"You know how this goes. They'll choose the jury. Have motions and opening statements. I'll begin my testimony, probably this afternoon." He paused and the weight of the earth pressed down on them in the silence. Now his gaze settled on the floor, somewhere near his bare feet. "I'll probably finish up tomorrow. Unless something . . . happens."

Something happens. What a nice euphemism, useful to cover anything from the judge getting a flat tire and being delayed on his way to court to Jack being shot and killed in the street on his way to the courthouse.

"So," she said, needing and yet dreading clarification, "if everything goes as planned, you'll be finished with your testimony as early as . . . tomorrow."

Silence from Jack, which was confirmation.

She waited, not wanting to ask it, until she couldn't put it off any longer.

"What happens then?"

Jack cleared his throat, paused, and cleared it again. "You go back to Mount Adams and I go back into hiding. We all think that the danger to you will have passed by then. It's probably passed now, especially if

Kareem Gregory never knows how close we've gotten. And life goes on like it did before. For both of us."

"Kareem Gregory?" A nice name, as long as she didn't think too much about the man behind it. "You've never said his name to me before."

"Like you don't know the name." Amusement crinkled the edges of his eyes but never quite lit up his face. "Like you haven't hit Google and learned everything you could about the case by now."

Damn straight, and she wouldn't apologize for it. There was only so much knitting and twiddling of thumbs a person could do before her brain shriveled and died.

Defiant, she shrugged and hitched up her chin. "I have to pass the time, don't I? Crabby Patty and Billy Bob didn't object when I sat down with my laptop yesterday. If you don't like it, blame them."

"I'm not blaming anyone." He hit her with that tone of quiet reproach, the one she hated so much because it made her feel like a slug trailing slime across the floor. "And everything isn't a fight, so stop looking for one all the time."

"Great. Since you're feeling so agreeable, tell me where you're going when you leave Cincinnati."

Just like that, the brick wall sprang up between them again, invisible but solid and impregnable as Fort Knox. For good measure, his face closed off and he turned to snatch his jeans from the floor. "I can't."

"You won't."

"Yeah." Furious now, he wheeled around on her, eyes gleaming and feral and every word clipped and dangerous. "You're goddamn right I won't. You've already been shot because of me. Do you think I'm going to do anything to put you in danger again if I can help it?"

They stood toe to toe and she refused to back down before his raging anger. "This is *my* life and *I* make the decisions about what I need to know and what I can handle—"

"No. You sure as hell do not."

Amara opened her mouth to scream at him in her frustration, to vent and let him know what she thought of him and his lousy pronouncements, but the subtle but absolute change that came over him had her snapping her jaws shut.

More light was creeping in through the windows now, letting her see him in more detail, and what she saw scared her. She saw him stiffen his spine until he stood at his full height, and the added quarter inch seemed to make him twice as big as he'd just been.

She saw his features harden until even the Sphinx showed more soft emotion than he did. Worst of all, she saw his back teeth clench and his jaw tighten down, and she knew that he would happily die rather than lose this particular fight with her.

Time to face facts.

This time tomorrow, or the next day at the outside, would be the last time she laid eyes on Jack, ever. She would not change his mind. They had gotten a little closer, true, but their affair, or whatever it was, was almost over, and when it was over there would be no messages reassuring her that he was okay, no occasional secret visits, no nothing, just like he'd always said.

They would never lay eyes on each other again.

In fact, they could go their separate ways tomorrow, he could be killed the next day, and she could spend the whole rest of her life wondering about him, not knowing he was dead. Tomorrow or the next day, when it was over, it would be over forever. The end.

"Jack," she said, anguished.

Turning his head, he looked away without answering.

To hell with not wearing her heart on her sleeve. To hell with her dignity. "You won't sneak away, will you? You'll tell me good-bye, right?"

No answer.

"Jack?"

With a cry, she launched herself at him and held on as tight as possible. Against her lips she felt the frantic thump of his pulse at the base of his throat, and beneath her fingers she felt the strain of his muscles as he struggled against doing the right thing and touching her. The right thing won, to her everlasting dismay.

Reaching up, he pried her loose and set her aside, his face turned away, but the choked emotion in his voice wasn't as easy to hide. "I don't have time for this."

He strode into the bathroom and shut the door, locking himself away from her.

Chapter 24

Kira couldn't read Kareem's mood this morning.

That was always a bad sign.

She hadn't slept, and she wasn't the only one with nocturnal wanderings. Around two A.M. the sound of Kareem's light footsteps outside her room had nearly sent her into cardiac arrest. Paralyzed with fear, she'd held her breath and prayed. If he ever decided to, say, come in or break down the door, there'd be nothing she could do.

Luckily, after a minute or two of lingering outside her door, his footsteps had continued on and then she'd heard the low, distant murmur of his voice mingled with Wanda's as the two went downstairs, probably to get a drink and commiserate about the unfairness of things like a new trial and the country's entire justice system.

Once she'd all but worn a hole in the carpet, she studied for her exam because, yeah, her life wasn't stressful enough or anything and she had her final nursing exams this week, too.

Now here they all were, clustered around the kitchen

table like three jittery cats in a shopping bag, pretending to eat breakfast.

"You need to eat something, baby."

Kareem looked at Kira across the top of the *Cincinnati Enquirer,* his brow furrowed in lines of such husbandly concern that her heart panged. He was unspeakably handsome in his fine navy suit and red tie, the picture of a wrongfully accused man who paid his taxes and loved his wife and wanted nothing more than to be left in peace while he ran his above-board auto-customizing empire. Even now Kira wondered at her sanity for doubting him, he was that convincing.

"You need to keep your strength up," he continued. "It's going to be a long day."

Didn't she know it. Ignoring Wanda, who sipped her coffee, Kira put on her devoted wife smile and hoped it worked. "I think I'll be able to stay at the trial through the afternoon break," she told Kareem. "But then I'll have to leave for my final. It's at three-thirty."

"My wife. About to graduate college with her bachelor's of nursing. I'm so proud of my baby."

He looked proud. His smile was proud. On the surface, anyway. But there was a disquieting gleam in his eyes and an ironic note in his voice. Or did she imagine it all? With Kareem there were always enough illusions and sleights of hand to make Houdini jealous.

Still, there was a game in progress here and it was her move. "Thank you. I'm just ready for it all to be over."

"So am I."

There. There it was again and she didn't imagine it this time. That enigmatic note that didn't quite match the conversation, as though he knew secrets she couldn't begin to fathom.

Agitated, Kira poured more juice and tried to take another bite of eggs. Wanda hummed absently. Kareem read. Kira was just checking her watch, wondering how bad the morning traffic would be and if it was too early for them to head down to the courthouse, when Kareem gasped, lowered his paper to the table and bent his head over it with rapt attention.

The women exchanged a bemused look. Then Kareem looked up and his face was alight with a terrible excitement that sent shivers racing along Kira's spine.

"What is it?" she asked.

"Nothing," he said quickly. "Nothing." But he looked down at the paper again, reread something and got to his feet with the vibrating restraint of someone who's in a big hurry and trying not to show it. He tossed his napkin to the table and wheeled around, heading for his office down the hall. "I just need to make a quick call. And then we'll go."

"O-kay, then," Kira said to his departing back.

Wanda, naturally, looked worried and trailed after him. "I'd better see what that's about."

"Okay."

Kira waited until the sound of Wanda's clicking heels disappeared down the hall, and then she lunged for the paper, desperate to see what had provoked such a reaction from Kareem. She hurried inside the pantry and scanned the headings.

To her surprise, it was the classified section.

What the—?

Nothing she saw at first glance looked the least bit interesting. Autos . . . autos . . . autos . . . Boats. Computers. Furniture. Singles. The next page went into real estate. Big freaking deal. What on earth—?

And then she saw it. Under the Singles column, a

few lines so insignificant that they would never mean anything to anyone unless he or she knew what to look for. Two words snagged her attention: *Kayjay* and *Muirwood.*

Kayjay, today is the day.
C U L8R? Meet me on Muirwood, ok?
—L.C.

The words swirled through Kira's mind in an indecipherable jumble and finally crystallized with a lightning flash of clarity, making perfect sense and solving mysteries that the DEA had spent countless hours and dollars trying to unravel.

Kayjay. Oh, God, *K.J.* Short for Kareem Jason Gregory. *K.J.,* the nickname Wanda had called Kareem as a boy, the one they were all strictly forbidden to use now.

And Muirwood was the name of a street in an underdeveloped section downtown where several abandoned factories stood. Where Kareem had once, years ago, looked at a warehouse and considered buying it for his auto-customizing business. Where he'd rejected the property as a money pit too run down to be worth the effort.

Or so he'd said at the time. Oh, God—could it be?

Shaking with excitement now, crumpling the newspaper between her clenched hands and getting newsprint on her fingers, she forced herself to smooth out the folds, breathe deep, and *think.*

A beautifully wonderful and simple solution came to her.

Kareem communicated with his suppliers—the Columbians, Russians or Mexicans; L.C. or whoever the hell was supplying his network with kilos of cocaine and heroin and God knew what all—through these messages in the newspaper.

This was why all the DEA's wiretaps and searches had turned up nothing. *This* was why they couldn't nail him on federal drug or racketeering charges. *This* was why he'd eluded the feds for so long.

She laughed—a single, hiccuping bark of surprised relief, too wonderful to keep inside—and immediately clamped her hand over her mouth lest anyone hear her.

And the warehouse on Muirwood. That was where he received his shipments and stored them. That was the mother lode, the hidden stash of so many drugs and probably guns that a conviction on possession with intent to distribute and illegal weapons charges would put Kareem in federal prison for a hundred lifetimes with no possibility of parole.

Jesus, God.

This one newspaper ad was the solution to all her problems, the tiny bit of luck she needed to get protection from the feds and begin a new life free of Kareem Gregory and his evil. And Kareem never had to know she'd been the one to turn him in.

Hands still shaking, she fished her cell phone out of her dress pocket. Not the regular cell phone, the one that Kareem called her on, but the secret one, the prepaid, disposable one that she only ever used to call Dexter Brady. She hit speed dial and waited for him to answer with so much uncontrollable excitement bubbling up in her that she could hardly stand still.

"Brady," he answered.

"I've found the stash," she told him. "The big one. I know where he keeps it all, and he's getting a shipment today. I know how he communicates with his suppliers."

There was a long pause. She could almost hear the whirring of Dexter's clever mind, feel his skepticism warring with his desperation for a breakthrough on this case.

"How?" he asked sharply.

She explained.

Another long pause and then Dexter said the words she'd been hoping for:

"I'll get a search warrant."

Chapter 25

"State your name and title, please," Assistant U.S. Attorney Jayne Morrison said.

"Special Agent Jackson Parker Jr., DEA."

"How long have you been with the DEA, Mr. Parker?"

Jack, sitting on the witness stand, didn't answer.

Almost everything in the soaring paneled courtroom had a surreal quality that Jack couldn't quite bring into focus: black-robed U.S. Circuit Court Judge Roberta Sheldon, who sat on the bench slightly above him with the court's enormous golden eagle seal on the wall at her back; the jurors in the box to his left, all waiting attentively for him to tell his story; the attorneys at their respective tables; the spectators in the gallery at the back; and the armed guards offering their protection from the man determined to hunt Jack down and kill him like a dog in the street.

Only Kareem Gregory was focused and real to Jack now.

The two men stared at each other across the space of fifteen feet or so, neither blinking. Nothing had prepared Jack for the shock of being in the same room with Kareem Gregory again.

Part of the problem was the man's outward appearance. He had on a dark suit and red tie that were more expensive versions of Jack's own clothes, a commanding but respectful presence—as though nothing delighted him more than the chance to show up here at court and clear up this whole misunderstanding about money laundering, which was something he would never do because he was an honest and hardworking businessman—and a face that didn't have green scales or vertical red pupils or anything else to clue the general public in to the fact that a monster walked among them.

Kareem Gregory had a remarkable ability to look like a regular man. Like a crouched lion eyeing a herd of antelope from a patch of tall grass, Kareem Gregory was expert at camouflage.

But Jack knew what he was. He could also see beneath the man's bland expression and read the banked message in his eyes.

I'll walk free, Jack.

I always walk free.

And I'll kill you if it's the last thing I ever do. Not because you set me up and trapped me, but because I always have the last word. Always.

Jack stared back and telegraphed his own silent message:

Not this time, motherfucker.

"Mr. Parker," said Jayne. "I was asking how long you've been with the DEA—?"

Jack blinked. "Twelve years."

"Tell us about your background, Mr. Parker."

Speaking directly to the jury, he explained growing

up in Memphis, his years in the corps, his subsequent criminal justice degree from the University of Louisville and his decision to join the DEA.

"Why did you decide to become a DEA agent, Mr. Parker?"

Staring at Kareem Gregory and sparing a quick glance at his beautiful wife and his doting mother, both of whom sat behind Kareem in the gallery and both of whom were complicit in every evil act Kareem had ever committed just as surely as they were both sitting there in designer clothes bought by the tainted drug money, Jack gave the answer he'd been dying to give.

"Someone had to have the balls to try to get drug dealers off the street. And I was tired of seeing what illegal drugs do to people. So I signed up, did my training and went to work in New York City."

Jayne murmured sympathetically. "Do you personally know someone who had a problem with drugs?"

Jack shifted, uncomfortable now. "My father. He had PTSD when he came home from Vietnam, but they didn't call it that back then. They called it cracking up. And he eventually OD'd on heroin."

He couldn't quite meet the jurors' eyes at this point, but he was aware of their somber expressions and quiet nods of understanding. And he was aware of Kareem Gregory's hard, unblinking gaze, relentless in its intensity.

"Mr. Parker, were you involved in an undercover operation that concerned Mr. Gregory?"

"Yes."

"Tell us about it."

* * *

After months of investigating and working with a confidential informant, the identity of whom Jack had never been told, the Cincinnati task force investigating Kareem Gregory had called for outside help.

Word was that Gregory, who quietly paid his taxes and made a good living running his auto-customizing business, was the kingpin of a ring that ran from Cincinnati down through Tennessee and up through Canada, with possible Mexican ties, but they didn't have jack or shit on Gregory.

They'd rarely seen such a well-organized and close-mouthed ring and, in desperation, they set up a bogus bank that served a "discreet and select clientele," hoping to get Gregory for money laundering, if nothing else, because, hey, when you're making money hand over fist selling drugs by the kilo to little kids and addicts, you're going to need a bank to clean it up real nice, aren't you?

Mostly they wanted to identify Gregory as the right man. Their Mr. Big.

Cincinnati needed an agent to go undercover to play the banker and they wanted someone from outside the city so there was no question of anyone in Gregory's organization recognizing him or being suspicious.

That was where Jack and Ray Wolfe came in—literally flew in from New York.

Introductions were made. Meetings arranged. Terms decided.

Then came the big night, in a private room at Cincinnati's priciest steakhouse.

Jack walked in with Ray as his "lieutenant." To the unsuspecting, they probably looked like professional athletes in town for a few days because they'd spared no expense on the clothing budget and were suited up real nice in Armani, just like Gregory's crew.

This was a rare switch from their usual UC work, which more often ran to T-shirts and jeans, setting up small-time dealers and raiding squalid dope houses for a few grams and a few weapons here and there.

The clothes were great. Walking in without wires, with only the surveillance van down the street to come rescue them if things went south, wasn't.

Jack heard the faint but familiar rumble of Air Wing, DEA's Cessna Citation, as it flew in the black skies overhead, surveilling the area, trying to keep them in sight for as long as possible and providing real-time commentary to the team in the van. It wasn't much comfort at that moment to have the full might of the DEA protecting him when he knew damn good and well that if things went bad during this meeting, Jack and Ray could be shot and killed long before that jet radioed for help.

Energy and tension ran high.

"Shit." Ray, the class clown, echoed Jack's thoughts exactly. "I should have gone to business school."

The hostess in black led them through the fancy-schmancy bar area, skirted the dining room with its well-dressed crowd schmoozing over the finest food to be found in Cincinnati, and led them down a hallway into the private room, where several overlarge gorillas in designer suits already waited, drinks in hand.

Very civilized, were these drug dealers.

Everyone froze. The low murmur stopped. Absolute silence fell.

The first gorilla went right to Jack, three hundred pounds of menace stitched into a thousand-dollar suit with enough firepower strapped to his side under his jacket to blow Jack to Kingdom Come six or seven times.

"Name's Yogi," he said. "We've been waiting for you. Back here."

They waded through the goons to what seemed to be the main table. Jack kept his shoulders squared and made eye contact with every one of those punks. They all returned the hard-ass stare.

Jack also kept one eye on the table. Two men were there, the first one standing, the second one sitting. Both waiting. As soon as Jack and Ray came into sight, the second man stood, too, like he was an underling same as everyone else, but it was too late for blending in with little Spartacus moves like that and Jack already knew that he was the one—the top dog.

What was the giveaway? Not the dark suits they both wore. Not their looks or age, because both seemed to be thirty-something-ish with the kind of dark appeal that women creamed for on sight.

No. In this case, as in most cases, body language told the whole story. The first guy was no joke and had the shrewd eyes of a man capable of causing more than his fair share of trouble for the DEA, and not the Yogi sort of brute force kind of trouble, either.

The first guy was a player, but the second guy was the boss.

There'd been something in his relaxed posture, with his arm resting across the back of his chair and his legs crossed. When everyone else was hopped-up and nervous, this guy was relaxed—probably because he knew any of his men would protect him with their own sorry lives before they let anything happen to a single hair on his head.

He was the one.

The other guy nodded a curt greeting. "I hear you run a discreet bank. We might be able to use you."

Jack, who was sweating bullets and well aware that either of these guys, boss or underling, could kill him for what he was about to do, huffed out an irritated breath and tried to look pissed off.

"Uh-uh," he said.

Dismissing this guy, Jack looked to the kingpin and felt the unwelcome shock of recognition, the can't-prove-it-in-court-but-know-it-in-my-gut thrill of realizing that he was right. Training had nothing to do with this certainty; instincts did.

This man, out of all the assorted thugs and killers in the room, was the one he needed to keep his eye on.

"I gave the word that I would only deal with the top guy," Jack continued. "If we can't agree on that, then we have nothing to talk about."

Wheeling around, Jack headed back toward the door and half expected a bullet between the shoulder blades with each step he took, public place or no. It never came. Four steps out, someone called, "Wait," and, after taking another step, just to make it look good, Jack turned back around.

The kingpin was smiling at him.

It was a relief and a horror, as though a dragon had taken a liking to him and wanted to be his special friend. That smile had power, menace, respect and brilliance all rolled up into one flashing white package. That smile chilled his blood.

"Let's talk." The kingpin jerked his head. "You and me. Over here."

Jack exchanged a quick glance with Ray and then met up at the table with the kingpin. The man, to Jack's fascinated surprise, put his arm around Jack's shoulders in a brotherly gesture and leaned close, as though they had secrets to tell and could understand each other in a way no one else ever could.

Up close, his eagle eyes were brown, his skin smooth, his breath minty fresh. His magnetic energy ran down his arm, across Jack's shoulders and permeated the entire restaurant and, probably, the night sky.

Against all odds Jack found himself wondering if he could be wrong about this guy and wanting to like him, to be the friend of a brother this cool. But then that smile flashed brighter and Jack knew he might just as well climb in bed with Satan himself as fall under this guy's spell.

"I like you." The kingpin had a perfect voice for giving speeches and commands.

"Really?"

"We can do business."

"That remains to be seen," Jack told him.

"I think we can come to terms. I've got a little cash I need some help with."

Jack snorted and shot him his best who the fuck do you think you're messing with? *glare. "I'm not real anxious to do business with someone who plays me for a fool, pretends he's not in charge and then still doesn't bother to tell me his name. Doesn't put me in a trusting mood, you feel me?"*

The kingpin's grin was wry, his shrug nonchalant. Watching him, you'd almost think they were negotiating the price of a used car rather than the laundering of millions of dollars. "A man has to protect himself."

"I'd say you've got that part nailed."

The kingpin dropped his arm and his smile and walked, head down, several paces away. Jack waited.

They all waited. No one spoke while the kingpin studied the polished tips of his shoes. Finally he meandered back, taking all the time in the world, and when he caught Jack's gaze again it was with eyes so malevolent and flat it was as though he'd had his soul surgically removed and replaced with a black hole.

Jack had served with distinction in the Gulf and been trained by some of DEA's finest. He'd faced down thugs of all descriptions and even a Russian drug lord, no problem. Fear was part of the deal. If you didn't have a healthy fear of the people you were dealing with, you most likely had a short life expectancy.

No biggie.

Staring into this man's face now, though, Jack didn't feel the garden-variety fear that got him through each day. He felt the sharp edge of terror. It ashamed him, but he did. In the second before he wrestled it back and mastered it, Jack felt the screaming, middle-of-the-night terror of a kid who's had a boogeyman-under-the-bed nightmare.

Then it got worse.

"Here's the thing." The kingpin stepped closer, stopping only when he was all up in Jack's grille and aiming for maximum intimidation factor.

It worked. Jack, calling on all his years of training, every ounce of self-control and borrowing against his future reserves, stood firm and didn't back away.

The kingpin's voice was low and rough now, as though someone had taken sandpaper to it. "If you're a fed, or a snitch, or even just a guy who forgets what he promised to do and doesn't keep his word, here's what you need to know." The man's unblinking eyes glittered with ice and his voice dropped. "I will kill you. I don't give a fuck who you are. I will kill you. *And before I kill you, I will kill your mama and your daddy, your kids and your dog and your old woman. If you have a goldfish and a houseplant, I'll kill those motherfuckers, too. I don't care if I go to jail for it. If someone betrays me, he pays with his life. That's how it works if you do business with me. Period."*

Jack's knotted gut was a screaming warning: tell him thanks, but no thanks, shithead. Do what you can to get out of here alive and never face this monster again.

But all of a sudden, the arrogance in the man's face pissed Jack off. So did his utter lack of regard for human life and Jack's own fear. Who the fuck did this bitch think he was? God? Jack was the motherfucking DEA. A federal agent doing his job. And this SOB thought he could intimidate him*?*

Fuck that.

Squaring his shoulders and planting his feet wide, Jack smirked. "Fascinating. Now what the fuck is your name?"

The kingpin grinned, all animosity forgotten, and extended his hand. "Kareem Gregory."

Holy shit. They had a name at last. Jack, who had no hopes that it was his real name, shook hands with the man who was about to ruin his life.

"Did you subsequently receive money from Kareem Gregory?" asked Jayne.

Jack didn't look at the judge or the jurors as he answered, didn't even register their presence. All his attention focused on Kareem and he wished, with all his heart and soul, that he could vault out of the witness box, lunge across the desk, and rip the man's heart out with his bare hands. The world would be a better place.

"Yes," Jack said. "He arranged for us to pick up four-point-nine million from a couple of his lieutenants. Part of the task force completed the transaction and executed a raid of the warehouse where the money was."

"You had a search warrant?"

"Yes."

"What were you looking for?"

"Drugs. Additional money. Weapons. Records."

"Did you find any?"

Even now the bitter disappointment sat on the back of Jack's tongue, thick and nasty. All that time and energy wasted, a huge opportunity lost. "No."

Twenty feet away, amusement lit Gregory's eyes as he listened to Jack's testimony.

"Did anything else happen that night?"

"I participated in a simultaneous raid of Kareem Gregory's house. We were there to arrest him and execute another search warrant looking for the same things."

"How did that raid proceed?"

"Like clockwork."

"And it turned up . . . ?"

"Some money in a wall safe."

"Was the defendant home?"

"Yes."

"Did you have any interaction with him at that time?"

"Yes."

Jack paused and tried to steel himself.

The dark memories, which he'd stored so neatly

away and locked in a secure location inside his mind—not unlike the endless storage facility at the end of *Raiders of the Lost Ark,* where the incompetent government bureaucrats dump the precious relic in with millions of other unmarked boxes—climbed out, one after the other.

"He was home, having dinner with his wife."

Jack's unwilling gaze flickered to the gallery, where Kira Gregory sat listening intently, as a good drug lord's wife should. She had the young face, cool beauty, drop-dead body and designer suit and purse for the role. She also had the quiet look, caged and desperate, of a woman dying to escape; a woman who might die if she tried to escape.

"What happened?"

What happened? His life changed forever, that's what happened.

They struck just after dark, at a time when neighborhood traffic was low and the likelihood of bystanders being caught in the potential crossfire was minimal. The team moved with the synchronicity of fingers on a hand, lining up in single file outside the massive front door of the Gregorys' mansion without so much as the scuff of a pebble to give them away. Two blocks over, the backup van waited, just in case. Air Wing circled a couple thousand feet overhead, providing aerial surveillance.

Jack, his adrenaline spiked and his pulse thundering, watched as their team leader, Dexter Brady, gave the signal, and it was all over in ten seconds.

The first agent in line used a fireman's Hallagan to work on the front door's brass dead bolt. The second agent attacked it with a battering ram. Agents three and four entered the impressive foyer with a shotgun and an assault rifle, sweeping the area for any signs of life, which weren't hard to find. They all yelled.

"Police!"

"DEA!"

"Search warrant!"

Jack and the rest swarmed inside to see the remnants of a touching scene in the dining room, which was right out of Architectural Digest *in terms of over-the-top expensive furniture—no roach-infested, filth-strewn crack house here, no siree.*

Candles flickered on the mantel and table. Flutes filled with still-fizzing champagne sat waiting. Half-eaten food filled the fine china plates, a nice roast of some kind, by the smell of it.

And leaping up from the chair, where she'd been straddling her husband, was a flushed, terrified and mostly uncovered Kira Gregory, her black dress falling from where it had been bunched up around her waist to cover her bare ass in the back and gaping open on some small but glorious dark-nippled tits in the front.

Kareem, whose shirt was unbuttoned to the waist, stood, shoved her behind him, and worked his rapidly deflating erection back into his pants.

"Oh, my God. You can't just break into our house! Who do you think you are?"

Kira Gregory's shouts seemed to go on forever as she faced the federal agents invading her dining room, and Jack had to admire her guts for facing down this occupying army, which was pretty much what they were.

Everyone was in full regalia, with dark jackets with DEA emblazoned on the back in huge yellow letters, badges pinned to waistbands, helmets, goggles, gloves, Kevlar vests and assault weapons, but her righteous anger outweighed any intimidation that she might have been feeling.

Jack would bet his right nut that this was the first concrete encounter she'd had with her husband's real line of work. Maybe she'd had suspicions, but she didn't have any firm knowledge. Not before this.

Welcome to the real world, Mrs. Gregory.

"You're under arrest, Mr. Gregory."

Dexter stepped forward with the handcuffs. If Gregory had any thoughts of running, the agent standing in his face with the rifle locked, loaded and pointing right at Gregory's bare chest persuaded him otherwise. He put his hands on his head and submitted to a pat-down, docile and cooperative as a newborn lamb. He showed zero surprise and absolute composure, as though dessert, fucking his wife and being arrested were what he'd planned all along for his evening.

"You have the right to remain silent. If you—"

Kira Gregory now had her dress tied in front and was decent, although Jack was willing to bet that no one present would forget the sight of her delicious and nearly naked body anytime soon. She watched the handcuffing of her husband with growing horror.

"What's this about?"

"It's okay, baby," Kareem murmured. "A big misunderstanding, that's all."

"But why is the DEA here?" Jack heard the rising hysteria in Kira's voice and saw the growing comprehension in her wide eyes. "You run an auto-customizing business. Why is the DEA *doing this?"*

Dexter tightened the handcuffs around Gregory's wrists and spoke to Kira with respect and sympathy in his tone. "Your husband did this, ma'am."

"What are the charges?"

"Money laundering. Conspiracy."

"No." Kira's gaze locked with Dexter's over the top of Kareem's head. "The DEA is for drug dealers and—"

"Your husband is a drug dealer, ma'am," said Dexter. "His money is dirty."

"No." Kira shook her head but the righteous conviction was leaching away now, leaving only a bewildered young wife in its place, one who wanted to have faith but was finding it increasingly difficult. "You're wrong. Tell him he's wrong, Kareem."

Kareem, who had his shirt and pants more open than closed and his arms restrained behind him, wasn't in much of a position to tell anyone anything, but he gave it the old college effort.

"They set me up. We'll get this straightened out, baby, okay? Right now I need you to call my lawyer and—"

"You don't sell drugs, though, right, Kareem?" Reaching out, she tried to touch Kareem's face, but Dexter held up an arm, forcing her back. "You told me you don't sell drugs. You told *me—"*

"I don't *sell drugs." Kareem's voice was low now, tinged with frustration and desperation, and even Jack, standing ten feet away, could see how the man's gaze skittered away from his wife's. "I don't—"*

But Kira was backing away from him now, shaking her head and whispering no, *and it couldn't have been more obvious that this woman's innocence was yet another casualty of Kareem Gregory.*

"Let's go," Dexter said. He frog-marched Kareem

toward the front door, through which the flashing lights of several blue and whites could now be seen, along with the craning necks of neighbors lining the street.

They passed the K-9 unit, a beautiful German shepherd being led by his leash, and Jack, who'd been lingering by the hall door, waiting for Kareem to clear out so he could begin searching the house with the rest of his team.

It wasn't against the rules for Jack to be there, but it wasn't the most brilliant idea he'd ever had, either. The other members of the team could handle the raid just fine without him, and drug dealers being confronted with business partners who turned out to be undercover federal agents tended to react badly.

But Jack had wanted this confrontation. He'd wanted Kareem Gregory to know who he was and who'd brought him down at last. He'd wanted the SOB to regret the threats he'd made the other night, to back down in the face of the full might of the United States government. You couldn't get away with treating federal agents that way. Maybe that shit flew in Columbia or Afghanistan, but it didn't work on American soil.

Then Kareem Gregory paused on his way out the door and his expression told Jack that he'd never in his life miscalculated as badly as he had by engaging this monster on the playing field. You didn't want to be on Kareem Gregory's radar and, worse, you didn't want to be in his sights.

Jack was now both.

They stared at each other for one beat . . . two . . . and then a twisted mockery of a smile curled one side of Kareem's mouth. "You scared my wife, man."

Like Jack gave a shit. He raised his eyebrows. "Sorry about that."

Kareem leaned close and Jack saw so much violence in his gleaming eyes that the fine hairs rose all along Jack's arms. "You remember what I told you, don't you, man?"

Dexter jerked Kareem's arm and marched him out before Jack could respond. "That's enough with the chitchat, Gregory."

Kareem seemed not to hear. He walked on past but turned his head as he went, staring at Jack over his shoulder and refusing to break eye contact until he was led down the stairs of his own front porch.

Behind them in the dining room, Kira Gregory began to sob and, between the sobs, to scream. "Kareem," she cried. "Kareem."

"Did you have any further contact with Kareem Gregory?"

"Not until I testified at his trial," Jack said.

"Why is that?"

Jack stared at Kareem, fixated on and obsessed with the gleaming light of satisfaction on the man's face. If it was the last thing he ever did in his life—if it required his dying breath—Jack would wipe that look off the man's face one day.

Oh yes. He would.

"Because," Jack said, "my mother was murdered two days later."

A murmur of surprise rippled across the courtroom, drawing Jack's attention to the jury and spectators for the first time in what seemed like days. What he saw made his heart freeze and then contract into a painful knot of terror.

There.

Way in the back, near the door, sat a woman wearing glasses and listening intently. She had her hair pulled up and no makeup on and looked utterly unremarkable except that she was the most beautiful woman in the world trying to look like she wasn't, which was about like a young Lena Horne pretending she was a farmhand.

Jesus Christ.

Amara.

Sitting four rows back from Kareem Gregory, the man who would torture and kill her if he had the slightest idea what she meant to Jack.

Chapter 26

The text was short, only two words:

Law library.

It was enough.

So when court broke for the recess, Kira was ready with her excuses.

"We knew Parker was going to be good." Jacob Radcliffe spoke in the pumped-up tones of a high-school football coach giving his losing team a half-time pep talk. For emphasis, he clapped a supportive hand on Kareem's shoulder and steered him out of the courtroom and toward one of the private conference rooms down the corridor.

Kira had the strong urge to tell the man that Kareem hated this kind of condescending speech, but why bother? If Kareem's negative energy was focused on his lawyer, then that increased her chances of slipping away for a few minutes.

"We'll take a bite out of him this afternoon, on cross," Jacob continued. "We've still got a long way to go."

Wanda swooped in. "How're you holding up, baby? You need anything?"

"I'm good, Mama." Kareem focused on Kira, pinning her with the full intensity of his attention until she felt x-rayed. "How you doing?"

"I'm good. But I need some fresh air."

"Oh?" Kareem raised his brows with mild concern. "You're not coming with us to the conference room, Kira?"

Kira tried to look pained, as though the thought of missing one second of any aspect of Kareem's life was enough to double her up with grief. "I'll be there in a minute. I might walk to the corner store and get some mints or a granola bar. Can I get anyone anything?"

Everyone shook their heads and Kareem and his entourage headed off down the hall and disappeared into the conference room. She watched them go, waiting until she heard the satisfying bang of the shutting door before she wheeled around, punched the elevator button, and ducked inside the car.

When the elevator stopped, she hurried out and followed the signs to the law library, which, she saw to her dismay, had windows that looked out into the hall. Great. All she needed was for some passing person to glimpse her in there and it'd be all over for her. Not to mention all the security cameras that had probably captured her every step on tape. Kareem didn't have access to the security tapes in the federal courthouse—at least not as far as she knew—but that was the problem with Kareem. You just never knew.

Her heart thudded into overdrive as she sailed past the information desk and a couple of eager-beaver women who were probably reference librarians and glanced up from their computers looking anxious to help.

Kira gave them a quick smile and kept moving since she wasn't a legal professional and didn't know what she'd say if confronted; she didn't know the name of a single law book and asking for the romance paperbacks would probably be a dead giveaway.

Kira marched past what looked like a million sets of reference books. Trying not to look like a tourist, she scanned every row out of the corner of her eyes and was almost at the emergency exit at the far end in the back, when a hand reached out from one of the rows, grabbed her wrist and snatched her between the stacks.

The momentum brought her up against the unyielding and disturbing wall that was Dexter Brady. With a startled squeak, she pressed her palms against the starched white cotton of his dress shirt, caught a whiff of the soapy freshness of his skin, and registered that it was him. Whether her body or her mind registered it first, she didn't want to think about. All she knew was that he was here and on her side now, and her future was much brighter.

After one arrested second staring down at her, he pushed her away as though she contaminated him and then, for good measure, took a step back and dropped his hands. His obvious revulsion for all things Kira Gregory caused an odd pang in her chest, but they both had more important things to think about.

"Did you get the search warrant?" she whispered.

"It should be ready by the time I get back to the office."

"What are you doing here?"

"I wanted to come and support Jack while he testified."

"When will you raid the warehouse?"

His expression sealed off, revealing nothing. "Soon. So you need to be careful."

"Do you think you'll find anything?"

"We're hopeful."

"Will you participate in the raid?"

"Yes," he said.

Oh, God. It was one thing to know she was sending a group of faceless agents into a dangerous situation based on nothing stronger than her gut feeling, another to know that *this* agent could get hurt or killed.

"Stay safe," she told him.

Those unfathomable black eyes bored into her. She had the unsupportable feeling that something was right on the tip of his tongue, something important, but he must have wrestled it into submission because he nodded once and turned to go.

"Wait here," he said over his shoulder. "I'll leave first and then—"

A sudden wave of gratitude rolled over her. Here, finally, was someone to help her get away from Kareem. She'd laid all the groundwork and done everything she could think of to help herself, true. She'd have her last two exams today and tomorrow and then she'd have her degree and be a self-supporting nurse. But Dexter Brady was about to give her that last little boost she needed, the help and protection that could give her half a chance at building a new life far away from Kareem, and she'd never forget this kindness.

A burst of courage—or maybe it was sheer stupidity—propelled her to stop him by touching his arm. He paused, glancing back at her with a question in his eyes.

"Thank y—" she began helplessly, but *thank you*

was for the neighbor who picked up your mail while you were out of town. *Thank you* wasn't for the man whose belief in you gave you a second chance at life.

So she moved her hand to his cheek and, when he started but didn't jerk away, stood on tiptoe and kissed his jaw. "Thank you." Then she hugged him with her arms tight around his neck, and that, finally, put him over the top.

His entire body went rigid enough to support a highway overpass. Reaching up, he wrenched her hands loose and pushed her back. He shot her one glittering glance and immediately looked away.

Without another word, he stalked off and Kira stared after him because the way he hated her stung, and she'd be a liar if she said it didn't. But now wasn't the time to nurse hurt feelings.

She counted to a hundred and twenty and then slipped out of the stacks and out of the library. Back to the elevator, her mind full of plans for the future and her exams and the home she would build for herself and Max as soon as she got her divorce and Kareem was out of her life forever.

When the car stopped, she ran into a man for the second time that day and her faint hopeful smile froze on her lips like a gargoyle's grimace.

"There you are, baby," Kareem said. "I was wondering where you'd gotten to."

Kira stammered and flushed and finally recovered enough to reach into her skirt pocket and pull out the pack of Wint-O-Green Life Savers she'd luckily thought to put there this morning before she left the house. "I got some mints," she told him. "Want one?"

* * *

Jack got back to the safe house after ten that night, nearly blinded by his anger or his fear, he couldn't quite tell which. His sky-high blood pressure had never recovered from the shock of seeing Amara sitting up in court—sitting right there in court like a fucking spectator—and he now had a pulsing headache in his temples and a roaring in his ears that sounded like an endless bullet train streaking by.

There'd been no chance for him to confront Amara or the unspeakably stupid chimps with guns who'd allowed her to leave the confines of the safe house and go to court like she was catching the latest Will Smith movie.

After the morning recess, he'd testified further, and then after lunch he'd been cross-examined by Kareem's mouthpiece. His fun-filled day had continued with a session at the U.S. Attorney's Office to prepare him for tomorrow's redirect examination, and then he finished off with a debriefing with Dexter Brady and the rest of the team about today's raid of one of Kareem's warehouses.

He was running on less than fumes because all he'd had was three packs of cheese crackers for dinner, and all it would take was one rolled eye or pursed lip to make him blow.

Some of his murderous intent must have shown on his face because all conversation stopped dead the second he walked into the kitchen. Everyone was gathered in their usual spots around the table, Sammy at the computer, Anthony bent over his paperwork, and Amara, the cause of all his turmoil, sitting there knitting some fluffy purple scarf-type thing, her face blank, sweet and politely puzzled, as though he was the one with the problem.

"We'll be out front," said the two agents who'd escorted him home, and then they filed out, clearly preferring the chill outside to the one in here.

Sammy cleared her throat and waited; Anthony kept his head bent low over the paperwork; Amara met his gaze with a defiant one of her own.

She looked stronger today, he thought, ripping and jerking his way out of the Velcroed black Kevlar vest he wore whenever he left the safe house. Her color was brighter and she looked rested, although God knew he hadn't let her get much sleep last night or the night before.

Free at last from the oppressive thing, which somehow weighed much heavier on him than three to five pounds, he held it over the table and let it land with a satisfying thud, right in the middle of all their shit.

They all froze.

"Does someone want to tell me," he said carefully, keeping an iron fist locked around his temper, at least for now, "who the genius is that brought Amara to court today?"

Amara surged to her feet, her chin hitched up. "Don't talk to them that way. I was the one—"

The second that calm voice registered in his ear drums, he lost it. So much for the whole remain-calm plan. *"I am getting to you."* His roaring reverberated in his throbbing temples, as though someone had clapped a set of cymbals to either side of his head. "For now I want you to sit down and shut up so I can talk to these fucking idiots—"

Anthony stood up, saddled his white charger and rode to the rescue, coming to stand between Jack's raging mania and the women. "Okay, chief," he said reasonably, not looking at all scared, which did nothing to smooth out Jack's mood. "You're going to need to calm down a little—"

Jack was ready to take off the man's head if he inched so much as a hair's width closer, but then Amara hurried around and put her hand on Jack's arm. "Can I talk to you upstairs?"

"Talk?" Snarling, Jack ripped his arm free from her touch. "What a brilliant idea. Where were all your brilliant ideas earlier today, do you suppose?"

Amara kept quiet, exchanged glances with the two clowns who apparently didn't understand that protecting Amara from Kareem Gregory necessarily entailed keeping her out of the same room with him, and headed for the steps.

Jack followed, trying to calm down, but his absolute terror got the best of him. All he could see were nightmare images, some that had already happened and some that could still happen.

Amara, shot and bleeding on the ground, passing out from the pain. Amara in the hospital, with surgery and tubes and bandages. Kareem, sitting in his chair in the courtroom, happening to glance around and get a peek at Amara and then putting two and two together. Kareem dispatching another assassin, one with better aim this time. Amara, bleeding . . . dying. Amara, dead. Her amazing light extinguished for no good reason, and all because of her unfortunate association with Jack. They'd been lucky once, but everyone's luck ran out sooner or later and he wasn't trusting Amara to Lady Luck anyway because Lady Luck was a raging bitch.

He followed her into their bedroom, clicked on the light, and shut the door.

She paced a few feet away, apparently bracing

herself, tossed the knitting on the dresser and then turned to meet his gaze with those big brown eyes that tied him up in knots every time.

Jack's emotion tightened his throat until it felt raw and the words came out hoarse. "Why—" he began, broke off and had to try again. "Why did you do that?"

This wasn't going to come out easy. He could tell by the way she stammered and yet her eyes still flashed defiant, as though she wanted to fling whatever it was right in his face but also didn't want to give too much away. In the end, she just came right out with it.

"I wanted to know what Kareem Gregory has done to you." That name coming out of that mouth was the kind of unholy combination that generally sent people running for a priest. "You wouldn't tell me everything. What else was I supposed to do?"

The momentary relative calm he'd managed to produce exploded in a shower of *what the fuck?* "What were you supposed to do?" he shouted. "How about stay here, nice and safe, in the *safe* house—I was kind of hoping the name would tip you off about that, but I guess I was wrong—take a nap, and recover from your gunshot wound? Did you ever think that might have been a better use of your time, Bunny?"

Now she had the mulish, crossed-arm look of a sulky child. "I'm not a prisoner. How much knitting do you think I can do in a day's time? You can't keep me locked away here—"

He could not be hearing this. Those words could not be coming out of that woman's mouth. "Keep you locked away? We're trying to keep you *alive*! Do you not get that?"

"I get that everyone was paying attention to your testimony. No one gave me a second look and Kareem Gregory didn't even—"

This was her explanation? *This* was supposed to make him feel better?

"But he *could* have, Amara. That's the point: he *could* have—"

"—notice me and I had on my glasses—"

"Your glasses?" His snort was so violent with sarcasm he nearly choked on it. "Well, that's fucking brilliant. When you and Clark Kent put on your glasses, God knows no one could ever recognize you."

"You yourself said you thought I was probably safe—"

"Probably?" His anger was so great that he needed to hit something. Since he didn't want it to be her, he pounded his fist against the wall and, when that didn't give him the head-clearing burst of pain he needed, pounded it again. "I don't deal with *probably* when we're talking about your life."

"Look." Taking a deep breath, she smoothed out her voice, ran her hands through her hair and worked at a tiny reasonable smile that never quite made it. "Look. Here I am, safe and sound. There you are. Nothing happened, so why are we—"

He was so not feeling the reasonable thing. He and reasonable weren't even in the same zip code at the moment. "Something *did* happen," he yelled. "I looked up and saw you sitting right behind Kareem Gregory and my heart stopped, same as it did when you got shot. How do you think I feel—"

A weird sound came out of her mouth and it took him a beat to realize it was a raw, ugly laugh rather than a sob. "Well, that's just the thing, Special Agent

Parker. I don't know how you feel. So you can understand my confusion."

The air swooshed out of him, deflating his lungs like a squeezed balloon. Even worse than the laugh was the new brightness in her eyes, the unspeakable wet that looked like tears. If she cried now, tonight, it would kill him the same as one of Kareem Gregory's hired bullets. Not tonight. Not tonight, God.

"Do you want to know how I feel?" she asked.

Yes. "No."

A light went out behind her eyes and it felt like the whole world fell into shadow. "Of course you don't." She turned away to stare at the blank wall rather than him.

He crept closer, needing to touch her or, if he couldn't do that, to smell the fresh sweetness of her skin. "All I want," he said, trying his damnedest to lock his emotions away where she couldn't hear them in the unnatural huskiness of his voice, "the only thing I'm hoping will come out of this whole mess, is for you to go back to life as normal when this is over."

She looked over her shoulder at him, wooden as a marionette. "So, just to make sure I have this straight, I'll wave good-bye to you, hop a plane back to Mount Adams and go right back to work on Monday without missing a beat. Is that it?"

Was that irony in her voice? Jesus, he was so spiked out on adrenaline and emotional overload he couldn't tell. "Yes." There was no way he could express, even if he wanted to, how much it meant to him to know that she was safe. "Everything I'm trying to do is to protect you."

"Protect me?" she said dully. "Because you couldn't protect your mother?"

Jack froze. Hugging a power line couldn't have shocked him more. He gaped, too stunned to muster up any of his usual bullshit bravado, and she just stood there, shining her spotlight into every black corner of his damaged soul.

When the anger hit him again, he pounced on it because he did anger real well and it was way easier than dealing with the endless aching guilt that nipped at his heels like a terrier.

"Don't," he snarled.

She widened her eyes with so much pure innocence her halo practically glowed. "Don't what?"

"Don't psychoanalyze me. Don't project emotions onto me. It won't work. That's not what we're about."

"Oops." She covered her gaping mouth in an impressive imitation of Betty Boop. "You accidentally said the word *we're.* I'll just pretend I didn't hear it, okay?"

And to think he was going to miss this woman soon. To think that he'd be roll-up-in-a-ball devastated once she was out of his life. All that was pretty hard to remember right this second, when the idea of drop-kicking her into next week was so appealing.

"Don't try to make this emotional, Amara. That's what I mean."

"Don't try to get to know you?"

He tried not to see the misery in her face or to feel his own. He wished this straightforward transaction, sex between two consenting adults for a few days and then buh-bye forever, would stay straightforward. He wished he didn't want her so damn much and that hiding his feelings didn't take every ounce of his strength.

"Why bother?" he wondered. "You already know everything you need to about me."

She paused as though she knew where this was going. The energy between them shifted into something other than anger, although the anger was still there, simmering and waiting to bubble over. "I don't know one thing about you, Jack."

Ah, but she did. Just the way he knew that the glittering excitement surrounding her now meant that she was ready and he wasn't the only one wanting.

Sex had been the last thing on his mind when he came up here, but now it was the only thing on his mind. All it took was the mere thought in her presence and his body was beyond his control.

Why were they arguing?

"You know *this*."

Taking her hand, he pressed it, hard, to his groin.

Chapter 27

A tiny, shameful part of Jack had wanted to shock her, to distract her with sex so she'd drop all her questions and stop trying to worm her way into his head, to light the fuse and see how big the resulting explosion would be. It worked.

Jerking her hand free as though she'd touched the blue flame of a lit gas stove, she squawked with outrage and tried to hit him. *Too slow, Bunny.* He grabbed her forearm, wrenched it down between them and taunted her because he didn't know what else to do.

"What's wrong?" He gave her a pointed once-over, fixing his most insulting leer on her heaving breasts, which were well hidden and yet prominent beneath her ribbed turtleneck sweater. "I thought you were all about being all up under me. I thought you wanted to be *close*."

A quick yank had her right up against him, belly to belly, and the last of his good sense died on the spot. He clamped his hands on the faded blue jeans over her tight ass and ground against her, seeking that soft sweet spot that was—he circled his hips and she gasped and bit back a moan—*there*. Right *there*.

Unfortunately, hanging on to her ass meant that he couldn't hang on to her arm, and she hauled off and slapped him. The pain was sharp and good, just what he'd needed, but she was winding up again and a slap was one thing but an uppercut was another.

"I don't want you," she cried. "I don't—"

"I don't believe you."

Snatching her arm out of the air, he twisted it behind her, wrapped his arms around her middle, trapping her, and swung her off her feet and around to the bed. It wasn't fair of him to use his training against her, true, but he didn't feel that bad about it because she gave as good as she got, grunting and kicking at him in her fury, her teeth bared and ready to bite.

They tumbled down together and she scrambled away on the bounce, crawling to the edge of the bed, and he laughed because he admired her strength and determination even if both were futile.

There was nothing he wasn't capable of tonight, nothing he wouldn't do to get inside her. But he wouldn't have to do it because she'd surrender. She always surrendered.

Grabbing her ankle, he jerked her and she collapsed face first onto the bed. Then he crawled over her, mounting her from behind, working his thigh between hers, thrusting his erection against the flexing globes of her ass and settling his weight on her. She didn't like it, or maybe she liked it too much. She screamed with frustration, her cries muffled by the linens, and writhed to get free of him.

"Shh."

He sank his nose deep into her hair, breathing her

into his body, and used a skimming touch to stroke that hair away and bare the tender curve of her neck and shoulder. Going still at last, she whimpered, and her melting vulnerability drove him out of his fucking mind.

He bit her. Not hard enough to hurt—just hard enough.

"Oh, God," she gasped.

A renewed burst of writhing wracked her body, but her hips were definitely undulating against his now and were as much a plea for more as they were a plea to stop.

"Don't fight me."

He tried to sound soothing, but apparently she wasn't buying it because she growled and jerked her head back, trying to break his nose. It almost worked. Cursing, he ducked out of the way just in time, rolled her to her back, pinned her hands overhead, high above her arching back, and stared at her. Both of them were panting.

"I hate you, Jack."

Maybe there was hate in her glittering eyes, but there was a whole lot of passion there, too. He could almost smell it on her, taste it in the damp sweat on her brow.

To get to the passion, he'd deal with the hate.

"I don't care whether you hate me or not."

Ducking his head, he kissed her.

This was some good shit. Some really . . . outstanding . . . shit.

Marian Barber's head disconnected from her body and drifted away, circling and hovering somewhere above her, hyper aware of the bathroom . . . of the blue tile . . . of the annoying *drip-drip-drip* of the faucet, which somehow didn't seem so annoying at this second. On the other hand . . . she was aware of nothing at all. Her head was heavy, her limbs leaden and clumsy, her lids tired.

Rest. She needed rest.

She leaned back against the wall near the bathtub and let the nothingness wash over her. It was good . . . so good.

But the weight of her weightless body got to be too much, so she slid and slumped her way to a seated position on the floor, being careful to keep the tiny bottle clutched in her hand and take it with her so she could find it again when she needed it. There was nothing worse than losing track of her medication or dropping some of the precious pills on the floor. These little babies were worth every dime she'd paid for them and more, oh yes indeedy.

Although . . . she didn't think they were her usual or even the improved shit Jerome sold her last time.

They were a different color, for one thing. The difference hadn't hit her until she'd crunched her first few and felt the welcome rush of relief, but, yeah, they were definitely a different color.

Using all of her concentration, she raised her heavy arm to look at the bottle. After that came the struggle to focus her eyes. Squinting, she held the bottle in front of her nose and stared, good and hard.

Yeah. She saw it now. These were red. Wasn't that red? She looked again. Yeah. Red. The ones she normally took were . . . pink.

Did that matter? Maybe, but . . . right now she couldn't think why it would.

She should go to bed.

Tilting her head back, she scanned the distance to the closed door. She thought about opening the door. She thought about the distance between the open door and her bed. She thought about getting up off the floor and the effort that would take. Then she thought again about how tired she was and how nice it felt just to close her eyes, just to breeeeathhhhhe.

The floor wasn't so bad.

But . . .

This pill thing.

It worried her.

Didn't that matter, if you took pills that were a different color?

And . . . the numbers on these pills . . . they were . . . different, too.

Her old pills said 20. The last batch from Jerome had said 30.

This batch from Jerome said—she squinted down at them and focused her eyes again—60.

Did that matter? Had she taken too many? The possibility tried to alarm her, but her precious Oxy wouldn't let it. That was why she loved her Oxy. It made everything okay.

Anyway . . . it wasn't like Jerome would sell her anything that wasn't safe.

Sliding down that last little bit, she rested her head on the rug. Ahhh. Perfect.

Not as good as the bed . . . but not . . . so bad . . .

Time for some sl—

Amara didn't seem to know whether to kiss or bite him and Jack was happy with either option. Sweeping his tongue as deep into the sweet depths of her mouth as he could, rabid with hunger, he nipped her back and soon tasted blood. Whether it was his or hers he didn't know and didn't give a fuck.

There was a lot of noise in the room. Her breathy cries . . . his low growls . . . their joint moans. And then she seemed to catch herself in this moment of weakness and pulled back.

"Don't."

Don't. Yeah, sure. He'd be sure to stop in another year or so.

He laughed and followed her, kissing her with such bruising force that he felt her head sinking further into the pillow. Maybe she hated him, but she damn sure had her thighs wrapped around his waist and her tongue in his mouth. Freeing her hands, he stroked down over her breasts, filling his palms, and then went to work on her jeans.

The sound of her zipper doused a little ice water on the proceedings and she disentangled her legs, trying to scoot away again. The continued struggle at this late stage of the game infuriated him. Who did she think she was fooling? What was the point of this whole denial exercise? Did she not know that this was probably their last night together?

"I don't want you." Levering herself up on her elbows, she glared at him, defiant to the last follicle of hair. "*No,* Jack."

The word checked him for half a second. No meant no, right? When a woman said no, that was the end of it. Except that he looked back in Amara's eyes and there was no *no* anywhere in sight.

If she didn't want him to work on her jeans, he'd work on his. It took two seconds for him to unbutton and unzip, three to shove the front of his boxer briefs down, pump himself a time or two—God, he was ready to explode—and four to grab a condom from the nightstand, open it with his teeth and work it on.

That gleaming gaze of hers tracked his movements the whole time, saying nothing.

When finally he was ready, he paused, trying to pull together some modicum of self-control before he touched her again. The way things were headed now, he was liable to hurt her.

"Please." The tiny whisper was all her mouth said, but her body was doing most of the communicating. The bright eyes, the straining lungs, the way her gaze dropped to his jutting erection and she swallowed hard, almost like she was salivating for him—they all told the rest of the story. "Don't do this to me, Jack."

Jack struggled against himself, his mind wanting to do the right thing and his body straining to take what it needed. Need won. Flashing her a hard look, he reached again for her jeans and jerked them down her hips. Not all the way off, but out of his way. Something in his expression must have scared her, because she made one last bid for freedom, flipping to her belly and trying to scramble away.

Jack lashed out and grabbed a hank of hair at her scalp. Not pulling—he would never pull her hair—but holding her in place. If she wanted to pull her own hair out to get away from him, that was certainly her prerogative.

The lust making him shake, he waited to see if she would struggle.

* * *

Kareem waited for Kira in her bedroom.

Actually, it used to be *their* bedroom, and that used to be *their* bed. Until the terrible day when Jackson Parker and his team tricked, trapped and arrested him, and his beautiful wife looked at him with horrified new eyes.

Just the way he was going to look at her when she finally got home.

They'd been happy together in this room. How many times had they made love under that fluffy duvet? He ran his hand over the fine cotton, remembering. Every single time had been glorious. There'd been nothing like making love with his wife. It was good to fuck the occasional other woman, sure, but he only ever made love to his wife.

Until that day when she realized the truth about him and cast him from the Garden of Eden straight into the flames of hell, where he burned. To this day, he still burned. And he'd been so stupid, so criminally foolish, that he'd wanted to make it up to her. He'd tried to be understanding while she came to terms with who he really was, tried to give her time, tried to be a patient and loving husband and let her come to him on her own.

Those days were over.

The bitterness collected on the back of his tongue and he swallowed it down. Then he swallowed another hard gulp of the Cabernet he'd brought upstairs with him and drained the crystal goblet dry. Wait—dry? Yeah, dry.

Infuriated because nothing ever went his way these days, he wheeled around and hurled the goblet into the mirror over the dresser, shattering both with an ear-splitting explosion of glass that sent shards in every direction.

The release felt so good that he looked around for something else to throw and was startled out of his fury when Mama poked her head in the door and shot him a glance full of that worried mother hen shit.

"Is everything okay—"

Losing it, he did something he almost never did: roared at her. "Get the hell out of here, Mama." Her eyes widened with alarm and that made him feel a whole hell of a lot better. *"You stay away from this room tonight."*

She faltered, her jaw flapping. "But—"

Here he dropped his voice because sometimes speaking softly scared people worse than anything else, and if there was one thing he wanted to do tonight it was scare some people. "Don't make me tell you again, Mama."

Some combination of his voice and the look on his face seemed to do it. She scurried off down the hall, leaving him alone in Kira's bedroom with only her belongings and his memories of the days when she'd been a loving wife.

The bitterness rose again, nearly choking him this time.

Kira was many things now, but loving wife wasn't one of them.

Passing the bed, he came to the chair where, just like always, she'd thrown her nightgown, a pale blue one. He picked it up in a slither of fine silk, pressed it to his nose, and dropped to the chair as the sweet familiarity of her scent swept over him. No one smelled like Kira. She wore some elusive combination of flowers and sex that gave him a hard-on every time he whiffed it. Like now.

Despair hit him in sudden, giant waves, and he propped his elbows on his knees and buried his hot face in the nightgown. For one terrible second he actually thought he might cry—he was that upset. But then he heard a welcome sound and it gave him something else to focus on: Kira's light footsteps in the hall.

His loving wife. Returned to him at last. What a fucking joke.

Standing, he tossed the nightgown aside and smiled at her. "Hi, baby."

"Hi." She lingered in the doorway, obviously not knowing what to make of finding him in her precious off-limits sanctuary. He imagined her expression would be the same if she found a turd in her bowl of ice cream but, to give her credit, she recovered pretty fast and plastered that fucking Stepford wife smile on her face. "What're you doing here?"

"Greeting my wife. Seeing how her exam went. Come here."

To his surprise, she came. Wow. She was full of surprises, his Kira was. Holding out a hand, he took hers and marveled at the perfect fit and the smooth coolness of her palm. He stared down at their fingers twined together and thought that it was the perfect representation of their lives, which were twined together until death and, as far as he was concerned, beyond.

He kissed her wrist, enjoying the leap of her pulse. "How was your final?"

"Pretty good, I think. Only one more tomorrow."

"And then you'll be a nurse?"

"I won't be a nurse until I pass my boards, but I'll have my bachelor's."

"My baby." He said it with pride because he was proud of her, his beautiful, treacherous wife. A man like him shouldn't have anything less.

She blinked as he cupped her cheek, no doubt detecting a note of turmoil in his voice. "Where's Max?" she asked.

"Don't worry about that dog." Tipping up her chin, he kissed her.

There was a moment's hesitation before she responded, but she always responded.

That was because no one could do it for Kira the way he could, just like she always did it for him. The minty-sweet taste of her, the tiny mewls of pleasure she could never quite silence, the willowy feel of her body, curved just enough in all the right places, filling his hands. Oh, yeah. She did it for him.

Breathless now, she pulled back and tried to speak, but he didn't care about that. He cared about untying the belt of her wrap dress and touching the hot satin of the skin beneath. He fumbled with the belt and she stopped his hands, but only for one second. Distracting her with his mouth on her lips, her neck, the wonderful fragrant valley between her breasts, he drove them both higher and even Kira couldn't fight it. Not now.

Putting her hands on his cheeks, she slowed him down a little and he was caught by the earthy beauty of her flushed face, bright eyes and swollen lips.

Finally he tugged that belt free and got his hands on her.

Jesus, Lord. Touching her was like holding the

universe in his hands. She felt *that* good. Still she tried to speak, to put a little distance between them.

"Kareem," she said, panting now, "I can't. I need to find Max and he needs a walk before I can go to bed. And I'm tired from my exam and—"

"No."

God, her tits were incredible. She wore this filmy little bra that showed every detail, and what he saw pleased him no end. She was aroused. Her nipples were dark with it, tiny hard points that told him exactly what he did to her. Murmuring some nonsense because he couldn't think to connect two words together when he had her like this, he bent, sucked one nipple between his lips and used his tongue to rub it against the roof of his mouth.

She went wild and her knees nearly gave way. It went just like clockwork, every single time, and you'd think he'd be tired of the predictability of her responses by now, but no. Seeing that he did this to her was a primitive thrill, every single time.

"Kareem, please stop." There was a little more steel in her voice this time, a little thrust in her palms as she pushed him, but he outweighed her by an easy hundred pounds and if he didn't want to stop, he wasn't stopping. "I need to walk the dog and I'm—"

"What, baby?" Irritation prickled at the edges of his sensual high, a buzzing fly that he couldn't quite see to swat. "Still on your period?" He crinkled his face in an exaggerated frown. "You better let the doctor know about that."

"No, I just—"

She paused and let her head fall back and her eyes roll closed, caught between the pleasure of his hand circling lower on her belly, heading toward the edge of the black scrap of lace she called panties, and her determination to keep this from going any farther.

"—I just don't think I'm ready—"

"You feel ready to me, baby."

"—and I'd really like for you to stop. Please."

"No."

Ahh, there she was. He slid his hand under that elastic band low on her hips and found the thick patch of wiry hair that he remembered so well. Shaking now with the force of his need, he zeroed in on that hard nub and Kira gasped and squirmed.

She was creamy and wet, hot and slick for him, just like always. For one perfect second she surrendered and the low moan rose up from her chest, but then the sound seemed to startle her and she came out of her sensual haze.

For the first time, she got mad.

Not that it mattered. Not tonight.

Anyway, she was mad at herself, not him. Mad because she couldn't resist him. Mad because she hated and wanted him, and it was all wrapped up together in one tangled knot she couldn't untie.

"Kareem." Going rigid, she shoved his hand away and glared, her eyes sharp now with focus. "I asked you to stop."

Kareem took his time about looking up from the juicy curve of her thighs, the triangle between her legs and her honey on his fingers. He stroked over her belly again, and her hips, and her ass, and he gloried in the fact that all this bounty belonged to him and always would. He was a starved man and he was about to feast.

Finally he met her gaze, saw her dark pupils dilate,

and knew the second her bravado gave way to fear. "I told you," he said. "No."

An arrested moment passed and things between them teetered between possible outcomes. Not the fucking—that was nonnegotiable tonight. The issue was whether she'd cooperate or not.

When she broke and ran for the door, he figured she'd decided on the not.

It made him sad to see her streak away from him like that, with real terror. It really did. And of course, what she'd done made him really, really sad. Angry too, but mostly sad, because how had it come to this ugliness between them?

It made him sick to think of it.

He still wanted to fuck her, though.

Sighing, he looked to heaven for some guidance about how to deal with his wife, but God, as usual, didn't have shit to say to him. That being the case, Kareem took matters into his own hands and ran after her.

They met at the door and, catching her around her waist, he hefted her off her feet and she screeched with some combination of fear and frustration. "No, Kareem!"

She kicked out at him, and maybe he was a twisted fuck, but he liked it. He liked the high pitch in her voice. He liked her healthy new respect for him when she'd been leading him around by the nose for months. He liked her emotions, which were finally raw.

But then she kicked him again and it got on his nerves because they had overdue business to attend to and his dick was like granite in his pants. Clamping his hand down on the crown of her head, he grabbed a big hank of hair and spoke calmly because his yelling too would escalate the situation and it was already escalated enough.

"Stop," he told her.

When she didn't stop, he got a little more irritated and pulled that hair until he felt it give way and rip away from her scalp in a clump. She screamed again, but that was too damn bad. It was her own fault for not listening when he told her to stop; everything was her fault. But she'd learn her lesson before the night was through. She certainly would.

Taking only enough time to kick the door shut with a crash that shook the rafters, he swung her around and slammed her into the dresser, which was just the perfect height for what he had in mind. She roared like a trapped bear, trying to kick him, trying to get his hand out of her hair, trying to stop the inevitable.

But that was the thing about the inevitable, wasn't it? There was no stopping it.

Bending her at the waist, he mashed the side of her face against the wood. Not to hurt her or anything—just to keep her still. She cursed him with language he'd never heard her use before, and it amused him. For a minute.

Then he thought about how she'd lied to him—how she'd betrayed him, how she obviously thought he was a fool—and he focused in on the lesson he needed to teach her, which was this:

Kareem Gregory always had the last word.

Wedging one thigh between hers, he widened her stance and took a minute to grind his dick against her ass, getting harder the more she writhed to get away.

Then he went to work on his zipper.

Chapter 28

Amara surrendered in the end.

To Jack's immense satisfaction, she settled on all fours and offered herself, just the way he'd known she would. She held still, quivering like a mare in heat, and tilted her hips back to receive him.

Coming up behind her, inhaling the musky freshness of her slick body's fragrance, he took his length and ran it through her thick folds, lubricating both of them. She was soaking wet, soft and swollen. Beautiful.

With a cry, he grabbed her hips and drove home, sheathing himself in her tight heat, nearly blinding himself with the pleasure.

There was one arrested moment when they both reeled with the shock of joining, the absolute perfection of it, and then she breathed, "Oh, God," and they started to move.

He wasn't sure whether he was driving her or she was driving him, but they were both loud and frantic, both beyond shame or embarrassment. He took her as hard and fast as he could, until great slapping sounds mingled with their cries, and she swiveled her hips, giving as good as she got.

He reached for her breasts and nearly roared with frustration when her sweater blocked the prize from his hands. Shoving the sweater up and out of his way, he stroked over her breasts in the satin cups of her bra, and then the bra irritated him too. Jerking one cup down, he squeezed and rubbed her, running his palm over her nipple, and her cries rose, both in pitch and volume.

Yeah. He needed more of *that.*

Waiting until her body began to stiffen and he knew she was coming, he rolled the engorged nipple between his thumb and forefinger and squeezed it.

She yelled and bucked, nearly pitching him off the bed in her frenzy.

He came for what felt like ten minutes, the ecstasy surging on and on until he was destroyed and exhausted. Her arms and his knees seemed to give way at the same time and they collapsed to the bed in a heap of sweaty bodies and winter clothes.

Over their harsh panting and the steady thunder of his pulse as it roared through his ears, he heard her voice, which was soft but relentless as the Colorado River carving its way through the Grand Canyon.

"Tell me about your mother."

He could almost laugh at his own foolishness for thinking either that he could distract this woman with sex or that he could keep her at some emotional distance. As though Amara the Fierce would let him get away with that kind of nonsense. Resigned to his fate, he slipped off her and smoothed some of the silken black strands away from her damp face.

"Come to bed," he told her, "and I will."

* * *

Kira's cries finally brought Wanda out of her room. They were too terrible to ignore.

Wanda kept one ear to the ground at all times, but she knew when to keep quiet and when to disappear. The last thing she wanted was for Kira to convince Kareem to kick Wanda out because where would Wanda go then?

Kareem had told her to leave, so she'd left.

Now she was back, in the dark hallway outside the master bedroom door, shaking like a leaf in a tornado, her heart going a thousand beats per minute. She didn't know what was going on in that bedroom, but she knew it was nothing good.

Kareem's mood earlier had worried her, of course, but Kareem was always in a mood of some sort and they often passed before she could diagnose them.

Then Kira came home and there'd been yelling, which Wanda ignored.

Next came running feet and the slam of a door, and Wanda ignored that, too.

Kira's high-pitched wails, though, like she was in pain—Wanda couldn't ignore that.

She listened, disbelieving, sick to her stomach, paralyzed with fear, and horrified to the depths of her soul because her son, her Kareem, couldn't have anything to do with noises like *that.*

The guttural grunts of male excitement and satisfaction. The relentless *slap-slap-slap* of flesh against flesh. The heavy bang of furniture into the wall.

And soaring high over the rest, Kira's wails.

No, God. Please, Jesus, Lord—no.

Wanda slumped against the wall and clapped her

hands over her ears, but the sounds were inside her now, church-bell clear whether she wanted to hear them or not.

And then, for the first time in years, she began to cry in great hiccuping sobs that burned her throat. They doubled her over and ripped her apart, but they kept erupting with the force of an angry Hawaiian volcano.

Kira. She swiped her eyes and swallowed her nausea. *Help Kira. Call the police.*

No—don't call the police because Kareem is already in trouble.

Go in there, Wanda.

Yes. That was what she should do. Raising her hand, she knocked, but they were three pitiful little soundless knocks with no hope against the noises coming out of the room.

She reached for the knob, praying for it to be unlocked and for the courage to open the door and walk inside, but God only saw fit to answer half her prayer: it was unlocked, all right, but Wanda was too gutless to go in there and see exactly what kind of monster she'd raised.

She was still wavering when, abruptly, it was over. Kareem finished his business and said a few low words to Kira, who answered back. Then the door swung open and Wanda scurried back as if there was any possible way she could disappear or hide what she'd been doing.

Kareem came out.

His pants were zipped but unbuttoned, his belt unbuckled, and there was an insistent bulge there that a mother should never see. Sweat shone on his face.

His eyes . . .

Wanda shrank against the wall and wondered for one terrified second if Kareem would hurt her because a man with that kind of look in his eyes was capable of anything. Those eyes were glittering and wild with an edge of ruthlessness so hard it could pound granite to dust. Worst of all, those eyes gleamed with grim satisfaction.

Their gazes met and held, and Wanda knew she was looking into the face of the devil.

"I told you to stay away from this room, Mama."

There was no inflection in his voice. No embarrassment, no emotion whatsoever. They might have been discussing the weather. *I told you not to go out in the rain without your umbrella, Mama.*

In no particular hurry, he passed by and went to his room, leaving Wanda to tend to her daughter-in-law.

"My mother," Jack murmured. "Where should I start?"

They were in the bed now, naked and twined, and Amara had one sleek leg slung over his hip, so he didn't give them much time for talking, but they'd give it a shot for now.

Other than testifying in court today, he hadn't talked about his mother in forever and barely allowed himself to think of her. The probability of collapsing to the floor and crying like a baby was just too high. But this one time, with Amara, it might be okay.

"What do you most remember about her?"

That was easy. "She smelled like Johnson's Baby Powder."

"What do you most miss?"

Jesus. Maybe he wouldn't get through this conversation after all. "Everything."

With a low croon of sympathy, Amara cupped his face and brought it down for a forehead kiss. That felt pretty good, so he shifted around so he could lower his head and rest it on her breasts.

They gathered each other closer and held tighter.

"Tell me what happened to her."

Jack blinked against the hot burn in his eyes and pretended it was dust and exhaustion rather than tears. "She was a teacher. She worked hard every day of her life. She loved me. She loved my father, even though he had a needle stuck in his arm most of the time. She tried to get us to love each other. We never did."

"Maybe you—"

"No," he said firmly. "We never did."

Amara didn't like that. He could feel it in the subtle new tension in her muscles. Thank God she let it drop, though. He wasn't up for a debate on all the possible hidden ways his father had showed his love over the years.

"He wanted me to be a doctor," he continued. "I probably had a subconscious desire to be like him—well, like the old him, anyway. The one in all the pictures on the mantel, with the uniform on. So I joined the Marines."

He paused because his throat was getting tighter, his voice hoarser, and those tears sure weren't showing any signs of evaporating.

"About three years after my father died, she retired. She'd been looking forward to it. Two days after we arrested Gregory, I flew to Memphis for this big dinner they were planning for her. And I—"

Jesus. He couldn't do this.

Amara's soothing hands stroked over his back. "And you what?"

Breathe, Jack. Breathe. A memory can't kill you.

"And I went to her house and I knew something was wrong. She was there, on the floor in the kitchen." He swallowed. "Shot in the head." He tried to swallow again but, man, that lump in his throat just wasn't going anywhere. "She was still alive."

"Oh, my God."

"So, you know . . . I called the police and got her to the hospital, where they said—big surprise—that there was nothing they could do for her. So I held her hand and she died."

"Kareem?" she whispered.

"Who else? You think it was a coincidence that she was shot a couple days after he threatened me?"

"But, Jack—it wasn't your fault."

Hah. Funny. "Whose fault was it, Angel Eyes? The boogeyman's?"

"But—"

"So that's why you shouldn't have been in the courthouse today. It's too dangerous. I don't want Kareem to figure out what you mean to me."

Beneath his fingers, he felt her lungs expand and catch as she held her breath. "And what do I mean to you?"

Did she think he wasn't going to say it after he'd just told her every other secret he had? Raising his head, he looked her straight in the eye. "Everything."

Kira had never thought there was a unit of time longer than forever, but apparently there was. That was how long it took for Kareem to finish with her.

At last he pulled free. At last he took his hands off

her. At last her knees gave out and she fell to the floor in a heap.

An unnatural silence stretched out, filling the room between them. She dialed her anger back a notch and breathed deep and dried her face because Kareem had had enough satisfaction for one night and he didn't need the additional thrill of seeing her tears.

When she was ready, she pressed her palms to the dresser and heaved herself up. Pain shrieked at her, starting in her lower half and shooting out of her torn scalp, but there was time enough for pain later. Now she had to face Kareem and let him know he hadn't won. Wincing, turning, she hitched up her chin and stared him in the face.

Unsmiling, he raised one eyebrow and waited.

"Where's my dog?"

He stared at her. She thought she detected surprise, but they were so good at this poker-faced cat-and-mouse dance, she and Kareem, that it was hard to know what he was thinking. And of course you could never know what a sociopath was thinking.

"Max ran away when I took him out for his walk." Kareem shrugged as he lied and pulled a *what can you do?* face. "I called him, but . . ."

Translation: he let Max out of the house in the subfreezing cold and/or drove him somewhere and kicked him out of the car. She knew it. Add that to the growing list of reasons she hated Kareem.

He stepped closer, his expression so icy it dropped the temperature of the room into the negative digits. "Now I have a question for you, my loving, trustworthy, loyal wife."

Something was trickling down her inner thighs now, dripping to her ankles and the floor, and she wrapped her dress closer, covering her nakedness while she waited for the accusation that was surely coming.

"Who do you suppose tipped the feds off about my warehouse over on Muirwood?"

Kira froze.

"They raided it this afternoon. Did you know that? Guess what they found?"

Kira kept her mouth shut, praying they'd found a thousand kilos of heroin and arrested Kareem on charges that could put him away for consecutive lifetimes with no possibility of parole. But then he smiled with genuine amusement and the brief surge of hope she'd felt shriveled to dust.

"They found an empty warehouse."

No.

If ever in her life her poker face slipped, it was then. Because she understood it all in that one moment, and Kareem had won everything. It was a trap—the whole scene this morning, the paper, the ad, his reaction. All of it had been a test of her loyalty and she'd failed in the worst possible way.

Ironic, wasn't it? The man who'd claimed entrapment had entrapped her. The circle of life was in full effect, wasn't it? Now he'd taken her dog, her body and her hope. She didn't have one damn thing left.

"The thing you need to understand, baby," he said, smoothing her cheek with the gentle touch that had brought her so much ecstasy over the years, and she was so stunned that she couldn't even move away, "is that Kareem Gregory always wins. The feds have got nothing on me and there's nothing you can tell them about me. I'm going to be acquitted and then my life will go on as usual." He paused to run his thumb over her bottom lip and press a soft kiss to her mouth. "And you will be my wife until the day you die."

Finished with her at last, he turned and walked out. "I'm sorry it has to be like this between us."

Yeah. She was feeling pretty sorry herself right now.

Chapter 29

Jack was asleep.

He'd put his head on her chest and they'd talked. Then his voice slowed and eventually tapered off altogether. Now she heard the even and unmistakable deep breathing of a man sleeping like a baby.

What a beautiful sound.

A fierce feeling of protectiveness pulsed in her veins as she stroked his head. Those clowns out there better be quiet. That was all she could think. If anyone flushed that loud toilet or did the slightest thing to—

Outside the bedroom window came the sudden *thud-thud-thudding* of something coming closer, growing louder. Not the quiet footfalls of their two outside guards as they made the rounds through the night, circling the perimeter. Uh-uh. This was the sudden violent sound of something bad.

Oh, shit.

Her sudden jerk of fear woke Jack up with a start, or maybe the approaching unidentifiable danger did it for him. Whatever it was, he was suddenly wide awake, sitting upright and reaching for his gun on the nightstand, a warrior heading off to battle at a moment's notice.

Down below, men were shouting now, their voices raised with alarm.

Jack jumped out of bed, yanked his underwear on and tossed her his T-shirt.

She was just pulling it on when they heard the reverberating crash, as though a million full-length mirrors had dropped from the Empire State Building.

For one uncomprehending moment, they stared across the bed at each other.

Had . . . had someone just thrown something through the bay window in the living room?

And then Sammy's high-pitched screams rose through the night and the most unwelcome smell in the world hit their nostrils:

The sharp, head-rushing fumes of gasoline.

There was a noise behind her, and for one terrible moment Kira thought that Kareem had come back. Standing upright but still hanging on to the dresser because her spongy knees wouldn't support a flea right now, she looked in the mirror and saw her mother-in-law in the doorway, staring at Kira with an awful mixture of pity and shock on her face.

Wanda. Just the picker-upper she needed right now.

Kira's first instinct was to fake a smile and act like she and Kareem had just had a little spat, but her reflection looked so bad that that would be impossible.

Her hair was wrecked and the spot on her crown alternately stung and ached. Mascara streaked down her face in twin strips of tarry black. Her lipstick was smudged up to her nose and down to her chin. Her dress was gaping open again, her underwear ripped. And the bodily fluid that continued to trickle down her legs was, she now saw, blood. It had dripped onto the floor in a growing puddle that would never come out of the expensive oatmeal Berber, no matter how much scrubbing she did.

The only thing Kira could do at the moment was pull the halves of her dress together and tie the belt, so that's what she did.

The women's eyes met in the mirror and Wanda started to cry.

Kira knew how she felt, but now wasn't the time.

"You need to go to the emergency room, Baby Girl."

Wanda's use of an endearment was so startling that Kira gaped for a minute, words sticking in her throat. Wanda had never used a nickname for her, and if she'd been so inclined, the choice probably would have been *bitch* rather than *baby girl*.

"No," Kira said. "I need to find my dog."

"Your dog?" Now it was Wanda's turn to be speechless. She hurried inside the room, turned Kira to face her and gripped her shoulders. "You could call the police—"

"The police?" Wanda hadn't meant it as a joke, but damn, it sure was funny. Raw, hysterical laughter shot out of Kira's mouth, projecting ugliness in every direction. Wanda tightened her grip on Kira, supporting her. "Great idea, Wanda. The feds can't keep Kareem in jail, but I'm sure the local police will solve all my problems with a domestic violence charge. And while I'm at it, I'll get a restraining order, too. That'll scare Kareem."

The laughter continued until Wanda shook Kira,

and then the hysteria took over. There was something about seeing concern in this woman's eyes and feeling a motherly touch from Wanda, of all people, that was more than Kira could handle tonight.

"What do you need?" Wanda asked, and that was when Kira burst into tears.

Hating herself for it, she sobbed for five seconds and rested her head on Wanda's shoulder. Wanda smelled like comfort—like powder-freshness, flowers and rain. Kira wanted to stay there forever, but staying there wouldn't bring Max back.

"I need to put my clothes on and go find my dog."

Wanda was aghast as Kira pulled away and rummaged in a drawer for some jeans.

"You can't go out in the cold in the middle of the night looking for that dog, Kira. You can barely walk."

"That's what I'm doing," Kira said flatly. "You can't stop me."

After a long look and a frustrated sigh, Wanda seemed to decide that there was no talking Kira out of this decision. "I'll help you. Let me get my shoes."

Come again? Kira would sooner expect Wanda to run Max over with her car than help find him.

Kira was so unspeakably grateful that she couldn't quite stop another surge of tears, embarrassing as they were. Wanda brought her in for a kiss, and the women were standing together when Kerry Randolph appeared in the doorway, making them both jump.

Whoa.

Kerry had no idea what he'd walked in on, but it was some serious shit. Serious and bad. Staring at the boss's wife was never a good idea, especially when the boss was a known killer and the wife was standing half naked in her bedroom, where Kerry had no right to be, but Kerry couldn't help staring at Kira Gregory on a good day, when she was fully dressed.

This was nowhere close to a good day.

The women jumped with surprise and then huddled together, trying to hide Kira without being obvious about it. Kira did something with the belt on her dress, but it was too late and the neurons had started firing in Kerry's brain. Blinking, he added it all together: the dress . . . the hair . . . the puffy eyes and streaked makeup.

Trying to be discreet about it, he shifted his gaze lower, to what he'd thought he'd seen. And, yeah, it was . . . Blood. On the insides of her legs.

Holy fucking shit.

Kira had been attacked. Probably worse than that, but let's go with *attacked* for now. The boss's wife had been attacked and the boss wasn't screaming for anyone's head. That must mean that . . .

"Kareem did this to you."

It wasn't a question, so Kerry didn't treat it like one. If he'd had any doubts about what'd happened, they disappeared when he saw the way the women's gazes skittered away from his.

Then Wanda started lying, to protect her piece of shit son, no doubt. "There's nothing here for you to worry about, Kerry." Wanda handed Kira a tissue from the pocket of her slacks and finally looked at Kerry with anger flashing in her eyes. "What are you doing here?"

Kerry barely heard her because he was so focused on Kira and his sudden, blinding need to kill Kareem. Something about the way she kept her head low, as though she needed to be ashamed or something, infuriated him worse than he'd ever been in his life.

Kareem had taken this woman, his *wife,* who was proud and strong and had delicate bones and fine skin and probably didn't weigh one-twenty-five soaking wet with four layers of clothes on, and used her the way no one should use a ten-dollar pro on the street.

Kareem had killed Yogi, too, but this was somehow worse.

This was *Kira*.

Kerry wanted to find Kareem, clip his balls off with a pair of gardening sheers and shove them down his throat, one at a time.

"Did Kareem do this to you?" he asked, his low voice vibrating with the effort it took to remain calm. "Did he touch you?"

She flinched and turned away, to look at a blank stretch of wall, and Kerry felt like a slimy-ass garden slug for making her feel worse than she already did, but, Jesus, he had to know.

"No," she said.

"Bullshit." Kerry wheeled around, heading for the door with murder in his heart. "Where is he? In his bedroom?"

Both women cried out and Wanda hurried over to dig her manicured nails in Kerry's arm. Kerry shook her off, but she just grabbed him again. *"Don't."* Wanda all but dropped to her knees in a full-out beg. "He'll kill you. You know he will."

If Kerry had been in his right mind, he'd've taken a moment to reflect on and laugh at the irony of Kareem's mother finally opening her eyes to the fact that she'd raised a murderer for a son. But the only thing on his mind right now was Kareem's blood, and how satisfying and hot it would feel flowing through his fingers.

Jerking free a second time, he stalked out of the room and ignored the women calling after him. It was all he could do not to roar with bloodlust like the Incredible Hulk or a rampaging tyrannosaur. He thought of Kira's abused body and the slump to her shoulders. He thought of the blood and her tear-streaked face. He thought of the quiet despair in her eyes and knew that she was irreparably damaged if not ruined. And he thought of how sick to death he was of being scared and doing nothing and letting his life be ruled by Kareem Gregory, psychopath.

"Kareem."

Kerry banged into the bedroom, not bothering to knock. That in itself was a serious offense punishable by beating, if not death. Looking around, he took a minute to get his bearings. The place was an Egyptian palace, with all kinds of moody lighting, black and gold furniture and chairs and shit, and a massive four-poster bed that could fit half of Texas in it.

There was no sign of Kareem, but . . . whoa, the heavy-sweet smell of wine hit him in a wave and he reeled from it, nearly getting a contact high. Was Kareem shampooing his carpets with the stuff?

"Kareem," he said again, and that was when he heard it.

The soft, broken sounds of a wounded animal or a man crying.

The shock glued Kerry's feet to the floor and he paused, listened, and heard it again—quiet but unmistakable sobbing.

It was coming from the walk-in closet, which was one of those deals like the men's department at Nordstrom, with lighted wooden shelves and the clothes hanging in neat rows, separated by color.

In the far corner, sitting on the floor with his back to the wall, a spilled bottle of wine next to him and his shoulders heaving with his face buried in his hands, was Kareem.

Kerry stared.

Kareem looked up. His face was a destroyed mess of snot and tears that he didn't bother to hide. Apparently he was beyond pride at this moment, beyond dignity. "She doesn't love me, man. She doesn't love me."

Kerry said nothing.

Kareem seemed to take this as encouragement to continue wallowing in his self-pity. "I've got nothing."

Kerry glanced around at the dozens of thousand-dollar suits, the shoes, the ties. He thought of the money, the house and the cars. All of it might well be seized by the DEA at any second, but it was Kareem's at the moment and it was worth a pretty penny.

Then he remembered Kira's blood and tears.

Yeah. Kareem had nothing.

After a while, Kareem's crying tapered off to sniffles, and then he got himself together and stood. Producing a tissue from somewhere, he swiped at his face, taking care of most of the snot, but not all.

Kerry tried not to vomit and wondered why he wasn't man enough to pull out his piece and shoot Kareem through the eyes right now. God knew he'd be doing the world a favor.

Kareem slung his arm around Kerry's shoulder. "You're a good man, Kerry. I know I can trust you. You're all I've got left."

Resisting the urge to throw off that arm, Kerry listened. Waited. Hoped.

"My trial should end tomorrow," Kareem said. "Hopefully by tomorrow I should have my life back."

"Right."

"Are you ready to do some work with me?" Kareem continued. "Get some new responsibilities?"

At last. Kerry's heart rate kicked up with relief and excitement, but he kept his expression blank and, he hoped, humble. He nodded. "Yeah. I'm ready."

"Good." Smiling with satisfaction, Kareem clapped his free hand to Kerry's jaw, pulled him in, and planted a kiss on his cheek, the twisted fuck. "Let's go."

Chapter 30

Get her out of here.

That was all Jack could think.

It was all a trap; he knew that.

Assassin 101: throw a firebomb in the house, wait for the targets to run for their lives, and pick them off as they stream out. Either a bullet kills them or the fire does.

Simple.

So if they ran out now, there was a pretty good chance of being shot. On the other hand, if they stayed in here, they were certain to burn. Already smoke was seeping under the door and he could almost swear the floor felt hot against his bare feet, which meant that the flames below were soaring to the ceiling already.

Not good.

Sammy's scream was bad news, but Jack's responsibility right now was making sure Amara lived even if no one else did.

So he took a chair and smashed it through the back window, the one that faced the small woods behind the house. Then he grabbed her arm and swung her around.

"We're going out this way." He tucked his gun in the waistband of his underwear. "We can't risk the stairs. I'll go first so I can break your fall. It's not that far."

"Jack—" Terror was wide in her eyes. A gun was one thing but the roaring flames of hell were quite another and damn if he couldn't hear them coming closer.

He shook her. "Don't argue with me, Bunny."

"Okay." She took a deep breath and, just that quick, got herself together. "Okay."

"Okay." Pressing a quick kiss to her lips, for luck, he swung himself over the sill, cutting his legs all to shreds in the process. He ignored the pain. Flipping over, he eased himself out until he dangled by his fingers. Then he said a quick prayer and let go.

The ground and the outstretched branches of a tree rushed up to meet him and he landed in a crouch that strained his tight ankles nearly to the breaking point.

Straightening, he looked to the window for Amara, well aware that the house was now an inferno that lit up the night sky, so hot that he almost couldn't stand even being in its perimeter. Soon the flames would burn through to the second floor and this whole place would be a smoldering heap of embers.

"Jump, Amara," he roared, holding his arms out to catch her and break her fall.

She had her head stuck out the window and nodded. Raising one foot to climb over, she was almost out when she screamed.

Jack's heart stopped dead.

A shadow of a figure moved behind her and suddenly she disappeared, yanked back away from the window. Jesus. No.

"Amara," he screamed. "Amara!"

Nothing.

No. He wasn't going to let that woman go. No, no, NO.

And if she was going to die tonight, he was damn sure going to die with her.

Wheeling around in his panic, he spotted the tree and its beautiful, beautiful branches.

Climb, motherfucker.

He climbed.

Scraping his already torn legs, he gripped the rough trunk with his bare toes and shimmied for all he was worth. Then the ledge was under his fingertips again and he was vaulting back inside the burning house.

He wasn't prepared for the scene:

Amara and another dark figure in black, struggling. Amara screaming and raising her hand—what the hell was she holding?—high overhead. Amara lowering her arm with a slash. The man's horrified and disoriented surprise as she buried her knitting needles in the side of his neck, near the shoulder.

One stunned moment passed. The man teetered, wide-eyed and stunned, not quite sure what'd happened to him. Then he lunged for her again.

Uh-uh. Not on my watch. Jack grabbed his gun from behind his back, steadied his hand, aimed and fired.

This latest killer grimaced and dropped, hard, leaving a sobbing and hysterical Amara to collapse into Jack's waiting arms.

* * *

"Honey?"

Dwayne Barber stretched and yawned that first jaw-cracking yawn of the morning, the one that always felt so good and got the day started just right. That, and sex, which was why he'd woken up. His morning erection was the size of the oak in the front yard and if they were quick about it, he wouldn't have to jerk himself off in the shower right before he left for work.

Where was that woman? "Honey?"

No answer.

But . . . oh, yeah, there was a thread of light seeping out from under the bathroom door. She was definitely in the bathroom. Again. Clearly some digestive issues were going on there. He'd have to ask her about it later. For now, he slipped out of bed, tiptoed across the cold floor and tapped on the door.

It was ajar.

"Honey?"

The silence was becoming a little weird when the smell saturated his nostrils with the slamming force of a poorly executed dive into the deep end.

It was a catalogue of the most disgusting stenches in the world: shit, vomit and urine, all layered together.

Jesus—no. Please, *no*.

The finality of it registered before the sight did.

Marian. His beautiful wife. Lying on the floor in puddles of her own filth, a bottle of prescription pills at the tips of her outstretched fingers.

"Amara," Jack said.

Amara couldn't bring herself to look at him, so she

stared out the window instead. They were at their third hotel together, where the agents had smuggled them after they'd all nearly been killed. Sammy had been badly burned and Amara and Jack had jointly killed a man. Another hotel. Funny, huh? A hotel was where she and Jack had begun their short-lived non-relationship.

Would they also end it in one? This one?

She tried not to hear the agents moving around in the other room, getting ready to take Jack to court to finish his testimony and let him watch the rest of the trial. She tried to pretend she'd see Jack later, but the stark terror in her gut and the silent knowledge in her heart said otherwise.

"Amara," he said again. "It's time."

Time. Yeah. Okay. She could do this.

It took more strength than she'd known she had to turn around and face him and then more again to muster up a quarter smile. She wouldn't tell him. What would she say? *I think you're going to die today, so be sure to drive safe, you hear?*

He had on that awful bulletproof vest over his clothes and she tried to let that be some comfort, but it wasn't. She almost wanted to tell him to take it off and be comfortable. A bulletproof vest wasn't going to stop Kareem Gregory. If she'd learned anything since this whole misbegotten adventure began, it was that. How many times already had Jack dodged Death? Three—no, four. Death would only be denied for so long.

Their gazes held across the distance of the room and he hovered just inside the doorway as though he felt, like she did, that getting too close right now wasn't the brightest idea in the world. He had no smile for her, reminding her of the days back at the Twelfth Street Diner, and his dark eyes were filled with darker emotions that she couldn't read.

Did he feel it, too, this overwhelming sense of impending doom?

"I don't want you to go," she told him.

"It's time."

"I still don't want you to go."

"I have to."

Yeah. She knew that. Not that the knowing made the understanding any easier.

"You'll be careful, right?"

"Yeah."

She nodded, as satisfied as she could be under the circumstances because that was all she could ask for. Neediness wasn't her thing, or at least it hadn't been until she laid eyes on Jack, but there was one thing she needed to know.

"If we'd met . . . I don't know . . . in a bar or at a wedding or at the bookstore . . . do you ever think about that?"

"Not much." A flicker of amusement lit his eyes. "Just a hundred times a day."

Laughter tried to bubble up from her throat but it jammed with the repressed tears already trapped there until she felt the burn of both. "Is—is there anything you'd have done differently?"

He paused, hesitating for so long she began to feel foolish and felt the color rise across her cheeks. *Brilliant, Amara. What'd you expect him to say? That he'd've dropped to one knee and proposed on the spot the second he saw you?* Now she'd embarrassed him and the only thing that remained was for him to weasel out of answering at all or come up with a lame-o answer that didn't hurt her feelings too much.

Yeah, sure, Amara—I'd've asked for your number so I could text you.

Something like that.

"I'd've walked up to you and told you that I can't breathe when I look at you. And then I'd've hustled you out of wherever we were and had you flat on your back with your thighs around my waist in fifteen minutes or less. That's what I'd've done."

Jesus. The man didn't play around, did he?

The answer surprised her, and the look on his face when he said it devastated her. There was no humor or smarm, no attempts to avoid her gaze or hurry out of the room before she asked something worse. Only the blazing intensity of a man who meant both what he said and what he didn't say.

"Come here."

He held out a hand and she edged around the bed to slide her palm against his cool one, still careful not to come too close. He respected the distance but reeled her close enough to rest his lips against her forehead, kissing her and holding her hand and wrist in both of his.

They stood like that for a long time, until one of the agents—Amara didn't bother looking around to see who—walked by with a discreet cough. "We need to go, Parker."

Jack nodded.

Amara stared down at their intertwined hands through the hot tears she'd sworn she wouldn't let fall. "You won't leave for good without telling me goodbye, will you?"

"No," he whispered.

"This isn't it, is it?"

"No," he said again, and she heard the blocked emotion in his voice.

Okay. Deep breath, girl. Take a deep breath.

If this wasn't good-bye, then she could let him go and she could fight back all the screaming demons telling her that this was good-bye whether they knew it or not.

She could do this.

She looked up and smiled into his face, which was blurred from her tears. "I'll see you later, then."

"I'll see you later."

Kerry Randolph stood at the Kentucky side of the Purple People Bridge over the Ohio River and stared at the skyline. Cincinnati. His city. He'd grown up here and gone wrong here and now he wanted to take another look from the bridge he'd just trekked half a mile across.

Purple People Bridge. How stupid was that?

It was a pretty bridge, though, and a pretty city, even under today's cold gray skies.

From here he could see all the familiar landmarks: Paul Brown Stadium, where he'd watched the Bengals lose more games than he could count and kept going back for more, the Underground Railroad Freedom Center and Great American Ball Park, where he could keep one eye on the Reds while eating the best cheesy nachos in the world.

The cell phone in his hand weighed him down and he thought about chucking it into the river. That would be fun, wouldn't it? And satisfying even if it wouldn't solve a damn thing. He looked at the lighted display, as if that would help him decide, but inspiration did not strike.

Thoughts jockeyed for position in his mind.

Like how he'd tried to do something with his life but was now little better than Kareem. Like Yogi, and how he'd been shot in the back of his head for an imagined wrong against the man he'd faithfully served for years. Like this city he loved and whether he'd ever see it again if he did what he was thinking of doing.

Like Kira. Always Kira.

Last, he thought about how nice it would be if, for once, he managed to look himself in the face when he shaved at the mirror.

That last thought decided him.

Taking a deep breath, he dialed.

"Brady."

Another deep breath. "It's me. I know where the warehouse is."

An exasperated sigh, and then, "And I've got four pairs of balls."

Kerry kept quiet, waited.

Brady's voice, rapid-fire now with excitement, came back on the line. "Are you shitting me—?"

"No."

"—because I spent yesterday getting a search warrant and tossing a warehouse that didn't have anything in it but warehouse, so I don't have time—"

"He took me there this morning," Kerry said. "He's got two hundred kilos of horse."

"Where is it?"

This was it. The part where Kerry either fished or cut bait. He could hang up now, toss his phone in the river and later claim it had all been a mistake.

Or he could man up, grow a pair at this late stage of his life and do the right thing.

Taking a last minute to linger in the first half of his life, the half spent in plain view, he looked across at the city he loved and said good-bye because soon he'd never see it again.

"Not so fast," he told Brady. "I want immunity. And I want to go into WITSEC."

"Has the jury reached a verdict?"

"We have, your honor."

The moment had all the hushed-silence drama of a TV movie of the week. Jack shifted on the balls of his feet, waiting, his nerves stretched to the snapping point. On either side of him stood the two agents who'd escorted him to court for the second half of his testimony. The plan was for them to hear the verdict and leave. Immediately. Normally he wouldn't have stayed, but he needed to be here and see how this whole fuck fest turned out.

The jury had come back way too quickly.

Reading juries was like reading tea leaves while blindfolded, but Jack had this one nailed. They looked too upbeat for a group about to send a man back to federal prison, which could only mean one thing: Kareem Gregory was about to walk.

He knew it too. Up at the defendant's table, the motherfucker stood with his lawyer and tried to look humble, but from where he stood in the gallery, Jack could see the smug smile hovering just beneath the surface. Maybe Gregory felt the daggers Jack was staring into his back, because he glanced over his shoulder, caught his gaze and held it.

Then he winked.

Something went off inside Jack's head, a lightning flash of rage that had him in motion before he could even register what he was doing. All he knew was that it was long past time for that piece of shit to stop taking up space on the planet, and if the judicial system wouldn't take care of him, then Jack would.

With a low growl, he took two steps to edge past the agent on his left and into the aisle, but they each caught an arm and held him back. He jerked free, seething, and reminded himself that Kareem's time would come.

Up at the bench, the judge read the various counts and charges and blah-blah-blah, finally getting to the piece of information they'd all been waiting for:

"Not guilty."

No.

The protesting voice inside Jack was quiet compared to the controlled pandemonium erupting all around him. On Kareem's side of the courtroom, people shouted and laughed and received stern warnings about decorum from the judge, as if they cared about that now that their boy had just walked. On the fed side: lots of long faces and dark mutterings among the U.S. attorneys. Inside Jack: utter disbelief.

No.

He had not sacrificed his life and career for this moment. This moment was supposed to be about justice, about avenging his murdered mother and putting a drug-dealing killer behind bars. It wasn't about that sorry-ass bitch getting away with one more thing in his accursed life.

Jack blinked and stared at the flash of movement

and colors all around him, seeing nothing, understanding nothing.

He thought about Mom. He thought about Amara being shot. He thought about the fire last night and how they all could easily have been killed because of that one man's vendetta. He thought about the life he'd given up and the one he'd never have, one with Amara in it, and children . . . a home . . . comfort . . . safety. Everything had been for nothing.

No.

Once again, his feet started moving with no conscious thought on his part. His babysitters tried to stop him, but he shook them off and shoved his way through the crowd surrounding that walking, talking, breathing piece of shit.

And then they were face to face, staring at each other, with Jack flanked by his sputtering and unhappy escorts who probably wanted to wring his neck for such an egregious breach of the procedures put in place for his safety.

Jack didn't care.

They stared at each other, he and Kareem. Jack choked back his rage as the man's triumphant smile widened, as though the only thing that could make this wonderful moment better was sharing it with his favorite DEA agent.

Sticking out his hand, Jack smiled, too.

Surprise widened Kareem's eyes, but he was a player through and through, always ready for a game. He took Jack's hand in his firm grip and Jack grabbed his shoulder with his free left hand, pulling him in hard to murmur in his ear.

"We'll get you in the end, motherfucker."

Kareem tsked. "Don't hate the player, man. Hate

the game. You remember what I told you, don't you, Jack?"

"You remember this: I'll get you if it's the last thing I ever do."

Kareem pulled back to look Jack in the eye with that flat gaze of his that was blacker than the heart of hell. "You've already done the last thing you'll ever do, Jack."

Chapter 31

"This way, Parker."

The escorts on either side steered Jack down the steps into the narrow alley behind the federal courthouse, which was good because Jack was too numb to manage any personal navigation himself. The night air was so cold and harsh that he could almost feel his pores shrink and his blood turn to ice. The vest on top of his coat weighed him down more than his disappointment already did, pressing his shoulders and reminding him—as if he needed any reminders—that he would never be safe while Kareem Gregory lived.

His days were numbered, and for all he knew he'd hit the big zero already. Now that the trial was over, he and Amara would go their separate ways and never see each other again. Tomorrow, maybe, or the next day at the outside.

She'd return to Mount Adams, safe and free, thank God. But he'd never lay eyes on her again and the few precious days they'd had together weren't enough. His mouth soured with the vile bitterness of it. *Weren't. Fucking. Enough.*

Trudging down the alley toward the idling SUV that would take them back to the hotel, he thought of all the things he'd've said to her in another life, if he'd had one:

You're mine.

I claim you. I want you. I need you.

I love you.

Let's make a baby together. Tonight. Now.

All things he'd never get to say and she never needed to know. What was the point in telling her? He was selfish, but he wasn't that selfish and he wouldn't whisper words to her that could make her hope or tie her to him. Even he wouldn't be that much of a bastard.

They had tonight, though and—

A flash of movement above them snagged his peripheral vision.

Ah, shit.

He looked up, but there was nothing on top of the building but black on top of black layered with black. The men on either side of him apparently noticed nothing because they never broke stride. And they were almost at the SUV.

Pulse kicking and pounding, in his throat, temples, chest and ears, Jack stepped up his pace. This was going to happen one day but, Lord, not tonight. Please, not tonight. Not before he saw Amara a last time.

He scanned the alley, looking . . . looking . . . and that was when he saw it.

There. On his chest. A red pinpoint ball of light that shouldn't be there.

Stark terror froze the breath in his lungs and his feet in their tracks.

No. Not tonight, God. He'd promised her he'd say good-bye.

"Amara," he whispered.

Amara sat on the edge of the bed in the dark, knowing.

She knew before one of the agent's cell phones rang in the next room and she heard their hushed, urgent murmurings. She knew before the knock on the open bedroom door disturbed her thoughts. She knew before she looked up and saw the quiet sorrow on Billy Bob's shadowed face.

Jack was dead and he hadn't even told her good-bye.

Jack, just like everyone else in her entire life, had left her.

"Amara," Billy Bob began gently.

The room spun and Amara slid off the bed to the floor, where she screamed and screamed and screamed.

Kareem sipped from his fizzing flute of Krug, watching his guests and experiencing the kind of satisfaction he hadn't felt since this nightmare began.

It was just a small and late dinner party with a handful of people because a big blowout tonight would be tacky and Kareem was all about class and taste. That was why he'd brought out the Krug, which he'd been saving for a celebration. A moment like this needed expensive wine.

What did he have?

An acquittal, with his whole life in front of him.

Jackson Parker dead at the hands of Hector's shooter

and in a zippered bag on his way to the coroner's office, with a bullet in his chest and a tag on his big toe; and, best of all, a fresh chance with his wife.

They still had some problems to work through, though, and last night hadn't gone well. That was why she was upstairs rather than here by his side. But everything between them would be different now that he was free. Now that she knew he'd never let her go, they could work on their marriage from the ground up and everything would be okay.

Picking up his fork, he went to work on the lamb chops. He was chewing with pleasure when he glanced up and caught Mama's eye down at the other end of the table.

What the hell was she looking at him like *that* for?

Like he had a big smear of shit on his face. What was wrong with her? She'd been acting funny all day, but he wasn't about to let anything harsh his mellow tonight. Not tonight.

Kerry was late, though. The party couldn't hit full swing until his top man got here, but he'd slap Kerry on the wrist for his tardiness later.

Wiping his mouth, he replaced the heavy linen napkin in his lap and tapped his glass with his knife. Everyone paused and looked around, and he smiled benevolently on them like the gracious host he was. "I just want to thank you all for coming tonight on such short notice—"

"We heard there'd be food," someone called, and they all laughed.

"—and for being here with me celebrating this wonderful night. The judicial system works, right? Go figure."

They laughed again, and he raised his glass for the toast. "To the American justice system—"

A sudden, violent pounding on the front door stopped him dead.

Around the big table, everyone froze, their eyes wide.

No.

He'd heard that sound before, but . . . No. It couldn't—

Kareem started to rise, tried to flash his guests a reassuring smile, but that was when the shouts of what seemed like a hundred voices came through the walls, loud and clear.

"Police! Search warrant!"

"DEA! Search warrant!"

And then, right before his disbelieving eyes, while he was crouched over his chair, half up and half down, the heavy front door with its beveled glass detail shuddered, splintered and flew open.

A stream of people paraded in, an invading army right here in America, all suited up in dark gear with helmets, goggles, boots, gloves and assorted battering rams and assault rifles, all pointed at Kareem and his scared-shitless guests, who couldn't hold their hands up and hit the floor fast enough.

Everywhere Kareem looked, he saw a snarling face over a weapon pointed at his chest. Everywhere he looked, he saw three tall letters on every jacket, emblazoned in yellow and taunting him here, at his dinner party to celebrate his renewed freedom:

DEA.

No.

Kareem stood all the way up and squared his shoulders. They weren't going to take him out like this. Not in his own damn house in front of his friends and—

The goon in front stepped up and gestured to the floor with his pistol, which he held in both steady hands. *Brady;* Kareem recognized him through the goggles and the gear.

"Get down, Kareem," he said.

Behind him, the other agents fanned out to loom over the facedown guests and search them for hidden forks or some shit.

Fury such as he had rarely known roared up from Kareem's chest, burning his neck and face with its heat. "What the fuck do you think you're—"

Without warning, Brady flashed into movement and elbowed Kareem in the gut. Kareem sank to his knees like a cinder block, winded, and Brady's heavy and hard foot in his back helped him the rest of the way down. Before Kareem could even blink, Brady'd cuffed his arms behind him.

He kept his foot on his back as though he enjoyed it.

Gasping with the pain in his ribs, which was bad enough, and the frustrated humiliation, which was worse, Kareem turned his nose out of the Indian rug and glared up at Brady with his one available eye. "Tha—that's unnecessary force, isn't it, Brady?"

Brady shrugged, clicked the safety back on his weapon and holstered it. The pressure of that boot between Kareem's shoulder blades increased. "Yeah. I'll feel terrible about it, too, when they put a warning letter in my personnel file."

Kareem's lungs pumped harder, trying to adjust. "Raided another one of my empty warehouses today, have you?"

"Actually, no."

Brady removed his foot and, bending down, hauled Kareem to his feet so they could face each other. Kareem had the terrible sinking feeling Brady wanted to see his reaction when he told him this next part. "Today we raided one of your warehouses with drugs in it. Guess what we found?"

Despite himself, despite all his best efforts, Kareem felt his jaw drop with horror.

"We're still logging it all, but we figure it must be, oh, two-hundred-and-fifty kilos of the Mexicans' finest heroin and coke. Oh, and there was some Mary Jane in there, too, wasn't there?"

"Yeah," said a passing agent.

"So," Dexter continued with that smug sarcasm that made Kareem want to rip his face from his skull with his fingernails, "I'm not real good on the math, but I'm thinking at, say, twenty-eight large a kilo, we're looking at a haul of about seven mil. That's a pretty good day for me."

Kareem couldn't help himself. "Yeah, but you lost Parker today, didn't you?"

They stared at each other.

Then Brady elbowed him again in the same spot and renewed agony erupted, shooting out of every pore in Kareem's body.

"That's for Parker," Brady said as Kareem dropped to his knees. "And for Wolfe and Reed."

Kareem gritted his teeth, refusing to cry out. "I'm going to sue you for every last fucking dime—"

"Feel free," Brady said, looking around. "Anyone see how poor Kareem here got injured?"

The answers came in a chorus from the nearby agents.

"Not me, boss."

"I didn't see nothing."

"I was looking the other way. Sorry."

Through the searing pain and the taunting, one thought crystallized for Kareem.

The one new person who knew about the warehouse. The one person who should have been here tonight, but wasn't. The one person he'd trusted.

"Kerry," he roared.

Kira packed two hours later, after the agents had finished searching the house.

It didn't take long.

A toothbrush and other toiletries, a couple pairs of jeans and a few sweaters were all she threw into her rolling carry-on. All the designer clothes and shoes stayed right where they were in her Mariah Carey closet.

She took off her fake diamond ring and left it in its crystal bowl on the nightstand. Too bad the feds wouldn't recover any money off it if they seized it. The taxpayers could stand to recover a little something after all the damage Kareem had done.

Standing in her bedroom for what she knew would be the last time, she felt nothing but relief. That, and emptiness.

Now was the time to do it because it was now or never. How long was she going to wait for the perfect moment? Until she was seventy and they'd celebrated their golden anniversary?

She'd wanted to get past the trial to see if he was convicted. Well, he wasn't convicted but the trial was over. She'd wanted to sell her ring for the money, but she didn't have the ring. She'd wanted to get her degree and now she had her degree because she'd sailed through her last finals today.

"Going somewhere, Mrs. Gregory?"

Dexter Brady's slow drawl came from the doorway and it sparked prickles of something—she wasn't sure what—along her skin. Even so, she couldn't face him. She took one last look around, and then she was ready.

"I'm leaving my husband." She edged past him, wheeling her suitcase behind her. "Maybe you can call me Kira now."

He pivoted to watch her go. "We can give you a ride. I've spoken to the U.S. Attorney's Office about getting you into WITSEC—"

Well, there it was. Everything she'd hoped and prayed for and she no longer gave a damn. No one had protected her last night, had they? There was no protection from Kareem. None at all. Anyway, she knew nothing that would help the feds, other than she'd once seen Kareem take too many aspirin.

So Kira kept walking toward the staircase. "No thanks. I don't need your help."

He called after her with alarm in his voice, but she ignored him. At the bottom of the steps, she turned into the living room, where Kareem sat, handcuffed, on one sofa, and his mother sat on another. Kareem's lawyer, Jacob Radcliffe, had arrived, and they all looked around when she walked in.

She only had eyes for Kareem. "I'm leaving."

He smirked. Even handcuffed, arrested and facing

the prospect of hard time in federal prison, no one did smug quite like Kareem. "You're not leaving. You belong to me. We settled that last night."

There was no point arguing with him. Whether he believed she was leaving for good or not was his business, not hers. Either way, she'd be gone.

Without another word, she headed for the front door, which, conveniently, hung at a crooked angle off its hinges, and pulled her cell phone out of her pocket to call for a cab. She didn't have much money, but she had enough to get her started.

Behind her, reality finally seemed to be sinking into Kareem's thick skull. When he yelled at her, she heard the rising panic in his taunting voice. "*Kira.* You can't go nowhere. You're *nothing* without me. You don't have *shit* without me. Now get your ass back here. Kira. *Kira!*"

Kira paused to think about what she had and whether he was right.

She had her degree. She had a few clothes and a little money. Best of all, she had Max—whom she and Wanda had found shivering in the woods behind the house last night—waiting at the kennel for her where he was safe.

No, she decided. Kareem was wrong.

She left, walking out the door without a backward glance.

Chapter 32

Mount Adams, Washington, One Month Later

"So, we've got a deal?" Katie O'Farrell recapped her pen and extended her hand over the table.

"We've got a deal," Amara said.

They shook and Katie grinned the grin of the well pleased, as she should. The old Amara generally didn't bargain and encouraged her clients to take their chances on the jury and Amara's skills as a lawyer. The new Amara realized that life was short and not all fights were worth fighting.

This case, where Amara's client was caught dead-to-rights selling to an undercover vice cop, fell squarely into that category. Better for her idiot client to plead out than face serious jail time.

Not that Amara gave half a rat's ass one way or the other.

If forced at gunpoint, Amara doubted she could come up with anything she cared about, starting with the watered-down red dreck in her bowl that someone in the kitchen was calling chili. Dispirited, she swirled her spoon in it and wished—God, she *wished*—she had a bowl of Jack's chicken and noodles instead.

Over at the grill was the new fry cook, a woman who didn't know which end of a spatula was up. Her soups were thin, her pork chops tough. To add insult to injury, she didn't fill out the white T-shirt, jeans and apron anything like Jack had.

Katie followed her line of sight. "Things aren't the same without Chef Hottie, are they?"

"No," Amara agreed.

"And I miss J-Mart. His brother's an ass. He only gave me two packs of crackers with my salad the other day."

"I know."

Katie twisted back around and settled against the booth. "How was your vacation?"

Amara stared at her.

Vacation. Hah.

She thought of the shootings and near-shootings and the absolute terror. She thought of the white-hot pain of a bullet tearing into her flesh. She thought of the would-be assassins. And then she thought of Jack's arms around her and his whispering voice in her ear. She thought of his smile, his kiss and his touch.

"Vacation was perfect."

"I'm thinking you need to get your money back. You don't look so good."

Amara knew how she looked: thin and wan with dull eyes and a mouth that had forgotten to smile. If she lived another fifty years she imagined she'd look the same way.

"I'm a little tired," she said.

Tired was such a small word to describe how she

felt now that even the simple acts of rising in the morning and dressing for work were as monumental as clawing her way to the top of Denali with only her fingernails to keep her hanging on.

Maybe tomorrow would be better. This was the mantra that kept her putting one foot in front of the other. Maybe tomorrow.

Scooting to the edge of the booth, she stood and grabbed her coat, the purple scarf she'd finally finished knitting, and her briefcase, desperate to be anywhere but here in her own skin.

"I think I'll just go on home," she said.

Katie called after her, concern contracting her brows as though Amara had announced plans to undergo a lobotomy. "I thought you had more work to do tonight."

"Nah." Amara waved and kept moving. "I need to work on my knitting. I just started an afghan."

Pausing only long enough to shove her arms into her coat and sling her briefcase over her shoulder, Amara went out into the night, ducked her head against the wind, and trudged down the sidewalk toward her car. After twenty feet or so, her brain registered the sound of a big engine pacing her right at the curb and she looked to her left in time to see a dark SUV roll to a stop and the passenger side door fly open.

Out climbed a big guy with dark pants and a jacket emblazoned with her least favorite letters of the federal alphabet:

DEA.

"Well, well, well." Watching him approach, she wrestled with the primitive urge to smash his unsmiling face with the business side of her briefcase. "If it isn't Special Agent Mateo Garciaparra."

"If it isn't the DEA's biggest pain in the ass."

"What are you doing here? I thought you belonged to the Cincinnati office now."

"I've got business here." He jerked his head at the car and held the door open for her. "Get in. We need to talk to you."

For the first time in a month, she felt the kick of adrenaline as it surged through her body and reminded her she wasn't dead—not physically, anyway. Planting her hands on her hips, she stood firm with no intention of getting into the car with this idiot.

"Why's that? Have you finally decided to explain why I couldn't attend Jack's funeral? Or maybe you're going to explain why the DEA's finest walked him out of the courthouse in full view of a sniper rather than sneaking him out through the underground garage, which is the normal procedure when there's a threat?"

Cocking her head, she tapped her lip with mock concentration and hope. "Or could it be that you're going to explain why he was issued a vest that was so faulty it let a bullet right through, no problem. Is *that* what you want to talk—"

"I want to talk about your letter-writing campaign, ma'am. Complaining to our senator and every other higher-up with a mailbox? Not cool."

"What?" Oh, this was too much. Waaay too much. "You have the nerve to complain about my behavior when I am merely trying to get to the bottom of your administration's incompetence and—"

"Shut up and get in."

Ex*cuse* me? Federal officers weren't supposed to talk to taxpayers like that, and she was about to tell him so when he grabbed her upper arm, swung her around and all but threw her into the passenger seat.

"Ma'am," he added, like that one polite word could disguise the fact that she was being abducted off a public street. Before she knew what'd happened, Mateo Garciaparra, kidnapper extraordinaire, had jumped into the seat behind her and they were pulling away from the curb and speeding off into the night.

"What the hell are you doing?" she screeched, addressing the driver, Mateo, the guy sitting beside Mateo in the backseat, God, and anyone else who might be listening. Her legal training kicked in and she asserted her rights. "Where are you taking me? Because if you're charging me with something, you need to charge me. And if you're not charging me, then you should release me—"

The driver, a dark-skinned guy with no traces of mercy or humanity in his expression, looked over at her with his implacable gaze. "You might want to do a little less yakking and buckle your seat belt," he drawled. "Ma'am."

It was on the tip of Amara's tongue to tell him exactly what he could do with his seat belt, but then they turned the corner onto the highway entrance ramp, whereupon he stomped the accelerator into the floor.

She buckled up and lapsed into a seething silence while she made a mental list of all the things she was going to sue the federal government for—false imprisonment, for one, assault if a bruise showed up on her arm, for another.

Cheered slightly by this prospect, she stared out the window and was surprised when, less than ten minutes later, they exited and followed the signs to a small private airport.

Great. They'd found a way to deport her even though she was a U.S. citizen.

She was eyeing her briefcase on the floor and wondering about her chances of fishing her cell phone out and punching 9-1-1 without anyone noticing—not good, probably, but what other options were there?—when they bypassed the terminal and zoomed straight into the open doors of a hangar and pulled up beside a small plane.

Determined not to miss a single detail for when she filed her formal complaint, she twisted around in her seat in time to see the massive doors close behind them, sealing them all inside with more swarming DEA agents and busy-bee mechanics, who seemed to be getting the plane ready for takeoff.

Now what?

Not fully up to speed with whatever plan they had for her—were they sending her back to Cincinnati, or maybe to Washington for some kind of debriefing?—she floundered and belatedly realized that everyone had gotten out of the SUV but her.

She got out, too, glancing around the hangar, which was lit like the Vegas strip on New Year's Eve. Though she had zero to no familiarity with private planes, she could see that this one was fairly new and decent-sized. Had they seized it from some Columbian drug lord? That was a happy thought. It was probably a Cessna or a Lear, not that she knew one from the other, and it was big enough that she wouldn't be white-knuckled with terror to fly anywhere in it.

Which was apparently the plan because Garciaparra jerked his head toward the steps. "Get on."

"Now wait just one minute—"

Whoa. The rest of her sentence shriveled and died. One good look at the flashing light in his eyes told her that something unpleasant was in her immediate future if she didn't climb those stairs. "Get. On." His teeth were gritted this time.

Fine, she thought. *Fine.* Wheeling around, she stomped up and into the plane with her chin in the air as if it'd been her idea in the first place.

Wow. Nice. Through the doorway were several spacious seats and the kind of wood paneling she might find in a Lexus. Huh. She hadn't known the federal government rolled like this. No wonder her taxes were so high.

There was a noise behind her, the small scuff of an approaching footstep or some such, and she stiffened with renewed annoyance as she tossed her briefcase on the nearest seat. This was bullshit. Bull. Shit. The DEA couldn't dispatch goons to track her down just because she'd ruffled a couple of feathers by asking some questions that needed to be asked. This was the United States. People didn't do things like that here.

Was this the guy in charge? Great. They needed to have a little chitchat. Pronto.

"Could you please tell me what I'm doing here?" she began, turning in the narrow aisle to face this latest looming DEA bully in all his dark finery. "Because I really don't appreciate—*Oh, Jesus, God.*"

The plane dipped and swayed, and she staggered back a step, grabbing for a seat back to keep from toppling over.

Her peripheral vision registered the sandy curls and skin underneath the DEA baseball cap, the five o'clock shadow, the endless height here in the cabin's tight space, and the broad shoulders that practically spanned the width of the plane.

The image hit her with the sudden sharp snap of a cracking whip.

He looked like Jack.

She froze, afraid to turn all the way and more afraid to take a good look because Jack was dead, which meant that he wasn't up and standing around on government aircraft, and she was losing it because she saw him everywhere she looked. Every face was Jack's these days and he hid around every corner, just out of reach, but *this* . . .

The shakes hit her in a terrible wave and the sobs were already coming, great, choking sobs that she couldn't control because . . . oh, God, he looked just like Jack.

The ghost or whatever he was moved closer until he was right there and she swiped at her eyes, well aware that she was making a fool of herself.

Look, Amara. Just look. Deep breath. You can do it.

She turned her head quickly so she could get it over with, like ripping a bandage off, and she stared into his face. Their gazes connected and understanding hit her in a lightning flash of clarity that had her doubling over.

Those eyes. Brown crystal with long lashes, shining now with tears, intelligence and something she could almost mistake for love. No one else could have eyes like that.

"Jack."

He caught her before she collapsed, crushing her against the body that was so achingly familiar. They clung to each other, grappling to get close enough, his hands settling in her hair and his face in the hollow of her neck. His tears were hot, his sobbing breath against her throat even hotter.

The words poured out and his hoarse voice was like angels singing in her ears.

"Amara. Amara, Amara, *Amara.*"

The shock of his touch was still vibrating through her when the anger came. Black and bitter, it stretched from the center of the earth to the far corners of the universe and back, strangling her in its hold until she lashed out at him and ripped away from the hands that didn't want to let her go.

"How could you do this to me?"

There weren't enough accusations to hurl at him, no words ugly enough to convey what he'd done to her, no punishment bad enough. She went bat-shit haywire, hissing and kicking and hitting with the intent to maim so he never pulled a stunt like this again.

"How could you do this to me?"

Apparently he'd expected something like this. She got one good slap in, right across his beautiful, beloved, treacherous face, and then he caught her arm when she raised her hand again.

Infuriated, she twisted and writhed because she wouldn't be satisfied until she'd drawn a gallon or two of his blood, but she'd have had more luck attacking the side of a bus. He subdued her easily, catching her around the waist with her arms trapped at her sides, and staggered back a step or two to the nearest seat, where he collapsed with her sprawled across his lap.

She raised her hand again and he jerked it out of the air again, and then everything shifted in that one arrested moment.

Openmouthed and panting, they stared at each other for one beat . . . two . . . and then she scrambled to straddle him between her legs, where he belonged, and kiss him with the pent-up passion and grief of this last agonizing month.

They held each other's faces, nipping and licking,

their tongues surging deep. He tasted like tears and clean sweat, hope and joy, and every delicious thing she'd remembered about him since he'd left her.

After a minute his hands began to search, roaming under her coat to her breasts, hips and butt, pressing her up against his raging erection until she moaned with the perfection of it.

"You're so thin." Worry creased his brow and she could almost laugh to see it. "You've got to eat. You can't waste away on me, okay?"

This was no time for lectures.

"You didn't say good-bye," she cried, trying to catch her breath, her tears streaking wet against her cheeks. "You promised you'd—"

"I'm sorry." He said it over and over again and she could tell that he was; pain shone in his dark eyes, a festering wound that was still taking a terrible toll on him. "I didn't know when they were going to do it."

"Why didn't you tell me?"

"Because." Frustrated tension tightened his body into marble. "How many times have you almost died since you hooked up with me? How much longer was our luck going to hold out? And besides that—I wanted you to be free. I wanted you to live your life and be safe to walk down whatever street you want to walk down. I wanted you to forget about me and find someone who—"

"Forget about you?" Amara gaped at him. "Are you that stupid?"

"This isn't a joke—"

"Do I look like I'm joking?"

They glared at each other and she felt a real urge to continue her assault. There must have been something amusing about her mulish expression because his mouth softened into the beginnings of a smile.

"God, I've missed this face, Bunny." He stroked her cheek. "You have no idea."

"I have some idea," she snapped. "Where have you been?"

"They moved me to the Detroit office temporarily. Now they're transferring me again to one of the foreign offices."

God, she couldn't breathe to get the words out. "Where?"

"Panama City."

Panama City. Great. And wasn't that an easy commute from the greater Seattle area? She could feel her body shutting down again, the cold washing over her and locking her inside a place so still and empty that hell would be a welcome change.

"And why have you resurrected yourself to give me this news flash, Jack? You want to make sure I have your address so I know where to send your Christmas card?"

The attempt at sarcasm hit a sour note with him because his lips thinned and stretched into a fearsome thing that was just this side of a snarl. "I want you to stop stirring up trouble and drawing attention to my tragic and untimely death. Otherwise, you're going to blow this whole—"

Of course. Ignoring the disappointment plummeting to the deepest pit of her belly, she focused on her anger as she jerked free and tried to get her wobbly legs under her.

"So that's it, then?" The rising screech would add to her humiliation later, when she had a chance to think about it, but for now there wasn't a damn thing she could do to control it. "You just popped in for a quick, 'Hey, how's it going, I'm still alive so don't screw things up—'"

Jack watched her rant from under his lowered brows, his eyes flashing as he tracked her arm-waving and pacing. Then, all of the sudden, he reached some invisible limit. Lunging to his feet with a cry, he chased her down, backing her up against the galley counter, where she cowered and he trapped her between his arms.

"Shut the fuck up, Amara."

Bravado kicked in. Inflated with outrage, she pointed at his nose. "How dare you—"

Wrenching her hand aside with a muttered curse, he kissed her, long, hard and deep, and everything inside her responded with a fierce primal urgency. When he pulled back enough to let her breathe, she didn't even think of arguing.

"Here's the thing," he said, trying to catch his breath. "You drive me out of my freaking mind. You're so bossy and annoying I spend half my time wishing I had some duct tape to slap over your mouth. You feel me?"

She nodded, light-headed with excitement because his words sure didn't match the blazing light in his eyes.

"On the other hand . . ." Lowering his head, gentle now, he kissed her again with the kind of feather-light brush that made yearning tie a knot in her belly. "You're the bravest, smartest, sexiest woman I've ever laid eyes on and you're under my skin. I can even sleep when I'm with you."

"Oh," she said.

"I'm so in love with you I can't see straight."

"Oh." Crying again, she swiped at her eyes and

prayed he wasn't about to ask her to be a special pen pal when he moved.

"So, even though I'm obviously crazy for thinking of it and you'd have to be insane to say yes, I want you to come with—"

"Yes."

He paused.

She knew what he was thinking. Hell, she knew what *she* was thinking:

Was she insane? To give up her home and her career to head off to parts unknown with this man who had to live in hiding for the rest of his life? To say good-bye to everything she'd worked for?

Hesitating for a minute, she tried to make it into more of a choice. Tried to really think on this and make a reasoned decision while considering everything she was leaving behind. Then she looked back into his brown eyes and there was no choice at all.

"Yes," she said again.

"Think about—"

"Yes."

He gave a disbelieving snort of relieved laughter that lit up his whole face, but then he sobered just as quickly, looking determined to talk some sense into her. "It's not a good idea. You know that—"

"I know. I don't care."

"—and I'm talking about marriage here, because if anything ever happens to me, I want you to have the benefits—"

She raised an eyebrow. "You want to marry me so I'll get the flag at your funeral?"

"I want you to marry me so you'll be my *wife.*"

The subtle inflection he put on the word made it

sound like the most precious position in the world, better than queen or empress.

"I'd be thrilled to be your wife."

They stared at each other and she watched the heartbreaking array of emotions cross his features, the joy warring with the sorrow. "You say that now, but we'll have to change our names. They're putting together new passports for us."

"I know." This was a solemn, serious decision and she was well aware of it.

"We can't have children, Amara. There's too much at risk—"

"Yeah." She took a moment to be sad for the children they'd never have, but she was pretty sure there wasn't a maternal bone in her body anyway. "I know."

He pressed his forehead to hers, and she relaxed into him, savoring the moment. "We're leaving as soon as they've fueled the plane and finished with the preflight stuff. Are you ready for this adventure?"

"I'm ready."

Cupping her face, he kissed her again and it was slow and sweet, achingly perfect. Then he pulled back and smiled, and it was the wide, happy smile that she never saw enough of. She intended to change that.

"I forgot to ask you the most important question," he said.

"What's that?"

"You speak Spanish, don't you?"

Laughter bubbled to her lips for the first time in a month and she tilted her head back to let it come. "Yeah. I speak Spanish."